GARGOYLES

BOOKS BY ALAN NAYES

Gargoyles
The Unnatural

GARGOYLES

Alan Nayes

TOR®

A TOM DOHERTY ASSOCIATES BOOK
NEW YORK

GARGOYLES

Copyright © 2001 by Alan Nayes

AMOREENA
Words and music by Dave Crawford and Richard Downing © Copyright 1970 Universal—Dick James Music, LTD., a division of Universal Studios, Inc. (BMI) International Copyright secured. All Rights Reserved.

A Tor Book
Published by Tom Doherty Associates, LLC
175 Fifth Avenue
New York, NY 10010

www.tor.com

Tor® is a registered trademark of Tom Doherty Associates, LLC.

ISBN 0-765-34056-9
EAN 978-0-765-34056-6

First edition: August 2001
First mass market edition: January 2006

Printed in the United States of America

0 9 8 7 6 5 4 3 2 1

For
Mom and Dad

Acknowledgments

I wish to thank the following persons, who generously lent their time and/or expertise to this book:

Michael Hamilburg
Joanie Kern
Stephanie Lane
Alfa Creative Service and Staff
Celeste Lauro
Linda Mackey
Isabel Salam
Blaine L. Smith, MD
Sara Schwager
Ava Solis Altina

Prologue

Somewhere near Itzimté Ruins, Guatemala, rainy season

She turned her first trick four months shy of her thirteenth birthday. Patricio had been a small man, only a boy really, being just two years older than she. His father had been a *teniente* in the security police that patrolled Mexico City, and he'd paid sixty pesos for Gabriella's services. Gabriella wasn't her real name then, but it was the name she'd used while plying her trade, and it was how she was currently registered at Las Canas.

Now, three years later, the teenage girl with the truculent almond eyes sat huddled under a gnarled tree limb, seeking refuge from the tropical shower. Her skin glistened moistly from sweat and precipitation, and she could smell her own fear above the pungent odor of the earth.

Gabriella stroked one hand across her gravid abdomen, then quickly climbed from the security and cover of the lush vegetation to resume her flight along the muddy *carretera carretera* that would eventually lead her to San Andres. Nightfall was fast approaching. She pressed onward, prodding herself another half kilometer, though her feet and thighs cried out for rest. Surrounded by miles of unfettered jungle that comprised the Guatemalan lowland rain forests, she longed for a shortcut. There was none. And carved out of this most intimidating habitat in all of Central America was Las Canas.

Wump. Wump. Wump. Wump. Los helicopteros. The choppers.

"Mi bebé!" My baby. Gabriella dashed back under the gloomy cover of the rain-forest canopy. She would rather risk an encounter with *el tigre* or even *Desmodus rotundus,* the loathsome bloodsucking vampire bat.

Wump. Wump. Wump. Anything but the choppers. She could never return to Las Canas. *Never.*

Gabriella clutched desperately at her stomach. It heaved with each laborious breath. She couldn't maintain this frenetic pace; it was impossible. She forced herself to think through the tears, through the pain. She might still stand a chance if she could thwart their initial assault.

Wump. Wump. Wump. Wump.

"Que mierda," Gabriella cried out.

Her hands protected her eyes as she stumbled farther through the thick underbrush. Thorns ripped at her skin, and vines threatened to ensnare her ankles as if they possessed wills of their own.

She tripped, stumbling forward. Terror gripped her like a giant anaconda. Her breaths catapulted from her convulsing chest in short gasps.

Oh Dios, por favor, she prayed. Please, God. If she could just make it to the Itzimté Ruins before dark.

High above her head, the canopy of epiphytes, vines, and towering ferns gyrated into a living tempest. The powerful downdraft from the Sikorsky's blades created a whirlwind of flying debris.

Gabriella threw herself on the forest floor, cowering under the onslaught of tangled vegetation.

Wump. Wump. Wump. Wump.

"No!" she cried. *"No!"*

With nothing to cling to but remnants of past dreams, Gabriella began to pray. She prayed for herself. She prayed for Las Canas. But mostly she prayed for the *bebés*.

The men from the *plantación de azúcar* were coming.

Chapter One

Amoreena Daniels gazed at the woman retching into the plastic emesis basin and struggled to visualize her mom as she once was, her mom prior to the diagnosis, her mom minus the cancer. It was a difficult if not futile exercise.

Wearing a hospital gown that appeared two sizes too large, Geneva Daniels adjusted her brightly flowered scarf with one hand, the cloth a replacement for her once-vibrant tresses. Seated next to her, Amoreena counted another fresh bruise coalescing under her mother's limpid skin, where an IV line replenished her fluid stores.

Room 441 on the University of California Medical Center oncology ward no longer seemed just a hospital room; rather, a bleak reminder of what physical devastation a disease run amuck could wreak on the human spirit. Even the astringent, aseptic smell failed to eliminate completely the specter of illness and suffering.

"Amoreena Daniels." It was the ward clerk. She waited outside the door as if what lay inside was contagious.

"Hold on," Amoreena said curtly, throwing her thick mane of auburn hair out of her face with a toss of her head. "You okay, Mom?" she asked, helping steady the basin.

Geneva coughed twice and nodded. "How 'bout a cigarette?"

"Not funny." Amoreena checked the basin. No blood, only

thickened saliva. She carried the basin into the bathroom.

Geneva heard the water in the sink. "You're just like your dad. No sense of humor." It required two breaths and a coughing spell to expel the words.

Amoreena returned, setting the clean basin on the nightstand. "I'll develop a sense of humor when you develop an appetite," she said, studying her mother's skin. She thought the sallow hue had lessened, or maybe it was just the fluorescent lighting. "And will you stop with the 'Dad jokes.' He doesn't deserve it."

"Ms. Daniels." It was the clerk again. "Dr. Gillespie's waiting."

"Sure, all right." Amoreena feigned a smile. It wasn't the ward clerk's fault her mother had metastatic cervical cancer. "Mom, I'll see you before I leave."

Geneva coughed deeply and spit into a Kleenex before finding some renewed vigor. "Amy . . ." She called her only daughter "Amy" with a short 'a' whenever their discussions centered on the serious. "When you're through with Dr. Gillespie, I have something to tell you."

"Tell me now. He can wait."

"No, later. Dr. Gillespie's very busy." She attempted a weak grin. "I'm not going anywhere. Yet."

Amoreena bent low and pecked Geneva on the cheek. Her skin felt cold and dry on her lips. Not the way she wanted to remember her mother. "See ya."

The conference room for the oncology ward was situated adjacent to the central nurses' station. Amoreena was very familiar with it. It was in this very room six months ago that Dr. Gillespie had unleashed the appalling news that her mother's cancer was a stage IV, metastatic. It had already invaded the liver and lungs. The revelation had given new meaning to the term shitty Monday. But there was still a fighting chance, he'd said. More out of a sense of duty than any realistic expectation of success, Amoreena surmised. Only later that night when she and her mom were alone did the real tears flow.

Dressed in faded denims and a loose scooped-neck T-shirt, Amoreena approached a man in a wheelchair. She moved with a certain aloofness that was both enticing and ingenuous.

The man waved.

She returned the gesture. She'd seen him several times before during her prior visits, and each time he appeared thinner and more cachectic. Acute myelocytic leukemia.

"Heya, gorgeous," he said, as she passed.

Amoreena allowed a smile. "How's it going?"

"Another day, same old shit."

Momentarily, she wondered how long he had. She didn't even know his name. Quickly, she dismissed the thought when she observed the blinds to the conference room drawn shut. Ignoring the stares from the nurses and resident physicians, Amoreena paused at the door and inhaled. *Fuck cancer*. She knocked.

"Come in." The voice sounded apologetic.

She entered and shut the door behind her.

Dr. Gillespie sat alone at a long table. Balding and bespectacled, he was an African-American with a well-trimmed gray beard. A medical chart lay open before him. He motioned her to a seat.

Finding the chair directly across from him, she didn't miss the gyn-oncologist's pained expression. The same expression he failed to mask six months ago.

In that one instant, Amoreena knew the news, whatever it was, was not going to be pleasant.

"So how's premed these days?" he asked, breaking the ice.

Amoreena stifled saying 'same old shit.' "Fine," she answered.

"Interviews?"

"Next fall with UCI, UCLA, and USC."

"Want to stay in California."

"UCLA's my first choice. It all depends." She left it hanging.

"Hm-hm." Dr. Gillespie's eyes scanned the blackboard.

Amoreena followed his gaze. Limned in chalk were clusters of cancer cells—she presumed they represented cancer cells—the big CA on an oncology ward was usually a dead giveaway. Adjacent to the diagram, a list of drug names had been scrawled. A second sketch demonstrated how these specific drugs attacked the foreign cells' replicating system. Curing cancer was simply that. Stop the unauthorized replication and the patient survived. Amoreena wished it were that easy.

Dr. Gillespie lightly tapped the chart on the table. "Your mother's weight's down."

Amoreena felt a tinge of undeserved guilt. "I know, it's almost like I have to force-feed her at home. This last round of chemo really took a lot out of Mom."

"You and Geneva are waging a tough battle." He hesitated, as if unsure how to proceed. "Amoreena . . ." he started again, but pursed his lips at the knock on the door.

Amoreena turned to find the door open and a woman filling the empty space. She was large, not fat, and exhibited an androgynous figure. She sported a business suit, one of those styles illustrated in catalogues targeted toward female corporate types who seemed to believe that becoming as successful as a man entailed dressing like one. The woman carried a thick satchel.

Without waiting for an invitation, she strode imperiously into the room and took the chair at the head of the table.

Dr. Gillespie made the introduction. "This is Ms. Rosalind Cates. She chairs our hospital's utilization review committee. Her specialty is medical oncology."

Amoreena sat in silence, staring at the only medical chart in the room. Her mother's. With no prior experience, she suddenly knew she despised utilization review committees.

"It's come to our attention, Amoreena," the oncologist continued haltingly, "that . . ." There was another disquieting pause.

At this juncture, the imposing Ms. Cates grabbed the reins. "I'll take it from here, Doctor," she said.

The tone of the woman's voice exhibited a callous knifelike quality very much like a personal-injury attorney Amoreena had seen pitching on late-night television.

Ms. Cates set her satchel on the table but remained standing. She placed both hands on the back of the chair. "Ms. Daniels, I believe your mother's health-care coverage had been provided by the Standard Care Insurance Company."

Amoreena nodded. "That's correct. And still is," she added in rejoinder to Ms. Cates use of the word "had."

Ms. Cates grunted. "Well, that's the purpose of this meeting. As of the end of this month, Standard Care will no longer cover Geneva Daniels for health-care needs. This includes any catastrophic coverage."

Amoreena felt her face grow hot. "What do you mean?" She swiveled to face the oncologist. "Dr. Gillespie, what's she talking about?"

"Ms. Daniels," Ms. Cates interjected.

Amoreena ignored her. "What's this lady got to do with Mom's treatments anyway?"

Before the doctor could reply, Ms. Cates had removed a spiral-bound notebook from her satchel and placed it on the table. "Ms. Daniels, your mother was employed as a secretary for H&M Printing Press for fourteen years. Is that correct?"

Amoreena refused to make eye contact. "And she'd still be employed if her pap smears had remained normal."

"When did her leave of absence commence?"

"Six months ago. After the diagnosis."

Ms. Cates gave a satisfactory nod. "That partially explains the confusion."

"Confusion?" Amoreena blurted out.

"Ms. Daniels, as of five months ago, H&M Printing has been in receivership, they've declared bankruptcy, and are no longer paying premiums for their employees', including any retirees', health-care coverage. As per the law, Standard Care, as well as the human resources department at H&M, notified your mother numerous times that her medical coverage would be her responsibility. Unfortunately, Geneva Daniels failed to respond appropriately, no premiums were paid, and therefore, as of this moment, she is without coverage."

Amoreena's mouth felt gummy. No coverage. *My God, she has metastatic cancer.* She barely heard Ms. Cates continue.

"I took the liberty of presenting Geneva Daniels's case to a group of other insurance agencies for gap coverage. However in light of your mother's current situation, they felt it would not be in their best financial interests to intervene. One did agree, though, to issue a policy, however, it would not cover any preexisting conditions. I've referred her case to Social Services."

Amoreena shook her head. "That's fucking great."

"Pardon."

Amoreena stood. "What is this shit? This is a damn hospital isn't it, or did I drive into the wrong parking garage?"

Ms. Cates cleared her throat. "There's no need to be obscene, Ms. Daniels. I understand—"

"You don't understand crap."

"I understand this," Cates retorted. "I've reviewed the chart and doctors' notes regarding your mother's treatments and at this stage of Geneva Daniels's illness, her cost/benefit ratio fails to fall within the curve of a successful outcome. Unless you can devise alternative means to finance her treatments, I regret to inform you, your mother will be forced to seek care elsewhere once she is discharged."

"What do you mean you couldn't tell me?"

Geneva stared at the ceiling. "I couldn't, that's all."

Amoreena listened incredulously, sitting on the opposite bed. "Mom," she started again. She forced herself to remain calm. "Do you want to end up on a county ward with the homeless and derelicts and have some first-year medical student practice drawing your blood. Jesus, why didn't you just pay the premiums?"

Geneva swallowed. She remained silent as a single tremor ran the length of her body.

"Mother, are you listening? You're not that sick you can't answer me. Why didn't you pay the damn premiums?"

Geneva's voice was soft. "I didn't have the money."

"What?"

Geneva turned and faced her daughter. A tiny flame smoldered behind her languid eyes. "I said I didn't have the money."

"Mom." She leaped off the bed. "You have over four grand in the bank. I know."

Geneva shook her head.

"Don't shake your head. I saw the last statement." Amoreena detected a staid look on her mother's face and instantly interpreted its meaning. "You knew about this meeting, didn't you? Did that Cates lady already talk to you?"

Geneva's refusal to answer was answer enough.

"That bitch."

"Amy."

"Don't 'Amy' me. You had four thousand dollars in the bank, and you didn't pay the premiums. Yes, Cates is a bitch, and it's all right for me to be pissed."

Geneva's expression hardened. "Amoreena, that money's yours. For your schooling."

"I'm on a scholarship."

"Partial."

"Just semantics. That money still should've been used for your insurance." She felt her face growing hot again. "Do you realize what you've done? God . . ." She pushed her thick hair from her forehead with both hands. "God, I'm angry at you. I'm really angry."

"Amy."

"Mom, I'm really—"

"Amy, shut up." Geneva sat up so fast it shocked Amoreena. Geneva coughed once and pointed to an empty glass. "Make yourself useful and get your mom a glass of water please."

Pouring from a pitcher, she handed Geneva the glass.

Geneva sipped twice. "Now listen to me. I'm dying."

Amoreena began to protest but was quieted by her mother's hand.

"Just hear me out. Please."

She watched her mom's face. She'd seen the same tough-as-nails expression before. It was when she'd told Amoreena her father was leaving. Amoreena had been a shy six-year-old, and she still recalled the same odd combination of combativeness, sympathy, and hopefulness. She suddenly felt like a little girl again.

"Baby." Geneva smiled. "You're the best thing that I've ever done. And I love you dearly, more than anything in the world. Even more than life itself." She paused for a breath. "Amy, do you know what the five-year survival is for a case like mine? Minimal. I'm not a gambler. Any money spent on my premiums would be like throwing it off a train. It'd be wasted. God, I'm so proud of you. And I'm proud of me. For my contributions. In some ways, I worked as hard as you to get you where you are, and I'll be damned if I'd do anything that might jeopardize your goals. Because goddamn, you *are* going to graduate from college and then go on to medical school and become the best doctor you know how."

Amoreena wiped at her eye. "Mom, you're all I've got."

"And you're all I've got." Geneva reached for her daughter's hand. "Come here."

Amoreena felt a wave of fatigue roll across her. "If you think I'm just going to let you die when there are options out there, you don't recognize your own flesh and blood. There's that research protocol."

Geneva brushed a stray strand of hair from her daughter's face. "I'll make you a promise. I'll hang around long enough to see my only child graduate. Providing . . ."

She met her mother's gaze.

"Providing, no matter what happens to me, you do nothing that risks your future goals. Promise me, Amy."

"I promise."

"We'll think of something, baby. We always do," Geneva said.

Amoreena closed her eyes. "I love you."

Tomorrow she would worry about the rest.

Chapter Two

The slide reminded Amoreena of a giant ugly tadpole. The tiny fetus stared out at the audience of a hundred biology majors from bulging, yet unopened eyes.

She made a quick notation to her diagram. *It was sucking its thumb*.

Setting aside her human embryology notes, Amoreena pulled a sheet of paper from her backpack. These last twelve hours had been absurd. From the time she'd left the hospital at 9 P.M., she'd mulled over financial options, yet no matter how she worked the variables, the numbers just didn't add up. Four sessions of chemo at $6,400 a pop. In addition there would be antiemetics to control nausea, analgesics for pain, and laboratory costs: blood work, urinalysis, chest X rays. The list went on ad nauseum.

"Perhaps Ms. Daniels would like to enlighten us on the origin of the human egg and sperm." Professor Stanton stood at the podium. "The origin of egg and sperm, Ms. Daniels?"

Amoreena slid the list under her notes. "Both the human egg and sperm are derived from large, round primordial germ cells."

"And . . ."

"These germ cells can be identified in the wall of the yolk sac as early as the fourth week of gestation, and their differentiation is complete prior to the conclusion of the first trimester."

Professor Stanton gave a perfunctory nod and shut off the projector. "Midterms in six weeks."

Instantly the Hashinger Science Center lecture hall exploded in a burst of activity. Students gathered their notes and books and moved en bloc toward the exits.

Amoreena hurried to the rear stairwell.

The seasonally warm September sun was not yet high enough in the sky to be uncomfortable and reminded her of days spent in Newport Beach. High school had been such a cakewalk. How to become valedictorian on Diet Cokes, beer, and french fries.

She found Millie Fontana waiting on the steps of Argyros Forum. They'd been roommates since their freshman year and rented a renovated antique two-bedroom house several blocks from the campus. Though the girls contrasted starkly in physical attributes, they shared common backgrounds. Each had been raised under financially disadvantaged conditions and both had received academic honors their freshman and sophomore years, Millie majoring in computer science and Amoreena going premed.

"Hey, roomie," Millie said. "You saw my note."

Amoreena dropped her pack and opened a small zippered compartment. She found her car keys and tossed them. "Silver needs gas, and when you shift into third you have to jerk it hard or you'll stall." Silver was Amoreena's '88 Mustang, which devoured as much oil as gas.

"Don't I know." Millie picked the keys off the steps. "I almost forgot. Some lady called asking for you this morning while you were in class. Ramona something. I left the name on your desk."

Amoreena watched her somewhat overweight, bespectacled roommate shuffle away. "Don't ride Silver too hard."

Millie turned briefly and waved.

Amoreena fished out a pack of Montclairs and lit up. On the breeze a trace of salt lingered, reminiscent of the coast, only twenty miles away. The forty-two-acre campus, founded in 1862, the day of Abraham Lincoln's inauguration, was tiny compared to UCLA, Amoreena's first choice. But Chapman University was much closer to her mother's apartment in Orange—they'd never owned a house—and scholarships and loans paid for 80 percent of the hefty tuition. Plus it had a good premed program, and the educational style was very personal. Most professors knew their students by name. Case in point, Professor Stanton. Also the tranquil nature of the campus made the grueling hours of study more palatable. Not that she didn't have fun anymore. Just not as often. It was difficult enough maintaining a 4.0 grade point average without the partying. The competition for medical school slots was intense. And failure wasn't an option.

The Student Legal Aid office was located in Roosevelt Hall, along with the Financial Aid Department. It was a relatively new enterprise and was run by law students from Chapman University's Law School. No one was available at the moment, so Amoreena made an appointment with the receptionist to return at 2 P.M. Her class in anatomy would be finished, and she'd dash over before her biology lab started at two-thirty.

The Student Employment Center was housed back in Argyros Forum, and, as Amoreena fully anticipated, the opportunities were not bountiful. Most of the jobs—clerical, lab assistants, and librarian shelvers—were minimum wage. She needed bigger money, faster.

For the next several hours, she forced herself to concentrate on anatomy and embryology. It was difficult. Reviewing the mophogenetic development of the human embryo only reminded her of the three things her mother had told her when she'd started college. 'I want to see you graduate with honors, I want to see you complete medical school, and I want to hold my very own grandchild.' The corners of Amoreena's mouth turned up just a bit when she recalled her own response. 'The first two are a shoo-in, Mom, but the third, don't hold your breath.' Marriage wasn't even listed in her distant plans, much less a child.

Anatomy wasn't any better at occupying her mind. The anatomic illustrations of normal liver and lungs only underscored how her own mother's organs would appear if represented on the textbook pages. She could easily visualize the ugly irregularly circumscribed lesions of metastatic disease punctuating the hepatic and pulmonary parenchyma.

Amoreena shut the text. Exams were still weeks away.

She returned to Roosevelt Hall, where she found one Mr. Jerry Fallwell, no relationship to the television evangelist as he strongly emphasized in his introduction, perched on the edge of his desk, flipping paper clips into the trash bin. Upon her entrance, he instantly came to attention, while providing a brief synopsis of his life in the legal profession. A sharply dressed, urbane young man and several years older than she, he exuded a certain hauteur that Amoreena decided all attorneys learn to nurture early in their careers.

However, he did appear genuinely eager to listen to her story while perusing the Standard Care policy spread across his desk.

"Let me be sure I have all the facts." Jerry pensively crossed his hands in front of his face so that the tips of each digit just touched. They sat in a small private counsel room adjacent to the Financial Aid office. "Your mother, Geneva Daniels," he began, staring at some point just above Amoreena's head, "has terminal cervical cancer."

"I didn't say terminal," she interrupted.

"You said metastatic."

"Metastatic does not mean terminal."

Fallwell acquiesced as if contemplating some deeper thought. "Yes, you're correct, and I'm not a doctor. Anyway. Your mother received, on several occasions, letters warning her of loss of Standard Care benefits if she did not pay the required premiums that at this point were no longer covered by her former employer, H&M Printing Press." He paused. "Exactly how many letters?"

"Six."

"I assume you have access to them."

"Mom threw them out."

Fallwell grunted. "You ever read *The Rainmaker?*"

She shook her head.

"It's about a boy dying of leukemia who gets screwed big-time by a large insurance company. They refused to treat him though all the premiums *had* been paid. A typical bad-faith case. These cases are egregious and occur thousands of times in this country."

Amoreena leaned closer. "Is my mother's a bad-faith case?"

Fallwell frowned. "Nope. The difference is your mother did not pay the required premiums."

She exhaled. "So where does that leave us?"

"Tell you what." Fallwell's alacrity to assist had not waned. "I just completed a course in Insurance Law. Let me make a copy of your mother's Standard Care policy, and I'll run it by my advisor. If he has any additional recommendations, I'll call you."

"Thanks. I'd appreciate it."

Fallwell smiled and dashed out of the conference room.

Amoreena sighed. At least she hadn't run up a large bill just to have a real lawyer tell her the same thing. The Chapman Student Legal Aid service was gratis. Couldn't beat that price.

When Fallwell returned, Amoreena gave him her pager number before leaving, in case anything else developed.

Academic Affairs was on the way to the biology lab, so Amoreena stopped in to pick up applications to the UCLA and USC medical school programs. It was a spacious office on the first floor of Wilkerson Hall, furnished in the modern venerable decor worthy of the Office of the Dean.

Mrs. Garcia, a pleasant Hispanic lady, staffed the reception desk. "Amoreena, I'm glad you dropped in. Dr. Sheffield wished to have a word with you."

Amoreena tensed. Dr. Wesley Sheffield taught genetics and was her premed advisor.

She found his office and knocked lightly, sensing a knot developing in her stomach. The last time she heard of a student getting called into a meeting with a premed advisor, it was to notify the student that he'd flunked the Medical College Admission Test.

She waited. He sounded like he was on the phone. She was on the verge of knocking again when the door opened, revealing an office in moderate disarray yet adorned with mementos of academic achievement as well as personal life—diplomas, certificates, and family vacation photos.

"Come in, Amoreena." Dr. Sheffield shook her hand and pulled her in. He was past sixty, gray-haired and three inches shorter than Amoreena's five feet eight inches. "Please sit. How is life?"

Amoreena chose one of the two plush chairs in front of the large teakwood desk. "Fine. Embryo's gonna be a challenge." So far, she hadn't told any of her professors about her mother's illness.

The advisor took on a more serious demeanor. "How are the grades?"

"All As last semester."

"Excellent. Outstanding academic record, Phi Kappa Honor Society, Hearst Scholarship recipient." He named off Amoreena's honors.

She gave a modest grin.

Dr. Sheffield began again. "I wanted to run an opportunity by you." He opened a folder containing her academic scores. Seemingly satisfied, he closed it. "Are you familiar with Dr. Jerome Pike?"

"Dr. Pike of the Pike Hypertension Studies?" One of her professors last semester had discussed an article Dr. Pike had authored.

Sheffield appeared impressed. "He's the one. Every year one of the large pharmaceutical concerns, this year it's Merck, contracts with his department to oversee a large, random, double-blind hypertension study. And every year, he requests a student at one of the local premed programs to assist."

Amoreena's expression lightened.

Sheffield raised both hands. "Nothing major, just minor record keeping. Mostly you'll be taking blood pressures. You can take a blood pressure?"

Amoreena smiled. She'd taken her mother's enough over the last six months. "Like a doctor," she said with confidence.

"Great," Sheffield said, clapping his hands. "Dr. Pike's secretary called asking for our most promising candidate. How would you feel about representing Chapman University?"

Amoreena wanted to burst. "I'd be honored."

"Wonderful, it's done then. I'll make the official recommendation." Dr. Scheffield stood. "Oh, there's one more item I think you should be aware of. Because Dr. Pike chairs the UCLA Medical School Admission Committee, I think I can say with virtual certainty, if you impress Dr. Jerome Pike during this study, you'll be a shoo-in for their freshman med class."

The premed advisor's auspicious prediction rocked her. She wanted to leap across the desk and plant a kiss of gratitude on Dr. Sheffield's face. Instead she settled for a hearty handshake.

"Thank you so much. I promise I won't let you or the university down."

Amoreena floated out of his office. *A virtual shoo-in.* And Sheffield had picked her, though she realized he still had to run it by the premed committee. Fantastic.

She picked up the applications she sought and was almost to the exits when her pager went off. Checking the number sent her crashing back to earth.

She groaned. It was Room 441 on the oncology ward. Borrowing Mrs. Garcia's phone, she called.

"Hello." The voice sounded flat.

"Mom, it's me."

"I'm not interrupting a test or anything?"

Amoreena looked away from the receptionist. Her mother with metastatic cancer worried about interrupting some damn test. "No, it's cool."

"Amy, a woman from the Hospital Social Services came by and was asking all these complicated questions about our finances. She was trying to explain about this option and how much time it would take and it was so confusing."

"Don't worry. I'm coming up there this afternoon. I'll talk to her. Just eat, okay."

"Thank you, baby."

"I love you, Mom."

During biology lab, Amoreena was content to let Gladys Peterson and another premed student work on the pig's heart dissection while she memorized the pertinent facts from the laboratory manual. Amoreena chose not to reveal her good fortune regarding the Pike study to them. She figured the news would get around soon enough.

Her mother was resting quietly, eyes closed, when

Amoreena looked in, so she let the nurse know she'd return after the visit to Social Services.

Social Services occupied the second floor of Building 25, a sadly decrepit building adjacent to the main hospital structure. The hall smelled of stale coffee and doughnuts.

Amoreena approached an open office and knocked. "Hello."

A waifish woman in her forties with thick bifocals looked up from behind a stack of charts. Numerous fine wrinkles lined her face as if all the sad and difficult cases she'd handled were indelibly etched in her skin. "May I help you?"

"I'm Amoreena Daniels."

The woman's expression lit up in recognition. "Geneva Daniels, yes. I apologize for not getting by today but as you can see"—she motioned to the imposing pile before her—"I'm inundated." She noted Amoreena's puzzled look. "Is something wrong?"

"No, it's just Mom said some lady from Social Services came by earlier and was asking a lot of questions."

"Wasn't me. Could have been Jenny Stiller, though I doubt it because I'm the one assigned to your mother's case." The woman rose. She was barely five feet. "Please sit. I'm Dolores Finney, and frankly"—her expression grew somber—"we have our work cut out for us, dear."

Amoreena accepted her offer of some day-old coffee and listened as Dolores outlined the plan.

"I've reviewed the chart and have spoken with both Dr. Gillespie and Rosalind Cates." Amoreena let a soft groan escape at hearing Cates's name. Dolores ignored it and continued. "It's going to be difficult, especially in light of the special time constraints, but options are available. After checking firsthand, I concur with Ms. Cates's verdict that the HMOs and insurance companies are out. The calls I made were answered politely but in no uncertain terms. Your mother's illness would be classified as a preexisting condition."

Amoreena simply nodded. She was thankful Dolores's attitude gave no trace of being judgmental or even reproachful. The nonpayment of premiums never came up.

Dolores reached into a file and pulled out two applications.

She handed the forms across her desk. "These are disability forms for Medi-Cal and Social Security." Abruptly she asked, "You're how old."

"Twenty-one."

"Good. And Geneva Daniels is," she paused checking a printout.

"Forty-eight," Amoreena answered.

Dolores nodded. "Fine. And no other children under twenty-one I presume."

"I'm an only child."

"Fill out the Medi-Cal form and present it to this address"—she handed Amoreena a card—"with proper identification and resident status—your mother's, that is. Simultaneously, complete and mail the Social Security disability application. Dr. Gillespie will need to fill out portions of both forms delineating your mother's diagnosis, prognosis, treatments, etc. Oh." Dolores leaped to another file and produced a third form. "This is an MSI application. MSI is a medical service program for the indigent. It can be pending while the others are being reviewed."

"Reviewed?" The word suddenly wreaked of bureaucrats and dullards with nothing better to do than sit behind a desk pushing paper.

Dolores cast Amoreena a genuine look of empathy. "Unfortunately that's the process. It can take up to three months, though thirty days is the norm."

"My mother has metastatic cancer. She doesn't have three months. She doesn't have thirty days. What about the county hospital?"

"They still require forms and approvals. Unless . . ." She paused a beat. "Well, I suppose you could wait till your mom suffers an acute emergency, then rush her in. They can't refuse to treat then." Dolores's voice trailed off.

Amoreena grimaced.

"I'm sorry. It's the best we can do," the social worker finished.

Amoreena folded the forms and slid them inside her pack beside her medical school applications. Whereas earlier she'd felt like floating, now she experienced a smothering sensation of sinking, pulled down by piles and piles of paper, filled with endless lines of inane questions.

"There's no other options?" she asked languidly.

"There is one." Dolores frowned. "Somehow come up with the necessary funds yourself."

Chapter Three

If her bedside radio alarm had not malfunctioned the next morning, Amoreena would have missed the call.

Millie was closest to the phone when it rang. She glanced across the breakfast table. "Sure, she's right here." Cupping the receiver, she spoke softly. "It's that lady who called yesterday."

Setting her purse on the counter, Amoreena frowned. She was already late for her first class and pressed for time. "Hello," she said curtly.

"Ms. Daniels, am I interrupting?"

"Depends. If you're selling mutual funds, my cash reserves wouldn't interest you."

"Amoreena, my name is Ramona Perez. I work for the Women's Clinic."

"I'm not in need of a doctor."

"But your mother is."

Amoreena stiffened.

The woman didn't skip a beat. "If you're willing to listen, I'm willing to offer you the necessary funding for your mother's cancer treatment. And please believe me, there's nothing illegal, unethical, or risky concerning our proposal."

Amoreena tried to imagine Ramona Perez in a boiler room with twenty other marketers, but somehow the image didn't match. This call was *too* personal. "I'm listening," she said with a feigned nonchalance.

"This is something I'd prefer to discuss in person. Are you free this afternoon?"

"My last class ends at four."

"That works for me. Are you familiar with the Women's Clinic?"

"I don't go to the doctor much."

"We're in Santa Ana on Spurgeon, not far from UCMC." Ramona recited the address and phone number. "Across the street, you'll find a park. I'll wait for you by the rose garden. I'll be wearing a black skirt and red blouse."

"Who was that?" Millie asked.

Amoreena leaned her back against the counter staring at the phone. "Someone who says she can solve all my problems."

Through her entire lecture on evolutionary theory, one question nagged at the edges of Amoreena's mind. Ramona Perez had never asked for her description. What if she sent Millie instead? Or a cop? But then the woman would surely check for some valid ID. Then again, maybe Ms. Perez already knew what the real Amoreena Daniels looked like. That thought bothered Amoreena at least as much as the mysterious phone call.

The class concluded with a series of equations used in defining population mechanics. Once these were added to her notes, she followed the herd from the lecture hall.

Near the exit, snippets of conversation drifted back over the heads of competing premeds.

A girl voiced, "I can only hypothesize what *she* had to do to luck into Pike's study."

Another male student quipped, "Check her knees."

Amoreena ignored the cheap banter. So the word was out. *BFD.* Big fucking deal.

Her next class was human genetics, one of her more fascinating courses, and commanded her rapt attention for the full fifty minutes.

The lecture topic was inborn errors of metabolism. Following the professor's concluding comments, a pop quiz produced the requisite groans and grimaces. Amoreena aced the twenty-question exam.

Keeping close tabs on the time, she decided to ditch her last class. She drove to the Medi-Cal office, which was buried on the first floor of a three-story redbrick building in the city of Orange. Though the staff behaved courteously, they worked in that predefined automatic mode set by all governmental bureaucratic standards. Which meant her mother's application for medical coverage and concomitant entry into the Medical Service Program for the Indigent would wend along a lazy meandering river of red tape. The elderly clerk confirmed thirty days minimum.

The news from the Federal Building at 34 Civic Center Drive was no more promising. Three months at the earliest before Social Security disability benefits kicked in.

At ten past four, Amoreena parked Silver in front of 517 Spurgeon. The sign on the two-story gray-stucco building read *Clínica de la Mujer*. Beneath, in smaller letters, THE WOMEN'S CLINIC. The local neighborhood was a combination of light industrial, retail, and residential. In the immediate area she counted two large apartment complexes. Most of the people she observed were Hispanic.

The medical clinic building appeared well maintained and professionally landscaped, as was the small city park located directly across Spurgeon.

Amoreena had no difficulty picking out the rose garden. Nor the woman in black and red. She was the lady watching her.

Chapter Four

"You look like the actress from that movie, the one with the call girl and the rich man," Ramona said, standing as she proffered her hand. "Ramona Perez."

"*Pretty Woman*." Amoreena accepted the gesture and introduced herself. "It's the mouth." Both women sat on the concrete ledge.

Ramona shielded her eyes with one hand. "You're really quite stunning. Have you ever been photographed?"

"Is this about modeling?"

"No."

Nearby several children played. Amoreena turned just as a young boy began his descent down a kiddie slide. He landed, spraying sand over his bare feet. Two other children shrieked gleefully in unison, their high-pitched screams somehow grating against Amoreena's nerves. She felt tense.

When she swiveled back to face Ramona Perez, she caught the older woman's intense gaze. Amoreena sensed she was silently being evaluated for something, though she had no idea what. The woman's expression revealed nothing.

"Kids are beautiful," Ramona said.

"Yeah, when they're someone else's." Amoreena's comment must have struck a chord because Ramona removed her sunglasses and laughed.

The levity was infectious. Amoreena found herself laughing, too, and in that single fleeting moment she felt as if some type of bond had formed between herself and this woman she barely knew. It was strange, almost scary.

Ramona stopped laughing and placed her sunglasses in her purse. Amoreena noticed how thin and dainty her fingers were. In fact, everything about Ramona Perez was petite. She had a slender, attractive face and her hair was black and cut short, with only the softest hints of graying. She couldn't have weighed much more than a hundred pounds. And height-wise, Amoreena towered over the woman's small frame.

Ramona sighed once and patted Amoreena lightly on the leg. "I'm sorry, it was just that your comment echoed my own thoughts in the past so accurately." Her accent came across stronger in person, yet her English was flawless. "I have two children, grown, but I can't count the times when they were young, I would say to myself, my two *hijos*, you are so precious, yet I think you would be more precious if you belonged to my neighbor." She chuckled once more.

Amoreena smiled. Across the street, a pregnant woman entered the medical clinic.

Ramona watched her disappear behind the smoked-glass doors before continuing. "First, I wish to thank you for taking the time to visit with me. Especially in light of your situation."

There it was again, the subtle reference to Amoreena's *situation*. How much did this woman know?

Ramona removed a business card from her breast pocket. "We specialize in the entire gamut of female conditions having to do with the reproduction organs. This includes all preventive medicine, treatment and evaluation of infections, pregnancy terminations, and prenatal care."

Amoreena wondered how the clinic dealt with metastatic cancer.

Ramona's next comment touched on that very issue.

"Of course, the more serious diseases, breast cancer, ovarian cancer, and other malignancies are best handled at a tertiary-care center. Once one of our physicians makes the diagnosis, the patient is promptly referred out."

"How did you get my name?"

"From your mother's former employer's insurance carrier."

"H&M Printing Press?"

Ramona nodded. "The company I work for, Meechum Medical Corporation, compiles a database that lists local companies and their insurance carriers, both private and worker's compensation, and the employees who subscribe. It's these subscriber lists that can be so valuable for marketing provider services.

"Which brings us to your situation. We know your mother was an employee for the now defunct H&M Printing Press. We also know she was, but is no longer, listed on the Standard Care Insurance enrollee lists. In addition, your mother listed one dependent. And if our research is accurate, this particular dependent was never covered by a Standard Care policy."

"I'm covered at school." Amoreena found herself developing a whole new conceptual image of Ramona Perez, not necessarily good.

"That fills in the blank," Ramona said. "We didn't know where you received health coverage, we just knew it wasn't with Standard Care."

"Thank God."

Ramona smiled empathetically and continued. "And most significant, at least from our standpoint, we knew Geneva Daniels's dependent was twenty-one and of childbearing age. And in need of financial assistance."

Ramona slowed the pace, letting this last point sink in.

Amoreena met the woman's gaze, wondering how a first impression could have been so inaccurate. The transformation was complete. Ramona Perez was no longer a nice petite Hispanic lady, but a tough shrewd businesswoman here for a specific purpose. The nature of which, Amoreena was fully confident, would soon be revealed.

Ramona's tone segued from the impersonal and calculating to a more personal and tender quality. "Amoreena, our work at the Women's Clinic is in the business of giving. We give good service, we give good care, and we give infertile couples who desperately desire a child a chance to have a baby of their own."

* * *

"A surrogate mother!" Millie said, nearly choking on a bite of pepperoni pizza.

It was dusk, the sun barely below the horizon. Birds chirped in the surrounding trees, and nearby a neighbor's television played the evening news.

Daryl, a classmate and reserve forward on the school's basketball team, had furnished the large pizza with three toppings and the beer. Amoreena and Millie supplied the company and the setting.

Daryl chugged down a third of a Corona before reaching for the fourth slice. "I volunteer to be the donor," he said in mock seriousness.

"Don't be an ass," Millie chided him. "They don't do it *that* way. They use artificial insemination."

"My method's more stimulating."

Throughout the friendly banter, neither noticed that Amoreena had remove herself and wandered off the porch into the middle of the small secluded backyard. She stood staring at the sky, blowing smoke rings. The scent of barbecued chicken wafted over the tall cedar fence.

"Hey, Amy, eat the last piece or it's a goner," Daryl said, finishing off his Corona.

Amoreena watched the last puff of smoke dissipate in the air before returning to the porch. She doused her cigarette in Daryl's empty bottle.

"You know, I never asked how much," she said.

"Don't be crazy." Millie popped the top off another beer and handed it to her roommate. "You were never serious anyway."

Amoreena took a slow sip. Her expression was pensive. "I agree the scenario is preposterous. But if you can separate yourself from the total absurdity of it all, the logistics are not too unreasonable." She repeated how Ramona Perez had presented the facts. "I wouldn't miss school, I wouldn't have to take on a job, I *would* be doing an act of altruistic nobility, and on a more secular level, I'd be able to finance Mom's hospitalization and treatments."

Millie considered momentarily. "I still think it's gross."

"I think Amy would make a great mom," Daryl countered.

Amoreena held up one finger. "But you see in reality, I wouldn't be a mom. I'd be more like a"—she searched for the right words—"a human incubator."

"So how did you leave it?" Millie pulled her chair closer.

"I said no. But I kept her business card."

Millie confiscated the last slice. "Did this Perez lady ever reveal what the clinic found so tantalizing about you?"

"Why not me?" Amoreena asked, and suddenly felt two pairs of riveting eyes. "No, that's what *she* said when I asked essentially the same question. Basically, the point was moot because I'd already declined."

The phone interrupted any further discussion.

Millie was up first. "Freeze the conversation till I return."

Through the kitchen window, Amoreena saw her roommate's expression turn somber. Millie set the receiver on the counter and walked back to the porch.

"Amy, it's the hospital."

The intensive care unit was on the second floor of the medical center. Dr. Gillespie stood at the nurses' station, dictating his admission notes, while Rosalind Cates hovered beside him talking with one of the ICU nurses.

When Amoreena entered, Cates shot her a curt glance before rambling for the exit. The woman reminded Amoreena of an obese vulture.

Dr. Gillespie interrupted his dictating and took Amoreena by the arm, moving her to a more private sector of ICU. He appeared fatigued; however, the overriding emotion his face portrayed was a disconcerting concern. She wondered how much of his concern was tapped for her mother and how much was attributable to the pressure he was surely feeling from the hospital's utilization review board. She then admonished herself for her cynicism.

Dr. Gillespie motioned her to a chair. "Your mother's suffered a setback, but it could've been much worse. We think one of the tumor nodules eroded through a small vessel in the pleura. That's the lining covering the lungs."

Amoreena already knew this fact from her anatomy class. She listened in silence.

"This has caused some bleeding into the space between the lung and chest wall," the specialist continued, "resulting in the formation of a pleural effusion. Your mother was experiencing some respiratory difficulty so, as a precaution, we transferred her to the ICU. I've removed the fluid. In the morning, we'll repeat a chest X ray to see how much, if any, has reaccumulated."

"And if it has?"

"We'll keep her in ICU until we get a handle on the situation." Dr. Gillespie attempted to sound hopeful.

Amoreena only shook her head. Now tacked on top of the escalating costs of chemotherapy, there'd be additional charges for the ICU stay. And no telling how long this could last. *At $1,500 a day.* She rose. "What did Ms. Cates want?"

Dr. Gillespie gave her a reassuring pat. "Don't worry about Rosalind Cates. The doctors still own the medical degrees. Now go pay your mom a visit. She's been asking for you. She's in Bed 4."

Geneva Daniels lay in a spaghetti maze of tubes, her head elevated. An IV snaked from one bruised forearm; the nasal cannula delivering oxygen wound away from her head in serpentine fashion; and an array of electrical wires, connecting her body to various instruments, monitored every vital function.

The sharp lines of her heart rhythm traveled across an oscilloscope screen in regular fashion.

Stepping to the side of the bed, Amoreena detected the aseptic smell of disinfectants, their astringent odors permeating the stall like huge invisible alcohol swabs. Her mom's respirations were slow and rhythmic, and she did not appear to be in any distress, though her skin appeared more pallid. Her eyes were clamped shut. She looked so frail, more so than on the ward, but Amoreena figured everyone appeared more frail with tubes and wires growing from their bodies.

"How ya doing?" she said softly.

Geneva's eyes opened. "Amy." She smiled. "I was dreaming."

Amoreena clutched her mother's hand, wondering for a second if her mom's dream included utilization review committees.

Geneva attempted a wan smile. "You were in it, and so was your dad. I don't remember much else."

"That's okay, Mom." The last thing she desired to hear was a dream about her dad. Since running out on them years ago, he'd never called, written, or given any kind of financial or emotional support. As far as Amoreena knew, he was living somewhere on the East Coast and worked in the gaming industry. To her, that was tantamount to being dead.

"You in much pain?" she asked, changing the subject.

Geneva shook her head. "Feel good. Dr. Gillespie was a sweetie." Then her forehead furrowed. "We're not going to argue are we?"

Amoreena gave her a gentle squeeze. "I got some good news."

"Tell me."

"I'm going to work in a medical research study at UCLA. The doctor who heads it is chairman of the school's admissions committee."

"I'm so proud of you, baby. See, I told you things would work out."

Mom, things are so far from working out you wouldn't believe.

Geneva suddenly looked fatigued. "I think I'll rest for a little bit."

Amoreena bent down and kissed her mother good night.

Chapter Five

Amoreena parked Silver in the patient lot located behind the *La Clínica de la Mujer* building. Less cars than she would have expected occupied the fenced-in area. The lot was barely a quarter filled.

She was fifteen minutes early for her 10 A.M. appointment with Ramona Perez. She used the time to calm her tense nerves with a cigarette.

In the park across the street, she heard a woman screaming at her two children. The language was Spanish, but the woman's angry inflection was clear. Kids. Until last week, children had been the last thing on Amoreena's mind.

Over the weekend two things had cemented Amoreena's resolve to follow up on the Perez woman's offer. Saturday morning, Geneva Daniel's thoracentesis result had returned positive for malignant cells in the pleural fluid. Not an auspicious sign. Though the oncologist had done his best to impress upon them that this finding was not totally unexpected, it did radically shrink the time frame for treatment options. He planned to enroll her mother in a combination chemotherapy–radiation therapy protocol in two weeks—if other *factors* did not provide a hindrance. His last statement had hung in the air like a rancid cloud. Amoreena interpreted the implication as "show me the money, baby," realizing it wasn't Dr. Gillespie's fault. He'd always treated her mother with dignity and respect. Amoreena attributed the bulk of the crisis to Rosalind Cates.

Later that same day, Jerry Fallwell had delivered the second of a one-two combination. Paraphrasing his professor of insurance law, he'd said that because her mother had failed to pay the required premiums, she'd essentially forfeited any chance for a speedy recovery. Most assuredly, the courts would take months to arrive at any type of verdict and, after piles of money spent, it may not even be in her mother's favor. The professor had suggested pursuing other options if time was a significant factor. Then, after the bad news, Fallwell had promptly asked Amoreena out on a date, which she'd politely declined.

Monday morning, her mother had been discharged home only to experience two episodes of severe nausea and vomiting. She'd refused returning to the hospital, and Amoreena had treated her with some Compazine prescribed by Dr. Gillespie. Then to make matters worse, a woman with a tinny voice had called to say her mother's Medi-Cal application for financial assistance had been denied because Ms. Daniels's signature was missing on line twelve, page three. Amoreena nearly exploded when the woman suggested a new application be filed.

Last night, the financial reiterations had played in her mind until past 3 A.M. When she awoke, she felt like she'd been dragged through an IRS audit. The numbers just didn't seem to add up correctly, and unless something was seriously juggled, they never would.

Amoreena snuffed out her cigarette on the asphalt and strode to the clinic entrance. Upon entering the Women's Clinic (she preferred the facility's English translation), she was immediately impressed by how much the center's interior contrasted with the two-story building's staid brick exterior.

A blue-marble fountain, replete with decorative stones and climbing ferns, occupied the lobby's central area. The gurgling sound of cascading water presented a soothing background for the large-screen television broadcasting an instructional video on breast self-examination. Several small children frolicked at the fountain's edge under the watchful eyes of their mothers. The floor was white marble and, adorning two entire walls, hung woven tapestries depicting figurines reminiscent of the Mayan era. Magnificent potted plants filled each corner, all real, and each exquisitely manicured down to the last leaf and petal. The unique interior design made Amoreena feel as if she'd entered a tropical paradise, minus the animals. It was far easier for her to envision a setup of this magnitude in Beverly Hills, not Santa Ana, California.

A security guard sat at a circular booth situated at the far end of the waiting area. Amoreena met his gaze, then watched him check a monitor before reaching for a phone.

Almost immediately, Ramona Perez appeared from behind double swinging doors.

"Amoreena," she said animatedly. She greeted her with a warm handshake.

Amoreena noted the woman's title printed on a gold name tag—CLINIC COORDINATOR.

"Nice setup," she said with an awkward grin. "I'd hate to be responsible for your interior-design bill."

Ramona's eyes sparkled. "Everything you see in here is authentic."

"Even the tapestries. They look museum quality."

"Especially the tapestries. We're an extremely successful company." Ramona stepped back, motioning Amoreena beside her. "How is your mother, dear?"

"Better. She suffered a bad episode yesterday, but she's at home now and holding down food. Dr. Gillespie, her oncologist, placed her on a liquid diet for two days."

Ramona acknowledged the summations with a few empathetic nods while leading them through the double doors.

Amoreena noted both were equipped with smart card security locks, and she did not miss the video camera mounted near the ceiling. She assumed the city's propensity for crime made the surveillance necessary.

The corridor widened near an elevator bay across from

which stood a four-foot onyx statue of a woman. Her highly polished facial features reminded Amoreena of the evil witch from the *Wizard of Oz*.

Ramona patted the statue's head. "Meet Ixchel, the Mayan goddess of medicine. In Mayan culture, she was also known as the old Moon Goddess."

"She doesn't look very happy," Amoreena said, gazing at the gaping mouth and irisless eyes.

"She has her days."

"Don't we all." Amoreena moved to catch up with the clinic coordinator, who'd resumed walking. "Is this a common theme?" she asked, seeing more paintings with Spanish motifs.

"You're referring to the tapestries."

"And Ixchel."

Ramona grinned. "So you're on a first-name basis. That portends well for you."

The coordinator's expression turned more serious. "Much of our business is transacted in Mexico and Central America, as well as Europe. But with this location, our newest addition to the Meechum Medical chain, we thought the decor tied in nicely with the largely Hispanic clientele we serve in Southern California."

The administration suite was located at the end of the hall, which placed it near the rear of the building. One entire half was devoted to a series of partitioned cubicles, each equipped with a computer, fax, and a phone line. Most were occupied, almost entirely by female employees working the phones, and Amoreena could hear fragments of conversation, though the majority of the speaking was carried on in languages other than English. She recognized Spanish and French but not several of the others.

Ramona escorted Amoreena past the cubicles into a well-furnished office suite, replete with more indoor plants and impressive reproduction wall prints.

The coordinator approached a receptionist, said something in Spanish, then motioned Amoreena to a plush sofa.

"Irene Leggett will be with you shortly. I hope your meeting progresses satisfactorily, and I look forward to speaking with you again." She shook Amoreena's hand and departed.

Setting her purse beside her, Amoreena reached for an issue of *People* on a coffee table but changed her mind when she realized it was the Spanish edition. When she looked up, the receptionist was watching her. Amoreena smiled, and the young woman returned to her typewriter.

With no desire to read, Amoreena began to review some biochemistry notes in her head.

She'd reached midway through the Krebs Cycle of enzymatic reactions when a door opened. A tall, lissome, neatly dressed woman stepped forward, offering one hand.

"Good morning, Amoreena. I'm Irene Leggett, the clinic administrator. I apologize for your wait, but in deference to your heavy academic schedule, I promise to keep this first visit as brief and informative as possible. Please come in, we'll talk in here."

Irene's office was enormous and lavishly furnished in a modern executive style. Adjacent to a large oak desk sat a fully equipped computer workstation. A voluminous library of texts and journals filled one entire wall, while mounted behind the desk hung a huge intricately detailed map of the western hemisphere. It was the largest map Amoreena had ever seen. The layout was all quite impressive on one scale, but left Amoreena with no feeling for Irene Leggett as an individual, other than that she was successful. There was nothing personal visible—no family photos, framed diplomas, not even a name plate for the desk.

Watching the clinic administrator with her precise movements, she couldn't help but entertain the idea she'd seen the woman somewhere before, though she was confident this initial impression was inaccurate. Amoreena partially attributed this feeling to the fact that Irene Leggett was an extraordinarily handsome woman. Approaching fifty, with exquisitely molded features, white hair cut short around the ears, and a noticeably feminine figure, Irene could've easily passed for a spokesperson for some corporate product or political cause. She exuded the confidence of someone who expected to get her way and usually did.

"Amoreena." Irene said the name more in musing. "I don't believe I've ever heard that name before."

"It's from an old Elton John song. He's one of my mom's favorite artists."

"It has a pleasant ring." Irene opened a file drawer and placed a folder on her desk. "So let's begin. First, it's very important to me that you feel relaxed today. And as the administrator of the Surrogacy Procurement Program, I encourage you to ask as many questions as you like during our time together. My role will be to provide you with the information necessary in order to make an informed decision. Now, I understand your mother is quite ill."

"She was diagnosed with metastatic cervical cancer six months ago. She's already had one course of chemotherapy, but her doctor says more are necessary." Amoreena finished, hoping she hadn't sounded too bitter.

"I'm sorry. My own son died of liver failure. It was very difficult." Irene paused appropriately before opening the folder. Inside, Amoreena saw pages of Xeroxed documents, each including a photograph of a woman. Much of the printed material had been blacked out.

"Many of our women are foreigners," Irene explained while positioning the folder across the desk. "The majority reside in Mexico and Latin America though we do have requests from Europe and occasionally as distant as Vietnam." She gave Amoreena a chance to look a moment before continuing. "More recently, our organization has been noticing an escalating demand for our services by well-to-do Caucasian couples, some of whom are American."

Amoreena listened while studying the photographs of the young women of varying ethnicities and ages. Most appeared of Hispanic descent, but she also counted Asians, several pretty African-American girls, and more than a few Caucasians who looked European in dress.

With each page she turned, Amoreena found herself wondering what the story was behind the face. The eyes, some bright, some hopeful, and some even fearful, gave no clue to the driving force behind each woman's decision. One girl looked to be barely in her teens. She was a dark-complected beauty with brown eyes that appeared too large for her face.

Except for a small ovoid scar on her forehead, her skin appeared flawless.

"Initial impressions?" she heard Irene ask.

"So young," Amoreena said.

Irene glanced once at the particular photo and gave an understanding smile. "You must consider that it's quite common in some countries for women to complete their families prior to their twentieth birthdays."

Amoreena closed the album. "Where's she from?"

"Mexico. Her actual file is confidential, of course." Irene pulled the folder to her side of the desk. "Amoreena, the initial introduction to our organization will be quite informal. Informality fosters trust, I believe. If at its conclusion you're still interested, I'll give you a copy of the contract and a psychological profile questionnaire to fill out. You'll be provided with as much time as you like. Take them home." Irene rose and opened a second file drawer, removing a small pamphlet. "This contains some background information about our clinics. Actually the Women's Clinic or Clínica de la Mujer, as it's called south of the border, is a subsidiary of a much larger organization, Meechum Medical Corporation. The Women's Clinic is our first in the US; however, we're currently negotiating to open a much larger facility in San Diego sometime next year."

As Irene explained, Amoreena's attention fell on the pamphlet's glossy cover. Under the printed logo was inset a photograph of an impressive modern compound, reminiscent of a secluded resort or college campus. Several large concrete structures with sharp architectural lines sat partially hidden in a valley of lush vegetation. Rising above a plantation-style house, the azure peaks of mountains almost touched the clouds.

"Looks like Club Med," Amoreena said.

"That's our Las Canas facility in Central America. We're extremely proud of the research carried on there." Irene gave Amoreena a moment to review the packet. "Meechum Medical was founded twelve years ago by a geneticist. We've grown tremendously and now have clinics in Mexico, Central

and South America, Europe, and the United States. In the last
two years, we've conducted business in over thirty countries."

Amoreena felt overwhelmed. She'd never have expected an
operation of such immensity behind the plain two-story brick
facade. "What do you do besides the surrogacy services?"

"Meechum specializes in pharmaceutical and medical research, concentrating on the genetic treatment of inheritable
disease. We envision someday treating the fetus before birth,
thereby obviating expensive neonatal hospitalizations.
Meechum Corporation also manages a number of clinical-
related provider services throughout Mexico and Central
America."

"I never heard of you."

Irene smiled. "Amoreena, there are literally hundreds of
biotechnology companies with annual revenues exceeding
fifty million dollars that you're unacquainted with. Meechum
Corporation is not traded on any exchanges, and the majority
of our research is financed from within. The remainder is conducted exclusively through private grants and foundations."
Irene let this last point sink in before rising from her chair.
"Allow me to show you a little of our facility."

"All our clinical activity is conducted on the second floor,"
Irene explained, as they rode the elevator one story up.

Amoreena mostly listened as the administrator conducted
the tour. She could tell Irene was proud of the clinic's physical
plant and rightly so. There was money here. The halls and
exam rooms sparkled pristinely, and all the medical equipment appeared to be top of the line.

Irene pointed out a sonogram machine. "Third-generation
ultrasonography. We can tell the sex of the fetus at eight
weeks."

Amoreena wasn't sure whether this was the norm, but the
way Irene boasted, she had the impression it was way above
standard.

The second floor was partitioned into two main depart-
ments, gynecology/fertility and obstetrics. There were fifteen
exam rooms and four procedure rooms. In addition, the clinic

had two fully equipped operating rooms, with anesthetists and doctors on call around the clock. Amoreena somewhat nervously checked out the in vitro fertilization room, where the surrogate patients were evaluated.

Throughout the tour, Irene maintained the conversation low-key—no high-pressure sales tactics—and she spoke knowledgeably regarding all aspects of patient care and evaluation. She also inquired informally about Amoreena's background—a happy childhood, raised by a single mother, presently no boyfriend though plenty in the past, no plans for marriage, schooling takes first priority, and yes, Amoreena thought the premed opportunities at Chapman University were excellent.

In turn, Irene revealed parts of her past. After graduating as an English major from an eastern university, she eventually went on to receive an MBA from Princeton. She worked for several of the pharmaceutical giants—Merck and Bristol-Myers to name two—and was eventually recruited to oversee Meechum Corporation's medical services division. In her own words, it was a brilliant career move, and she enjoyed her work immensely. She was fifty-two and spoke Spanish and Portuguese fluently, the Portuguese an advantage in various locales in South America where they hoped to expand. On a more personal level, she revealed she'd never remarried after the death of her son.

"What interests you about becoming a surrogate?" Irene asked. They'd stopped outside one of the obstetrics procedure rooms.

"The money," Amoreena answered candidly.

Irene reacted as if she'd expected this exact answer. "Financial incentives are the number one motivational factor in the vast majority of our cases. However, surrogacy is far too complex an issue to be relegated to a series of bank deposits. We're not bartering books, automobiles, or computer software. We're in the business of lives, Amoreena. Human lives. And I'm not just alluding to the babies involved, but also to the commissioning couple. And to you, dear. If you're fortunate enough to be chosen as a Meechum surrogate, you'll find yourself so deeply involved in the entire process, the money may even become secondary."

Amoreena resisted rolling her eyes. "The money second-ary?"

"No, it's true," Irene said, touching Amoreena's arm. "You'll find yourself asking questions about the baby. What does she look like? What color is his hair? Will she grow up pretty? Will he need glasses? Braces? Will she be smart? Will he be good at calculus? And there'll be a thousand more thoughts inundating you at every turn. And you must be emotionally prepared to deal with these issues. Because that's what surrogacy is all about. Raw emotions. Strip away the basic science and you're left with love, caring, happiness. Even regret, though we do our best to mitigate this possibility by ensuring all our girls are mentally equipped to handle the emotional impact of surrogate motherhood."

Amoreena experienced a moment of regret of her own for having been so blatantly honest with the clinic administrator.

Irene smiled. "Listen to me going on like that. It's just that I feel so strongly about the Meechum family. In no way was I attempting to disparage your financial wishes, Amoreena. In fact, it's no accident that one very important consideration in determining the location of our clinics is the economic status of the clientele we'll serve. Indigent clients are hungrier, have more mouths to feed, and therefore have greater incentives to participate in our surrogacy programs. And demand has never been greater, what with the inordinate delays couples face through conventional adoption agencies. Our surrogacy programs work for all parties involved. We have happy clients on both sides."

The obstetric procedure room door swung open, and an orderly wheeled a young Hispanic woman out in a wheelchair.

The first thing Amoreena noticed, other than the patient's fifth- or sixth-month pregnancy, was that this girl did *not* look happy. She appeared frightened and on the verge of tears. Their eyes met momentarily, and Amoreena suddenly felt the urge to reach out and touch her. Just as quickly, the feeling passed and Amoreena realized that the girl's emotional state could easily be explained by her physical condition. After all, pregnancy was frightening, especially if experiencing it for the first time.

Irene hastily moved Amoreena down the hall.

"We have three delivery suites fully equipped to handle any conceivable emergency, including performing caesareans if necessary." She saw Amoreena tense and quickly added, "C-sections are performed in less than five percent of our cases, far below the industry average."

Irene steered them down a second hall leading to a conference room. She touched Amoreena lightly on the arm. "Our last stop. I want to introduce you to two people."

She ushered Amoreena inside. Around a large oak office table were eight chairs, two of which were occupied by the second and third members of the clinic's executive committee.

Irene introduced Dr. Ross Becker, Meechum Corporation's medical director, and Mr. Tom Volkman, the attorney for medical affairs.

The two men sat directly across from Amoreena, and she immediately noted one of the men, Dr. Becker, was quick to smile while Mr. Volkman simply nodded dismissively and returned to a stack of notes before him.

Amoreena instantly liked Dr. Becker more. He was handsome, looking every bit like the quintessential television doctor actor—fiftyish, gray hair, nattily dressed, and exuding confidence and empathy with the slightest movement of his eyes.

In contrast, Mr. Volkman, though not unattractive, was dressed more slovenly, tie askew, sleeves rolled to his elbows, and his disquieting demeanor seemed to reach out to her across the table.

Reflexively, Amoreena pushed back against the spine of her chair.

In a reassuring show of support, Irene took the chair immediately to Amoreena's right. "It's not often we get a doctor and lawyer on the same side of the table," she said, smiling at the two men.

Amoreena sensed the line sounded rehearsed, but there was little time to dwell on the thought before Mr. Volkman launched his first question.

"Ms. Daniels, you've never been married, is that correct?"

Quickly Irene intervened. "Amoreena, before answering I

want to assure you this interview is strictly informal and entirely confidential. It just gives us a chance to get to know our girls a little better."

"I understand," Amoreena said, swallowing the lump that had suddenly bloomed in her throat. She inhaled, decided against asking for an ashtray, and met the attorney's steady gaze. "That's correct, Mr. Volkman."

"And no children?" he asked.

"That's correct."

"Healthy?"

"Yes sir. Other than an appendectomy when I was ten."

Mr. Volkman made a couple notes on a card. Then he asked, "Ever been pregnant?"

Amoreena felt Irene tap her leg with the tip of her shoe. It gave her a sense of camaraderie.

"Never," she answered calmly.

"And your occupation?"

"I'm a student."

"Major?"

"Premed. I want to become a doctor."

Volkman gave a noncommittal grunt, then continued. "Your mother has metastatic cancer, correct?"

"Yes sir, cervical."

"That's unfortunate," Volkman said, devoid of empathy. He touched his lower lip, studied a notation, then looked up. "Thank you, Ms. Daniels. I wish your mother a speedy recovery."

"Dr. Becker," Irene said.

The physician tacitly perused Amoreena a moment. "Ms. Daniels, how do you feel about children?"

Amoreena sensed a trick question but couldn't determine the trap. Not wishing to show any hesitation, she answered as best she could. "I like children, and one day I'd like to have a family. But right now, my mother's health and my education come first." She finished with a forced smile.

Dr. Becker rubbed his chin, seemed on the verge of posing a second question, but instead left her with an approving nod.

"We appreciate you coming in, Ms. Daniels," he said.

* * *

Back in the administrator's office, Amoreena was handed a folder containing some papers, along with the promotional pamphlet.

"Read the questionnaire carefully and thoughtfully," Irene instructed. "It's designed to make you think. Will I be happy as a surrogate? What do I think of carrying another couple's baby? Is this right for me? And study the contract. The compensation terms are spelled out on the back pages."

Irene escorted Amoreena out the door.

In the reception area Amoreena saw Ramona Perez, who smiled and waved.

Irene placed a hand on Amoreena's elbow. "I want you to be sure this is right for you, dear."

"I understand, Ms. Leggett."

"Irene."

"Irene," Amoreena corrected herself.

"That's my girl," Irene said. "We look forward to seeing you again. And we all wish your mother the best."

After a brief embrace, she turned Amoreena over to the clinic coordinator.

"How'd it go?" Ramona asked on the way to the car.

"I'm impressed."

"I'm glad."

For a full two minutes after Ramona departed, Amoreena sat alone on the front seat of Silver with the engine idling. She'd actually done it. And she felt not just a little proud for having kept the appointment, though she was relieved the ordeal was over.

She reached for the folder and removed the contract. Recalling Irene's words, she turned to the last pages where the terms of compensation were elucidated.

She read the numbers.

"Oh shit."

Becker moved a stack of charts aside and swung one hip up on the corner of Irene's desk. "Volkman's concerned she's too smart."

"Who?" Irene asked, scrolling down a list of the clinic's most recent patient census.

"Ms. Daniels."

"She's a second-year premedical student, not a Ph.D in biogenetics."

"Whose *uninsured* mother is dying of cancer," Becker added aloofly.

Irene tapped the mouse and the monitor went blank. "Our numbers are up ten percent this quarter."

Chapter Six

"Fifty thousand dollars!" Millie pushed aside a plate of cheese nachos. "It's baby selling."

"It's not baby selling," Daryl countered.

Amoreena yanked the contract from in front of both their faces. She'd picked a secluded table at Los Vacitos to break the news. Other than herself and her two close friends, there were no other college students present, only shift workers. Her mom had once celebrated a birthday at the local pub with some former employees of H&M Printing.

"I'm not selling a baby," Amoreena said, settling the argument. "I'm performing a service."

Millie eyed her roommate. "Maybe you should try prelaw instead. You're beginning to sound like one."

Letting the comment slide, Amoreena reviewed the specifics out loud.

"Ten thousand dollars when I'm fertilized. Another ten grand each at the successful conclusion of the first and second trimesters, and twenty big ones at delivery."

Millie slid her chair over and finished reading. "The final fee will be disbursed upon delivery of a viable healthy infant to Meechum Medical Corporation."

"Sounds legit to me," Daryl said, finishing his beer.

Millie frowned. "I don't know."

Amoreena looked up. "What do you mean you don't know?"

"I said I don't know."

Amoreena was beginning to feel just a little perturbed at her roommate's attitude. Millie could at least be more understanding. It wasn't *her* mother with metastatic cancer.

A vintage song by CCR began to play on the jukebox. Amoreena listened to a line. After Elton John, Creedence Clearwater Revival was probably her mother's favorite vocal group.

She felt a hand on hers.

"Look, Amy," Millie said. "I'm rooting for you and your mom as much as anyone, and if I had the money, we wouldn't even be discussing this damn contract. I just don't want you to do anything foolish or something you might regret later. I love you and Geneva and . . ." A smile began to break at the corners of her mouth. "Plus, Daryl and I don't want to see you get fat."

Amoreena feigned a punch. "You jerks."

Early-afternoon traffic was lining up around the Orange Circle when they emerged from the pub. Across the street, *mariachi* music blared from a Mexican restaurant. The air carried the savory scents of corn tortillas and quesadillas.

"I appreciate the embryo notes," Amoreena said, pecking Daryl on the cheek.

"Anytime." They began to walk.

Millie saw the feathers first, splayed against Silver's windshield. "Shit," she groaned.

Amoreena walked to the driver's side of the Mustang. "It looks like a pigeon."

The dead bird lay with one wing wedged down under a wiper blade. A single drop of coagulated blood clung to its beak.

"It must've been blinded by the sun's glare and flown into the glass," Daryl said.

Millie stepped closer. "How odd."

Daryl disengaged the bird. "I think its neck's broken."

Amoreena watched him discard the pigeon along the curb.

"Poor thing," she said. She was glad she didn't believe in omens.

* * *

After dinner, Amoreena studied for an hour before setting her notes aside. She dug up the surrogacy questionnaire and wandered out to the kitchen table. She found a CD of Matchbox 20, turned the volume to low, and hit PLAY.

She poured herself a glass of wine, grabbed an open box of cookies, and returned to the table. Earlier she'd called Jerry Fallwell, who'd eagerly given her the name of a friend who practiced family law. She would call the attorney, a Mr. Stein, first thing tomorrow regarding her surrogacy contract.

She consumed two cookies before embarking on the questionnaire. Do you consider yourself in good health? Do you have any siblings? How is their health? Most of the questions were straightforward. She breezed through the first two pages.

Page three began with an inquiry into past psychiatric care. Amoreena scribbled a no. *Ask me again in six months.*

From that point on the questions required a modicum of thought. When you were a child did you ever find a baby bird and attempt to raise it as your own rather than return it to its nest? Amoreena thought of the dead pigeon. She wrote no. More questions dealt with the period of childhood. Were you adopted? No. Ever reside in a foster home? No. Did you know both your parents? Yes. Did you love both your parents? No.

"When are you going to tell Geneva?" Millie stood in the hall, wearing a Lakers T-shirt that hung to her knees.

Amoreena yawned. "Have you ever been required to give up a family pet and been unable to do so?"

"What?"

"Some of these questions are really stupid."

Millie took a seat and pulled the questionnaire to her side of the table. She read briefly before looking up. "Well, have you?"

"Have I what?"

"Been unable to give up a family pet?"

Amoreena reached for another cookie. "I remember I once had this turtle, one of those little green ones with the red ears.

One weekend, Mom and I took a trip to San Diego, and I had to leave it with a neighbor. I cried the entire trip worried how poor Herman would survive without me."

"And?"

"The lady's son who was supposed to watch Herman ended up letting it go in Irvine Lake. When I found out, Mom had to hold me back from kicking the shit out of the little bastard. Girl, I was the angriest eight-year-old around for about two weeks."

Amoreena pulled the page back and jotted an answer.

Millie stretched across the table. "You put no. I thought you said you cried."

"But I was never officially *unable* to give up Herman," Amoreena said with a trace of defensiveness.

"True." Millie went to the refrig and returned with a cup of nonfat yogurt. "Ever thought of getting a dog?"

"What for? They eat and then go out in the yard and make a mess."

"Just an idea." Millie said, walking toward her bedroom.

Amoreena waited until her roommate's door was closed. "You clean up after it?" she called out. "And any pet sleeps outside unless the weather's bad."

Millie stuck her head out. "Deal."

Jacob Stein leased a converted three-room bungalow several blocks from the Orange Mission in old Orange. The placard posted on the front lawn indicated his practice specialized in family law and personal injury.

For fifteen minutes, Amoreena waited impatiently, seated in a rusty brown leather chair in an unpretentious office of wood-paneled walls and oak-beamed ceilings. If Mr. Stein didn't hurry, she would be late for her morning's ethics class, which started at nine-thirty.

A glance upward from her coffee cup met Mr. Stein's intense gaze.

"You've indicated you're an acquaintance of Jerry's, Ms. Daniels?" His tone was noncommittal.

"I consulted him on another issue," Amoreena said. "He spoke highly of you."

Mr. Stein grunted indifferently and returned to perusing the Meechum Corporation contract. She wondered if he would have grunted similarly if this initial visit had been for a wrenched back or twisted ankle.

"You mentioned this is for a friend," he said without looking up.

"Yes."

Amoreena watched him reevaluate one particular paragraph before setting the paperwork aside.

"It's your standard business contract, Ms. Daniels." Stein tapped the paper as he reeled off specifics. "Natural father is married, desires his sperm inseminated in surrogate by means of artificial insemination. Surrogate represents she is capable of conceiving child. Surrogate understands and agrees not to attempt to form a parent-child relationship with any child she conceives, carries, and delivers, pursuant to the aforementioned." He stopped tapping. "Where this contract varies from the norm pertains to two points."

Amoreena leaned forward in her chair.

"Typically," Stein began, "any compensation for services shall be paid upon surrender of the child. Not so here. Moneys begin distribution at inception.

"Also, the father usually agrees to pay all expenses incurred by surrogate pursuant to the pregnancy. However in this case, Meechum Corporation, acting as the intermediary, assumes all financial responsibility, which I might add exceeds the upper limits of what has been standard and customary in the surrogacy business in terms of direct compensation."

"Is that cause for concern?" Amoreena asked.

"Actually, both points benefit the surrogate." Stein gathered the contract and handed it across the desk. "Good luck, Ms. Daniels," he said. Then with a sly grin, he added, "And I wish the same for your friend."

"Thank you, Mr. Stein."

* * *

Amoreena had just parked Silver in the student lot when her pager beeped.

"Damn," she said, reading the number to her mom's apartment.

Amoreena delved into her purse for her cell phone and called.

"What's wrong?" she asked as soon as Geneva answered.

"Amy, can you talk?"

Amoreena immediately picked up on the distress in her mother's voice. "I'll be right over." She hung up before her mom could protest. She hated missing another class but as long as she could scrounge notes off someone she'd survive.

Geneva Daniels rented a small two-bedroom unit at the Terrace Apartments.

As soon as the door opened, Amoreena noticed her mother's red eyes and tear-streaked cheeks.

"Should I call Gillespie?" she asked, stepping inside.

"No, no dear, I'm feeling okay."

"You don't look so hot."

"Look at this." Geneva handed over the written notice. Amoreena walked to a chair and read the two neatly typed lines.

"The bastards are raising your rent."

"Amy, please."

"What do you want me to do, call up management and thank them for gouging you two hundred dollars more each month?" Amoreena folded the paper and deposited it under the kitchen sink with the rest of the trash. "This really sucks."

"What are we going to do?"

Amoreena shrugged and opened the refrigerator. The quart of Gatorade she'd bought her mom was three-quarters empty and two eggs were missing from the dozen that were there two days ago. She checked a cabinet. Two cans of soup were gone.

"What are you doing?" Geneva asked.

"Making sure you're eating."

"You think I'd lie about my appetite?"

"Yes," Amoreena said without hesitation. She turned for the door. "Mom, I don't want you worrying about the money. Use what you have to out of the savings account, and I'll come up with the rest."

"I don't want you working."

"Nothing I do will affect my grades."

"You promised."

"I know."

Amoreena felt her mother take her arm as they walked out to the car.

"One day," Geneva said, "this will all be behind us. You'll be a successful physician, married, and I'll be the proudest grandmother in my bridge group."

"You don't play bridge." Amoreena adjusted her mother's scarf. "Blue really looks good on you. It highlights the color in your eyes."

"How are your classes?" Geneva asked suddenly, changing the subject.

"Fine."

"You always say fine."

"You've seen my grades."

"All right, Ms. Einstein," Geneva said, embracing her daughter.

Amoreena unlocked the car and climbed in. "I'll call you tonight."

"Love you."

Silver's engine backfired once before idling roughly.

Geneva frowned. "What's that smell?"

"Silver's burning a little oil."

"How long have you been driving like this. Is it safe?"

"It's safe. Now go back inside and rest. I'll have a mechanic take a look under the hood." She began to pull away. "And don't forget to eat. Plenty of fluids. And I want you increasing your activity some. Don't lie in bed all day."

Geneva waved. "My daughter, the doctor."

Amoreena honked a good-bye, wondering if it was just the rearview mirror that made her mother appear more frail.

She found Daryl and Millie on the steps of the Science Center.

"Ah, Chapman's famous student la absentia," he said, surrendering his ethics notes.

"Miss anything important?" she asked.

"It's all there."

Amoreena made a short detour to the library, where she Xeroxed the lecture notes. She'd just made it back to the exit when she heard her name called.

She froze, recognizing the voice. Turning, she saw Dr. Sheffield homing in on her like a heat-seeking missile. Millie and Daryl politely excused themselves.

"I tried to catch you after ethics class," the premed advisor said.

"Morning, Dr. Sheffield," she said, hoping he didn't have bad news regarding the Pike Hypertension Study. She'd been told her scheduled start date would be early November.

"I was wondering if we might talk," he said pleasantly.

"Sure."

"My office?"

Amoreena nodded through an avalanche of thoughts, all bad. Could the university have found out about her her mom's medical condition and the possible untoward financial repercussions for one of their scholarship recipients? Surely, Sheffield knew nothing of her visit to the Women's Clinic. Maybe Stein had spoken to Fallwell. But then Fallwell wasn't acquainted with Sheffield. Was he?

Doing her best cool and composed imitation, Amoreena sat and waited for Sheffield to make himself comfortable behind his desk. She was sure a bomb was about to detonate. The only unknown pertained to her chances of survival.

Dr. Sheffield imbibed a long drink of coffee. "Amoreena," he began slowly, "have you given much thought to graduating in three years?"

The question took her by complete surprise. "No," she said taken aback. "I mean, it'd be nice, but . . ."

"I've been reviewing the curriculum for the beginning junior premeds. I wasn't aware you'd undertaken such heavy loads your freshman and sophomore years. Now if you were able to squeeze pathophysiology and neuroanatomy into your spring semester, you'd satisfy the requirements for a three-year graduate."

Momentarily stunned, Amoreena sat mesmerized by the

possibilities. She could enter medical school a year early, become a doctor a year early, and, most significantly, the chances of her mother being present at her graduation would increase by one entire year.

One whole year. Unbelievable.

"What would this entail?" Amoreena asked. "Besides the two additional courses."

"Nothing major. Just wanted to get your feelings on the issue before I place your name alongside Gladys Peterson's on the list of students taking the Medical College Admission Test this fall. The date is"—he checked a calendar—"December fifteen, a Saturday. That is if you concur."

"I concur," Amoreena said, unable to disguise her eager anticipation.

Dr. Sheffield escorted her to the door. "I want you to understand three-year students are judged more stringently than the typical four-year college applicant. Your grades are your ticket, Amoreena."

Almost as an afterthought, he added, "And let's not neglect class attendance."

The entire afternoon blew by Amoreena like a stiff breeze. The prospect of graduating in three years had energized her to a new level. There was no doubt in her mind she could handle the added stress and workload. Next week, she would shop at the campus bookstore for a study guide on taking the MCAT, the standardized Medical College Admission Test by which all premed applicants were ranked. A high score would guarantee her acceptance.

Deciding the oil leak could wait, Amoreena parked Silver under the carport and ran inside, where she found Millie's hand-scribbled note by the phone to call Dr. Gillespie.

Fortunately, the oncologist was still at his office.

"Amoreena," he said, his voice animated. "A spot has become available on the advanced cervical cancer investigational protocol. I've convinced the Utilization Review Committee that Geneva Daniels should be offered this option."

"That's fantastic."

"It gives us a fighting chance," Dr. Gillespie continued. "On the negative side, since this is classified as an experimental model, no insurance will cover the treatments, including Medi-Cal. I didn't discuss the actual cost with your mother for fear she might refuse the treatment since there is only a predicted twenty-five percent five-year survival rate."

"That's twenty-five more percent than we had before."

"That's the only way to look at it."

Bracing herself, Amoreena asked, "Dr. Gillespie, what are the actual costs?"

There was a moment's hesitation.

"Thirty thousand dollars."

Chapter Seven

"Welcome aboard," Irene said with a wide grin.

Amoreena watched the clinic administrator examine the signatures on four different pages. The turning point in the decision-making process had been Dr. Gillespie's news that the investagational cancer treatment protocol had become available for her mother—sequential cisplatin and 5-Fluorouracil in combination with radiotherapy. The hospital bills would escalate rapidly.

When she'd turned in the psychological profile, a part of her had secretly hoped she wouldn't be accepted, perhaps the clinic psychologists would unearth an aberration in her mental makeup nonconducive to surrogating. But when Ramona called yesterday evening, an immediate sense of relief rolled over Amoreena. She could almost see the check for that first ten thousand.

Irene stamped the contract with the official Meechum Corporation seal, made a copy, and handed the original to Amoreena.

"For your records, dear. Don't lose it."

Folding it quickly, Amoreena slid it down into her purse.

"Nervous?" Irene asked.

"Some."

"I'd be somewhat concerned if you weren't." She stood and

held out her hand. "We're proud to have you as a member of our organization."

Almost reluctantly, Amoreena asked, "What's next?"

Irene smiled. "Your physical."

Ever since her first gynecologic examination when she was fifteen, Amoreena had hated placing her feet in the metal stirrups. But with each exam, she'd grown to realize the importance of the annual checkup.

If only her mother had submitted to more regular . . .

"Ms. Daniels." A nurse removed a thermometer from Amoreena's mouth. "Your temperature is normal." She completed the blood pressure, pulse, and respirations and noted the findings in a chart. "Doctor will be in shortly."

After a polite knock, the door opened and a man in a white lab coat entered.

"I'm Dr. Louis Rafael," he said. The introduction involved a brief handshake, and, though his accent was Spanish, the enunciation was precise. He must've picked up on the change in Amoreena's expression because he added, "I realize you were expecting Dr. Becker; unfortunately he's involved in another case. I'm an associate. If you'd prefer to wait . . ."

"I trust you," Amoreena said. She watched Dr. Rafael check the instrument tray. He was a handsome man, tall, and built like a triathlete. With thick black hair that touched his collar, he was much younger than Dr. Becker, possibly in his early thirties.

When he turned, she was immediately attracted to his brown eyes. They were both bold and friendly. She could almost hear them saying *relax*. Amoreena decided she liked him.

Dr. Rafael stretched on a pair of latex gloves. "There's an old Spanish saying. *Dios hizo desnudes, nosotros nos avergonzamos.* Roughly translated, God made us naked, man made us ashamed, which roughly means, take it easy, Amoreena, this portion of the exam will be very brief."

Amoreena lied back. "I hope everything's in order," she said. "Roughly translated, let's get this over with."

Minutes later, Amoreena sat dressed in the laboratory while a technician drew her blood and ran a urinalysis. When she inquired regarding results, he simply smiled with hollow eyes and escorted her past a procedure room to a cramped office.

Dr. Rafael motioned her inside. "I apologize for the disorder. Please, sit."

Amoreena waited for him to slide behind a small desk piled high with charts, before saying, "What's the verdict, Doc? Do I pass?"

He smiled affably. "You're in excellent health."

"That means I'm acceptable."

"Yes."

"Thank you." Amoreena held his steady gaze for a few awkward moments until her attention diverted to a framed photograph on the desk. She leaned closer. "Where was this taken? It's beautiful."

Dr. Rafael moved aside a stack of charts. "Guatemala. The lost Maya city of Tikal slept for over a thousand years until its discovery in 1848." He picked up the photo. "I took the picture when I was eleven."

"The couple are your parents?"

"Yes, my mother was English, my father full-blooded Indian. The English ruled in our household," he said.

"They still live in Central America?"

He repositioned the photo. "They're deceased."

"I'm sorry."

Without further elaboration, he opened a file drawer and retrieved an envelope.

"Amoreena, this contains your temperature chart, calendar, and instructions. Your last menstrual cycle was when?"

"One week ago. It ended September ninth."

Dr. Rafael removed the calendar and placed an "x" on the appropriate date. "All set then. You're familiar with how to use this?"

Taking the packet, Amoreena concisely reviewed what she'd learned during the history and physical. "I monitor my temperature every day at the same time. Morning is best. And I record it here." She pointed to the correct area on the ovulation chart. "When I see a half degree drop in my basal body temperature, I schedule an appointment for that day."

"You learn fast." Dr. Rafael walked her into the hall. "Don't worry, Amoreena, you'll do just fine."

After directing her to the elevators, he returned to his desk and picked up the phone.

Speaking in fluent Spanish, he said, "The American is on her way."

Standing outside Irene Leggett's office, Amoreena smoothed her skirt and shoved the pack of Montclairs deeper into her purse.

I did it. Almost on the verge of being light-headed, she took a few deep breaths to calm her nerves. Though her sense of accomplishment was less than when she aced an exam, just the idea that she'd come a step closer to financial security for her mom made her feel as if a lead weight had been removed from her neck. She'd never been so close to fifty thousand dollars.

She was just about to knock when the door opened.

Tom Volkman stepped around her. "Hello, Ms. Daniels."

"Hello."

He passed without another word.

"Amoreena, please come in." Irene sat behind her desk, reading over some documents.

"Is he always so controlled?" Amoreena asked, finding her chair.

Irene continued to read. "Who, Tom?" She looked up with an amused pose. "I think, yes. However, his legal mind is brilliant so we excuse his apparent aloofness." She set the file down. "And as for you, dear, it appears everything's a go. The corporation has agreed to hire you as a surrogate. If at any time during the coming months you have any questions or problems concerning your role, please call either me or Dr. Becker. One of us is always available. Concerns?"

"Just one."

Irene's eyes narrowed.

"Will I ever meet the prospective parents?" Amoreena asked.

"Section six, paragraph two," Irene paraphrased. "At no

time will surrogate come in contact with or attempt to establish contact with future parents."

"That sounds like a no."

The administrator's expression softened. "Dear, as callous and impersonal as this may sound, it's extremely important you understand that you're being hired as one party in a business transaction. Nothing more. At no time will you attempt to form a relationship with either the parents or the baby. Given the voluminous amount of press devoted to past legal battles pitting surrogates against parents, I hope you can accept our position. This includes discouraging any personal bonding with the infant as well, though recently I have relented somewhat and allowed viewing of the baby's sonograms. I might add," the administrator said, raising her index finger, "by avoiding any potential legal problems, Meechum is able to offer our surrogates more financially satisfying contracts."

On the way out, the administrator paused. "One final comment. Section fourteen. Surrogate agrees not—"

Amoreena finished, "agrees not to smoke, drink alcoholic beverages, use illegal drugs, or take medications without written consent."

Irene stepped back. "I'm impressed. That was verbatim."

Opening her purse, Amoreena pulled out the open pack of Montclairs and dropped them in a wastebasket. "Mom wanted me to quit anyway."

The lobby was virtually deserted when Amoreena strode to the exit.

Chapter Eight

The two-month-old scars ~~stood out~~ as thin white lines against her bronze skin, creating ugly latticelike patterns over her lower legs and ankles. A few remained fiery red and elevated, an indication the infectious process from the toxic thorns and insect bites had not yet totally abated.

The doctor had been correct in his diagnosis, Gabriella thought ruefully. Just not aggressive enough in his treatment. He should have prescribed the little white pills earlier and in larger doses. But then who was she to question the actions and motives of the local medical personnel. She was but a *vaca*. Now she was a marked *vaca*, scarred for life because of a foolish and futile romp through the jungle. Next time, she'd have a better plan.

The line began to move, and Gabriella looked up in time to see another girl disappear into the *vampire* room. The room, really a small cubicle attached to the main laboratory, was where all the routine blood work was collected, thus the macabre christening. The column of females numbered close to fifty women and Gabriella stood at the forty-eighth position, near one end of the narrow corridor.

She moved one girl closer. Beneath her bare feet the tile felt cool and comfortable, as did the air, courtesy of the building's efficient air-purification system. The doctors and nurses of Las Canas would never tolerate the sticky humid outside heat that smothered the compound from sunrise to sunset— the very same heat the girls bathed in, ate in, and at night, slept in.

No one spoke. One guard stood rigidly just outside the vampire room entrance, another leaned against the wall at Gabriella's end of the line. Both sported military fatigues rife with perspiration stains and AK-47 assault rifles. Both were unshaven, reeked of body odor, and neither smiled.

Gabriella averted her eyes from the closer guard's gaze and checked the crook of her arm. She hoped this technician was more adept at finding her veins. The two previous times since her aborted escape, her skin had been left bruised and tender.

The line moved once more, and Gabriella slid farther along the wall. Every month it was the same. Blood work, a urinalysis, and then back to the laboratory supply room to count bags of solutions, boxes of syringes, and glass collection tubes. Once the leg infections resolved, she'd be returned to housekeeping, her permanent station.

Today, though, she was not so averse to having her blood examined. This past month, the baby had been acting strange. At first she thought the ordeal of her capture had affected the fetus. But now, at almost sixteen weeks, the baby's movements had become jerky, at times causing extreme abdominal distress. She'd heard similar complaints from the other girls. When she brought her concerns before the medical personnel, they told her not to worry. Everything was fine. Gabriella didn't believe them. Something was wrong, and she hoped the blood tests would provide an answer.

"You." The muzzle of the guard's rifle touched her shoulder.

Gabriella flinched.

"This one?" he asked a nurse standing beside him. A crisp clean surgical mask hung around her neck. Gabriella hadn't heard her approach.

The nurse pushed Gabriella's hair away from the side of her neck and compared a six-digit number tattooed onto her skin and the number on a computer printout. "Please follow us, Gabriella," she said.

"My blood."

"Not today."

"But my baby's acting funny."

"We'll take care of it."

The guard escorted them down two different halls, neither of which was familiar to Gabriella.

"Where are we going?"

"Please relax," the nurse said.

"You're not thinking of running again?" the guard hissed.

"Quiet," the woman ordered.

Gabriella noticed the jerky movements in her abdomen increase. She guessed the baby was sensing her own fear. Using one hand, she wiped some perspiration from her forehead. This part of the building was warmer.

With a side glance, she saw the guard leering at her with that all-too-familiar look. But she knew she was safe from his hands. An unwritten rule stated the guards could not touch any of the girls if they were *carrying*. Vincinio, the Las Canas security chief, was the lone exception. But then Vincinio was a monster.

The corridor ended in two swinging doors. No sign indicated what lay beyond.

The woman pushed through first.

"Move," the guard said.

Gabriella stepped inside and felt her legs go weak. She'd heard about this room from the others. It was near the nursery.

"No," she said, her skin pallid.

The nurse took her by one wrist. "It's okay."

Two orderlies in green led her to an examination table. From the ceiling hung three high-intensity surgical lights and next to a wall of cabinets filled with medical supplies sat two trays of sterile instruments. The air smelled of sweat and disinfectant.

"Will it hurt?" Gabriella asked.

"No," the nurse said, pulling her mask over her face. She motioned to the guard. "Get the doctor."

Gabriella felt a tiny prick in one arm as the nurse started an intravenous line.

"This is to help calm you," she said, injecting a clear liquid into her vein.

Gabriella winced. The baby was rocking and rolling now.

She could taste her own bile in her mouth. She wanted some water but was afraid to ask. The room was spinning. No longer able to resist, she watched her arms and legs tethered with leather restraints.

The cramps began ten minutes later. And with the first sharp sensations of discomfort, Gabriella knew the nurse had lied.

It was going to hurt. And hurt horribly.

Chapter Nine

Even before Amoreena checked the thermometer, she felt the twinge in her lower abdomen. The half degree drop in temperature confirmed what she already knew. She scribbled a small "yes" in the September 16 square of her calendar and called the clinic. The operator instructed her to be in the lobby at 7:30 A.M.

"Ovulating means never having to say you're sorry," Millie said, watching Amoreena rush to get dressed.

"Oh that's original."

"What class you going to miss?"

"Evolution." Amoreena gulped down a glass of juice and ran for the door. "Don't say nothing."

"Good luck, roomie. Love you."

The Mustang stalled backing out. "Don't screw with me, Silver," Amoreena screamed. She punched the accelerator twice, turned the ignition, and the engine fired, belching a cloud of gray smoke. Ignoring the smell of burning oil, she shifted into drive and sped away.

Ramona Perez had already opened the doors when Amoreena parked.

"Welcome back," the clinic coordinator greeted her.

"You guys are efficient."

"We've done this many times."

Undressed and gowned, Amoreena waited on the examination table. She watched a nurse arrange a tray of instruments. The speculum she recognized, but the others were unfamiliar. One looked particularly threatening, a long needle-nosed pliers with teeth.

The door opened and Dr. Becker and a technician entered. After a cordial hello, the physician explained the procedure while checking the instrument tray. He paid close attention to a tiny opaque vial propped upright in a Styrofoam container.

"The actual insemination process," he said, "takes less than two minutes, and the only discomfort might be some mild cramping. First, we're going to dilate your cervix."

He said something in Spanish to the technician, who positioned the tray near the table. Amoreena would have preferred his speaking English, but she refrained from making her request. Both the nurse and technician appeared tense.

Positioned and stirrupped, Amoreena waited. Staring at the ceiling, she thought of her mother. It'd been a struggle, but Geneva had finally hit the magic number of ninety-five pounds, the weight requirement for entering Dr. Gillespie's research protocol. They'd celebrated last night with dinner at a small restaurant overlooking Newport Bay. Geneva's only concern, other than what scarf to wear, had been whether the three-year graduation program would be placing too much stress on her daughter.

My mom. Amoreena grinned.

"You're going to feel a warm solution," Dr. Becker began. "This is a disinfectant. Now I'm going to conduct a brief exam. Then the dilatation."

Amoreena felt the warm liquid followed by Dr. Becker's probing hands. They were larger and coarser than Dr. Rafael's. The first dilation caused no discomfort; however, with the subsequent ones, she noted a mild ache.

Dr. Becker spoke again and she heard shuffling near her feet.

"We're ready to commence with the insemination," the medical director said. "You might be a little uncomfortable while I manipulate your cervix. Please try not to move." He grabbed the long single-toothed tenaculum.

Amoreena felt something inserted into her vagina and then

a brief, sharp stabbing pain. Visualizing the pliers at work, she resisted the urge to pull away.

Minutes later, the ordeal was complete.

"You did fine, my dear," Dr. Becker said, removing his gown and gloves. "Twenty minutes on your back and you'll be free to go. Tylenol's okay for any pain but nothing else."

"Activities?"

The director paused at the door. "Other than weight-lifting and intercourse, your normal routine." He flashed a smile and stepped out.

After getting dressed, Amoreena met with Ramona Perez in her office. Except for a mild queasy sensation, she felt good.

The coordinator explained what to look for—bleeding, cramping, painful urination, fever. She said in two or three weeks they'd know the outcome of today's procedure.

"Good luck," Ramona wished.

A flood of emotions coursed through Amoreena as she crossed the lobby's marble floor. Trepidation, fear, relief, elation, and even pride—she'd accomplished what she'd set out to do. Also shock, what had she really done?

Momentarily distracted, she almost collided with a patient entering the clinic.

"Excuse me," she said.

The young woman held Amoreena's gaze for only a second but long enough for the recognition to click. It was the same patient she'd seen being wheeled from a procedure room during her initial interview. At that time, she'd guessed the girl to be about five months along. Amoreena easily recalled the fear registered in the patient's face then. Now the woman exhibited no real emotion at all. Her eyes were dull and her expression listless. If anything, she looked ashamed.

There was another major difference in the patient's appearance as well, but a second commotion distracted Amoreena's attention.

An Hispanic man, neatly dressed in a sport shirt and slacks, had broken into a heated argument with the burly guard manning the information booth. Though the angry exchange was in Spanish, Amoreena recognized Dr. Becker's name. For a moment, she feared the confrontation might turn physical.

When the guard reached for the phone, the man quieted. A second security guard appeared and led the man through the double doors of the administration suite.

Relieved the disagreement had been settled amicably, Amoreena looked around for the female patient she'd recognized. She found the woman waiting by the elevators. Alone and wearing a bright calico dress and sandals, she was staring Amoreena's way.

Amoreena took a step in her direction but stopped when she saw the woman slowly shake her head. The elevator door opened, and the patient stepped out of view.

Only after the door slid shut did it dawn on Amoreena what was so obviously different about the patient.

The girl was no longer pregnant.

Chapter Ten

The day her mother was scheduled to begin Phase I of the experimental cancer research protocol, Amoreena bled.

She prayed she hadn't started her period. The bleeding was scant, and it certainly didn't feel like a normal period. She experienced no cramping or bloated sensation.

She called the clinic and a nurse recommended she come in for a blood test. Reluctantly, Amoreena agreed, though it would mean missing another lecture. She wondered how long Daryl and Millie would continue collecting her notes.

Geneva was waiting outside her apartment door when Amoreena pulled up. Miraculously, her mother's weight had peaked at ninety-seven pounds and she looked almost *healthy*, dressed in her white slacks, a blue blouse, and matching scarf.

"You look nice," Amoreena complimented her. "How do you feel?"

"Like a slave being thrown to the lions. I've accepted the fact the next four months are going to be hell." Geneva frowned. "I still don't know how we're going to pay for all this hullabaloo."

"This hullabaloo just might save your life," Amoreena said, reaching for her mother's small suitcase. "It's never as bad as you imagine."

"When was your last chemotherapy session?" Geneva huffed.

"You know what I mean." Amoreena hoped she didn't sound too acerbic. With all that was going on, plus quitting the cigarettes cold turkey, her mood index was fast approaching a ten on the irritability scale.

Stretching from the passenger side, Geneva touched a hand to her daughter's cheek. "You feeling all right, dear? You look kind of pale."

"I'm fine."

"Still taking your vitamins?"

"Yes," Amoreena lied, thereby avoiding the confrontation the truth would have precipitated.

The outpatient oncology clinic, a single-story red brick building, resembled more an elementary school than an infirmary where the very ill waged daily pyrrhic battles against insurmountable odds.

While Dr. Gillespie explained the protocol again, this time stressing a list of potential complications that Amoreena thought would never end, a nurse brought in the consent forms to sign.

A wheelchair appeared, and Geneva waved good-bye as she and the oncologist vanished down a hall in a mix of lab coats, patients, and medical staff.

"I love you," Amoreena called after her.

She felt a touch on her arm, and her mood soured considerably when she turned to face Ms. Cates. The utilization chairwoman led her to an adjoining office.

"Ms. Daniels," she said, motioning to a chair.

Amoreena sat, doubting the purpose of this little powwow was to wish the Daniels family good luck.

Ms. Cates pulled a folder from her stout briefcase. "I'm sure you're aware that any experimental therapeutic interventions will not be covered by any insurance programs, most definitely not Medi-Cal."

Amoreena responded with an icy stare.

"You and your mother will be one hundred percent responsible for all hospital costs up to and including any costs secondary to complications of treatment." She slid a form across the desk. "This is a financial liability form, Ms. Daniels. In essence, it states the signee, in this case you, will be fully responsible for all expenses incurred."

Jerking the form around, Amoreena scanned the single paragraph. The wording was straightforward. There were two places for signatures. One said PATIENT, the other GUARDIAN/RESPONSIBLE PARTY. Something didn't jibe.

"Why doesn't Mom sign it?" Amoreena asked.

"We will have your mother sign it. We require your signature, too."

"Is this *routine*?"

"In a few cases."

Amoreena felt warm. She needed a damn cigarette. "But I'm not her guardian, I'm her daughter."

"You're twenty-one, Ms. Daniels. The hospital will accept you as the responsible party."

"And if I refuse?"

Ms. Cates reached for a phone. "All treatment will be postponed until this matter can be resolved."

"I can hire an attorney."

"That's your right."

The bitch is jerking me off. Sure, I can hire a lawyer. And pay him with what? And how long will that take? In a wave of realization, Amoreena suddenly understood the purpose of this charade. The utilization committee didn't think her mother would survive. And because Geneva Daniels's estate would not cover the costs of treatment, the hospital needed a recourse. *I'm their goddamned recourse.*

"You have me by the proverbial balls, Ms. Cates," Amoreena said.

"I beg your pardon."

Amoreena reread the form in silence, line by line. She felt the chairwoman's eyes burning the top of her head. She signs, and Mom gets treated. She doesn't sign, and there's no treatment. She didn't like the rules, but it wasn't her game. And her mother sure as hell hadn't asked to participate in this ugly game of bad chance.

Amoreena looked up slowly. "May I borrow your pen?"

* * *

She found her mother lying semierect in a ward similar to a dialysis unit. A curtain separated each bed.

Amoreena bent down and kissed her mother on the forehead. "I've gotta run. You'll be okay?"

Geneva scowled at the yellow infusion of cisplatin. "It looks like urine."

In the next bed, a man vomited. Amoreena wished her mom didn't have to hear it. Cisplatin and 5-Fluorouracil were legal poisons. In a short time, her mother would be suffering the same fate.

She felt Geneva touch her hand.

"Go, Amy, I'll be fine."

"You sure?"

"I love you, baby."

One bed over, the man vomited again.

Amoreena squeezed her mother's hand and left.

Still an hour away from her scheduled appointment at the Women's Clinic, she dropped by the campus bookstore to purchase a study guide for the MCAT. With midterm exams fast approaching and Pike's Hypertension Study to begin next month, she'd need to set aside some time to prepare for the Medical College Admission Test, no doubt the most important singular event in determining her future. She'd never bombed an exam before, and she was determined to maintain her perfect record.

Since her mother's diagnosis she'd learned to compartmentalize the significant factors affecting her life. It was the only way she could survive and continue to excel, by concentrating on one compartment at a time. The MCAT was an additional compartment. So was three-year graduation. There was her mother's cancer. And now a separate surrogacy compartment. Wonderful. Before long, her personal page would resemble a honeycomb.

From the bookstore, she walked to the library. Classes were in session, and she enjoyed the brief solitude. One day, she vowed, all the stresses would be behind her. She hoped the pressure didn't rise to intolerable levels before that time arrived.

She removed several medical journals from her pack and slid them toward the librarian. She'd researched everything she could about her mother's illness, and all she'd read seemed to confirm what the oncologist had told her. It was a steep up-hill battle, but steep uphill battles had been won before.

The librarian examined the titles. "Are you a medical student?" she asked.

"Soon." Amoreena turned to leave, but paused in mid-turn. If she hurried, she had just enough time to research one other subject that had only recently climbed to the forefront of her "must read" list.

Aware of the clerk's inquisitive stare, she went to the computer index and typed in the subject. She doubted Chapman Library would have anything pertaining to the topic but was mildly surprised when the monitor indicated one text.

She found the book on the second floor. Far from being a tome, Martha Field's *Surrogate Motherhood* was under two hundred pages. Scanning the inside back cover, Amoreena found it amusing that the book had been checked out only two times in the past, the most recent eight months ago. Probably for a research paper, she assumed.

"Due in four weeks," the librarian said, stamping the return slip.

Imagining a cloud of suspicion shading the staff woman's eyes, Amoreena mumbled something about a sociology assignment and shoved the book into her pack. Was she being paranoid?

With minutes to spare, she made the drive to the Women's Clinic and reported to the guard. Again, she was impressed by the efficiency of the medical staff. A nurse led her to the laboratory, where the same technician who had drawn her blood for her initial physical applied a rubber tourniquet just above her elbow. Amoreena watched her own blood fill two tubes.

As the tech whisked them to a centrifuge, she sensed a presence behind her. She turned just as Dr. Rafael closed a chart and stepped toward her.

Amoreena smiled awkwardly.

"How do you feel?" he asked. He seemed to look past her eyes in a way Amoreena found charming and a little scary.

"You heard?"

"A nurse reported to me as soon as you called."

"You requested the blood work?"

"Yes, and a brief physical. Dr. Becker's already set up in the exam room."

Amoreena suppressed a stab of disappointment that Dr. Rafael would not be more involved in her care.

"Any more bleeding?" he asked.

She shook her head.

"Cramping?"

"None."

"You should be fine." He patted her lightly on the shoulder, issued an order to the tech standing by the centrifuge, and disappeared behind a vaultlike door at the rear of the laboratory, but not before exchanging a few words with an older woman housekeeper collecting trash.

Amoreena watched another man and woman in lab coats follow Dr. Rafael inside and only when she looked away did she notice a tall guard stationed behind a nearby counter. His vantage allowed him a commanding view of the entire lab. She recognized him as the guard who'd escorted the angry Hispanic man from the clinic lobby after her insemination procedure. An ugly red burn scar punctuated his neck and one ear.

"Doctor is waiting," the nurse said, motioning Amoreena down a corridor of examination rooms. The few other pregnant patients she passed averted her gaze. It struck her as odd that none of the women patients appeared genuinely happy. She began to wonder if dour expressions were a requisite to becoming a surrogate.

"Tell me about the bleeding," the medical director said, once Amoreena was draped and gowned.

"It wasn't much," she said. "Didn't feel like a normal period."

"Any abdominal distress."

"No."

He finished the exam quickly. "You're okay. I find no evidence of miscarriage or active bleeding. Let's see what the blood shows."

A nurse returned with a white laboratory slip. She handed it to Dr. Becker. He scanned the results, then handed the paper back to the nurse, saying something in Spanish.

Amoreena almost snatched the slip from the woman's hand as she whisked out of the room.

Cognizant of her restlessness, Dr. Becker said, "Those belonged to another patient."

Amoreena let her breath escape in a long whistle. "I guess I'm just a little anxious."

He smiled and began to scribble a note in Amoreena's chart.

"Can I ask you a question?" she asked.

He nodded but continued to write.

"Dr. Becker, during my interview here, I saw a young woman coming out of a procedure room. She appeared really frightened. She was pregnant."

He stopped writing and looked up.

"Then on the day I ovulated," Amoreena went on, "I saw her again down by the elevators. But this time, she wasn't pregnant."

"And."

"It just struck me as odd. She didn't seem that far along . . ." Amoreena paused, suddenly regretting bringing up the subject. Becker's expression indicated it was none of her business, and he was right. It wasn't.

She shrugged. "I just wondered what went wrong. I felt sort of sorry for her. I guess I shouldn't have asked."

Becker sat on a stool, closing the chart in his lap. "Amoreena, gestational age can be very difficult for a layperson to judge. This woman you mention may have in fact been much further along than you believed, and she simply delivered. That's the most direct explanation. I hope this was the case. However many things can occur during a nine-month period. Unfortunately, not all are good."

Detecting nothing behind the intense blue of his eyes, hidden or otherwise, Amoreena watched Dr. Becker reopen the chart. He began to write again, indicating the topic was closed.

Though she could have sworn this patient had not been nine

months pregnant, or even eight, she chose not to press the subject. It really was none of her concern.

Thankfully, before the silence became too oppressive, the nurse returned, carrying another laboratory slip.

"Well?" Amoreena asked with some trepidation.

Dr. Becker surrendered the yellow paper. "This makes it official, young lady."

She read the results in disbelief. "I'm pregnant!"

"Congratulations."

Chapter Eleven

It had been that simple. Unbelievable. Amoreena sat through both her afternoon lectures, shrouded in a daze, oblivious to the discourses from the podium. At one point, she caught Daryl watching her. She turned away.

Today, she'd reached the first milestone and tomorrow she'd collect tangible proof. A check for ten thousand dollars made out in her name. She ran one hand over her belly, wondering how many weeks would pass before the flat contour began to change. Physically she felt the same. Mentally and emotionally, she was floating in a cloud of anticipation, suspended by the realization that a new life was growing within her. And it had been so incredibly easy.

Daryl caught up with her on the steps of Roosevelt Hall. "What's with you?"

Amoreena didn't look at him. "What do you mean?"

"Back there in anatomy, you looked like the Cheshire cat that swallowed a canary."

She gave him a quizzical glance.

"I know," he said. "I never liked Alice in Lalaland either. So you want my bio notes or not?"

Amoreena stopped. "I forgot," she said, placing the notes in her pack.

"Amoreena Daniels, the darling of Chapman's premed program, forget?" Daryl was watching her with an intense gaze. "Something's brewing. You never forget. Anything. Hey, I heard a nasty rumor."

She felt her face flush.

"Says you're going to be a three-year graduate."

"If I pass the MCAT."

Daryl smirked. "You've never *not* passed a test in your entire life."

"I suppose that's true," Amoreena said. The banter was growing tedious, and she wasn't in the mood for small talk.

Her tenseness wasn't lost on Daryl.

"Whoa, the girl's flying today." He swung his books to the opposite arm and moved away. "Enjoy my notes."

"Thanks, Daryl," she mumbled, though she doubted he'd heard her.

With no time to feel guilty, Amoreena rushed to the student lot. She'd already received permission to skip out of the afternoon's fetal pig dissection in biology lab. All it took was an ingratiating smile and a fake dental appointment for the male graduate student to grant her request. She'd collected a review handout and promised to be ready for the midterm practical.

Geneva Daniels was waiting in a wheelchair when Amoreena entered the radiation oncology suite.

The IV had been disconnected, and she was sipping from a glass of juice. "Am I glowing yet?" she asked, seeing her daughter approach.

Amoreena touched her mother's cheek. "She feels hot," she said to the nurse standing nearby.

"Temp's normal," the oncology nurse said.

"You sure?"

The nurse forced a smile at Geneva before using a handheld gauge to retake the temperature. After a few seconds, she removed the sensor from Geneva's ear. "Ninety-eight point six," she said.

Amoreena nodded, checking the digital readout.

"How'd it go?" she asked her mom, adjusting the colored scarf.

"Besides the vomiting, cramping, and feeling like my veins were filled with hot acid, it went well."

"It wasn't that bad. You look good. Dr. Gillespie says you tolerated the chemo well." Amoreena had spoken to the oncologist before picking up her mother.

"Do I get a prize?" Geneva asked.

"Yeah, you get to return tomorrow."

"Wonderful."

With an orderly's assistance, Amoreena helped her mother into the car.

"Hi ho, Silver," Geneva said, as they pulled away.

Braking at a red light, Amoreena looked over and felt a sudden surge of adrenaline. Her mother had opened her pack and was rummaging through its contents, partially exposing the Marsha Field text on surrogating.

"What are you doing?" She jerked the pack away and tossed it in the backseat.

"You're quite surly today," Geneva said. "What are you afraid of? All I wanted was to smell one of your Montclairs. At least, I deserve that."

"I don't smoke anymore."

"You quit. Just like that."

"Yup."

Geneva put a frail hand on Amoreena's shoulder. "I'm so proud of you. It took a death sentence for me to give it up. You're so much better than me."

"I'm not any better than you. It was just bad for my skin, that's all."

"You have flawless skin."

Amoreena glanced across the seat. Her mother really did look proud. She wondered how proud she'd be if she knew the real reason she'd quit.

The rest of the drive to Geneva's apartment remained subdued, and when Amoreena pulled next to the curb and parked, she noticed her mother staring oddly out the windshield.

"What are you looking at?" she asked.

Confusion marred her mother's expression. "I saw a flash. It looked like a shooting star."

"Mom, it's daylight. And overcast."

"It sounds strange, I know."

"Yes, it does."

Geneva continued scanning the sky as Amoreena helped her inside.

The apartment smelled of stale potpourri. Opening a window helped, and while Geneva reclined on the couch, Amoreena carried some trash from under the kitchen sink out to a Dumpster in the alley behind the unit. Before she returned, she'd already decided what her mother needed.

"Let's go out for dinner tonight," she said cheerfully.

Geneva remained still, staring at an etagere of knickknacks from past vacations and weekend trips.

"Dr. Gillespie said it'd be fine," Amoreena coaxed. "Pasta's good, and soup, whatever you want. My treat."

"I'm not really up to it."

"We don't have to dress up."

Geneva shook her head. In the gloom, her mother's tears appeared suddenly as if painted on by a child's hand, uneven streaks coursing haphazardly down her skin.

"What is it, Mom?"

"Amy, look at me."

"You look fine."

"No, look at me." Geneva ripped the scarf from her head. Her voice had taken on a plaintive tone.

Amoreena stopped halfway across the living room, letting a Kleenex drop to the floor.

Deep shadows circled her mother's eyes, and what little hair had survived the initial treatments had been decimated by today's combination session of chemo and radiation therapy. It took very little imagination to see her mother's scalp as smooth and white as a billiard ball within a week.

"I'll buy you a new scarf," Amoreena said futilely.

"I don't want a new scarf. I want my hair back."

In thick gulping sobs, Geneva's emotions roiled to the surface. The plaster cast had fractured, showering the tiny apartment with sharp fragments of pain and suffering.

Retrieving the Kleenex, Amoreena sat beside her, pulling her close. Her mother's trembling chipped and nicked at her own tough exterior, but the mortar and bricks remained strong.

"Stick it out, Mom," she whispered. "One day at a time."

Later that evening, lying on her own bed, Amoreena cried. And strangely, she didn't know why. She hadn't cried earlier at her mother's. Dinner had gone well enough, chicken noodle soup and a salad. They'd watched *Wheel of Fortune* together, and her mother had even laughed.

And though tonight's studies hadn't been easy, and the anticipation of meeting with Irene Leggett hung over her like a starter's pistol, she wasn't too concerned. This weekend she'd have plenty of time to catch up. And frankly, she didn't feel that upset. Her mother was enrolled in an advanced research protocol, the Daniels family would be ten grand richer tomorrow, and she'd graduate in three years. She was in total control of all her life's compartments. So . . .

"Toughen up, girl," Amoreena said aloud. The house was empty, lending her voice a sinister quality.

A key turning the lock and the front door opening caused her to tense.

"You hibernating or what?" Millie called from the hall. In succession, the lights in the kitchen, den, and finally her roommate's room came on.

Millie stopped in the doorway. "Sick?" she asked, seeing Amoreena in bed.

"Just resting."

"With all the lights out? It's not even ten."

Amoreena kicked the sheets aside. "Where were you?"

"Daryl's, studying. Said he saw you today. Used the B word."

Stretching, Amoreena went into the kitchen.

Millie followed her. "So what's wrong?"

"I'm hungry." She scanned the fridge but nothing looked appetizing. She wanted a beer and cigarette.

"What's really wrong, roomie?" Millie stood at the counter, her arms folded across her chest. "It's Geneva."

Amoreena shook her head. "I'm pregnant."

"Oh shit."

It was well past midnight before Amoreena finally drifted off to sleep. She dreamed of trees. Lots and lots of trees.

* * *

Friday morning arrived with a chill in the air. The overcast sky and unseasonably cooler temperatures sent a shiver through Amoreena as she dropped her mother off at the oncology clinic. Geneva was in better spirits; perhaps it was the new sweater she'd purchased last spring and was finally able to wear. Regardless, her mother's uplifting mood was contagious, which only added to Amoreena's verve.

She sped away from the medical center, for the first time feeling invigorated. She had one more appointment before classes began, and this one she was determined to be on time for.

Upon seeing her enter the lobby, the security guard immediately passed Amoreena through to the administration suite. The cubicles that had been so abuzz with activity during her interview sat idle and quiet. The computer monitors sat blankly staring at her and when she pressed the keypad on one there was no response. She stepped away when she heard a door open.

Dr. Rafael exited Irene's office with a small stack of charts under one arm. Without his lab coat he appeared thinner, but no less handsome. His face was drawn up in an expression of consternation; however, when he saw Amoreena, the lines of worry vanished, replaced by a wide grin.

"Good morning, Ms. Daniels," he said, shifting the charts so he could extend his arm.

"And to you." Amoreena took his hand briefly.

"I heard the news," Dr. Rafael said.

"Exciting, yes."

"How do you feel?"

"Like an Olympic athlete."

"I'm glad." He moved aside so she could pass. "Don't neglect the prenatal vitamins."

"No way."

Amoreena watched him back away a few paces, before turning to leave. Though she hadn't been aware of it on their initial encounter, now she noticed Dr. Rafael had a barely perceptible limp; so mild, in fact, she couldn't discern which leg he favored.

"He's a fine physician," Irene said.

Amoreena swung around, wondering how long the administrator had been standing behind her.

"He seems nice," she said.

Irene touched Amoreena's arm. "Shall we?"

Beyond the section of computers, they passed a series of offices, all closed up and locked. Briefly Amoreena thought she and Irene had the entire administration suite to themselves.

"It's so quiet," she commented.

"Nice, isn't it," Irene said, looking over one shoulder. "The ancillary staff aren't due in until nine. By then, it can become quite hectic."

Hectic wasn't what came to mind when Amoreena recalled the buzz of activity she'd witnessed several weeks before, emanating from each partitioned workstation. Efficient would have been a better description.

"What do they do?" Amoreena asked, referring to the employees she'd seen manning the computer terminals.

"They handle the inquiries."

"Inquiries?"

"You cannot imagine the volume of calls. And this clinic is relatively new. The demand for our services worldwide is at a record pace."

"That's good."

"Indeed."

An office adjacent to Irene's was open, and inside, partially hidden behind a cluttered desk, Amoreena saw Tom Volkman. Though talking on the phone, he acknowledged their presence with a cursory wave. This was the office she'd seen Dr. Rafael exit, mistaking it for Irene's. She had no difficulty imagining the Meechum Corporation attorney creating looks of consternation in all those he interacted with. Just doing his job.

Upon entering the administrator's office, Amoreena instantly detected the sweetly delicious scent of flowers. The small bouquet of roses, orchids, and several unfamiliar tropical species filled a wicker basket sitting on Irene's desk. Propped against the bouquet was an envelope.

Irene reached for the envelope. "To paraphrase a great American writer, 'within every child born, the potential for the human race is born again.' Amoreena, there's a tremendous obligation on both our parts to carry this through to a successful conclusion. Though the responsibilities may at times seem daunting, I don't want you ever feeling that you're alone in this endeavor." She leaned back against the desk's edge. "At the risk of sounding overly sentimental, I want to assure you, dear, anything you need is only a phone call away. You're part of us now. And we're a part of you."

Amoreena received the envelope. Turning it over in her hands, it felt as light as a feather and as heavy as a lead dumbbell.

"Go ahead, open it," Irene said.

Tearing open the seal, Amoreena removed the contents. Though she'd already known what lay inside, actually seeing the check gave her an unexpected warm sensation. She wanted to giggle as she read her name and the amount.

Ten thousand dollars and no/100.

She studied each letter of her name again, ensuring correctness of spelling. It was.

"Shit," she murmured under her breath. She looked up meeting Irene's gaze. "Thank you."

"You're very welcome."

Exhaling, Amoreena sat down, her legs suddenly weak. "You cannot begin to understand what this means." She softly chuckled. "I feel like I've been delivered. I mean, it's so incredible. It really is, Irene." Abruptly, she rose and embraced the clinic administrator. "You may have saved my mother's life."

"Not me, dear," Irene said. "You're the player. We just supplied the playing field."

"Do the parents know?" Amoreena asked.

"They're quite pleased. And yes, you can cash it today," she said, as if predicting Amoreena's next question.

"Now."

"Right this moment."

Amoreena carefully folded the check and placed it in her purse. She couldn't remember a day starting out this promising in years. "I appreciate all you've done," she said.

"The flowers."

Amoreena grinned. "I wasn't going to forget. Do you mind if I give them to my mother?"

"That would be nice."

Retrieving the basket and setting it in the chair with her purse, Amoreena could hear more activity from outside. She guessed the other employees were getting settled in front of their computer terminals.

"There is one other point," Irene said, her tone giving Amoreena reason to pause. "Dr. Becker mentioned you'd been concerned yesterday about another patient's welfare here at the clinic."

"I just asked," Amoreena said, not understanding why she suddenly felt the need to defend herself.

"No harm done. However the doctors have very busy schedules, so in the future, if you observe or hear anything that makes you uncomfortable, I'd like you to voice those concerns to me. Consider me a confidante. Anything unsettling to you is unsettling to me. Do we have a deal?"

"Deal," Amoreena said, searching the administrator's eyes but seeing only green.

Remotely feeling as if she'd just been gratuitously blindsided, she gathered her belongings and started for the door. The warm sensation had evaporated.

"Remember, dear," Irene called after her. "First prenatal checkup in one month."

All the way through the lobby, Amoreena tried to dispel the notion she'd just been subtly threatened. *Do we have a deal?* Yes, or *what*? She was sure she was reading too much behind the administrator's simple question. But she couldn't refute the fact it had come across sounding almost like a warning.

Exiting the lobby, Amoreena spied the note from halfway across the clinic parking lot. Initially, she thought it was one of those flyers hawking cheap stereo systems or free car washes. But Silver was the only car marked.

Amoreena pulled the scrap of plain white paper from her driver's side window. Unfolding it, she studied the six words, though their meaning was incomprehensible.

Lo siento por tus bebés, vaca.

Though Amoreena didn't speak a word, she recognized the language as Spanish. She looked around, but saw nothing suspicious. Across the street in the park, a group of children played. The note had not been written by a child.

She read the words once more, and though already deciding Silver had been erroneously targeted, she neatly folded the paper once and slid it inside her purse.

Chapter Twelve

The shuttle proved to be a bonanza in time saving. The van ran daily Monday through Saturday and provided transportation for the outpatient oncology patients receiving therapy at the medical center. Inexpensive and reliable, Amoreena had heard about the service from a social worker. She'd immediately signed Geneva up.

With some much-needed financial breathing room on the horizon (the Meechum check had cleared the same day it had been deposited) Amoreena once again attacked her studies with all the determination and vigor of a fighter in training. Thirty minutes extra each evening she devoted to her MCAT preparation. She was astounded at the amount of material the Medical School Admission Test covered. In addition to a science section emphasizing biology, chemistry, physics, and mathematics, there was a verbal reasoning portion and a written essay. Amoreena was confident she'd score well in the six-hour exam.

She imagined the prenatal vitamins giving her an energy boost, and she took them religiously.

One week before midterms the Pike Hypertension Study began. That morning Amoreena awoke with a mild stomachache, which she attributed to nerves. When she looked in the mirror, she thought her eyes appeared puffy. However, as soon as she stepped foot on the UCLA Medical Center grounds, any anxiety lessened.

An associate of Dr. Pike's, Dr. Erin Laslow, conducted the initial orientation. An immunologist by training, her alacrity for teaching made Amoreena completely forget her Saturday morning jitters.

"Dr. Sheffield mentioned you plan to graduate in three years," Dr. Laslow said while making sure Amoreena was comfortably situated at the research station. There was a small desk, two sphygmomanometers, and a data entry logbook.

"That's the plan," Amoreena said. Silently she rehashed the instructions she'd been given earlier. After logging in each patient's height and weight, she was to take blood pressure readings in each arm and record the findings in the logbook. A piece of cake. Because the study was double-blind, neither she nor the patient would know if a placebo or active medicine had been dispensed.

"The clinic ends at three," Dr. Laslow said. "It shouldn't be too busy today. The first Saturday is usually slow. All set?"

"It's pretty straightforward."

"Dr. Sheffield said you were bright. Any problems, page me."

The first patient was an obese African-American male. Amoreena used the large sphygmomanometer cuff and recorded the pertinent readings. He politely thanked her and departed. This is a breeze, she thought. Only an idiot could screw this up.

Sixteen patients later, her opinion had not wavered. She looked forward to meeting with Dr. Pike next week.

Ten minutes before the clinic's scheduled closing time, the last patient plunked himself down in the chair. Amoreena reached for the normal adult-sized cuff.

"I'm not in the study," he said.

He was Hispanic, and the large bruise coalescing under his right eye reminded her of an overripe plum. From the vermilion border of his lower lip, two black sutures hung like errant hairs. He didn't attempt to smile.

Amoreena felt her own blood pressure begin to rise. Despite his facial trauma, she recognized him. He was the same man she'd seen arguing with the security guard at the Women's Clinic over a month ago.

"Can I help you?" she asked.

"No," he said with an appraising gaze.

His breath smelled faintly of alcohol, and Amoreena didn't like him in spite of his neatly dressed appearance and precise English. The face didn't match the slacks, sports coat, and Jerry Garcia tie.

"Are you a patient at La Clínica de la Mujer?" he asked.

She didn't answer. She looked up and down the hall, but saw no one. She debated calling for security.

He must've seen the look of disquiet in her eyes because he raised one hand. "Relax, I only stopped because I'd seen you at the clinic in Santa Ana."

"What happened to your face?"

"Would you believe I was sweeping my apartment and the broom hit me?"

"Twice?"

"Actually I had a little problem with the locals in Ensenada, Mexico."

"What do you want?"

He reached over and tore a blank page from the logbook. He scribbled a number. "Call me if you feel the baby move before the third month." He folded the paper and set it on the desk.

Amoreena examined the note. The number was a 310 area code. Los Angeles. She noted the funny way he'd written the 0 with a line drawn diagonally through it. "From what I've read, quickening doesn't usually begin until after sixteen weeks," she said.

"Behold the young informed mother. I'm impressed." Standing, he turned to leave.

"What's your name?" Amoreena asked.

"Dr. Godinez!" However the voice belonged to Dr. Laslow, who stood in the hall opposite the research station. Her expression conveyed disgust.

The man gestured as if beginning a statement, but instead, made an awkward salute to the immunologist and departed down the hall. Amoreena thought his gait less steady than when she'd witnessed his tirade with the guard in Santa Ana.

Dr. Laslow watched until he rounded a corner, then stepped up to the station desk. "Did that man bother you?"

Amoreena shook her head. "Not really. He was only here a few minutes."

"Good."

"You called him a doctor."

Dr. Laslow pulled the logbook her way and made a cursory review, nodding approvingly. "Dr. Ron Godinez was an intern in the internal medicine program here, actually a very astute one, until about six months ago, when he began missing morning rounds. For reasons unknown to me, his behavior became more erratic—absences, prescription errors—resulting in not just a few patient complaints. When he failed a drug screen, Dr. Pike asked him to enter a drug rehab program. He refused and was removed from all patient care." The immunologist closed the log book. "Records look fine. Any difficulties?"

"None."

"Fine." Dr. Laslow gazed in the direction Ron Godinez had taken. "Seeing him here today tells me he's at least attempting to get his life back on an even keel. UCLA's Substance Abuse Clinic is held on Wednesdays and Saturdays. I hope so. He held a lot of promise."

Amoreena didn't mention the man's alcohol breath. She could have been mistaken.

The staff physician stood and shook Amoreena's hand. "Excellent first day. Dr. Pike will greet you officially next weekend." She stepped away, then paused. "Amoreena, I'm not one to make suggestions on a personal level, but Ron Godinez would not be a favorable influence on a premedical student's application process."

Amoreena saw the brief downward shift of the immunologist's eyes to the paper with Godinez's scrawled phone number and immediately understood where the staff physician was coming from.

She scooped up the paper and crushed it into a tiny ball.

Dropping it in the trash, Amoreena said, "Don't worry, Dr. Laslow, he's not my type."

* * *

As she'd promised her mother, Amoreena scored well on all her midsemester tests, actually acing her biology and embryology examinations. Her overall average was high enough to maintain her number one position in the junior class, just beating out Gladys Peterson, the daughter of a well-to-do cardiovascular surgeon in Newport Beach. Dissatisfied with the results, Gladys and several friends challenged the final numbers, as they'd done each semester before, and came up short.

Unperturbed by their petty complaints, Amoreena increased the time each day devoted to her MCAT preparation. December 15 would be upon her before she knew it. And it couldn't come at a worse time. Right before the grueling week of final exams.

"How do I look?" Millie leaped from her bedroom adorned in a yellow oversize sweatshirt emblazoned with the Disney's Mighty Ducks' logo, jeans, and a Bill Gates mask.

"Like a hundred billion dollars," Amoreena said. She sat at the kitchen table tabulating the most recent hospital charges.

Millie pretended to fly down the hall. "Come on, roomie. Halloween's only once a year. You need to get out."

"I *need* to study." Amoreena totaled the numbers and groaned. Her head remained above water, but just barely. She looked up, critically appraising Millie's costume. "You were someone else last year."

"I wore Andy Grove."

"Who's Andy Grove?"

"He runs Intel." Millie removed the mask, sticking two fingers through the eyeholes. "You think these guys get royalties for this shit?"

"Like hell they need 'em." Amoreena switched off the calculator and rubbed her eyes.

"You still taking your vitamins?" Millie asked.

Amoreena nodded.

Millie's expression grew more serious. "I heard you talking in your sleep the other night."

"What was I saying?"

"Couldn't tell."

"Was it in Spanish?" Amoreena smirked.

"What?"

"Nothing." She yawned. "I've been having these weird dreams lately. I see vivid colors, and there's always plenty of trees, almost like a jungle."

"Weird. Think it's stress?"

Amoreena feigned a wide-eyed innocence. "Who me, stressed?"

Both girls smiled and touched hands.

"I called last week to make my first prenatal checkup," Amoreena said, "and the nurse said Dr. Becker was out of town. They postponed it until next week."

"So that's what's bothering you."

"What's bothering me is I've gained seven pounds."

"Hell, roomie, you could gain twenty pounds and still make a drop-dead-beautiful vampiress. The Chapman Halloween-fest won't be the same without an auburn Elvira."

"Not this year."

"The entire male student body's going to starve."

"They'll have the hundred-billion-dollar woman."

"Oh yeah, right." Millie went to the refrigerator and removed a Corona. "Daryl and I thought we'd run by the animal shelter sometime."

"Choose one that cleans up its own poop." Amoreena wasn't too high on getting a pet, but she couldn't very well refuse her roommate the right.

A horn honked outside followed by several pseudoscreams of agony. Millie donned her mask. "Last chance."

Amoreena waved. "Elvira, Mistress of the Dark, wishes you a haunting night."

"Now that's a scary thought," Millie said, and slammed the door.

Halloween had transformed the residential streets into a maze teeming with little goblins, ghosts, and action figures. Amoreena negotiated the drive to her mother's place cautiously, careful to avoid all the howling and squealing creatures of the evening.

A plastic pumpkin by the front door was barren except for one caramel. Not usually a sweet-tooth addict, nevertheless Amoreena unwrapped the candy and popped the caramel in her mouth just as her mother opened the door.

"Amy, those are for the children."

"Sorry," Amoreena said sheepishly. "I had a sudden craving."

Geneva retrieved the pumpkin. "Well, it's late anyway." She stood, pecking her daughter's cheek. "You didn't have a party to attend?"

"Millie went. I was sort of tired." She followed her mother inside, locking the door after them. "It's starting to grow," she said, touching the fine hair on her mother's scalp.

Geneva smiled ruefully. "Now I just look like a fuzzy billiard ball."

Amoreena fixed them some tea and when they were both settled on the couch, she asked. "Did you ever mention to Dr. Gillespie those weird flashes you've been seeing?" Over the past two weeks, Geneva had experienced two other strange episodes involving her vision. She had called them "shooting stars."

"I forgot."

"It might be significant."

"Next time, I promise."

From the sidewalk rose the laughter of trick-or-treaters.

"I'm out of candy," Geneva said, suddenly concerned.

"Don't worry, I shut off the porch light. They won't bother you."

After replenishing their tea, Amoreena set the recliner back and listened to a CD. This was much better than some wild-ass Halloween party, though she did miss Millie and Daryl. She pictured Daryl as Frankenstein and chuckled. Besides, she couldn't drink anyway.

She watched her mother working on an afghan. Since the end of Phase I, her mom's energy level had increased significantly. It helped that throughout the entire four-week ordeal, her weight had not dropped below ninety pounds. Only the other day, Dr. Gillespie had informed them Geneva's latest laboratory results were within normal limits and after a short hiatus, she could begin Phase II.

Her mother's disability checks were coming in finally, which also helped. The total bill for the investigational protocol thus far amounted to just under seven thousand dollars.

Amoreena felt good about promptly paying it all off but realized another unforeseen emergency would put them behind the eight ball again.

She let her eyes drift closed. Her meeting with Dr. Pike during her second visit to the UCLA campus had gone well, too. He'd been pleased with her work, and her brief prior encounter with Ronald Godinez never came up, which was a relief. If the ex-intern was on the admissions committee chairman's blacklist, Dr. Godinez was the last person she wanted to be associated with.

If the baby moves before three months. . . .

His words still haunted her. What had he meant by if she felt any fetal activity in less than three months? She'd researched the numbers again, and the average time for "quickening," the term for fetal movement, was between eighteen and twenty-two weeks. What was so special about twelve weeks?

At one point she'd been tempted to look Godinez up at the drug rehab clinic, if in fact he was even in attendance, but decided against it. If someone looked and smelled like trouble, he probably was. Even so, a small part of her regretted having discarded his number.

Another option would be to discuss the entire episode with Irene Leggett. But for some ill-defined reason, she didn't feel quite comfortable with the clinic administrator as her confidante either. Perhaps . . .

Amoreena snapped alert. Her mother was talking, and she hadn't heard her.

"I'm sorry," she said sitting up.

"If you want to doze . . ."

"No, I'm fine."

"I was just wondering," Geneva said, pushing the afghan aside, "why I haven't received any of the hospital bills, yet."

"Because I'm having them all sent to my address."

"Amoreena."

"Don't argue, Mom. It's the only way I can keep track of all the separate items. You worry about getting well, I'll handle the finances. I thought we were settled on that issue."

"We were."

"Good, then." Amoreena saw her mother was still bothered by something. "I'm listening."

"Well," Geneva started. "A man called yesterday asking for Ms. Daniels. I said that's me, and he said he had some additional information on the clinic. I asked him what information; I assumed it related to my oncology clinic bills, since I hadn't received any."

Amoreena felt her chest tighten. "Go on."

"Anyway, he said, 'Ms. Daniels,' then he paused and asked if I was the Ms. Daniels at the Santa Ana clinic."

"What did you tell him?"

"I said I think you have the wrong Ms. Daniels."

"And."

"He apologized and hung up."

"That's it."

Geneva shrugged.

"Must've been a wrong number," Amoreena said, feeling as if she'd just dodged a bullet.

"I tend to agree, except for one thing."

"Yes?"

"Before hanging up, he asked if I had a daughter."

Chapter Thirteen

The nurse checked the urinalysis dipstick a second time. She shook her head. "No infection."

Amoreena frowned. She'd been positive she had a bladder infection. Since her midterms, she'd awoken two or three times a night and gone to the bathroom. No burning, just frequency. One day last week it'd been so bad she'd barely been able to sit through an hour lecture.

"Diabetes?" she asked.

The nurse indicated no while assembling a series of glass tubes. Amoreena watched her unsheathe a needle attached to a syringe.

"More tests?"

"Doctor's orders." The nurse arranged the various lab forms on the counter.

Amoreena hadn't expected this first prenatal checkup to be so thorough. Just a blood pressure, weight, a few questions, but not an extensive laboratory workup.

She picked up one of the lab requisition slips. Across the top, she read *La Clínica de la Baja. Ensenada, Mexico.* Two lines down, a box was X'ed out—human leukocyte antigen.

"What's this one for?" Amoreena asked.

"To check on the baby," the nurse said, politely taking the slip from Amoreena's hand.

"An all the others are for the baby, too?"

"Some are for you." The nurse positioned Amoreena's arm and applied the tourniquet. "You must save your questions for the doctor."

Amoreena barely felt the needle penetrate a plump vein. Adroitly the nurse filled six tubes of blood, packaged them along with the appropriate requisition slips into an insulated container, and motioned to an orderly, who set the container on a tray with four more similar containers. The man scribbled in a chart, then wheeled the tray away.

"Where's my blood going?" Amoreena asked, while the nurse applied a Band-Aid.

She smiled, and said, "I take you to the doctor now."

The examination room table was cold, but Amoreena was relieved she hadn't been asked to get undressed. Alone, gazing at a wall of instructional posters, all in Spanish, her thoughts returned to the laboratory slip. Ensenada, Mexico, had been its destination. She'd never heard of La Clínica de la Baja. She assumed it was part of the Meechum vast chain.

During her senior year of high school, she and some friends had driven to Ensenada to party and watch a surfing contest. They'd had fun. The town was clean, the locals friendly, and the beer cheap.

That's not the reason Ensenada piqued her interest now though. Ronald Godinez had mentioned Ensenada during their brief conversation the first Saturday of the hypertension study. He'd insinuated he'd had some trouble in Mexico and the appearance of his face at the time had seemed to substantiate that, at least the trouble part.

She wondered if his time in Ensenada had anything to do with her mother's odd phone call. Amoreena felt certain the caller had to have been Godinez. No other males she was acquainted with knew she was a patient at the Women's Clinic. Except Daryl. And he wouldn't have called her mom's apartment. Plus, her and Millie's number was unlisted while her mother's wasn't. Anyone searching for a Ms. Daniels would be directed to her mother's place, in addition to the twenty or thirty other Danielses in the phone book.

Amoreena supposed it could have been Dr. Becker or Dr.

Rafael, but that didn't make sense. She'd revealed her own number, plus her beeper, on her medical history form. Why call her mother?

Assuming it was Godinez, then, what could be so important he'd go out of his way to attempt to contact her? What 'more information about the clinic' was he alluding to? She'd been paid, the check didn't bounce, the medical care first-rate. So what was the problem?

A light knock interrupted any further contemplation. The door opened, and Dr. Rafael entered with a nursing assistant.

"I hope you don't mind," he said. "Dr. Becker's still away on business."

"No," Amoreena said, a little more eager than she would've wanted. She added, "Dr. Becker must be very busy."

"He flew to Brazil. We're opening a new clinic in São Paulo."

"How exotic?"

Dr. Rafael smiled. "I suppose. If you speak Portuguese." He waited while the assistant finished recording Amoreena's weight, temperature, and blood pressure. "How do you feel?" he asked.

"Fine. Maybe a little fatigued."

"Vitamins?"

"Every day. Also I'm always running to the bathroom, but the nurse said there was no infection."

"That's correct, Amoreena. No gestational diabetes either." Dr. Rafael moved to one of the posters. Using his pen, he explained, "As your uterus enlarges, it presses on your bladder, resulting in the sensation you describe. As your body becomes accustomed to the changes, your symptoms will improve. Any nausea?"

"I've been waiting, but nothing significant yet."

"Good."

Amoreena watched him perusing her chart. "My weight was one twenty-three today. That's eight pounds. Isn't that too much so soon?"

Dr. Rafael wrote something and closed the record. "I wouldn't be too concerned. Every patient varies."

"I just don't want anything to go wrong."

He stood, patting her knee. "You're doing fine, Amoreena. Next month we'll get an ultrasound."

He turned to leave.

"Dr. Rafael." Amoreena jumped off the table, nearly colliding with him when he turned. Only inches apart, she stepped back awkwardly. "I did have one more question. Actually two."

"Yes?"

"Are the parents excited?"

For a brief moment, he didn't respond, and Amoreena thought he hadn't understood. She was on the verge of repeating herself when she saw him grin.

"Yes, they are quite anxious. And pleased."

"What are they like? I mean, are they . . . ?" She noticed her own hesitation.

Dr. Rafael raised his hand in a reassuring gesture. "The woman is Caucasian, of Dutch ancestry I believe, and the husband is Hispanic. They are well off financially."

The news gave Amoreena a pleasant feeling. She nodded. "I'm real glad. I want the baby to have a good home."

Dr. Rafael reached out and gave her arm a gentle squeeze before letting go. "And the second question?"

Amoreena's tone grew more serious. "They took a lot of blood today."

"All routine," Dr. Rafael said, glancing at the laboratory section of the chart. "There's blood type, we monitor for anemia, diabetes, check for hepatitis B and C, and HIV, and screen for rubella immunity." He closed the chart. "We also run several genetic tests."

"Such as."

Dr. Rafael smiled. "Alfa fetoprotein for one and a few others, all monitoring the status of the fetus."

"How many others?"

"It's all standard protocol," he said, picking up on Amoreena's puzzled expression.

"Is human leucocyte antigen a genetic test?"

"Why do you ask?"

"I saw one of my requisition slips. It was being sent to La Clínica de la Baja in Ensenada, Mexico."

"Hm." Dr. Rafael rubbed his day-old beard. He opened the door for the assistant to leave, then once alone, he said, "I can only assume what you observed is related to the corporation's rush to integrate all the clinics under one computer program. Our facility in Ensenada is the largest and oldest in Mexico. Irene wants this integration process completed prior to the opening of the new San Diego clinic." He shrugged. "Feel better?"

"Some." Amoreena debated bringing up Ronald Godinez's name but decided against it. After her last experience with Dr. Becker, she didn't want to risk another near confrontation with Irene Leggett. There was something else she wanted to show him though. She reached for her purse and unfolded the scrawled note she'd found on her car.

"*Lo siento por tus bebés, vaca,*" she read slowly.

His response wouldn't have been more severe if she'd slapped him across the cheek. Dr. Rafael's jaws tensed for a scary second, and Amoreena envisioned him lunging at her. Reflexively, she moved back.

His demeanor rapidly cooled, leaving only a strain in his voice. "Where did you find that?" he asked.

She handed the note to Dr. Rafael. "It was left on my windshield." She watched him slowly shake his head as he examined the paper. He looked more hurt now than angry. "Did I say something wrong?" she asked.

"Amoreena, do you understand what you read?"

"I was hoping you would tell me."

"It means, I feel sorry for your babies, cow."

"*Vaca* is 'cow'?"

"I'm afraid so."

"Not very complimentary. I'm not that big."

Dr. Rafael didn't smile. "Have you mentioned this note to anyone else?"

She shook her head.

Relief spread across Dr. Rafael's face. "I'd request that you not do so."

"If that's your wish."

"Amoreena, *vaca* is a very derogatory term. As you're aware, we serve a largely Hispanic clientele. Merely mentioning the word might cause some misunderstanding. You don't know who wrote this?"

"I assumed it'd been placed on my car in error."

"I believe you're right." He opened the door. "Let's agree it never happened."

Amoreena smiled and shook his hand. "Agreed."

He waited until she'd entered the elevators before storming down the hall.

"Did you leave this message on the American's car?" Even in Spanish, Dr. Luis Rafael's voice came across as a stertorous hiss.

The Latina housekeeper held his gaze, unfazed by the young physician's lividity. "Your mother would not be pleased with your tone, Luis." She casually folded the note three times and dropped it in the wastebasket.

"The dead have no opinion," Dr. Rafael said.

"Ah, nephew, but they do. If you choose to listen."

With one foot, Dr. Rafael lashed out, kicking the door to the small break room shut. In two strides, he crossed the linoleum and yanked the woman to her feet.

"Did you leave the note?" His fingernails dug into her uniform.

She winced in discomfort, but her hard brown eyes remained locked on his face, only inches from her own.

"Yes," she said and smiled.

Dr. Rafael recoiled in shock. "Why?"

She went to the cupboard, found two Styrofoam cups, and filled both with coffee. She handed one to Dr. Rafael.

"The Anglo is different, Luis. I follow her. I know where she lives." Her tone abruptly changed from disdain to optimism. "She will help break the curse. You must trust me on this."

"You will get her killed. Like—"

"No. No. She is special. I feel it here." The woman gestured roughly to her chest. "I know this to be true."

"You are an old housekeeper." Dr. Rafael said, shaking his head. "You know nothing." His shoulders sagged heavily, and he used the back of a chair to help support his weight. "You know nothing," he repeated.

"She is very pretty, yes? Like Polita."

Dr. Rafael fixated on the chart in his hand. Amoreena Daniels's chart. No longer wanting to hold it, he laid it on the table.

"Keep away from the Anglo," he ordered.

"She can help."

"No!" The veins in his temples swelled with the outburst, stretching the skin thin.

The woman's gaze turned demonic. "I've seen *them*, Luis. Two years ago in Las Canas I saw them. Their tiny faces, their—"

"Shut up!" He cursed. Grabbing the chart, he whirled for the door.

"Please," the woman pleaded. She stalked him to the exit. "No, Luis. Listen to your heart."

Dr. Rafael's hand had just grasped the doorknob when she said, "Polita comes."

The named stopped him in his tracks. "When?"

"Soon."

Dr. Rafael made no verbal response. Only his clenched jaws indicated he'd heard. He opened the door and stepped out, leaving the woman alone.

She smoothed her uniform. "One day, Dr. Luis Rafael, you be big American doctor. But at what cost, *mi hijo*. What cost?"

The reception area was a madhouse—women accompanied by strollers, children playing tag around the fountain, and patients standing three deep at the reception desk. Upstairs, Amoreena had also noticed all the exam rooms filled in addition to three of the procedure rooms. It suddenly dawned on her as she stepped into the lobby that the clinic had only two doctors, Dr. Rafael and Dr. Becker. And with the medical chief out of town, no wonder the patient flow was backing up.

She felt a little guilty at having taken up so much of Dr. Rafael's time. But what she'd perceived as excessive diagnostic tests had bothered her. And though the explanation provided had not allayed all her concerns, it did help.

Genetic tests. She hoped the results didn't indicate she harbored some deleterious gene.

Backing Silver out, Amoreena turned and drove toward the exit. A guard patrolled the parking lot. She'd seen him before, standing watch in the laboratory. Today he wore a cap with a flap that shielded the scar deforming his ear from the sun. He stood near the sidewalk carrying on some sort of discussion with a younger Hispanic woman.

Amoreena braked at the street and waited. She recognized the woman. The girl was the same patient she'd questioned Dr. Becker about resulting in Irene's subtle admonishment.

She was in tears, and when she attempted to enter the clinic grounds the guard rudely blocked her way. A second attempt was met with a more forceful result.

Amoreena rolled down her window. "Hey," she called out.

"Un momento, señorita," the guard responded with a baleful stare, before turning his attention back to the woman. He said something, inaudible from Amoreena's vantage, and pointed.

The woman backed away suddenly and then sprinted into the street. It was a wonder she wasn't hit by oncoming traffic. Amoreena watched her dashing across the park.

"Can I help you?" The guard stood just outside Silver's driver's side door. His lips curled into a malignant grin beneath a bushy mustache. He smelled like cigar smoke.

"No," Amoreena said. "I thought there might be trouble."

The guard's grin widened. "I am in no need of assistance, but I welcome your worry."

"Concern," Amoreena said, correcting his minor semantics error.

"Ma'am?"

"Never mind." The girl was almost to the other side of the playground. Amoreena released the brake.

"You are a patient at La Mujer?"

"Adios." Amoreena squealed into the street and sped for the first intersection. If she hurried, she might be able to catch the girl before she reached the opposite boundary of the park.

She was resting on a bench when Amoreena parked next to a little league baseball diamond. She locked Silver and crossed the grassy infield.

"Hi," Amoreena said, shielding her eyes from the sun.

Breathing less heavily, the woman looked up and smiled weakly. She couldn't have been more than one or two years out of her teens. Her skin was a blotchy brown and except for some lipstick she wore no makeup. Her clothes appeared recently purchased, and she sported a conspicuous amount of gold jewelry.

"Do you speak English?" Amoreena asked.

"*Un poquito*, a little."

"My name is Amoreena."

"Isabel."

They sat quietly. Far across the park, Amoreena could see the guard watching them. He looked like a toy soldier.

"You work for *La clínica*?" Isabel asked.

"No," then grasping what the girl meant, Amoreena nodded. "Yes, I am a surrogate. You?"

"*Surrogatia. Sí. No mas.*" She wiped an eye. "I saw you inside. Two times."

"Yes." Amoreena slid closer. "Isabel, you were in trouble with the guard."

The woman gazed in the direction of the clinic. "I wish to talk with doctor, about *mi bebé*." She began to sob. "I so ashamed. Very bad things happened. Not know why. Sometimes I wish die." Her hands rose covering her small face. The tears dribbled down her fingers.

Amoreena reached out to her. "I'm sorry," she said.

In the distance, a police siren wailed.

The woman stiffened and abruptly stood. She looked like a frightened animal. "I leave. No good here." She backed away.

Amoreena walked after her. "What happened?"

The girl raised a fist and let fly a slew of invectives, all in Spanish, all aimed at the guard across the park.

"Isabel."

She paused to regain her breath. Her expression had turned stony and cold.

Amoreena took another half step. "Where will you go?"

"Mexico." The tears were returning. "I so ashamed."

"Isabel, what happened to your baby?"

The girl's head begun to shake, faster and faster until her face, twisted into a mask of sheer terror.

"It wasn't *mi bebé*!" she screamed. "It not my fault." She stutter-stepped and began to run.

"Isabel!"

The woman didn't slow. Churning her legs, she couldn't have run faster if she were fleeing a ghost.

Chapter Fourteen

Gabriella sat on a weathered mattress supported by rusted springs, her knees hunched against her chest, waiting. The afternoon temperature in the barracks room hovered near ninety-five. There were over one hundred such rooms divided between two dormitories. Constructed of concrete and cinderblock walls, each unit included a bed, sink, mirror, a tiny closet, and a set of shelves for clothing, and in Gabriella's case, books.

Initially designed to house the large itinerant labor force once employed by the noble land barons, the original owners of the Las Canas sugar plantation, the two-story, rectangular structures currently provided shelter for a far different labor pool. Though austere by North American standards, each room had running water and electricity, when the generators weren't shorted out by a stray rodent or bird searching for a place to nest. A small square window—the bars were added only within the last ten years—allowed the occupant a scenic view of the verdant valley of the Peten, a junglescape of serried hills and cloud-covered rain forests.

A communal shower and bathroom located at each end of the centralized halls were the favorite posts for the Las Canas security personnel. The showers were made accessible each morning and accommodated up to ten women. An adjacent private stall was available if a guard suspected anything amiss, which usually required an in-depth *"inspection."*

Through the bars of the window a humid breeze floated the sweetly pungent scents of fresh cane and native bananas. Every so often when the wind came from the west, Gabriella could detect the aroma of coffee beans roasting in the sun. For many years, sugarcane, bananas, and coffee had been the region's leading cash crops. No more.

The wind shifted because now Gabriella could smell the coffee, rich and heavy in the air. It was her favorite. She inhaled, immediately evoking pleasant memories of a young child assisting her parents in their small *tienda* on the outskirts of Mexico City. Until two bullets from a *ladron's* pistol made Rosa an orphan at age seven. By age thirteen, the child Rosa had become the precocious Gabriella, a name borrowed from a famous Mexican actress, and the extra money she made lifting wallets provided the young woman the food and clothing necessary to live a comfortable existence.

However, it was a three-line ad in a local barrio *periódico* that provided the teenager with the inducement to vacate Mexico City's red light district. She was fifteen when she packed her few belongings, including three thousand pesos in cash, and headed south, crossing the border into Central America during the wee hours of dawn. The cost—one thousand pesos.

Las Canas welcomed her fecundity with open arms. The day she was escorted through the plantation gates was the day Gabriella considered her entry into hell. And one day she truly believed she would burn, but not before her tiny flame ignited a conflagration that would roast all of Las Canas.

A firm rap on the thick oak door startled her from her vindictive mindset. *"Entre,"* she said.

Unlocked, the door opened.

Gabriella's heart jumped when she saw the guard. Smelling his rancid perspiration, her stomach muscles tensed, but relaxed when a woman stepped around his squat form and into the room.

Tall for a Guatemalan, Polita Salinas carried her five-eight lithe frame ramrod straight, giving anyone watching the impression she was part soldier and part aristocrat. Her Indian ancestry had blessed her with handsome and dark-complected features, the high cheekbones accentuating her deep-set eyes to such a degree that her natural beauty would be appreciated anywhere in the world. She was thirty-one.

She looked down at the guard. "You may leave."

The man, his gaze never leaving Gabriella's *falda* draped over her knees, fingered a tiny gold crucifix dangling from a chain around his neck. He grinned lewdly before bowing his head to Polita.

"Watch yourself with this one," he warned. "I would hate to see the same scars on your face that cover Vincinio's arms."

"The young jaguar has claws, too," Polita rejoined, "but uses them only to hunt and in self-defense. Vincinio's own stupidity caused his scars."

"As you say, *señorita*." He backed into the hall and shut the door.

Gabriella started to speak but was silenced by Polita's raised hand.

She waited two seconds before drawing back her foot and kicking the door with a sharp *crack*. She then yanked it open, catching the guard in the process of holding his ear.

Smiling, she said, "Perhaps I should speak with Vincinio."

Fear infiltrated the guard's sheepish grin. He quickly spun on his heels and headed down the hall. "I'll wait outside."

Polita waited until his footsteps faded before closing the door.

Turning, she asked, "How are the legs?" switching to English.

Gabriella took a moment to stop giggling. "*Mejorando.*"

"In English."

Gabriella wet her lips and tried again. "They is improved, but at night my legs . . . eetch?"

"They are improved and itch. Say it again."

"They are improved but at night my legs itch."

Polita nodded approvingly. She walked over to the window. The sun's rays reflected golden off her skin.

"The itching is a good sign," she said. "I'll make sure the doctors don't neglect your antibiotics."

"*Gracias*. I mean, thank you."

Gabriella swung her legs over the bed and walked to a shelf holding a stack of paper and several books. In Spanish, she said, "It is so difficult, Polita. Why does English have to be so hard?"

Polita crossed her arms over her chest. "My friend, the more difficult a goal, the greater will be your reward. That I promise you. Don't give up."

"I won't."

Polita checked her wristwatch and when she looked up her expression had turned serious. "I don't have long, so we'll forgo today's lesson."

Gabriella followed Polita's lead and moved as far from the door as possible, relieved the rest of the discussion would be carried on in her native language.

Polita took one of the teenager's hands. "We require more proof. I've heard talk among the other girls"—she never used the word *vaca*—"about some of the babies. What I hear I have difficulty believing, and if I am skeptical, the world will surely brand us *locas*."

Gabriella wouldn't meet her gaze. "I've heard, too."

"I know you hate to talk about it, but I must ask you. You never saw your baby?"

"It wasn't my baby," Gabriella said, suddenly indignant.

"I'm sorry, I didn't mean it like that. *The* baby."

The teenager shrugged. "The nurses buried him in a blanket. I could hear it making strange noises."

"Describe them."

"I can't."

"Try."

"*I can't.*" Gabriella squeezed her eyes closed.

Polita waited, gently stroking the girl's hair. "One day I'll fix your hair the way the women in America do."

Gabriella sucked in several gulps of air. "It sounded like a wounded kitten. Or maybe a monkey. It was horrible."

"That helps. But I must have more. None of the others will go along."

"No. They're afraid of Vincinio."

Polita glowered. "Vincinio's an animal. But they're right. You must use extreme caution. The nursery's guarded like a fortress."

Pain creased Gabriella's face. She'd heard what Vincinio Calientes was capable of. A brute and the younger brother of the plantation's overseer, he organized the security at Las Canas.

"One day I'll kill him," she vowed.

Polita waved her off. "Don't speak nonsense. Vincinio's nothing, a cockroach." Her mood turned pensive. "Do you still have the camera hidden?"

Gabriella affirmed with a curt nod. Only she knew of the abandoned python burrow near the perimeter fence.

"Do you wish to back out?" Polita asked.

"Never."

"And Humberto?"

"He'll do what I ask."

Polita embraced her before stepping back. "Shortly I'll be traveling to the United States. I'll meet with my cousin and see where he stands. Unfortunately, he is as obstinate as a mule. A blind mule. He sees nothing."

Gabriella listened with envy. "Maybe one day I go to America and visit. I'll go to Disney Park and maybe see a famous actress."

Polita grinned affectionately. "Never lose sight of your dreams." The smile vanished with the sharp clip of approaching footsteps. Her tone became hushed. "I heard they hired another American, an Anglo. She's quite intelligent. She wishes to be a doctor. How ironic." Her last comment was delivered with a trace of contempt.

"Why did she do it?" Gabriella asked genuinely puzzled.

"Her mother is dying. I suppose she desires the money."

Both women's eyes shifted to the door. The footsteps had grown silent. The lock disengaged.

The only warning Gabriella had of what was to follow was the subtle nod of Polita's head. The older woman's hand swung around in a tight arc, impacting loudly against the teenager's strategically placed palm. A staccato crack split

the air. The force of the rehearsed blow whipped Gabriella
sideways.

The guard burst in, his fingers gripping the assault rifle.
"Vaca," he hissed, advancing toward the teen.

"No," Polita ordered, stepping between the two. "Punishment has been administered. There'll be no more trouble from
this one."

Chapter Fifteen

"Dear, we have a problem."

Amoreena studied Irene's somber gaze, feeling very much like a bear cub about to tread across a trap-infested meadow. She would have to step very carefully to avoid being caught.

"My lab results?" she asked innocently, though she already knew the blood tests from her prenatal checkup had returned normal. Dr. Rafael had informed her three days after they'd been drawn. She surmised the personnel running the Ensenada Clínica de la Baja were quite efficient.

Resisting the urge to squirm away from the administrator's cold stare, she had no difficulty determining how Irene had found out about her interview with the Mexican girl two weeks ago. The guard was the only one who'd seen them together in the park.

Irene stood and walked to the window. "You and I both know all your laboratory tests have been fine," she said. "I'm referring to Isabel."

Amoreena quelled a wave of nausea. Each morning the sensations grew worse.

"What about Isabel?" she asked, perhaps more surly than she would've liked.

"What did you two discuss? I'm sure it had nothing to do

with socioeconomic conditions of our sisters south of the border."

"I saw her having an argument with the guard," Amoreena said truthfully. "I stopped to help."

"Help?"

"See if there was a problem."

"Ah." Irene returned to her desk. "And who appointed you clinic liaison? Perhaps you'd prefer Ms. Perez's position."

This time Amoreena squirmed at the barb. "I didn't know it'd be a problem. I'm sorry."

The intensity of the green in the administrator's eyes settled down a notch. "There are many things at our clinic you're not aware of."

Amoreena remained silent.

"One of which is the subject of remuneration," Irene continued. "All the contracts that we enter carry different values. After all, Meechum Corporation is first and foremost a business."

"What do you mean, different values?"

"Answer this question, Amoreena. Do you think it unreasonable that a wealthy individual with a beautiful red-haired wife would find a beautiful auburn surrogate far more attractive, in a reproductive sense, than a woman with lesser attributes?"

"I guess not."

"Sprinkle in a high IQ, and you can understand then why we value your contract to such a degree. It's strictly a business proposition."

Amoreena listened, feeling like the traps in the meadow had just been transformed into mounds of manure. And Irene was spreading it on thick. She'd just been called beautiful and a genius in one sentence. But somehow, even if it was legal, it didn't seem quite moral. Paying her more because some stranger thought she would be a better mother than another woman. Yet in reality, she wasn't a mother. She was a commodity. And all commodities were not valued equally. Still . . .

"Are you satisfied with your contract?" Irene asked.

"Yes. Definitely." Amoreena hated to think where her mother would be without the ten thousand she'd been paid. Phase II was midway toward completion and already some of the tumor sites showed signs of regression. Dr. Gillespie was even optimistic.

"Then you wouldn't wish to jeopardize our agreement, correct?"

"No," Amoreena said, stiffening at the implied threat.

"Try to imagine," Irene said, "if the other girls found out how much your contract was worth. Wouldn't it be conceivable that they might all demand equal compensation?"

Amoreena sat in silence. Would Godinez have called her to discuss this inequality in payment issue? She doubted it.

Irene abruptly leaned closer. "Did you discuss your contract with Isabel?"

"No," Amoreena said.

"Then what?"

It dawned on Amoreena that she was in a chess match and Irene had just made this smoke-bomb maneuver, whether the economic explanation was true or not, to get at what she and Isabel had really discussed. And just as suddenly Amoreena realized there was no way in hell she was going to betray the Mexican girl's confidence.

'It wasn't my baby. It wasn't my fault.' What hadn't been her fault? Something about the baby. What bad things had befallen Isabel's baby?

"We didn't talk long," Amoreena said. "Her English was poor, and my Spanish speaking abilities range from *sí* to *no*. She said she was returning to Mexico."

"That's all."

"Yes." *Except for the fact she was scared to death about something.*

"Has anyone else made any attempts to contact you?"

Amoreena thought of the vague note left on her car and Ronald Godinez's call. More traps.

"No," she answered.

"You'll inform me immediately of any such attempts?"

"Yes," Amoreena said, suppressing more waves of nausea.

"That's all, then." Irene stood, leading her to the door. "I would hate to see any financial conflicts interfere with your mother's treatments," she added.

Amoreena nodded warily. There'd been nothing implied or subtle about that threat.

The morning sickness made studying virtually impossible. Since Irene's impromptu interrogation, the constant uneasy queasy sensation followed Amoreena around all day, not just in the morning. Finally, around dusk, it would dissipate, only to reinvent itself more intensely the next morning. And Irene's paranoia about the whole Isabel encounter only magnified Amoreena's disquiet. Why had Irene been so adamant in trying to find out what the Mexican girl had revealed? Had the Mexican girl known something that Amoreena didn't know? Perhaps regarding her contract. If that were the only issue, discussing contract terms, then Amoreena hadn't done anything wrong yet. One thing was certain. The girl had been scared. And Amoreena suspected the girl's fright had little to do with any contract clause.

Though sipping tea and munching pretzels did little to soothe Amoreena's mind, at least the snacks helped some with the nausea. But not much.

Amoreena had developed an unnatural habit of talking to the cause.

Rubbing her hand over her no longer flat abdomen, she would say, "Lay off, Buster. You're giving me a headache *this* big."

"How do you know it's a him?" Millie would ask.

"Because only a guy could be this rude."

Attending class was an exercise in sheer willpower. Amoreena had no choice. With Dr. Sheffield expressing his concern repeatedly regarding any skipped classes, Amoreena began to feel the Chapman University faculty were monitoring her activities as close as the staff at the Women's Clinic. Plus finals commenced in less than a month.

The MCAT was a black spot on the near horizon as well, growing bigger and blacker each day the test date neared.

She was thankful the Thanksgiving weekend would give her a welcome hiatus from the Pike Hypertension Study. The patients would just have to forgo gazing at her pretty and more puffy face for a week. They'd manage.

Amoreena applied some powder to the dark smudges of fatigue under each eye. The last two mornings, she'd doubled up on her prenatal vitamins hoping for an energy boost, to no avail. She still felt like she was walking around wearing a pair of ankle weights.

She stepped back, evaluating her reflection in the bathroom mirror. The shadows were well concealed but the generalized puffiness remained, more prominent over her cheeks and under her chin. Her weight had tipped the scale at 128. Thirteen pounds in barely eight weeks. Far more than the recommended weight gain of a pound per week. Yet only Dr. Rafael at the clinic had expressed any concern. He'd chided her for consuming too many bagels. Hell, she hated bagels. Just looking at one now, stacked with mounds of cream cheese, would wrench her gut.

The only good she perceived in her new self pertained to her breasts, if you could call going from a C to D cup in two months good. If she could bottle the technique, she'd put 90 percent of the plastic surgeons in line for food stamps.

But no matter from which angle she gazed into the mirror, nothing could alter the fact that this Thanksgiving morning she felt like shit. And for the first time she found herself questioning her sacrifice.

"Four more weeks," she muttered, rummaging through her closet. The end of the first trimester would almost coincide with the completion of her mother's Phase II therapy session. That, she convinced herself, would restoke her incentive, especially once she'd collected the second installment on her contract. Ten thousand dollars could ameliorate a lot of nausea.

She picked out a loose-fitting blouse and slacks, again critically evaluating how she looked. Satisfied that nothing showed, she grabbed the bowl of cranberries and tray of sweet potatoes she'd prepared and locked up.

She was already backing Silver out when the phone rang. The fifth ring triggered the answering machine. No message was recorded.

* * *

"Amy, let me help you," Geneva said, taking the bowl of cranberries.

"You look nice, Mom." Amoreena followed her mother inside the apartment.

Geneva beamed. "One hundred pounds, this morning."

"That's fantastic." Amoreena gave her a big squeeze, immediately regretting her ebullience.

Geneva stepped back, critically appraising her daughter. "Is it my imagination or are both Daniels girls filling out?"

"What do you mean?" Amoreena asked, making for the kitchen. She used the counter to partially conceal her abdomen.

"I just meant you feel more . . . womanly."

"Mother." Amoreena pretended to fuss around the sink. She suppressed a gag. The smell of turkey was the last thing she needed. "I've been snacking a lot with all the studying. I may have put on three or four pounds."

Geneva continued to stare.

"Mom, what?"

"You just look . . . different."

"I didn't drive over to receive a critique on my figure."

"Baby, don't be so sensitive. I didn't mean anything by it."

Amoreena watched her mother fiddle with a cornucopia on the table. "The apartment looks nice," she told her.

"Thank you."

Geneva was gaily dressed in a green two-piece cardigan dress and matching silk scarf. Amoreena thought her mother's skin appeared more vibrant, too.

"Are you retaining fluids?" Geneva asked innocently.

"No. Maybe." Amoreena avoided her stare. "I start my period next week."

"That must be it."

Geneva went to the refrigerator, passing Amoreena on the way out. "How 'bout some wine? I picked up a Tawny Port yesterday."

"I'm not really thirsty."

"It's your favorite."

Amoreena sat on the couch, pretending not to hear her. The holiday weekend wasn't beginning well.

On the television, the Dallas Cowboys were leading the Washington Redskins by two touchdowns. At that moment, football seemed the most insignificant thing in the world.

"Do we have to watch this?" she asked.

"You enjoy football."

Amoreena switched off the set. "The Pilgrims got along well enough without it."

"Of course, dear."

Amoreena felt like she was slowly smothering under the weighty aromas of turkey, corn-bread dressing, and baking sweet potatoes. She exhaled several times in succession.

"Are you feeling well?" Geneva asked.

"I'm fine." She turned on the stereo. The Christmas tune playing only seemed to irritate her. She looked up, catching her mother watching her, the Tawny Port in one hand, a glass in the other.

Amoreena forced a sheepish grin. "Maybe I am a little thirsty. Do you have any milk?"

"Milk?"

"I'll get it."

She poured herself a large glass and brought it to the table. Her mother had obviously expended some energy in setting out the family crystal, candles, and traditional Thanksgiving centerpiece. The least she could be was more appreciative.

Just as Amoreena inhaled, Geneva set a plate of baked yams on the table. Their rich aromas dived right to her stomach, where they seemed to expand at supersonic speed.

Oh God.

"Excuse me," Amoreena said, rising. She headed down the hall.

"Tell me when you're hungry, dear. I'll heat up the turkey and dressing."

Amoreena slipped inside the bathroom, shutting and locking the door. By some holiday miracle, the kitchen odors remained locked out. Irish Spring soap engulfed her nostrils. The clean lime scent refreshed her.

Amoreena turned on the faucet and splashed her face, checking the mirror. Had her cheeks swelled more in the last thirty minutes?

She waited for the nausea to pass, swearing she wouldn't vomit. Allowing the cool water to flow over her wrists seemed to mitigate her queasiness some.

She heard a soft knock.

"Amy?"

"I'll be right out."

"I fixed your favorite brownies, the ones with the sprinkles," Geneva said from the other side.

Amoreena leaned closer to the woman reflected in the mirror, so close her breath fogged the glass. "Happy Thanksgiving," she whispered to the stranger.

It was late when Amoreena parked Silver under the carport. The house was completely dark, and she admonished herself for not having had the foresight to leave a light on, especially since Millie was spending the holiday weekend with her family.

Tucking both arms around her chest, Amoreena walked to the front door, oblivious to the blue Volvo parked at the curb. She scrambled in her purse for the keys.

When the man approached from behind, he made no effort to hide his presence.

Chapter Sixteen

"The turkey dies because it's ignorant of its own future." Ronald Godinez stood in the front lawn, his hands shoved deeply into his jeans pockets, his flannel shirt untucked. "Happy holiday," he said.

He remained in the shadows of a rose-vine-infested arbor, requiring Amoreena to step away from the door in order to get a better look at his face.

She maintained one hand inside her purse, moving the contents about until her fingers closed around the small canister of pepper spray. She didn't trust him, and the unsavory odor of spent cannabis effusing his clothes made her distrust him even more. God, she could have at least left on the front porch light. The only illumination came from a streetlamp several houses down.

"I was hoping you hadn't left town for the weekend," Godinez told her.

He wore the familiar pathos of a man the world had bullied too often. The more Amoreena heard him speak, the more he reminded her of a disgruntled boy who'd lost his way home.

"I was visiting my mother," she said.

"How is she?"

"Fine."

"Really?"

Amoreena found herself repulsed by something intangible in the darks of his eyes. "Actually," she said, "she has metastatic cancer."

"Not good."

"Tell me about it."

"Caca pasa."

"Pardon."

"Shit happens."

"What do you want?" Amoreena asked testily.

Godinez reacted suddenly as twin beams of headlights cut a narrow swath across the front lawn, briefly illuminating him. The car, a late-model Cadillac, cruised by and turned into a drive a half block down.

Amoreena watched him scrutinize the vehicle until its engine stopped. "You expecting company?" she asked.

His attention shifted from the car to the street.

"Never know," he said, gazing right and left. Seemingly satisfied, he shrugged. "Mind if we talk inside?"

"If you try anything funny, I'll break your nose."

Godinez grinned. "I think I believe you."

Under the light of the living room, Amoreena thought the ex–UCLA medical intern appeared thinner than when she'd last seen him. He'd also forgotten or neglected to shave for several days, giving his face the scruffy look of a derelict. After he asked for a beer, she offered a Coke, which he accepted without fanfare. Watching him drink, no matter how hard she tried, she couldn't conjure an image of him sauntering into a hospital room, chart in tow, and inquiring about a patient's status.

He must've interpreted her misgivings for pity.

"Last year at this time, I was in the running for the Golden Caduceus Award," Godinez said. "It's awarded to the outstanding medicine intern."

"So what happened?"

Without moving his head, his eyes roamed around the room, touching on each furnishing. "You live here alone?"

"My roommate's visiting her family."

"Boyfriend?"

"He's six-five, two hundred fifty pounds, and plays linebacker for the San Diego Chargers. He's due over any minute," Amoreena deadpanned.

Godinez chuckled and scratched his nose. "If I'm not mistaken, Junior Seau's married. I'll take that for a no." He quickly added, "And no, I'm not interested."

"I won't take that as an insult."

"It wasn't meant as one." He finished the Coke in one long gulp and set the can on a coffee table, using a magazine as a coaster.

Amoreena held out the box of pretzels she was munching on. For the moment, her nausea was quiescent.

Raising one hand, he declined. "I didn't come here to raid your refrigerator. And contrary to second impressions, I'm not starving or destitute." With a burst of energy, he rose and walked to the front door.

Thinking he was leaving, Amoreena watched him step outside a moment, but then just as abruptly, he returned, closing and locking the door behind him.

"What was that all about?" she asked, more curious than concerned.

"The psychologists call it paranoia. I call it good old-fashioned caution." He resumed his position on the couch, draining the last drop from the Coke can. "How far along are you?" he asked.

Amoreena started to answer. Instead she minced her words. She was beginning to feel uncomfortable again, not just from the incessant queasiness, but also from being in such close proximity to this former UCLA resident physician, Golden Caduceus nominee, who now reeked of marijuana and looked like he belonged in an ad for the city's homeless and vagrants.

She set the pretzels beside her chair and leaned close. "We're going to play it this way, Dr. Godinez," she told him.

"Ronald."

"Fine. Ronald, I'm going to ask the questions, and *you're* going to fill in the blanks. If I'm satisfied, the game continues, if not, we'll call it an evening because, frankly, I'm tired, feel like shit, and want nothing more than to bury myself under my sheets and sleep."

Godinez's eyes flashed. "Not hearing me out would be an egregious error."

Amoreena suppressed a yawn. "I wasn't impressed with your turkey analogy. And I'm tired of being threatened."

"Who threatened you? My money's on Leggett, though Becker's very capable as well."

Amoreena reached for the phone.

"What're you doing?"

"You're outta here, or I'm calling the police. Now." She raised the receiver and pressed nine.

"No. No." Godinez leaped to his feet, holding out both palms in supplication. Panic lines creased his face. "Okay. Your rules. Promise. Just don't call the police. Please." He sat down languidly. "One more black mark on my record and I *am* through."

Amoreena replaced the receiver.

"Thank you," he offered weakly.

"Did you call my mother last month?" she asked.

"Yes."

Amoreena saw a film of perspiration coating his forehead. "Why?"

"I was hoping to find you."

"Why me?"

"Because you're a patient there."

Amoreena registered his discomfort. "I'm not the Women's Clinic's only patient."

"True. But the others"—he shrugged—"most are undocumented aliens and too frightened to talk."

"Like Isabel?"

"I'm not familiar with any Isabel."

Amoreena had no difficulty recalling the Mexican girl's panic-stricken face. "She's no longer a patient there," she said.

Godinez grunted to himself and returned to the couch. "I tried discussing my concerns with some of the other women, but they wanted no part of me. No trouble, they'd say—I guess it was the money."

"*I* need the money."

Godinez suddenly slid forward as if he wasn't listening. "Plus, they didn't have your medical background."

"I'm only premed."

"Don't underestimate a university education, Amoreena."

"Why was it so important to find me, Ronald?"

"I wanted to warn you. And . . ." He hesitated. "I also need your help."

Amoreena pondered briefly what he said. "How did you obtain my address?"

"Your medical record."

"My chart at the clinic," Amoreena said, registering genuine surprise. "So much for patient confidentiality. Go on."

Godinez cast a furtive glance out the window before continuing. "A clinic employee accessed your records and gave me your phone number and address."

"Not Dr. Luis Rafael," Amoreena said, hoping the answer a no.

"A custodial lady," Godinez explained. "It's not really important because last week I found out she was no longer there."

"Why?"

"The place is really bizarre. I heard she became ill and had to return home somewhere in Central America."

Amoreena detected more than sarcasm in his explanation. "And you don't believe this."

"Are you kidding me? I just pray she's still breathing."

Amoreena started. "Are you suggesting she was killed?"

Godinez shrugged wearily. "I don't know. I don't want to scare you."

"You're doing an exemplary job of not doing that. Is *this* how you warn people?"

The phone rang before he could respond.

Amoreena rose, accidentally knocking over the box of pretzels. From the corner of one eye, she saw Godinez staring intently at the answering machine. "Don't answer it," he warned.

Amoreena reached the phone midway through the third ring.

"Don't answer it," Godinez repeated.

"You are paranoid." But the urgency in Godinez's tone prevented Amoreena from lifting the receiver.

She waited for her prerecorded voice to complete its cycle.

Seeing the ex-intern sitting rigidly on the edge of her couch as if preparing to bolt for the door made her feel only slightly less foolish. The guy gave her the creeps.

Upon hearing Millie's voice, she breathed a sigh of relief. She hadn't realized she'd been holding her breath.

Amoreena greeted her roommate. During their short conversation, she noticed Godinez had relaxed considerably, though several times he pulled the drapes aside and checked out the window.

Replacing the receiver, she took her place beside the box of pretzels. "My roommate."

"I gathered."

"She said she's started looking for a dog," Amoreena remarked in a weak attempt to lighten the foreboding smothering the room.

Godinez grunted dismissively, obviously uninterested in any pet stories.

He reached out and crushed the aluminum Coke can with one hand.

"Another?" Amoreena asked.

Godinez shook his head. "I need your help."

The wall clock indicated it was after eleven. Late. She would've been well within her rights to call it a night, but a tenuous thread of camaraderie had begun to stretch across the room's empty space, and Amoreena would have been no more able to resist continuing than refuse telling the time to an inquiring stranger on the street.

"How?" she asked, instantly observing the intern's eyes brightening.

"I must obtain my girlfriend's medical records."

"I assume she was a patient at the Women's Clinic."

"A surrogate," he said, adding as almost an afterthought, "like you."

Amoreena didn't refute this last comment. Godinez evidently had sources unknown to her who kept him informed. Probably the disappearing housekeeper. Besides, she didn't wish to lie, at least right now anyway.

Instead she asked, "Why don't you have your girlfriend assist you?"

"She's dead."

"Shit," Amoreena mumbled. Subconsciously, she found herself checking the front door. The dead bolt was engaged. "I'm sorry," she said.

"Yeah, *caca pasa*."

"What happened?"

Godinez sat forward, his elbows resting on his knees. His tone conveyed little emotion.

"My family is strictly Catholic," he began. "The Catholic Church forbids surrogacy in any form, which made it difficult for Gretchen and me. Gretchen wasn't Catholic. I used to wonder if she even believed in God."

"Why'd she do it?"

"The same reason I assume you're doing it."

"Money."

Godinez nodded. "During a visiting rotation at UCMC last February, I admitted a man diagnosed with metastatic prostate cancer. Gretchen's dad. After he was discharged, she and I started dating. Man, I couldn't see enough of that woman. I wanted to marry her, which really shocked my family."

"Why?"

"Gretchen was black."

Amoreena was neither shocked nor uneasy about interracial couples. Of far more concern to her was why this girl she didn't even know had died. The fact that she'd been a surrogate at the same clinic created an invisible bond that spanned both the world of the living and the deceased. That she felt uneasy about.

Godinez continued. "In March, her father's insurance coverage ran out."

The bond just grew stronger.

"Her mother was unemployed," he went on, "and I couldn't very well help her on an intern's meager salary. Then one day a woman contacted Gretchen. Said she could solve all her problems."

"Recall a name?"

Godinez shot Amoreena a wicked smile. "Ramona Perez. Anyway, the money was right, and Gretchen signed on the dotted line."

"And?"

"In the beginning, things seemed to go smoothly. She was paid on schedule, which allowed her father's chemotherapy to continue. And I can't complain about the quality of care she received . . ."

"Until . . ." Amoreena was unaware her posture had turned rigid.

"I initially became suspicious when they began ordering all these tests that had nothing to do with the pregnancy."

"Human leukocyte antigen."

"That and other esoteric genetic tests, some of which I'd never heard of. Then last June, she'd just entered her second trimester, the bomb fell. The clinic medical director—"

"Becker."

"I call him Teflon Man. You could dump a bucket of shit over his head and he'd still come out clean, smelling like an orchid." Godinez shook his head. "Gotta hand it to him, though. The guy's brilliant. Anyway, when Becker informed Gretchen something was wrong with the baby, she freaked. And of course, the clinic required more tests. And this time, they suggested she come in alone."

"Why?"

"I'd become a nuisance."

"Did she go in alone?"

Godinez grimaced. "Against my wishes. We even had a fight about it. She told me if I continued to interfere, the clinic would declare the contract null and void."

"Can they do that?"

"That's not the point. Just the threat of having her father's therapy put at risk because of a legal tussle ensured Gretchen's complete cooperation. They might as well have been holding a lighted match to her toes." For a long moment, Godinez slowly shook his head. "That was the last day I saw Gretchen alive."

Amoreena's thoughts drifted to Dr. Rafael. Had he been involved in the girl's ill-fated care? "She died at the clinic?" she asked incredulously.

"On her way back from Ensenada, Mexico."

Amoreena shuddered involuntarily. "What was Gretchen doing in Ensenada?"

Either the man was Academy Award material, or what Godinez was about to relate affected him deeply. He took a few seconds to compose himself.

"I don't think I'll ever know," he said. "Her clinic appointment had been at ten. I was asleep that day because the night before I'd had a rough shift on call. At five that afternoon, I was awakened by a collect call from Ensenada. It was Gretchen, and she was hysterical."

"How so?"

"Crying. Laughing. It was like she'd slipped completely over the edge. I nearly didn't recognize her. It was scary. All she could talk about was how her baby wasn't a baby."

"Her baby wasn't a baby?" Amoreena reflexively touched her own abdomen. "She *was* pregnant?"

"Yes." Godinez wrung his hands. "When I finally calmed her enough to speak coherently, she actually apologized."

"Apologized?"

"Yeah," Godinez said, his face paling. "She apologized for not making herself more clear. What she'd meant to say was not that her baby wasn't a baby, rather her baby wasn't a *human* baby. Then the line disconnected."

Amoreena sat stunned.

"It gets more bizarre," Godinez said, chuckling, entirely inappropriately. "I dressed and immediately drove to the clinic. Becker refused to see me, but Irene did, feigning complete ignorance. When I threatened to go to the police, she said that was also an option their legal staff was considering if Gretchen failed to honor the contract. Supposedly Gretchen had violated some travel clause." His expression soured. "I waited at my fiancée's apartment all night, but she never showed. Early the next morning, her family was notified there'd been an accident. Somewhere between Ensenada and Rosarito, Gretchen had missed a curve. Her car plummeted two hundred feet down a rocky cliff."

A dark cloud had transformed the intern's expression. "During the ensuing investigation, everyone denied any knowledge of Gretchen driving to Mexico—the clinic, her family, and I sure as hell didn't know. The Mexican authorities did say it appeared she'd been returning to the US border, but couldn't explain how she'd lost control under such optimal driving conditions. The day had been dry and sunny. Until the autopsy."

Godinez clenched both fists. "Gretchen had been legally drunk." He gazed imploringly at the crushed Coke can. "How do you get a blood alcohol level of one point four without imbibing any alcohol?"

"She didn't drink."

"Not while she was pregnant. She'd never have done anything to harm the baby. Plus it was a violation of her contract."

"What about a US investigation?"

"Out of their jurisdiction. Our police only had what the Mexican authorities released," Godinez said, his voice animated. "When Gretchen's body was finally transferred north two weeks later, the Orange County coroner conducted his own examination. He confirmed the blood alcohol level, but get this. You ready? There was no mention of Gretchen being pregnant. It was like the preceding four months had never taken place."

For a split second the shocking revelation didn't register. When it did, Amoreena felt her entire body tingle unnaturally. "How could that be?" she managed to say.

Godinez shrugged lamely. "After the accident, I lost all track of time. I began devoting more energy to finding out the truth than to my own patients. Every day without her, my depression deepened until even the alcohol didn't help. The pot helps some." He grinned sheepishly. "Pike booted me off the service when I discharged a patient from the emergency room with another patient's meds. Fortunately, nothing came of it, but . . ." His voice trailed.

"How's rehab?"

"It's . . . rehab." Godinez stood suddenly and began pacing. "But that's why I need Gretchen's chart."

"And you want me to get it."

"If I show up at the clinic again, Irene threatened to have me arrested. And the cold bitch would do it."

Amoreena tried to push herself deeper into her chair. She didn't like it, not one bit. Her slate wasn't squeaky-clean with the Meechum administrator either.

"Ronald, I can't do it," she said, regretting each word. "My mother's treatments are dependent upon the clinic's continued financial support."

"I understand." Godinez had stopped pacing and was watching her with neither anger nor resentment. "I really do. But I had to ask."

"Didn't the Orange County coroner get her records?"

"You think Becker didn't doctor the chart?" he said cynically. "That's one of the first things they teach you in medical school. I want her *real* chart."

"I wouldn't know where to begin looking."

"Forget it. I asked and"—he exhaled into his hands—"believe it or not, that helps."

"What will you do?"

Godinez leaned against the wall. His eyes focused on some unseen point near the ceiling. "Be a hell of a lot more careful next time I go poking around Ensenada. There's a clinic down there—"

"Clínica de la Baja."

The intern appeared minimally taken aback.

Amoreena explained, "Some of my blood tests were sent there."

"Interesting," Godinez said with little conviction. "Don't mess with their security. The Ensenada guards are a bit more aggressive than their north of the border counterparts."

Amoreena recalled Godinez's beat-up appearance when she'd first talked to him at the hypertension study orientation. So that's what he'd meant by "trouble with the Ensenada locals."

"Ronald, why did you ask me to call you if I felt the baby move in three months?"

Godinez eyed her warily. "That's what Gretchen experienced. I just thought if you were dealt the same deal . . ."

"What deal?" Amoreena sat forward suddenly.

"I wish I could say. Except that once Gretchen noticed the baby begin to move, the pregnancy seemed to . . . accelerate.

By four months, she looked six months, her weight increased, she cried all the time, she . . ." Godinez ran one hand through his hair. "I just don't fucking know anymore. Maybe Gretchen did freak out like the clinic asserted, some paranoia of pregnancy, maybe she did get wasted on tequila, maybe she wanted to break up with me, who the hell knows. It's like chasing ashes in the wind. But I'll tell you this. For her to refer to the fetus as something inhuman, that I can't accept. No way. She saw *something* in Ensenada, and I mean to find out what."

Amoreena followed him to the door.

"Be careful," she warned.

"You too."

After a brief awkward embrace, she watched him dip back into the shadows, but not before accepting his phone number.

"Just in case," he muttered.

When he was halfway to his car, she called out his name. "Ronald."

He took one step back in her direction and stopped.

"What was your fiancée's last name?" she asked.

"Bayliss. Gretchen Bayliss."

"How's her dad?"

"He died three weeks ago."

Chapter Seventeen

The ultrasound table felt cold and hard under her back. Amoreena lay motionless while the technician applied some clear gel to her lower abdomen. The sonogram was the last item of her second prenatal checkup. The *routine* blood tests had already been collected and tubed. She presumed some would be sent to La Clínica de la Baja in Mexico. This presumption only added to the difficulty of determining her next course of action.

Amoreena forced herself to relax while a female tech went to work. The transducer head caused a mild discomfort as it passed over certain quadrants of her belly. She hoped that was normal.

Almost a week had passed since her late-night rendezvous with Ronald Godinez, and she still hadn't arrived at a decision. Though he hadn't come out and specifically said it, Amoreena had intuited that the intern believed his fiancée's car crash had been more than an accident. Just the idea of murder, as remote as it seemed, sent a shiver through her bones.

The tech paused. "You okay?" she asked.

Amoreena nodded. "How much longer?"

"Not long."

Visualizing her own sonogram was nerve-wracking enough, but coupling *seeing* the fetus with her knowledge of Isabel's and Gretchen Bayliss's bizarre comments about their babies, sent her anxiety level soaring. The two women's statements had been too similar to be coincidental.

"It wasn't my baby."

"My baby wasn't a human baby."

Amoreena suppressed a shudder. Yet she was unable to pull her eyes from the ultrasound monitor. By the tech's calm reaction, everything seemed to be normal. To Amoreena, the echoes of the sound waves bouncing off the fetus created an indecipherable picture. She hoped the doctor would be better at interpreting the shifting white shadows across the background of blue.

Watching the occasional jerky melting of one image into another, she figured the easiest course would be simply to discredit all Godinez had told her. Her recollection of the intern's disheveled appearance and marijuana-saturated clothing would not have made this a difficult task. But the man's frightened-animal intensity and emotional lability prevented Amoreena from doing this. Plus there was Isabel. There'd been nothing extraordinary about her appearance. Except fear.

She decided to let the ultrasound results be her guide. If abnormal, she'd immediately discharge herself from the Women's Clinic's care, get a second opinion, and pray Dr. Gillespie could influence the utilization committee to complete her mother's treatments on Amoreena's good credit. If normal, which she fully anticipated, she'd follow through with the decision she'd arrived at that morning during the embryology lecture.

The hand on her shoulder startled her. She shifted her gaze up and saw Dr. Becker observing the sonogram monitor. Dressed in a sports coat and slacks, he looked more like a businessman than a caregiver. She had no idea how long he'd been in the room.

The tech said something in Spanish and handed Becker the transducer. The physician gently guided it across Amoreena's lower abdomen.

"See his heart," Becker said, briefly adjusting the transducer head.

The tiny rhythmically pulsating mass was easy to pick out.

"Yes," Amoreena whispered, mesmerized by the beating organ. There really was something growing within her, something alive, and one day it'd talk and call for Mommy and Daddy. Her fingers began to tingle witnessing the real-time images.

"So it's a he," she said, amazed at how fast Becker had determined the sex.

"Yes." He moved closer to the screen, effectively blocking Amoreena's view. He appeared to be studying the monitor in more detail.

"Is everything all right?" she asked.

Amoreena thought he indicated yes with a brief nod but couldn't be sure. She wanted him to move aside so she could watch, too, however Becker remained rooted in front of the screen, periodically adjusting a dial.

After another minute, he removed the transducer from Amoreena's skin. "Clean her up," he ordered the technician.

With his customary pat on the knee, he said, "Everything's routine, Amoreena."

"What about the parents?"

The pressure of his grip increased slightly. "What about the parents?"

"Did they want a boy or a girl?"

She felt his fingers relax. "It doesn't matter as long as the baby's healthy."

"And he *is* healthy?"

With a grin he motioned to the monitor. "You saw for yourself."

After he departed, the technician wiped clean the gel and returned Amoreena's clothing. Before the tech exited, Amoreena asked, "Can I have a copy of my ultrasound?"

The question was unexpected because briefly the technician appeared flustered. "You must ask the doctor," she said.

"Can you get him?"

"Doctor is very busy."

"Please."

The woman held up one finger. *"Un momentito."*

She was only out of the room for a few minutes. Amoreena was relieved when she returned with Dr. Rafael.

"What happened?" he asked in mock seriousness.

Amoreena tensed. "What do you mean?"

"You put on a few pounds since I last saw you."

"Is that bad?"

He grinned. "That's good. It means you're eating healthy."

"The nausea comes and goes," Amoreena said, giving him an accusing glare. "You scared me for a second."

"I'm sorry." He pulled up a stool and sat down, glancing once at the sonogram monitor. "So what's this special request of yours?"

"I was wondering if I could have a copy of my ultrasound."

"Why?" For an instant he actually looked shocked.

"As a reminder."

Dr. Rafael pondered the request a moment. "Under normal circumstances, yes. However, under the surrogacy agreement, all the images of the baby belong to the clinic and the parents."

"If the parents give permission?"

"The final decision would rest with Irene and Dr. Becker, but I have to tell you it's never been done before."

"Can I at least see the ultrasound?"

"Didn't Dr. Becker show you?"

Amoreena feigned a pout. "He stood in front of the monitor almost the entire time."

"Sit tight." Dr. Rafael left the room briefly and returned holding an X-ray folder. He removed a film and slid it up on the viewing window. "See the head, and here's the torso. And get a look at those legs. He's going to make a hell of a soccer player."

Amoreena followed Dr. Rafael's index finger as he outlined the various other fetal structures—the heart, liver, lungs, kidneys—all in mosaic shades of black and white.

"Feel better?" he asked, returning the sonogram to the folder.

"Yes, thanks." It truly was a miracle. She couldn't suppress the urge to giggle.

"What's so funny?"

"I just feel good. No, relieved would be a better description."

"I'm glad for you, Amoreena."

She held his gaze. "What was Gretchen Bayliss doing in Mexico?" she asked. As soon as Amoreena saw Dr. Rafael reenter the room with the sonograms she knew she was going to press the question. It was only a matter of timing. She wanted to catch him off guard. She did.

After an awkward exchange between doctor and technician, the sonogram tech exited the room.

Amoreena scrutinized the younger physician's face but whatever had been there before, he'd buried.

"Were you friends with Ms. Bayliss?" he asked.

Amoreena shook her head. "My roommate went to school with her," she lied.

"Then you're aware of the accident."

"Yes."

"Horrendous," he said, checking his watch. "She was Dr. Becker's patient."

Suddenly, the door burst open. *"Emergencia!"* The sonogram tech said. *"Dr. Rafael, rapido."* Her eyes were wide as saucers.

Amoreena saw flashes of white as personnel in lab coats raced by the room. Dr. Rafael issued an apology and dashed out of the room. The door slammed shut. She was alone.

Outside, the commotion's intensity faded as whatever the emergency was had been transferred elsewhere.

Amoreena dressed and grabbed her purse. She opened the door. The hall looked deserted. She stepped into the corridor.

Passing two empty exam rooms, she approached a corner. Right would take her back to elevators. She looked left just as a nurse ran by.

Another shriek took her breath away. She watched the nurse enter one of the two delivery rooms. The patient's cries were much louder with the door open, hitting her like sharp slaps in the face. She blinked at the raw emotion.

Inside, she saw clinic personnel leaping around one another in response to orders as monitoring equipment and an IV setup were positioned around the table. She couldn't see the patient, but from the screams which persisted, there plainly was someone in dire distress.

A man in a surgical mask saw her watching and kicked the door closed. At the same time, a red bulb about the room's entrance began flashing angrily. A security guard entered the room.

The screams abruptly stopped. A deathly silence ensued.

Amoreena waited, knowing she should leave but unable to get her legs to move. Witnessing firsthand the pain and suffering had piqued the future physician within her.

"¿Puedo ayudarle?"

Amoreena jumped, not seeing the technician until she was upon her.

"Can I help you?" the woman repeated in English.

"No. I was leaving."

The tech nodded and began pushing the portable ultrasound machine toward the elevators.

Amoreena didn't move even after the technician had passed out of view. She noticed the delivery room light switch to a constant red glow. Sensing some new event about to take place, she ducked inside an empty procedure room. Closing the door partway, she positioned herself next to the doorjamb. The tiny gap permitted her to observe the delivery room entrance without being detected, unless someone happened to enter her room.

Silently she practiced her excuse. *I was lost.*

The delivery room door swung open and a man in surgical scrubs wheeled out a metal cart. He was followed by the security guard. Inside the room, the pandemonium had abated. Amoreena detected voices carrying on conversation in normal tones, until the door swung shut.

The guard, a beefy individual with thick, tattooed forearms, spoke quietly to the man in green scrubs. She watched the man affirm with a curt nod. Immediately, the guard positioned himself several paces away from the cart, his expression registering something akin to disgust.

Amoreena shifted her attention to the single white container on the cart, which she guessed was the object of the guard's disdain. Rectangular and approximately two feet long, the bassinet appeared to be made of plastic or fiber-glass. At one end, she saw several attachments, similar to the ventilation hose hookups she'd seen on the oncology ward. A fluorescent light fixture ran the length of the bassinet's cover, which resembled a shallow elongated dome. The cover was transparent and misted with condensation over its inner surface.

The man in scrubs pulled a blanket from a lower shelf and folded it across the entire apparatus.

The loud *mewling* started as soon as the man began to push the cart. Instantly, Amoreena sensed her arms prickle with goose bumps. So high-pitched, the cries actually seemed to ricochet off the ceiling and walls. Her knees began trembling uncontrollably, and her brain suddenly felt numbed by a men-acing sense of foreboding. She desperately wanted to turn and run, yet her feet remained cemented to the floor. All she could do was listen with morbid fascination, positive she'd never heard a sound quite like it before. *Something* was alive within the bassinet.

She waited until the footsteps had faded before entering the hall. She stepped quietly by the delivery room, then hurried to the next corner. Peering around, she saw the guard and man in scrubs waiting for another elevator. She'd never seen this one before, and if her sense of position was correct, she figured she was standing near the rear of the building.

The lurid crying continued until the man, cart, and guard vanished into the elevator.

Though she knew she should leave, she couldn't make her-self return to the lobby. The *pull* was too strong. Instead she found herself drawn to the strange ululations as if by an invis-ible magnet. Subconsciously caressing her own abdomen, she looked back over her shoulder toward the delivery room. The door was still closed, and the red light remained on. She hoped the patient inside was all right.

Summoning her nerve, Amoreena inhaled deeply twice. The adrenaline pumping through her veins had temporarily cured her perpetual nausea.

Before she suffered a change of heart, she stepped briskly to the elevator and hit the OPEN button. The delay seemed interminable. She stared up and down the corridor. She saw no one. She hit the button again, waiting. The door slid open and she leaped inside.

She began to descend automatically. To her chagrin, she could find no buttons to control the doors from the inside.

One floor down, the elevator door slid open, revealing a well-illuminated room with white-tile floors and walls. A small operating suite came to mind except for the shelves of boxed medical supplies and columns of empty plastic bassinets stacked vertically.

A warm air current swept by Amoreena's face, leaving her skin moist with perspiration. She felt like she'd entered a sauna turned to low.

Not ten feet across the tile floor, the scrub man stood, his back to her. Another man hovered at his side. Both men wore surgical masks and long-sleeved vanilla-latex gloves and were in the midst of engaging the infant inside the bassinet. The feeble crying persisted but only intermittently.

A thin tube carrying a clear liquid ran from an intravenous bag suspended from a pole to a small angiocath held in the scrub man's fingers. A sparkle of metal from the angiocath's tip indicated the presence of a tiny needle, further evidenced by a sharp wail moments after the man's hands dipped below the bassinet's sides. The other man quickly adjusted a stopcock valve. The squealing ceased.

The two men had been so busy concentrating, they'd heard neither the elevator door open nor Amoreena's whispered curse when the guard stepped from a cubicle adjacent to the elevator entrance.

Spying Amoreena, the guard reached for his gun belt.

"No!" she gasped.

Chapter Eighteen

"I got lost," Amoreena said, wearing her most convincing sheepish grin. She'd been escorted directly to the clinic administrator's office by the less-than-cordial guard and now sat in the same chair she'd interviewed from.

Behind her desk, Irene listened in stark silence to Amoreena's version of events. A folder lay open before her. Amoreena presumed the chart was hers.

The phone buzzed. The administrator picked it up, listened briefly, retorted snappishly in Spanish, then replaced the receiver. She shut the folder.

"So you inadvertently chose the wrong elevator, thinking it would return you to the lobby."

"That's correct."

Irene's eyes narrowed. "I don't believe you."

Amoreena shifted her focus to the computer monitor on the administrator's desk in a weak attempt to deflect Irene's ire. As in each of her previous visits, the screen was filled with data, mostly letter abbreviations and numbers. One line of data blinked from inside a highlighted area. Amoreena wondered if Irene ever shut the damn thing off.

"I thought the guard was going to shoot me," she said.

Irene snorted. "Don't be ridiculous. Meechum Corporation is not in the habit of harming its patients."

"What about Gretchen Bayliss?" Amoreena asked.

Irene casually shoved the file she'd been perusing across the desk. "Read for yourself," she said calmly.

Suspecting some sort of chicanery, but nevertheless retrieving the folder, Amoreena read the name typed across the tab. GRETCHEN BAYLISS. ID 12436.

The fact that Irene had been prepared for the inquiry, so prepared she'd actually had the file pulled, caught Amoreena completely off guard.

"How is Dr. Godinez these days?" she heard Irene ask.

"He's in drug rehab," Amoreena answered, making no attempt to deny cognizance of Godinez's existence. She realized there was no point in lying to Irene. After all, how else would she have heard about Gretchen Bayliss?

She leafed through the folder, stopping at the English translation of the *Reporte de Federales de México*. Most of the pages related to the accident were poor-quality copies of the originals the Mexican authorities had forwarded to the Orange County coroner. The Women's Clinic had been distributed their own facsimiles which seemed odd to Amoreena, until she recalled the clinic had been Gretchen's primary medical provider at the time of her death.

Irene recited some platitude regarding Godinez's tarnished future if he didn't get a better grip on his life, a comment Amoreena chose to ignore.

She'd reached the line listing the cause of death. She skipped to the US version.

Gretchen Bayliss had died of multiple traumatic injuries. Most noteworthy were the fractured skull, ruptured spleen, cardiac contusion, and severely lacerated liver, any one of which alone could have proved fatal. The human body was not designed to survive a straight dive down a 220-foot ravine in an '89 Honda Accord, seat belts or no seat belts.

Two additional findings proved more disconcerting than the causes of death. Amoreena could find nothing alluding to Gretchen's supposed inebriation.

"She wasn't intoxicated?"

"Of course not," Irene said. Her tone had become less surly and more conciliatory. "The anesthesia she received for the abortion in Mexico caused the spurious blood alcohol level. The county coroner's investigation proved that."

Amoreena closed the file and set it back on the desk. Had Godinez purposely fabricated the alcohol story pertaining to his fiancée's death in order to convince her to assist him in his quest for Gretchen's medical records? And if so, why? Nothing she'd examined would seem to be of much benefit to him. If anything, this accident report removed the mystery shrouding the girl's demise.

"How far along was her pregnancy?" Amoreena asked, dismayed that Godinez had mentioned nothing of his girlfriend's abortion. She wondered if he even knew.

Irene frowned. "It was a twenty-one-week termination. Totally unwarranted and *totally* in conflict with the policies of this medical corporation. For some unfathomable reason, Ms. Bayliss had become convinced something was horribly wrong with the baby. Even after witnessing her own normal sonograms, she refused to heed our advice. In the week preceding the accident, she'd become paranoid, prompting Dr. Becker's referral for psychiatric evaluation."

The administrator's tone became contrite. "On the day of her appointment with the psychiatrist, Ms. Bayliss drove to Mexico, where she checked herself into a private clinic south of Rosarito. There, she aborted the pregnancy. The accident occurred on her return trip."

"What happened to the fetus?"

"Disposed of by the treating clinic. Needless to say, the contracting parents were quite distraught."

So much for the enigma of Gretchen's nongravid condition at the time of her autopsy. There was something else Amoreena felt compelled to ask. "Was the infant normal?"

"Her baby, yes."

"But you never examined the body."

"Up to that time, all Ms. Bayliss's sonograms and laboratory tests had been perfectly within normal limits," Irene explained. "There were never any indications of an impending problem."

"That you were aware of."

"There was *never* any problem."

"Then why did Godinez request Gretchen's medical records?"

Irene shifted impatiently. "Actually what Dr. Godinez demanded was that the remainder of Ms. Bayliss's compensation package be paid to her family. That was ludicrous. Upon her death, the contract became null and void. When I refused, he became irate and threatened a lawsuit. Understandably, the man was upset. His girlfriend had just been killed, and Dr. Becker would be the first to tell you the stresses a busy internship can cause. We think some of Ms. Bayliss's paranoia had begun to rub off on him."

Amoreena pondered what she heard. Irene's explanation plus the coroner's report tied all the facts into a neat package. It wasn't too great a stretch of the imagination envisioning the poor woman becoming paranoid, driving to Mexico, then accidentally missing a curve on the return trip. Things happened. But to terminate her own pregnancy? And what circumstances precipitated this paranoia?

"Amoreena, what's really bothering you?"

"What did I witness upstairs?"

"A routine case of preterm labor. After a night on our obstetrics ward, the mother will be discharged tomorrow." The administrator's tone turned somber. "Unfortunately, the infant, a male, had to be transferred to an outside facility secondary to some respiratory complications. He should do fine."

"What I heard didn't sound like an infant with breathing problems."

"And how many preterm neonates have you cared for, Dr. Daniels?"

Irene's sarcasm felt like a slap on the hand, sharp and painful. Yet Amoreena had to admit the administrator had her there. She supposed an infant suffering from acute respiratory distress syndrome could explain the pitiful sound she heard coming from the bassinet. If so, Amoreena hoped the baby's condition was less serious than his labored crying might have indicated.

"One last suggestion," Irene offered. "If Dr. Godinez attempts to contact you again, I'd suggest you call the police."

Amoreena had already considered just that.

* * *

The unmarked gray van pulled out of the clinic lot just in front of Amoreena. She'd seen it several times before, parked at the loading dock at the rear of the clinic. It resembled some type of medical transport, except there were no flashing lights. She followed the van on Spurgeon to the Santa Ana Freeway where she lost sight of it when the vehicle turned south toward San Diego.

Amoreena drove north to the Garden Grove Freeway and headed west, exiting on Glassell.

The university's student lot was filled to capacity, and it took ten minutes before she secured a place. So close to final exams, parking spaces went at a premium.

She was late for her human genetics class, so she waited at the door of the lecture hall, catching Daryl as he squeezed out sandwiched in a pack of other science majors.

Before she'd even spoken, he pulled a page from his pack.

"You're setting a bad example for the other premed wanna-bes," he said, handing over the notes.

Gladys Peterson shuffled by with her trademark stack of textbooks. "Missed you in class today, Amoreena."

She ignored the verbal jab. Instead, she pecked Daryl on the cheek. "I owe you."

She turned, but felt a firm grip on her arm. "You okay?" he asked, studying her face. "Really?"

Amoreena saw that Gladys and several other premeds had stopped and were watching her.

She smiled. "I'll get these back to you tomorrow," she told Daryl.

"No rush," he said.

"See ya."

Walking away, Amoreena felt like the fat lady in a carnival sideshow modeling lingerie before a roomful of men. Though she knew they couldn't *know*—she trusted Millie like a sister—she still wanted to just disappear. Her self-perception had taken a real hit lately, and she had to remind herself that another ten grand would be coming her way again shortly. The first trimester payout was scheduled right after the final exam week and just before the Christmas holidays. Somehow the compensation package had lost some of its luster. Pulling her jacket around her, she detoured past the Student Center and headed for the library.

Even before collecting notes from Daryl she'd decided to skip her afternoon embryology lecture. She wasn't up to confronting magnified human fetal images in various stages of development projected up on an eight-foot-by-ten-foot screen. She felt confident she could catch up on any missed material later.

Amoreena found an empty study carrel on the second floor, plunked her pack of books and notes on the desk, and sat down. Her MCAT manual slid into view, a stark reminder that in nine days she'd be taking the most important exam of her student career. Today, she didn't care. She shoved the entire pack aside and leaned forward, resting her head on her arms.

She couldn't rid herself of the strange squealing noise she'd heard in the clinic earlier. Had there really been an infant in respiratory distress as Irene had intimated? If so, why hadn't an ambulance been summoned? She hadn't seen one when she departed. True, it could have arrived while she'd been talking to Irene, but she didn't recall any sirens.

When she'd left the clinic, she'd also felt fairly reassured regarding the circumstances of Gretchen Bayliss's accident. But alone again, seeds of doubt began to erode the edges of Irene's explanation. She silently replayed the entire conversation, looking for some discrepancy that would indicate Irene had lied. She found none. The facts as they'd been presented by the clinic administrator supported the official version of events, yet Amoreena still found it difficult to disregard all Godinez had told her.

Was it her turn to become paranoid now? Weren't the first symptoms of paranoia a belief that everyone was lying to you? She thought of the frightened Mexican girl in the park. Had paranoia been at the root of her terror as well?

Amoreena tried massaging the back of her neck, refusing to become trapped in the quagmire of doubts and uncertainties. Final exam preparation would be impossible of she didn't regain her focus. And that was a certainty she couldn't ignore.

For five minutes she forced her mind to remain blank. She tried practicing the relaxation techniques she'd read about in the *What to Expect* pregnancy book. She inhaled slowly and deeply through her nose, pushing her abdomen out as she did. She counted to four. Then she exhaled for a six count. After the third such series, she felt the tension in her neck and shoulders begin to dissipate.

She closed her eyes.

The dream was so real she could smell the hanging vines of tropical orchids and passion flowers. The absolute solitude of the forest frightened her. No matter in what direction she went, tree limbs obstructed her path. Darkness descended over her like a heavy blanket. Then the feeble crying began.

With a start, Amoreena jerked her head up. With one hand she caught the drop of saliva that had trickled from the corner of her mouth.

She glanced at the clock mounted above a neighboring carrel.

"Shit," she mumbled. It was past five. She'd dozed for *almost two hours*. She listened, half-expecting to hear the labored respirations of an infant in distress, but only the soft whispers of two students conversing reached her ears.

Gathering her books, she descended the stairs for the exit.

The house front door was open when she pulled under the carport. Expecting Millie in the hall, she reeled back in shock at the compact bundle of fur hurtling toward her.

The Labrador puppy bounded into Amoreena's legs, sniffing at her shoes. His feet looked like they belonged to his parents, they were so disproportionately huge.

Amoreena watched the mutt gyroscope around her ankles. When she bent down to pet the puppy, she caught a wet tongue. Looking up, she saw Millie posed with both hands on her hips wearing a what-do-you-think look.

"When did *this* happen?" Amoreena asked.

The boisterous pup began to yelp at the sound of her voice. Millie pointed. "Quiet, Byte."

"Bite?"

"Not B-I-T-E. B-Y-T-E." Millie squatted, slapping the hardwood floor. "Come, Byte." She glanced up as the pup rocketed her way. "Byte as in computer."

"I get it," Amoreena said, watching the puppy and her roommate fall against the wall together. "I just don't believe it."

"Try it."

Amoreena started to shake her head, but something in the dog's ingenuous exuberance made her want to smile.

"What the hell," she said. She clapped her hands together twice. "Come here, Byte. Come."

The pup's big head twisted out of Millie's grip. Momentarily out of control, he spun in one complete circle, unable to gain traction on the wood floor, before fishtailing in Amoreena's direction.

The force of impact nearly knocked Amoreena off-balance.

"God, I wish I had his energy." She cupped both arms under his belly and raised him partway in the air.

"Careful," Millie said.

"I'm not an old woman."

"I was warning Byte."

Both girls laughed.

"You are one chubby dog," Amoreena said, releasing the squirming animal. She dodged a pawed left hook as Byte frolicked between her calves.

"Okay, outside with you," Millie said, opening the back door. "Leave Amoreena alone."

The pup shot across the floor and stumbled into the grass. Bouncing to his feet, he zeroed in on the bird feeder.

Amoreena and Millie watched a flock of doves scatter.

"I can hear the birds now," Amoreena said. "There goes the neighborhood."

Millie tossed a Frisbee, sending it careening off a tree trunk. Byte gave the yellow disk a dismissive look, then returned to prowling the bird feeder.

"Some scumbag left a cardboard box full of puppies in a Dumpster in Costa Mesa," Millie explained. "The pound began releasing the dogs last week. He didn't cost much."

Amoreena watched the pup scamper and relieve himself on the Frisbee. "He doesn't seem *too* traumatized by the ordeal."

"Byte," Millie groaned.

"Don't worry, the Frisbee's Daryl's."

Amoreena helped Millie rig a shallow box for the dog to sleep in. Amoreena donated a ragged beach towel and a stuffed rabbit given to her by an old boyfriend. With the cooler nighttime temperatures, both girls decided to make Byte's temporary living area a corner next to the brick fireplace hearth. Millie pulled the rug back in case of any accidents. She promised to have the dog housebroken within a week. Amoreena had her doubts.

After dinner, Millie took a break from her studies to try the Frisbee game once more. This time Byte seemed to catch on, though he couldn't quite carry the plastic disk without dragging it across the grass.

Amoreena watched the dog's playful antics from the kitchen window. If nothing else, tending to the puppy had taken her mind off things she preferred not to dwell on. She wondered how the clinic newborn was doing, but her ruminations stopped there. It was out of her hands.

For the second time, she tried calling her mother. After the sixth ring she hung up. The hospital shuttle should have dropped her mom at home over an hour ago.

She informed Millie where she was going, then grabbed her MCAT review manual. She could study while her mother watched TV.

On the way to Geneva's place, she stopped at a pet shop and bought a rawhide bone. She figured the tough rawhide would be more appropriate for puppy teeth than the stuffed rabbit.

Any hopes of spending a quiet evening with her mom were dashed when Amoreena pulled into the Terrace Apartments. The revolving glare of the red-and-blue vehicle lights reflected ominously off the street's pavement. Her heart sank.

The ambulance was parked in front of her mother's unit.

Chapter Nineteen

"Mom!"

Amoreena flew through the open doorway, nearly colliding with a paramedic studying the portable heart monitor.

The senior EMT next to him reached out a burly arm. "Who are you?"

"I'm her daughter," Amoreena said, shrugging off the hand. "Mom!"

"I'm over here, Amy." The voice was weak, barely audible.

The stretcher took up the central portion of the living room. A coffee table had been shoved to one side to give the emergency team space to work. A code 99 equipment case lay open on the floor.

Amoreena stooped under an intravenous line and knelt at the head of the stretcher. Behind her, she could hear one of the EMTs conversing on a portable radio. "Sinus tachycardia, BP stable . . . ETA ten minutes."

A third paramedic finished applying strips of tape to the large temporary dressing covering the right side of Geneva's scalp.

"Mom, what happened?" Amoreena asked, taking notice of the coagulated blood spotting her mother's face and neck and staining the entire front of a blue blouse. She was close enough to smell its pungent odor.

Geneva reached out for her daughter. "I fell." Her tone lacked its customary feistiness, and it troubled Amoreena the way her mother's eyes remained unfocused on the ceiling.

After several attempts she found Amoreena's hand.

"Baby, the flashing lights."

"Mom?"

The senior EMT touched Amoreena's shoulder. "Your mother's sustained a scalp laceration which will need suturing. Her vital signs are stable, and there are no other obvious injuries. Does Ms. Daniels have any allergies to medications?"

"No."

"Any medical problems?"

Amoreena nodded weakly. "She's being treated for cervical cancer."

Her voice trailed off, though, as she scrutinized her mother's obtunded upward stare. She didn't hear the medic's next question because of the rushing noise of panic slowly rising between her own ears.

Passing one hand in front of the pair of unblinking eyes, Amoreena suddenly felt light-headed.

Her mother was blind.

By nine that evening, Geneva Daniels's MRI was read as abnormal.

Amoreena waited in the radiology suite while Dr. Gillespie finished arranging her mother's transfer to the inpatient oncology ward. The laceration had taken twelve sutures to close and, consistent with the senior EMT's initial assessment, no other acute injuries were discovered. Except her mother could no longer see.

The earlier panic had been replaced by anger. *Why, for god-sakes? Why now?* Amoreena wanted to scream so loud the entire utilization review committee would hear her. If Rosalind Cates had stuck her head in the room, she was sure she would have punched her.

Instead, she stood like a zombie staring holes through the flat images of the inside of her mother's head. From the hall, she heard the oncologist issue an order, then he was beside her.

"How bad is it?" Amoreena spoke in a monotone.

Dr. Gillespie repositioned one film. "Your mother has several metastatic lesions in the brain. Two in particular"—he pointed—"here and here, are the most likely causes for your mother's symptoms."

Studying the two dark irregular spots, Amoreena was keenly aware he hadn't said blindness.

The oncologist went on, "These lesions are located in the occipital region where the visual cortex is found." He moved his finger to a larger, less-defined spot. "This lesion is most likely contributing to Geneva's elevated intracranial pressure."

"Is that what caused her to fall?"

"That and her visual impairment."

Amoreena felt like taking a scalpel and cutting the ugly spots out of the films herself.

Fuck the little metastatic bastards.

"Is this permanent?" she asked.

Dr. Gillespie thought for a moment. "I don't know. The plan is to start some steroids and bring down her increased intracranial pressure. This should improve your mother's lucidity, but whether the sight returns, well, we'll just have to wait."

And see.

"We'll make every effort to ensure your mother's comfort," the oncologist said. He hit two switches, and the viewing windows went dark. "I'm really very sorry about this."

When he turned to leave, Amoreena saw the defeat in his expression but also something else. He paused, gazing appraisingly at her.

Interpreting this new look correctly, she didn't bother concealing herself with her coat. "Is it that obvious?"

Dr. Gillespie closed the door. "Amoreena, I practiced obstetrics for ten years prior to concentrating on gynecology. You're four, five months?"

"Not quite three."

This raised an eyebrow. "Guess I've been out longer than I thought. I trust you're receiving good prenatal care."

She averted his eyes. "Are you going to tell my mom?"

Dr. Gillespie smiled wanly. "I'm only Geneva's oncologist,

you're her daughter." He opened the door. "Your mother's waiting for you upstairs."

Geneva Daniels rested with her head semielevated. The intravenous line the paramedics had inserted had been replaced with an IVAC monitor, making it much easier to rapidly and accurately adjust the fluid-administration rate. A cardiac monitor tracked her heart rhythm. Her eyes were open, her face directed at the far wall.

Amoreena entered and dimmed the lights. She didn't know why.

"Mom, it's me, Amy."

"I can hear you." Only her lips moved.

Amoreena stood by the railing, desperately searching for a phrase that would lift her mother's spirits from the black pits of despair and hopelessness, but any words she could think of fell miles short of adequate.

Geneva raised one hand, and Amoreena lunged at it, curling her head and neck tightly around it as if she could return her mother's sight by pure osmosis. For a full fifteen minutes, the tears rolled down Amoreena's cheeks, the dam of frustration, anger, and fear bursting through the tough shell she'd erected over the past two months.

"Amy, baby, don't." Geneva moved and pulled her daughter down to her.

"I'm so scared, Mom."

"That makes two of us."

"Don't let go. I need you holding me." Amoreena wept.

"I've got you, baby. I always will."

"What are we going to do about these bugs in my head?" Geneva asked the next day when Amoreena stopped by after her last class.

Amoreena couldn't believe the change. Dr. Gillespie had warned her the intravenous dexamethasone possessed temporary mood-uplifting effects, but she was in no way prepared to hear her mother cracking one-liners.

She walked over and kissed Geneva on the cheek.

"You're obviously feeling better."

"The headaches are gone except for around the stitches. I think I like this stuff. What did the nurse call it?"

"Dexamethasone. It's a steroid."

"Will it give me big muscles?"

"It's not that type of steroid." The entire time she conversed, Amoreena studied her mother's eyes. They tracked symmetrically but seemed unfocused. She began to pass a palm in front of her mother's face, but Geneva's hand shot out and after two jerky attempts caught Amoreena firmly by the wrist.

"Please don't do that," Geneva said.

"I'm sorry. How did—"

"The orderlies do it, the nurses do it, Dr. Gillespie did it not a half hour ago." Geneva pulled her daughter's hand close and kissed the back of her fingers before releasing her grip. "I guess I'm just tired of it. At least tell me when you're going to test me."

"I will." Along with the drop in Geneva's intracranial pressure, Amoreena could see her mother's mental faculties had returned to normal. "Any changes?" she asked.

"I presume you're alluding to my vision." Geneva shook her head. "No."

"Dr. Gillespie said your condition might be temporary."

"Are you referring to the bugs in my head or being blind?"

"You know what I mean," Amoreena said, blaming her mother's sudden mood shift on the medicines. She saw Geneva's eyes directed at her and resisted the urge to test her sight again.

"Tell me how you're doing," Geneva said.

"I'm fine."

"That's all?"

Amoreena heard more in the simple inquiry than was there. If her mother knew, though, she gave no other indication. She was back *looking* at the opposite wall. Sooner or later, Amoreena realized, she would have to tell her. But not during the current crisis. Procrastination was a tool that Amoreena never felt comfortable using. But today, it was just what the doctor ordered.

As was lying. So Amoreena lied. "I'm ready for my MCAT next week. And finals should be a breeze. Genetics and embryology are going to be the tough ones, but I'm prepared."

"You'll do fine."

"I know. Oh, and the hypertension study is going well; I think Dr. Pike likes me." That was only a little lie. Actually the UCLA admission chairman had barely said three words to her since the first session. She hadn't asked why for fear of being branded a brown-noser.

"And Millie?"

"She's cool. We have a pet dog now."

"Really? What's her name?"

"Byte's a he. The name was Millie's idea. It comes from a computer term."

"I'd love to see him."

Amoreena winced but kept talking. "He's real cute, part Lab I think, and smart. The little bugger's already housebroken." Another little lie.

"Where does he sleep?"

"Inside."

"You're going to spoil him."

"It's okay. He's good company."

Amoreena was going to describe how Byte had chased the doves away from the feeder, but Geneva had drifted off to sleep. Checking first the heart monitor—the rhythm was regular, as was her mother's relaxed breathing—she sat in a chair and removed the MCAT manual from her pack and tried to study.

It was impossible. On every page she saw ugly metastic lesions poking little holes in her mother's brain. It wasn't fair. There were murderers on death row who could live to be a hundred, and not three feet away lay a woman who'd never harmed anyone in her life, being eaten alive by tumor cells resistant to drugs strong enough to kill a horse.

Fuck cancer. Amoreena filed a silent complaint with God and closed her book. There was too much to think about to cram. Yesterday, Dr. Gillespie had hinted he might withdraw Geneva from the research study. And there was also the question of living arrangements. Amoreena refused to even entertain the possibility the blindness might be permanent. Where would her mother stay? At the apartment? She'd require a part-time home-health nurse. How expensive were their services? Or a hospice. But didn't people go to hospices to die?

"God, God, God," she mumbled, feeling like she was drowning under the waterfall of decisions cascading over her. She just wanted to make it to Christmas, get the MCAT and final exams behind her, collect the second surrogacy installment, and somehow hope for a miracle.

Miracles can happen, she told herself, unconvincingly. Though the tightness of her pants was tangible evidence of the tiny miracle growing within her, she viewed the fullness as less a miracle and more a reminder that she'd need to consider embarking on some serious maternity shopping shortly.

Geneva slept through dinner. Not wishing to disturb her, Amoreena kissed her mom softly on the cheek and told the nurse she'd check in later.

As soon as she pulled into the carport, she heard Byte's barking from the backyard. Though more like yelping, the pup's vocal exuberance was a welcome sound nonetheless. Millie was studying late in the campus computer lab, and Amoreena didn't feel like being alone.

After refreshing the dog's water and food bowls, she sat outside on the back porch under an afghan she pulled off her bed. Across her feet, Byte lay curled in a compact ball, his nose pressed firmly against her ankle.

The puppy's dependence upon her for shelter and sustenance elicited within her a sense of inner strength that she would have never known existed if sitting alone. With one hand she scratched the soft fur just behind the ears. Byte responded with a stretch, and a single slurp of his small tongue before settling back to his state of temporary hibernation. Today's challenges behind him, tomorrow he'd confront a whole new set of animal challenges.

Amoreena hoped they would not prove as insurmountable as hers presently appeared to be. She thought of her mother, blind and dying, confined to a bed and sheets as impersonal as a highway motel room. The picture hurt so much, she recoiled in anguish.

With the weight of the gloom pressing around her, she gently cradled the sleeping puppy in her arms and settled him on his blanket by the fireplace. Then she went into her bedroom, quietly shut the door, and cried.

Chapter Twenty

Humberto Mungia squirmed forward in pitch-blackness, moving on his belly like the sand crabs he'd once seen near Puerto Cortes in the Gulf of Honduras. The dark, so heavy and complete it came at him from all directions, didn't bother the boy; nor did the acrid, stale odor of rat feces and bat dung, nor even the occasional rusted nail that protruded through the metal ventilation chute, tearing at his clothes from above and catching the leather strap of Polita's 35mm camera wound around his chest and shoulder.

What did bother him were the spiderwebs. Spun every few feet, the delicate strands always managed to find his open, unprotected skin, his face, mouth, hands, especially his eyelids. It was like each thread were alive and before he could swipe the air in front of him, it'd dart in and entangle him. Fortunately, so far, he'd received no bites. The spiders in the rain forest were larger, hairier, more ornery, and possessed longer fangs than the little brown ones he used to squash on the walls of the orphanage in Guatemala City.

Tonight was his fourth attempt at traversing the ventilation duct above the Las Canas Nursery. And his last. Of course, after his third failed effort, he'd told Gabriella the same thing. No more. It can't be done. Then she'd given him one of those please-just-for-me looks with her big brown eyes and a hug that sent electricity through his limbs, and here he was. So what if he was just a young *hombré*, a *chiquito*; he possessed the same feelings as a man, just on an eleven-year-old scale.

With his arms flexed under his chest praying mantis style, Humberto flexed his ankles and used his toes to propel himself forward another few inches. The crabs would've laughed at his snail pace. Small for his age group, his diminutive stature afforded him this *luxury* of crawling through a metal chute at two in the morning. The constant threat of being caught like a fat rabbit in a burrow by Vincinio kept his adrenaline circulating on overdrive. The *hombre's* forearms were thicker and stronger than the boy's thighs.

Humberto advanced another few inches, concentrating less on the fetid aroma of rat dung and more on the spot just over his right eye where Gabriella had planted her good-luck kiss. His forehead still felt hot and tingly where her lips had pressed against his skin only an hour earlier. One day, he vowed, the young *vaca* would be his and when that special time arrived, she'd no longer look upon him as a boy. He would be a man, and he would treat her as a woman. Just imagining the possibility sent a searing sensation from his head into his loins. If he wasn't careful, he might find himself wedged in tight, a prisoner of his own lust.

A short squeak in the dark and the scurry of tiny claws jolted Humberto back to reality. Reflexively he moved one hand to shield his face. An alarmed rat in confined quarters could wreak havoc on an exposed nose. Especially if hungry. Humberto had once seen a starving rat gnaw the eye from a python a hundred times the rodent's size.

Though nervous, he dared not use the flashlight for fear of being detected. One guard, casually looking up and noticing a metallic reflection from a vent, would send the boy to the Casa de Dolor, House of Pain. As far as Humberto knew, he'd heard of no *visitors* leaving Vincinio's abode under their own power. And many never left at all.

In ten minutes, he'd scooted another thirty feet. A vent lay ahead. From past attempts, he knew this particular vent would not yield visual access to the nursery. But he was close.

Below him resided the guards' quarters for the nursery security personnel. He'd discovered the room by accident during his first unsuccessful venture into the building ventilation system. His mistake, and partly Gabriella's, too, though he would never overtly toss blame in the *señorita's* direction, had been to embark too early. No one told him the *cabrónes* played cards till one in the morning.

Over a month had passed since he'd crept by the vent and looked down on the heads of two guards seated at a makeshift table not six feet away. Passing a bottle of hundred and eighty-proof *guaro* between them, neither had suspected Humberto's presence. But it would've been pure folly to slither past the vent and risk being heard. So he'd backed away.

The other two aborted attempts resulted from scheduled maintenance repairs being made to the nursery's vast air-purification system. Too much illumination and too many bodies poking in and out of the chute's corridors. Even Gabriella had agreed any venture would be too risky.

But tonight all he heard was light snoring from the dark room below. And though Polita had warned him of the night-vision video monitor mounted above the room's door, Humberto wasn't concerned. Its lens was directed away from the ceiling. Thirty seconds was all the time it took to put the vent behind him.

With renewed vigor, he inched ahead oblivious to the rat dung. He made an effort to ignore the spiderwebs. As long as the hairy creatures kept out of his face he'd be okay.

Ahead, he saw where the pitch-black had softened to a deep ocean blue. His heart rate accelerated. That gentle curve in the metal corridor was his final destination. The blue luminescence came from the ceiling lights of the nursery. They were never shut off. Special generators were designed to maintain the glow's integrity even during a power outage. Rumors described the lights as having a calming effect on the babies.

Humberto adjusted the camera strap pressing into his neck and pushed forward.

The vent overlooking the nursery was larger than the others, measuring three feet in length, and was covered with a fine mesh filter, in addition to the vertical metal slats. Because the crawl space offered more room there, Humberto found maneuvering somewhat easier. Twisting onto his side, he was able to pull the camera strap over his head and sidle up to the opening.

The newborn nursery stretched out below him under a veil of blue light. The eight-foot fluorescent bulbs, spaced several feet apart across the entire ceiling, made a monotonous buzzing sound, reminding Humberto of a dozing beehive. He quickly counted three nurses, each dressed in green surgical scrubs, moving between the rows of bassinets. Two were administering formula, while one sat before a console of computer monitors at the far end of the nursery. He didn't see any guards, though he was sure they were close at hand.

He also detected an odd smell, which he first attributed to the filter, but after using one finger to determine the mesh's surface was clean, he realized the almost musky scent was rising from the nursery below. The smell wasn't unpleasant, just *odd*. He'd never have associated the odor with a roomful of newborns.

He counted at least fifty white bassinets, separated into three uneven rows. Most appeared occupied, and each was supplied with a pair of flexible plastic tubes leading from canisters mounted on the bassinets' metal frames. The thin tubing snaked out of view under blankets draped over the tiny occupants.

Humberto's vantage didn't allow him to gaze directly into a single bassinet, though in several, he could make out portions of tiny limbs and isolated patches of flesh. What he saw bothered him, yet he blamed the apparent distortion of hands and legs on the filter and the blue illumination. He felt like he was looking into a giant aquarium. He hoped the specialized lighting didn't affect the photographs.

Quickly, he positioned the camera. Polita had been specific. Get photos of the babies. In rapid succession, he took three pictures. The camera contained film for twenty-four takes. He snapped three more.

Humberto paused while a nurse adjusted a blanket. He snapped another one. A high-pitched squeal shifted his attention to a different bassinet. Two more photos. More movement along the opposite row, limbs flailing. Another photo.

Reflexively, he cringed back from the vent opening when

he spied a guard entering the nursery. Directly behind the security officer, a man wearing a lab coat pushed a metal cart stocked full of sliced fruit. Humberto centered both in the viewfinder and snapped their picture. He included the cart.

He watched them approach a double door located near the rear of the nursery. The scientist's fingers moved nimbly over a keypad on the wall and the hydraulic doors swung inward, revealing a second room.

Through the camera's lens, Humberto could see structures resembling crude beds. There was a jerky movement and a blurred form suddenly filled the viewfinder. Humberto gasped. After snapping the picture, he pulled his eye away hoping for a better look at the half-adult-sized figure standing upright in the doorway. But the doors had already swung shut.

Gabriella huddled in the darkness against the velvety bark of the *la ceiba* tree. Its crooked trunk extended high above her head, passing within inches of the sidewall of the nursery.

The guard-tower lights swung her way, and she quickly skirted around the trunk like a squirrel, keeping to the shadows. Each minute Humberto was late increased their chances of being caught. Gabriella silently cursed. How long did it take to snap a few pictures? Humberto should've returned fifteen minutes ago. Where was the little shit?

She watched the infrared beams race across the ground away from her position and allowed herself to relax some. There'd be a full ten minutes of absolute darkness before their return.

Looking toward the jungle, she could just make out the irregular line where the tree canopy met the blackness of the sky. The forest was unusually quiet tonight. She slapped at a fly buzzing near her ear.

A sharp noise above her head startled her. She looked up in time to see the dark outline of two legs kicking out from the wall.

"Wait," she whispered in her native tongue and quickly scampered up the trunk to assist the boy's egress from the vent.

"Gabriella."

"Quit kicking." She guided Humberto's feet to the nearest bough. Sliding one arm around his waist, she pulled him out.

"Gabriella," he tried again.

"Shsh."

Together, they climbed to the ground.

Wedged against the building, Gabriella dusted the dirt, grime, and matted spiderwebs from the boy's face and hair.

"Were you successful?" she asked.

Humberto nodded, his eyes flashing with pride. "There's another room. I saw—"

"No time." Gabriella took the camera and began to pull away. "We must hurry."

Then almost as an afterthought, she stopped, turned, and kissed him on the cheek, before the pair vanished into the night.

Chapter Twenty-one

Goetz Auditorium on the University of California Irvine campus vibrated with the buzz of premed majors jostling for their assigned seats. Talking was minimal, as most of the students were too nervous to converse, in anticipation of the grueling six-hour Medical School Admission Test.

The front stage was starkly set with a single long table and four chairs for the test proctor and his three assistants. A large time clock was mounted on a separate stand, positioned to be easily visualized from every seat in the lecture hall. Seating capacity was 150. Every chair would be occupied.

Amoreena double-checked her printed name and the corresponding seat assignment on her identification badge—Row 15, Seat 42. Neither number sounded particularly lucky. She didn't envy the student in Row 13, Seat 13.

Squeezing by two other examinees, she found her designated seat and sat down. Her stomach churned from nervous energy. She no longer noticed the constant queasiness in her midsection that had dogged her the preceding four weeks. Steadfastly refusing to entertain any thoughts of becoming ill, she rubbed her belly and silently mouthed, "I will not get sick." Her entire future lay on the line today.

Momentarily, her concentration was broken by the image of her mother, attempting to butter a bran muffin earlier that morning. Amoreena had stopped by the hospital prior to her drive to campus and entered the room just as the medical assistant had been administering breakfast. Geneva's effort at feeding herself had looked pathetic and had given Amoreena another excuse to curse the fickle finger of fate that had singled out her mom for such suffering. Reliving the experience now put things in perspective. The MCAT lasted but one Saturday, cancer was for a lifetime. She vowed to get back to arranging Geneva's home-health care after the exam.

For the second time, she rearranged the eraser and three number two pencils on her desk. A fourth pencil remained in her purse. She felt ready and wanted to get on with the test.

More nervous murmurs filled the auditorium. The participants filing in reminded Amoreena of sheep herded toward a shearing. She wondered what percentage of the students were taking the exam for the second and third time.

"Hello, Amoreena."

Gladys Peterson squeezed into the empty seat next to Amoreena's.

Amoreena smiled. "Hi." She noted one of Gladys's eyelids jumping incessantly and wanted to reach out a finger under the girl's thick glasses to stop it.

She watched Gladys blink several times in succession while she removed a plastic pencil holder and five pencils from her satchel. When she saw how Gladys's fingers trembled while trying to insert the pencils into their proper notches, she actually felt sorry for her. The girl was *hyping out*.

"I'll be soooo relieved when this shit is over," Gladys whispered.

"Me too," Amoreena agreed, looking toward the stage.

The proctor and his assistants had gathered around the podium and were in the midst of a discussion. Separate piles of exams sat on the table.

Amoreena felt a sharp tap on her shoulder. She turned to find Gladys staring panicky-eyed at her.

"I forgot."

"What?" Amoreena said. She could see Gladys's tic had become more intense.

"The stages of meiosis."

Amoreena touched Gladys's wrist. The skin was moist with perspiration. "Relax. There's ten." She slowly clicked them off so Gladys could remember.

For a full minute, Amoreena could hear her classmate repeating the stages of cell division under her breath. Out of the corner of one eye she watched her fellow premed major fumble in her purse and remove a tiny white pill.

Gladys popped the tablet in her mouth and swallowed. "If I bomb this test, I'm dead."

In a gesture that seemed entirely natural, Amoreena reached over and patted Gladys's hand. "You're going to do fine."

"What if I freeze?"

"You're one of the smartest girls in the premed program. You're not going to freeze."

Gladys fidgeted with her pencil holder. "Did you sleep last night?"

"Four hours."

"I was up all night."

Amoreena tried to grin. "Relax, girl."

A silence fell over the auditorium as the proctor tapped three times on the microphone mounted on the podium, signaling his assistants to begin their march to the aisles with bundles of exams cradled in their arms.

Amoreena could hear Gladys inhaling and exhaling as if she were midway through a sprint.

"You're hyperventilating," she whispered.

Gladys's stertorous breathing persisted.

Amoreena gently nudged her, keenly aware of the stares from neighboring students.

"Your friend okay?" a man asked from the seat directly behind them.

The situation was rapidly becoming embarrassing. "Yes," Amoreena answered curtly. She nudged Gladys again, this time more sharply. "Can you hear me?"

Gladys nodded in rapid succession, her eyes glued on the stationary hands of the large time clock.

"I can't—," her voice choked momentarily, "stop."

"Jesus," Amoreena mumbled under her breath. The assistant assigned to their section was stopped six rows away. If the test administrator got wind of the problem, she felt sure he'd yank Gladys from the exam.

A mealy-mouthed girl on the opposite side of Gladys began to rise. "I'm notifying the proctor."

"Sit down," Amoreena ordered. "She's just a little nervous."

The girl reluctantly sat. "She's got one minute to calm down, or I'm requesting a seat change."

"Deal." With no paper sack handy, Amoreena grabbed the next best thing. She held her jacket in front of Gladys's face. "Breathe into this. Hurry."

She felt Gladys resist. "Do it," she said, positioning her classmate's hand around the jacket. "Now breathe slowly."

Within seconds, the physiologic effects of rising carbon dioxide levels became apparent. Gladys's respiratory pattern slowed, and the white outline of tensed tendons in her hands vanished.

A sigh of relief escaped Amoreena's lips. Gladys Peterson would survive to take the MCAT.

After another fifteen seconds, Gladys returned the jacket. "I thought I was having a heart attack," she said.

Amoreena deadpanned, "For a moment, so did I."

Both girls grinned nervously until they saw the exam booklets coming their way.

"Here goes," Amoreena whispered.

"I'm fine now," Gladys said. She touched Amoreena's hand. "Thanks."

"Good luck," Amoreena wished.

Reacting the way she did had briefly taken the edge off her own nerves, but now that the situation was under control, Amoreena experienced a new bout of queasiness. She closed her eyes until it passed.

When she opened them, the proctor was beginning the opening instructions. A text pamphlet lay on her desk.

From the podium, she heard the administrator say, "You'll have fifty-five minutes to complete this section."

A cacophony of tearing paper erupted in the auditorium as over a hundred booklet tabs were ripped open.

Amoreena inhaled deeply. Turning to the first page, she attacked the first set of questions.

Initially, the multiple choice questions were academic and straightforward, but the farther into the exam she plowed, the more vague and difficult they became. Amoreena found herself using more time than she wanted on some questions and forced her pace up a notch. The intermittent groans around her was all she needed to remind her today was the real deal. There could be no screwups.

Midway through the science section, one of Gladys's pencils rolled off her desk and struck Amoreena's left foot.

Amoreena bent over to retrieve it. Upon straightening, a sharp twinge zapped her abdomen. Silently she gasped.

The same twinge occurred a second and third time. Ignoring the running exam clock, Amoreena put down her pencil and palpated her midsection. She'd experienced aches and discomfort before, but these were different. She waited for the wave of nausea, but it never materialized.

Perspiration broke out on her forehead. It was far too early for . . .

The sensation repeated itself, and this time the tips of Amoreena's fingers felt a movement, releasing a sack of butterflies in her stomach. Then a second movement, more forceful.

My baby. The realization shattered her concentration into a million fragments.

Before she could stop, the words slipped out of her mouth. "I felt my baby move."

Gladys met her gaze with a quizzical stare, and returned to the examination, but not before taking in Amoreena's loose blouse.

The baby gave a jerky kick that made Amoreena want to grin. The life inside her was actually moving.

Any attempt at returning to the exam, though, was thwarted by additional fetal activity. Amoreena's elation quickly gave way to discomfort. She could no longer concentrate.

Fear, approaching panic, set in only after she realized she'd forgotten the ten phases of meiosis.

* * *

"Time." The proctor motioned his assistants to begin the final collection.

Amoreena quickly scribbled marks in the last remaining dots and put down her pencil. The auditorium echoed with soft murmurs and sighs of relief. Once the exam booklets were assembled in neat separate piles on the stage, the students were dismissed.

Amoreena mumbled a weak good-bye to Gladys, who returned her farewell with an odd stare and walked for the exit.

Mentally and physically, Amoreena felt totally numb, except for the intermittent jerky activity in her abdomen. Only during the physics section had the baby's movements moderated. But by then, four hours into the test, the damage had been inflicted. There was little doubt in Amoreena's mind—she'd bombed the MCAT.

The baby gave a particularly rambunctious kick, causing Amoreena to grimace.

"Damn you," she cursed, and immediately experienced a stab of guilt. It wasn't the baby's fault she'd just blown the most important examination of her entire life. Just like it wasn't her fault that her own mother was dying of cancer. Shit happened. At times, it just seemed she'd been granted inordinately more than her fair share.

Amoreena gently supported her belly with one hand, whispering a contrite sorry to the fetus inside.

An updated version of "Little Drummer Boy" drifted across the parking lot from someone's car stereo. The thought of Christmas a little over a week away brought Amoreena little merriment, though the second installment on her surrogacy contract, due sometime next week, would at least provide her with some extra cash for gifts. She and Millie hadn't even put up any house lights this year.

Unlocking Silver, Amoreena squeezed in and adjusted the seat as far back as it would go. The baby sensed the positional change and rocketed with a new burst of energy. Amoreena pressed both palms firmly against her skin, trying to visualize what the baby looked like, flailing about in its private pool of amniotic fluid. The bulge under her blouse was definitely going to be a challenge to hide. She recalled Gladys's puzzled expression during the test and winced. Maybe Gladys hadn't understood her, Amoreena hoped without much hope.

"Shit." She shook her head and let Silver idle, ignoring the smell of burning oil, while she dug in her purse for her cell phone.

A nurse on the oncology ward reported her mother's condition as unchanged.

Next she dialed the Women's Clinic. Though the fetal activity caused no undue discomfort, its prematurity bothered her. What if the baby wasn't getting enough oxygen? For a moment, Amoreena shoved aside her pessimism regarding the MCAT debacle.

Once the on-call operator answered, she asked to speak with Dr. Rafael.

"He's unavailable," the strongly accented voice returned.

"Can you page him?"

"Please hold." A moment later the operator inquired, "Are you a patient?"

"Yes." Amoreena began to identify herself but held back.

"If this is an emergency—"

"It's not an emergency. I just wanted to talk to him about my pregnancy."

"Please hold."

After a further delay of half a minute, a second voice came on. "This is Irene Leggett, the clinic administrator. How may I assist you?"

Amoreena silently groaned and pressed END. There was only so much shit she could take in one afternoon.

Though she'd wished to discuss the fetal movement with someone, Louis Rafael was the only individual at the clinic she felt comfortable with. Certainly not Irene or Dr. Becker.

Perhaps Dr. Gillespie. He'd been an obstetrician prior to his oncology practice. Just before entering the medical center's number, though, another name flashed in her mind, along with the ex-intern's warning. *Call if the baby moves before three months.*

Ronald Godinez.

Suddenly each fetal kick reminded Amoreena of Godinez's

dead fiancée, adding to her unease. What was so significant about twelve weeks? Godinez would know.

Scrambling in her purse, she found the number. She waited impatiently while his phone rang.

"Come on, pick up," she willed, but after the tenth ring she was forced to disconnect.

She checked the time. It was almost 4 P.M. If she hurried, she could make it to the UCLA Medical Center before five. She recalled Godinez had been attending a drug rehab class on Saturday afternoons. The session's exact location wouldn't be too difficult to determine once she arrived.

Traffic on the 405 was heavy for a weekend, and the drive took longer than anticipated. With some effort, Amoreena succeeded in not dwelling on the MCAT—until she glimpsed the sprawling medical center's grounds. The dying sun cast an orange hue off the main hospital's alabaster walls, and the symbolism of an evaporating sunset prompted Amoreena to consider how her chances of medical school would evaporate if her exam effort today was truly as weak as she feared.

If only she'd been better prepared to handle the baby's first activity. She realized now being a surrogate could never totally nullify all emotions between a biological mother and her unborn. Part of her was growing inside her and a poor MCAT score was not going to change that. She'd just have to accept whatever results returned—good or poor—and better strive to successfully mesh her pregnancy and her studies.

This afternoon she'd begin by finding Ronald Godinez.

She parked Silver in the same lot she used when participating in the hypertension study and approached a security shack. The guard directed her toward a nondescript, two-story, gray-brick building adjacent to the outpatient medical clinics.

The county mental-health facility provided mental-health evaluations for many of the city's indigents. It also housed the medical center's only methadone clinic. Amoreena entered through the smoked-glass doors and searched the empty lobby. She saw no one behind the reception desk and except for the monotonous din from a hallway buffer machine, she would have thought the premises vacated.

She passed a single elevator adorned with an artificial

wreath and looked down the first-floor corridor. The heavy scent of polishing wax buried any further reminders of holiday festivities. A man facing away from her worked diligently at the opposite end of the hall, swinging a cumbersome-looking machine in wide pendulous arcs across the gray linoleum. She also counted four doors, but each was closed. Straining to hear any voices, Amoreena debated going upstairs.

Any indecisiveness was abruptly truncated by the sound of a door opening behind her.

Amoreena turned to see a woman exiting the ladies' rest room. Both noted each other's presence at precisely the same moment.

The woman's hair was cut severely short around her ears and neck, accentuating her masculine appearance, and her piercing gaze gave Amoreena a cold clammy feeling. A satchel hung on one shoulder, and she used a cane when she took a step.

"The clinic's closed for the weekend," she said, moving tangentially to the exit.

Amoreena took a parallel path, slightly behind her. "I was looking for Ronald Godinez," she said, speaking loud enough to be heard over the buffer machine.

"Do you wish to join our group," she asked, "or are you simply a friend?"

"A friend."

The woman paused, resting her weight on the cane. "Over the last month, Dr. Godinez has developed quite a cadre of fans. You're the third request this week."

"Have you seen him?"

"No. And even if I had, I wouldn't be at liberty to say. I'm Jil Bastion. I'm one of the therapists for the county's outreach program, and unless Dr. Godinez has broken a law and you're an undercover cop, I'm afraid I won't be able to assist you." She turned back for the doors.

Amoreena started after her. "I'm not a cop. I just wanted to talk with him."

The therapist pushed against one door with her satchel.

"Ms. Bastion," Amoreena persisted.

"Doctor," the woman corrected her.

"Dr. Bastion. If you do see him, can you at least tell him Amoreena Daniels came by?"

The woman stepped back inside, letting the door swing shut. "Can I see some ID?"

"What?"

"A driver's license will suffice."

"Sure, why not?" With nothing to lose, Amoreena dug in her purse. Not wishing to antagonize the therapist further, she resisted making a reciprocal request. "Here," she said, holding out her photo.

Dr. Bastion scanned the likeness. When she finished, her expression had softened considerably. "We'll talk outside."

The cooler evening temperature forced Amoreena to pull her sweater tight around her. Standing on the clinic steps, she watched Dr. Bastion remove a business card from her satchel.

"Several weeks ago," the therapist began, "Ronald warned me some people might come inquiring about his whereabouts and that he wished to remain anonymous. I told him I would honor his request as long as drugs were not involved. He assured me they weren't." She paused to scribble something on the back of the card. "He described the only exception as an attractive auburn female. He said she would be pregnant and appear ill at ease. In my opinion, a fairly accurate description."

She handed the card to Amoreena. "That's his address. It's not far from the medical center, only three or four blocks."

"How is Ronald?" Amoreena asked, reading the unfamiliar street name.

"He's missed the last two sessions. When you see him, tell him the group wishes him happy holidays."

"I will, Dr. Bastion, and thank you."

With directions from the parking guard, Amoreena found the Four Oaks complex with little difficulty. Looking starkly out of season, Godinez's barren unit faced the courtyard sandwiched between two brightly festive apartments. Amoreena could see lights on inside through the tightly drawn curtains.

She knocked and waited. The kicking in her abdomen only added to her anxiety.

She was about to knock again when the door opened partway, revealing a middle-aged woman of Hispanic descent with small melancholy eyes and pursed lips. Amoreena experienced a sinking sensation when she thought the woman had been crying.

"Is Dr. Godinez in?" she asked.

The woman started to speak, shook her head, then stepped weakly out of view.

A moment later, the door swung open all the way.

"How can I help you?" an older man asked with a thick accent. Behind him, much of the living area appeared in disarray, with clothes and books piled on the floor and in chairs.

"Does Dr. Godinez live here?" Amoreena asked.

"He did."

"Do you know where I can find him?"

The man's face slowly twisted in shame. "Our son is deceased."

Chapter Twenty-two

Shock and disbelief clouded Amoreena's drive back to Orange County. Sadness, too, for after their last visit together, she'd actually come to like Ronald Godinez. And now he was dead of an accidental overdose.

Amoreena recounted the details she'd learned of the intern's untimely demise. According to the senior Godinez, who'd done most of the talking, Dr. Godinez had been found two days ago stretched out on the sofa unconscious. The television was still blaring when the landlord unlocked the intern's unit at the parents' request. They'd not heard from their son in over three weeks, and when he failed to return their calls they became concerned. The paramedics were unable to revive him, neither were the emergency room docs at UCLA Medical Center, and after a rigorous sixty-minute code blue, he was pronounced. The miscellaneous drug paraphernalia— needle, syringes, tourniquet, a combination of crack cocaine, crystal heroine, and one other drug the elder Godinez was unable to name, sealed the preliminary diagnosis for the coroner, though the final toxicology report would be weeks away.

While listening to their story, it had become clear to Amoreena that both parents blamed their son's ill-fated relationship with Gretchen Bayliss for his demise.

"How could he make such a mess of his life?" the elder

Godinez lamented when he escorted Amoreena to the door. By then it was dark outside.

"I'm sorry," she said, embracing them both.

Now cruising alone on the 405, she tried to recall when she'd last seen the intern. That Thanksgiving night at her house. And the impression he'd conveyed was of an individual slowly regaining control of his life. Ronald Godinez had been on a mission, and a person didn't jam a needle into his veins while in the middle of the race.

Amoreena shivered, and even the baby's kicking couldn't divert her line of hypothetical reasoning. Unless he'd uncovered additional information regarding his fiancée's death. Information so disturbing to him, Godinez had found it necessary to resort to a mind-altering escape. Or even worse—no, Amoreena would never consider he'd OD'ed on purpose. Accidental, a possibility, suicide, never. Ronald Godinez wasn't the type, though Amoreena had no idea what type did take their own lives.

Another possibility began to form as a hazy shadow in her mind, and as its image sharpened, Amoreena reflexively increased her grip on the steering wheel. What if Ronald Godinez hadn't jammed the needle into his own arm? What if someone else had applied the tourniquet and injected the drug into his veins? Someone who had some basic medical knowledge, maybe even worked for a medical clinic, someone who wanted Godinez to just go away. For good.

"Could I be that fucking blind?" she cursed in the dark.

Amoreena suddenly regretted not discussing Godinez's acrimonious relationship with the Meechum Clinic with his parents. In all likelihood, they'd probably known little anyway if she recalled correctly how Godinez had portrayed his family's uncompromising attitude toward surrogate motherhood. Yet asking couldn't have hurt either. The dialogue might even have assisted with any pending investigation.

"Goddammit, Ronald, what the hell happened?" Amoreena said, moaning.

She debated pulling off at the nearest exit and returning to Godinez's apartment, but the muffled signal from her purse sent a lacerating stab of alarm up her neck. Her pager made her immediately think of the hospital oncology ward.

While throwing a cursory look in the rearview, a vehicle with one headlight was trailing a little too close, she groped for the pager in the dark. The green luminosity of the digits gave her an instant sense of relief. It was only Millie. Her roommate could wait.

Setting the pager aside, she flipped on her right blinker and made the east transition to the Garden Grove Freeway. Directly behind her, a semi blared. Already approaching the upper limits of Silver's comfort zone, sixty-five, she swerved to the far right lane, allowing the diesel to rumble past. In the mirror, she saw the one-headlight vehicle, its silhouette depicting a van, make a similar move, though now it remained several cars back.

She stared ahead, cognizant of a vague sinking sensation developing in the middle of her gut, totally independent of the baby. In fact, since leaving Godinez's apartment, she hadn't felt any fetal movements, and she wondered if the smooth vibrations of the wheels on the pavement had produced the calming effect. Almost simultaneously she began to worry if something was wrong.

"You okay, kiddo?" she said, taking one hand off the wheel and patting her abdomen.

When the absence of activity persisted, Amoreena mumbled "God, how did Mom do it? You get concerned if they move too much and apprehensive when the kicking stops. And I have six more months of this." She sighed.

Amoreena reached for the radio but decided the silence was better. A second page from her roommate made using the cellular phone more tempting; however, in fifteen minutes she'd be at the medical center. She'd call Millie from the oncology ward before checking on her mother.

Passing the familiar freeway exit signs relieved some of the tension she felt, until she noticed that the minus-one-headlight van remained behind her, three cars back. She thought it was white. Still not overly concerned, she moved to the middle lane, keeping one eye in the rearview.

The van continued in the slow lane.

Nearing the 22 split, she waited until the last minute, then, shifting to the far left lane, she grabbed the Newport Beach Freeway transition north. Behind her, she heard the gripping squeal of tires and she glanced in the passenger-door mirror just in time to see the van swerve across two lanes of traffic, safely catching the same exit.

The sinking sensation had returned.

Amoreena told herself the van's presence was just a coincidence, but when the single beam followed her off the State College exit ramp, her suspicion of being tailed rapidly escalated into a disquieting realization.

She stopped at the exit light, checking her rearview. The van—she could see it was a dirty gray, not white, and had tinted windows—idled two cars back.

Her mind raced. No one she knew drove a gray van with tinted windows. If the vehicle was a tail, did that mean Ron Godinez's place was being watched, too?

The light turned green, and Amoreena sped into a sharp left turn. The UCMC Hospital stood less than a mile ahead.

The van made a similar turn. So much for coincidence.

On impulse, she turned right at the next intersection. One block down she took another left. If the chase persisted, her next stop would be at the local police station. Slowing, she drove past a school yard where kids were shooting hoops under a single playground light. Checking behind her, she saw a street devoid of traffic. Had she lost them that easily? She sure as hell was no speed racer, and Silver would be lucky to complete one lap in Indianapolis.

Feeling somewhat foolish, she approached a four-way stop and turned left, bringing her back to State College. She waited at the corner, looking east and west. Her pulse quickened at the sight of a van, but this one was definitely white, and had two working headlights.

Admonishing herself for being paranoid, Amoreena pulled back onto State College. Maybe she was reading too much into Godinez's death. She passed through two more traffic lights, with a constant eye in the rearview, yet no more sinister vans from Mars or wherever appeared.

Maybe the entire scenario had been just a coincidence.

She made it to the hospital unscathed, and, choosing a spot in close proximity to the parking guard, she braked. For several minutes she sat perfectly still, watching the passing traffic. The mystery van had suddenly become the disappearing van.

If the adrenaline boost had done nothing else, it had at least taken her mind off the MCAT debacle, though it seemed Silver's sudden turns had awoken junior. Amoreena winced at a sharp movement. Were three-month-old fetuses supposed to be this strong? She didn't want to consider how junior would feel at six months.

She waited until entering the lobby before returning Millie's pages. When her roommate didn't answer she began to leave a message.

"Millie, it's—"

"Don't hang up, I'm here," Millie broke in.

Amoreena instantly sensed the urgency in her roommate's voice. "What's wrong?" she asked, subconsciously lowering her voice. She stepped toward a vacant corner.

"The police are just leaving."

"The police."

"Hold on."

Amoreena overheard voices and then a door close. Millie returned promptly. "They're gone."

"Millie . . ."

"We were burglarized."

"Shit," Amoreena cursed under her breath. Surprisingly enough, her next question didn't allude to computers, stereos, or class books. "How's Byte?" she asked, fearing any more bad news.

"Scared but okay, I guess. I found him under Ms. Berden's porch next door. The bastards left the front door open."

"You sound good, too."

"Like the cops said, we're both fortunate neither one of us walked in on their little jaunt through the Emerald Castle."

Amoreena agreed, silently wondering what stroke of fate had driven her to UCLA first, instead of returning directly home from the MCAT. The baby's first fetal movement might have just saved her from serious injury or worse.

"What's missing?" she asked.

"Nothing, the place is a mess—"

"Nothing?" Amoreena interrupted, both shocked and puzzled.

"Everything's here, your computer, the stereo, VCR, my room's intact. The investigator surmises someone scared them off before they could get anything out. Lucky, huh."

Amoreena only nodded while a thought tried to take hold but failed to gain any solid footing. She'd been doing more of that lately, not forgetting, just failing to follow through. Pregnancy really did change a woman.

"Where are you?" she heard Millie ask.

"The hospital."

"How's Geneva?"

"Haven't seen her yet."

"Give her big hugs from me."

"Sure." *Nothing missing.* "Look, gotta go. I'll be home in about an hour," Amoreena said.

"Should I ask about the MCAT?"

"No."

"I won't. Luv ya, roomie."

All the way to the oncology ward, Amoreena couldn't deny the possibility that the house break-in and the one-beamed van were somehow related. She harbored little doubt she'd just been followed. The driver of the van hadn't risked a serious accident by veering across two lanes of traffic just because he'd inadvertently almost passed his exit. What she was missing, though, was the why.

"Nothing missing." This was even more bizarre. Someone doesn't pick your lock, ramble through your residence, and not take anything, unless . . . This time the thought found a firm grip and held on. Unless they were searching for something in particular. But what did she, or Millie for that matter, own that would be in such high demand to risk a burglary charge?

Still puzzled—the initial shock had worn off—Amoreena entered the cancer ward and approached the nurses' station. The baby's activity had calmed considerably—only periodic twitching—but seeing Dr. Gillespie scribbling orders this late on a Saturday evening caused a new round of abdominal tension. She guiltily hoped he was working on another patient's chart.

"Amoreena," he said, looking up from his notes, "we've begun weaning your mother off the steroids."

"That's good, I gather." She didn't miss the oncologist's wavering glance at her midsection. She resisted the urge to button her sweater.

"Yes, Geneva's intracranial pressure has normalized."

"Her vision?" Amoreena asked.

The oncologist's frown shattered any newfound hope. "Unfortunately, she remains blind. At this juncture, we just don't know how much damage to the optic apparatus is permanent and how much, if any, is temporary."

"Shit," Amoreena mumbled.

"I'm sorry." Dr. Gillespie capped his pen and slid it in his pocket. "There is one other matter I needed to discuss."

"If it's money," Amoreena started, but was politely quieted by the oncologist's raised palm.

"My decision has nothing to do with finances," he began. "Because of the chemotherapeutic agent's propensity to induce severe nausea and vomiting which might adversely affect your mother's already precarious condition, I've found it necessary to suspend the treatment protocol until she's become more stable."

Amoreena read the difficulty of Dr. Gillespie's decision in the deep creases radiating from the corners of his eyes like spokes on a wheel. "She's that bad," she said, already knowing the truth.

"I don't want to make her any worse."

"When can we begin again?"

The oncologist touched one of her hands. "Let's get your mother across this bridge first."

Amoreena hated the idea of interrupting the cancer therapy. Watching the clear fluid from the IV flow into her mom's veins—she guessed it was only dextrose now—she didn't begrudge Dr. Gillespie's decision, though she didn't entirely support it either. A small darker part of her wondered if her reservations could be ascribed to selfishness. After all, look what she'd sacrificed in order to obtain the funding for the cancer protocol. It helped to know Dr. Gillespie was only doing what was right for Geneva Daniels.

Amoreena's gaze shifted away from the IV tubing. In the shadows, her mother's face looked more gaunt, as if her cheeks had been scooped out with an ice-cream dipper. She stepped nearer the bed, and beneath the scents of fresh linen she could smell human flesh that had fought a battle too long and too difficult. It wasn't unpleasant, just depressing.

Geneva's eyelids fluttered out of synch, then opened. Her head turned in Amoreena's direction.

"How was the MCAT?" she asked.

Amoreena didn't question how her mom knew it was her; maybe it was her smell or the way she'd crept shamefully into the room like a misbehaving child. At the last instant, she decided not to lie.

"I didn't do well."

Geneva's expression softened as if reading far more between the four words. She patted the mattress. "Come here, sit."

Amoreena shifted a blanket aside and sat, taking her mother's hand and resting it in her lap.

"Tell me what happened. It couldn't have been that bad," Geneva said.

The words wanted to skyrocket toward Amoreena's open mouth. Well you see, it was like this, I felt the baby move, and then my brain turned to mush. Have you ever tried to concentrate with mush between your ears? Oh, by the way, I also found out a friend OD'ed on drugs, and a strange van followed me here.

Instead she said, "I guess it just wasn't my day."

Geneva offered a smile. "Mine neither. Give me a hug. The nurses and doctors are great, but they don't give good hugs."

Amoreena leaned over and in that one frigid second, she realized her mistake. Her sweater popped open. Geneva's palm froze on her daughter's abdomen. For an interminable moment, neither spoke.

When the baby kicked, both mother and daughter winced.

A million times, Amoreena had tried to visualize how her mother would take the news and an equal number of times,

Amoreena would have been wrong. Maybe it was the illness, maybe the steroids, but regardless why, Geneva neither removed her hand nor expressed any emotion approaching shock or disgust.

She stared flatly toward the ceiling. "My God, Amy, what is this? I'm going to be a grandmother?"

Though her mother's face brightened with anticipation, Amoreena couldn't pretend the profound hurt in Geneva's voice wasn't there.

"I'm sorry I didn't tell you sooner," she confessed, maintaining one vigilant eye on the heart monitor. Thank goodness, the rhythm remained regular.

Geneva's fingers tenderly probed. "What's wrong with now?"

Another jerky kick. Amoreena was glad her mother couldn't see how uncomfortable the movements were.

"You were very active, too," Geneva boasted with wounded pride. "Sometimes I worried you might crawl right out of me. Tell me, boy or girl. Feels like a boy, a strong boy."

"She's a girl," Amoreena lied, recalling her mom's desire to take a granddaughter shopping for dolls and fluffy pink petticoats.

"Amy, Amy, why did you keep this secret from me? I'm your mother."

"I know, it was really, really stupid of me." Amoreena squeezed her mother's palm. "Forgive me?"

"How could I not forgive you? You must be what, five or six months?" Geneva said, still unable to remove her hand.

After the first untruth, the others followed naturally. "Five and a half," Amoreena answered, suppressing images of a terrified Mexican girl screaming in a park, Ronald Godinez stretched supine on a metal gurney, and Gretchen Bayliss's coroner's report. There was no way in hell she'd reveal the truth.

Gillespie's decision to halt the chemotherapy never came up, nor the MCAT again. The remainder of the evening passed under a dark cloak of falsehoods and innuendoes as Amoreena maintained the facade of a happy mother-to-be. Yes, she could continue her studies, and no, her plans for medical school would not be adversely affected. It wasn't difficult, under the circumstances, and there were brief interludes where Amoreena actually felt this child she carried really was *hers*. She stumbled only once.

It was when she rose to leave and Geneva touched her hand. "When do I meet the father?"

The question hung in the air like a limp rag.

"Amy, you are in love?"

"Mom," Amoreena started, hoping the tightness in her throat was only temporary. *Say something, for godsakes.* In that one moment, gazing into her mother's face and seeing not the iniquitous ugliness of cancer, but only the beautiful caring person responsible for giving her life, she knew she could never reveal the entire story. Not now, not ever.

How could she have even considered telling this woman just diagnosed with metastatic brain lesions, who'd lost her sense of sight, how her only daughter had accepted recompense for carrying a child she never wanted, solely because someone had to pay the goddamn medical bills?

Amoreena held tight to Geneva's cachectic fingers.

"Yes, I'm in love," she said, praying the words didn't sound as hollow to her mother as they did to her.

Chapter Twenty-three

By midafternoon Sunday, the house was back in order. Millie had been accurate in her description over the phone, the place had been a mess. Not the kind of ransacking depicted in the movies, where china was shattered and walls and planks crowbarred loose, but the methodical disarray resulting from a meticulous search—personal items in drawers removed and then replaced incorrectly, pantries emptied, the contents strewn haphazardly over counters, and records, videos, and computer disks tampered with. Fortunately, nothing was damaged. And *nothing* was missing.

"Odd." Amoreena sighed, relieved all the same.

During the remainder of the cleanup, she updated her roommate on the halting of her mother's chemotherapy, though she chose not to discuss Godinez's death. Millie wasn't acquainted with him anyway, and the subject of the MCAT remained off-limits. Bombing the biggest exam of your life was not a topic she desired to elaborate on.

Millie was as excited as Amoreena had initially been at feeling the baby's activity.

"He's strong," she commented, the "he" coming naturally.

"That's what Mom said," Amoreena reluctantly agreed.

Byte took turns following each girl around until the roommates were satisfied that everything was back in its place.

Several times, after hearing a car backfire from the street or as some vehicle rumbled by, Amoreena went to the window and stole a look outside. Each time she parted the blinds, her pulse accelerated and the baby's activity quickened, yet she saw no sign of the mysterious gray van.

"Expecting company?" Millie asked from the kitchen while pouring two cups of hot tea. "You look like the proverbial old bag spying on the neighbors."

"Thanks a lot." Amoreena reclined on the couch. It wasn't easy lugging a water-filled volleyball around twenty-four hours a day. A volleyball that kept *growing*. Changing the subject, she asked, "What about fingerprints?"

"Very doubtful." Millie set two cups on the coffee table. "The cops said whoever did this were professionals, whatever the hell that's supposed to mean."

"That means they wore gloves."

"I dunno; they didn't seem too bright to me."

"Who?"

"The police. All they could talk about was getting back in time for some football game. Reminded me of Ren and Stimpy with badges. They asked if we had any guns."

"Do we?"

"I don't."

"Neither do I."

"Said we might consider one. Two single females living alone . . ." Millie shrugged.

"That's a reassuring thought."

"Also suggested we change our dead bolt. Gave me the name of a locksmith."

"Wonderful." Amoreena felt anything but wonderful. Godinez had known something about her baby, something she was confident wasn't good, and now he was dead. Was that the connection? Did whoever had gone through the house think Godinez had somehow given her information about the clinic, the baby, or maybe about his fiancée? The relationship, though plausible, appeared tenuous. Maybe. Surely if this had been a routine burglary, some items would've been taken. A VCR, jewelry, *something*.

"The cops suggested the robbers were looking for something," she heard Millie say. "They asked about drugs."

"Yeah, right." A car passed, and Amoreena parted the blinds. A red Camry. "Maybe they were after my prenatal vitamins."

"The way you're progressing, I'm beginning to think they contain a secret ingredient."

"You meant to say *swelling* and don't remind me." Amoreena said, watching the puppy sniff at her tea. She cautioned him with the toe of one foot. "What, you trying to burn your nose?"

Byte padded closer and rested his head on the cushion while Amoreena stroked softly behind his ears.

"He likes you," Millie grinned.

"Come here, you little rascal." Amoreena attempted to hoist the dog beside her, however at the sudden increase in fetal activity, Byte suddenly stiffened and growled, his two eyes fixed on Amoreena's midsection.

"Hey, don't be rude to my godchild," Millie scolded the dog.

Both girls laughed, though inside Amoreena didn't think it near as funny. She watched the puppy dash away from her across the rug.

That evening, she attempted reviewing notes for the week's upcoming final exams with little success. *The dog had been scared.* She was sure of that much. But of what? An unborn fetus? The air turned stale around her, and, finding it difficult to concentrate, she crashed early. At the least, she could get a good night's sleep.

When she wasn't dreaming of moss-infested trees laden with thick vines that encircled their boughs like snakes, she was fighting to find a comfortable position on a mattress that suddenly felt too hard and lumpy. At one point, past 3 A.M., she awoke and saw Ronald Godinez standing at the foot of her bed, his mouth opening and closing like a bloated guppy underwater. This image, too, was only a dream, but the low rumble of an engine outside her house was not. She listened until the vehicle drove away.

The first surprise Monday morning came well before her scheduled 9 A.M. embryology exam. Millie answered the phone while Amoreena was stepping out of the shower.

"Can you take it?" she heard her roommate call from the kitchen.

"The hospital?" Amoreena said, burying herself in a yellow-chenille bathrobe. She never used to feel this cold.

"Not the hospital," Millie's expression was one of curious concern. "Says he's with the California Medical Board."

:"Don't tell me they already heard about my MCAT."

It wasn't about the MCAT. Amoreena listened briefly, making brief comments where appropriate, then hung up. She stood pensively, aware of Byte's warm fur against her calf. The baby was quiet; maybe he hadn't slept so well last night either.

"Well?" Millie said.

Amoreena scribbled a notation on a pad. "He wants to discuss my written complaint against Dr. Ross Becker."

"I didn't know you filed any complaint."

Amoreena tore the sheet lose and neatly folded it. "I didn't."

Unlike the MCAT, the embryology final exam covered material that Amoreena was intimately familiar with and even though a part of her mind kept drifting to John Risken, that was the name the medical board investigator had used, she was able to maintain her focus enough to breeze through the hundred-question test in thirty minutes less than the alloted two hours.

Negotiating the steps to the lecture hall, she also found it easier than she would have anticipated to ignore the stares from the other premeds. The word was out, evidenced by the comments she'd already heard, "So Daniels did the dance," and "Who was the lucky bastard?" Not a half day into final exam week and Amoreena surmised the entire university already knew, at least those she was associated with.

Big fucking deal. Next time Gladys Peterson suffered an anxiety attack she'd lend her a plastic bag and help slip it over her entire head. The bitch.

She dropped the completed test booklet on the desk.

"Amoreena." The professor handed her a folded slip. She could read nothing behind his bifocals. "Have a safe holiday," he wished.

"Thanks."

Amoreena felt anything but festive when she saw the signature on the slip. Dr. Sheffield requested to meet with her at her earliest convenience. It didn't take much of an imagination to guess what topic was on the premed advisor's mind. She was sure it wasn't her grade point average.

Amoreena Daniels, student extraordinaire, maybe ex-student extraordinaire, future physician, and single mother-to-be, albeit surrogate. She was rapidly becoming the toast of the junior premed class. Wonders never ceased.

Dr. Sheffield let Amoreena seat herself before quietly shutting the office door. He returned to his customary position behind his desk, never allowing his eyes to drop below Amoreena's shoulders.

"Tell me about the MCAT," he started.

Today wasn't the time to bullshit. "I bombed it," she said matter-of-factly.

"That bad?"

"That bad." Amoreena shifted slightly to compensate for another round of tiny kicks. Recently she'd begun to wonder if she were carrying twins. "I don't know, Dr. Sheffield, my mind just went blank. It seemed the more I tried, the more jumbled the facts became. It wasn't a very satisfying experience."

The advisor gave her an empathetic nod. "If it helps any, the other students I talked to concur with your sentiments. Gladys described it as the most difficult exam she'd ever sat for."

"You talked with Gladys?"

"This morning. She relayed how you came to her assistance. Described your actions as 'real cool.'"

Skepticism crossed Amoreena's face. "That's all she said?"

"Yes."

Amoreena fidgeted nervously. If not Gladys . . .

"I also received what I consider to be a very special phone call earlier," the advisor continued. "From your mother."

Amoreena looked up quickly. She hadn't realized she'd been gazing at her own abdomen. "Mom called. Here?"

"We had an interesting chat." He let the statement hang.

In a flash, she knew. "It was Mom who told you."

Dr. Sheffield nodded slowly. "She's quite worried about you. And frankly, so am I."

Amoreena saw her own hands trembling on the arms of the chair so she crossed them in her lap.

"Are you okay?" Dr. Sheffield asked.

"I don't know." She tried to wet her lips with a tongue that felt like sandpaper. She didn't swallow for fear of gagging. She was confused. *Her own mother.* If she spoke she just knew she would cry and that would be unacceptable.

"I'll get you some water." Dr. Sheffield exited briefly and returned with a Styrofoam cup.

Amoreena sipped. "Thanks." The arid sensation in her mouth lessened. "Mom is very ill," she said.

The advisor's expression conveyed a melange of pity and commiseration. "She told me. I must say the news both shocked and confounded me. Why did you choose to carry this burden alone?"

Amoreena shrugged, meeting Dr. Sheffield's steady gaze. "She's one tough lady, my mother."

"It seems those same genes have been passed successfully to the next generation."

Amoreena smiled ruefully at the compliment:

Dr. Sheffield watched her a moment before speaking. "Your condition was only a portion of our discussion. Mostly she wanted to know about you, how your classes are faring, dates of upcoming medical school interviews, and overall chances of acceptance. I assured her that I've noted no drop-off in your superior academic achievements. However . . ."

The silence of the pause was like nails on a blackboard. Inside, Amoreena cringed.

"However," he went on, "I can't predict the response of the admission committee's members to a single pregnant female applicant. Your pregnancy is none of my or the university's business, but getting you into next year's freshman medical school class is. That was and still is my number one priority." He leaned closer. "Is it yours?"

"Yes," Amoreena answered.

Dr. Sheffield gave a sharp affirmative nod and rubbed his palms together. "That's exactly what I wanted to hear. Maintain your GPA, let's hope for a superior MCAT result and you'll do fine, Ms. Daniels. I also wish your mother the best."

Escorting her out, he added, "And please, keep me informed."

With an assurance that she would, Amoreena departed, feeling significantly better than when she'd climbed the steps to Wilkerson Hall. Dr. Sheffield knew, the school knew, and her mom knew. Now if only she could predict how the admission committee would take the news. Her first interviews would begin in several months.

She was halfway to the library when another burst of fetal activity forced Amoreena to a concrete bench. A lancinating pain was followed by a dull throb, which gradually dissipated.

"Someone needs to trim this kid's nails," she murmured, palming the left lower quadrant of her midsection. She could actually see her skin moving under her clothing. Or so she thought, but she knew that couldn't be right. Regardless, she'd search out Dr. Rafael at the clinic when she returned for the second installment on her contract following her first trimester checkup and ask if what she was experiencing was normal. If she didn't receive a satisfactory answer, she'd request a second opinion.

Forty-five minutes of human physiology was all she could take, and at eleven-thirty Amoreena packed her books and notes, keenly aware of her rising anxiety level. At 1 P.M., she was supposed to meet Mr. Risken at Watson Drugs. She was familiar with the establishment; in fact she'd chosen it. Adjacent to the Orange Circle and not far from the campus, the old-time pharmacy/soda fountain was always crowded, especially around lunchtime, and only several blocks from the city police station. If the meeting deteriorated for whatever reason, she'd have plenty of company.

She chose to walk, the exercise couldn't hurt: however, with each step she found herself hoping the medical investigator wouldn't show. Or maybe he couldn't find the place, though her directions had been explicit. Yet another greater part of her wanted to hear what he had to say about Dr. Becker. Had Ronald Godinez or his fiancée also spoken to someone from the California Medical Board? Now they were dead. The possibility was far from reassuring.

She passed the spot on the street where Daryl had removed the dead pigeon from Silver's windshield. Seemed like eons ago.

When she entered Old Town Circle, she found a packed Watson's sidewalk veranda, virtually every table occupied. She began to look for a tall man wearing a gray-wool jacket and yellow tie, the description the investigator had given her. She saw him standing next to a curbside mail depository.

She approached, waiting for him to catch her eye. It didn't take long. With a polite wave he motioned toward an unoccupied table under a blue awning, in plain view of the street. She nodded.

By the time she arrived, he was seated comfortably, one hand resting atop a business carryall.

He stood. "John Risken," he said, offering her his hand, then a business card. "I appreciate you takin' time off between exams to meet with me."

"No problem."

He held Amoreena's chair as she sat down.

She guessed him to be close to forty with prematurely gray hair. Not unhandsome, his most prominent features were his eyebrows. Bushy and salt and peppered, they met just above the bridge of his nose, suggesting either menace or an Einsteinian intelligence.

She introduced herself with her driver's license, while reading the card. "I'm not familiar with your organization," she commented, returning the card.

"Keep it. Hungry?"

Amoreena shook her head. The smell of fries and cheeseburgers were upsetting both her and junior. The baby hadn't stopped kicking since sitting down.

Risken ordered a Coke for himself, a hot tea for Amoreena, and then began. "The California Board of Quality Assurance is responsible for investigating any complaints filed against physicians who practice in the state of California."

"Is Dr. Becker under investigation?"

"Not officially, yet. The way the process works is to interview all parties involved first. We begin with the originator of the complaint."

"So Dr. Becker knows nothing of our meeting?"

Risken nodded. "That's correct. Everything is strictly confidential. Now"—he paused, removing a manila folder from his carryall—"according to our records in Sacramento, Dr. Becker has been practicing in California for less than a year; before that, New York and Washington, DC. Since opening his clinic here, there have been two formal complaints brought against him. The first one arrived in September and the most recent filing"—he looked up—"yours, was filed about four weeks ago at the end of November."

He started to speak again but stopped when Amoreena raised one hand. "Mr. Risken, I never filed a complaint against Dr. Ross Becker."

"He is your doctor?"

"True, but I never filed a complaint. There must be some mistake."

Two deep creases formed above the investigator's eyebrows as he reexamined his notes.

"May I see it?" she asked.

"Of course, it bears your signature." He pulled out another folder, removing a single page. He slid it across the table.

The complaint was typed and covered approximately two-thirds of the paper. Instantly, she could tell the style of the scripted signature bore little resemblance to her own.

"How far along are you?" she heard Risken ask.

"You seem to know a lot about me," she said, still examining the signature.

"The pregnancy is mentioned in the complaint."

"I'm three months."

"I would've guessed five. Have two children of my own." Amoreena looked up. "Mind if I read it?"

"Go ahead, you signed it."

"That's not my signature."

"You're sure?"

She gave him a do-I-look-stupid look.

"You're sure," he said.

"Can I still read it?"

Risken reached for his Coke, a dull expression on his face. The eyebrows hadn't budged. "I don't see why not."

Feeling the focus of the investigator's gaze, Amoreena began to read. The syntax was not what she would have used and hinted the author might have had some legal background.

Phrases such as "reckless exploitation of women" and "ethical and moral issues that fall contrary to our state's constitution and bylaws" did nothing in Amoreena's mind to clarify exactly what the author was complaining about. Whoever had written the memorandum had been vague. Whether this was foresight or oversight, she couldn't tell. All she could extrapolate was that Dr. Becker and the Women's Clinic were being accused of conducting exploitive experimentation on human subjects without proper consent. The complainant went on to request that the state investigate and intervene, if necessary, in the business practices of Meechum Medical Corporation.

Amoreena scanned it once more but gleaned nothing new. "I wonder what she meant by exploitive experimentation?"

"Why do you say 'she'?"

"Presumption, I guess. All the patients at the Women's Clinic *are* women."

"Yes, you're correct. I suppose I read it from a father's perspective."

"It could be interpreted from either side."

"True. So what do you think?"

Amoreena sat pensively a moment before speaking. Something in the wording had struck a nerve, yet how the complaint related to her she didn't know, just that in some way she knew it did.

"It almost seems," she said, "the author is taking an ideological stance against a practice in general rather than a single incident."

"My take exactly," Risken commented. "Most patients who take the time to draft a written complaint to the board cite specific details usually pertaining to one event—a missed diagnosis, incorrect therapeutics, etc. Not so here. That's what's so baffling. And that's why I wanted to meet with you."

"You mentioned another complaint."

"Plainly written by someone who had an ax to grind. Not enough to build a case on." Risken dug out another folder. "My team has been in San Diego initiating the accreditation process for another of Dr. Becker's clinics. This facility will include a small fifty-bed hospital. That's why it's so important these complaints are followed up in an expeditious manner."

"What about the person who filed the first complaint? She couldn't help?"

"Another dead end. The patient named in the report is deceased, and I've been unable to locate the individual who filed it."

Amoreena's curiosity was piqued. "Who did file it?"

"Confidential. At least until any formal hearings are held."

Amoreena sat quietly, feeling the baby move. She shifted the position of her legs. One foot had fallen asleep. "Mr. Risken, what do you know so far about Meechum Medical Corporation?"

"Based upon their licensing application, the medical side of their business is to provide obstetric and gynecological services to indigent populations in Mexico and Central and South America. They also distribute a wide range of pharmaceutical products worldwide. Only recently have they operated in the US. Dr. Becker is a geneticist by training."

"Anything about surrogacy programs?"

"Not that I recall."

Amoreena pulled her chair closer. "Mr. Risken, I'm a surrogate. The clinic hired me to carry another couple's baby." Frowning, she added, "I haven't been real comfortable with my progress so far."

The furrow had returned to the investigator's forehead. "I'm listening," he said.

In concise order, Amoreena related the specific details—the puzzling note left on her car, her blood being sent to Ensenada, Mexico, the terrified Mexican girl in the park who'd lost her baby, the gray van following her, her home break-in, Ronald Godinez's warning, and his fiancée's mysterious death in Mexico. At the mention of Godinez's name, she detected a barely perceptible rise in Risken's bushy brows.

"When did you last speak with this Dr. Godinez?" he asked.

"Around a month ago. He wanted my assistance in obtaining his fiancée's medical records. Why?"

The investigator responded by offering Amoreena another business card. "If Dr. Godinez contacts you again, have him give my office a call. It's quite important he do so."

"I'm afraid that's impossible. Last week Ronald Godinez died of an overdose."

Risken's expression registered his disappointment. "How unfortunate. His signature was on the first complaint."

Polita Salinas watched from the front seat of her rented Ford Escort. She'd parked less than a block away, having tailed her quarry from the time she'd left the campus. The Anglo carried herself well, she thought, considering her *condition*. Tall and statuesque, she could have produced a beautiful child. Under *normal* circumstances.

Polita waited, observing how the two conversed. She was thankful the state medical board was now involved. In this great Estados Unidos, a single signature really could get the ball rolling, as the classic Anglo cliché posited. Even a false signature.

Resting one hand on the shift lever, she debated when to attempt initiating contact with the Anglo. No doubt the girl was quite intelligent, but were brains enough to save her from her present predicament? And how much did she know? Not near enough to understand just what a high wire she was balancing on, Polita surmised. Any fall could be fatal.

Not for the last time, the Las Canas attorney tried to imagine what it would be like to carry one of those . . .

She couldn't bring herself to finish the thought. After all, she was a woman, too.

Chapter Twenty-four

Amoreena sensed something wrong as soon as she turned onto Spurgeon. She slowed, approaching the Women's Clinic. The parking spaces lay three-quarters empty and at the building's rear entrance she spied two long trailered U-Hauls. Next to these, almost out of view, was the medivan with its bright gold *Clínica de la Mujer* lettering painted over its side panels. Two security guards, not one, patrolled the entrance drive. A temporary fence had been constructed along the lot's perimeter.

She turned into the drive only to be stopped by one of the guards. He was large and Caucasian, with two lopsided ears and a nose that looked like it had been broken more than once. She didn't recognize him, though the other, a Hispanic man, she recalled from the incident with the young Mexican girl.

She rolled down her window. "I have an appointment with Dr. Rafael," she said, hoping her voice conveyed more bravado than she felt inside.

"Name," the guard said.

"Amoreena Daniels."

He carried a small computer notebook and punched in the name. His eyes scanned the screen briefly, before looking up. "Park as close to the front entrance as possible."

"That shouldn't be too difficult." Amoreena pulled forward. In the rearview she saw the guard speaking into a portable radio.

She picked a spot next to a Ford Escort. She locked Silver, but before going in she scanned the entire lot, silently chiding herself for being overly cautious when she failed to find any dirty gray vans.

Inside, the lobby was sparsely filled, with only a smattering of patients.

Ramona Perez escorted her upstairs. Amoreena thought the clinic coordinator appeared more emotionally tense than usual. She walked in short, rapid steps while her hands remained locked in her pockets. For a moment, Amoreena entertained thoughts of not getting paid.

"You're looking well," Ramona commented once inside the elevator.

"I feel like the Goodyear Blimp."

Even the coordinator's grin seemed forced. "That's entirely normal, dear. Trust me. And how is your mother?"

Amoreena shook her head. "Her doctor's had to halt the chemotherapy."

"I'm so sorry to hear that. Let me know if there's anything I can do."

"I appreciate your offer."

The doors slid open, and Amoreecna's face froze in shock. The entire hall was lined with packing crates. Even the statue of Ixchel no longer stood vigilant in her customary spot. Amoreena's stomach muscles tightened in a brief wave of panic.

"You're moving," she said in almost a whisper.

Ramona led her around two men pushing a dolly. "Yes. Our newest facility in San Diego is scheduled to open in February. Irene and Dr. Becker are down there now."

No doubt working on the accreditation process, Amoreena thought ruefully, and feeling not just a little bit abandoned.

"I was supposed to see Dr. Rafael today," she said.

Sensing her unease, Ramona lightly touched her back. "Relax, Amoreena. He's here. And this move won't affect you in any way. The Women's Clinic will continue to remain open as a satellite facility for the Meechum Corporation. We're just not scheduling any new patients until the transfer is complete."

Ramona passed her to a nurse, who led her to the laboratory. Amoreena never thought having her blood drawn and a urinalysis collected would give her a sense of reassurance, but it did. At least the routine remained normal.

Once in the exam room, she was placed in a gown and told to wait. The doctor would be in shortly. Since her unexpected meeting with Risken, the baby's activity had quieted, much to Amoreena's relief, though her level of awareness of the entity within her had grown considerably. Sometimes, especially lying on her back in bed, late at night, she felt more certain than ever there was more than one. A tiny thrust in one side of her belly would be followed by one equally quick movement on the opposite side of her midsection. Then in succession, more brief bursts of activity in different areas, some low in her pelvis and others higher up, almost to her ribs. Fortunately, the discomfort was less, or maybe she was just becoming more tolerant of the sharp jabs and kicks. Even the incessant bouts of nausea had dissipated.

Mentally, she was far less sanguine. The medical investigator's revelations regarding the formal complaints against Dr. Becker and the Women's Clinic, one allegedly signed by *her*, had done nothing to assuage her disquiet. Yet looking around the exam room, she saw nothing to indicate the level of care provided here was in any way substandard. The room appeared well stocked, the instruments clean, and the personnel knowledgeable.

The obvious answer, Amoreena decided, and she'd told Risken as much, was that Godinez had fabricated the second complaint himself and then signed her name, when his initial complaint had failed to generate the response he'd sought regarding his fiancee's medical care and subsequent accident.

In a way, it made her angry that he'd had the nerve to forge her signature. But only in a small way. She had to admit she was far less upset about Risken conducting an informal investigation, even under false pretenses, than she was about Godinez's overdose. The intern's actions only proved he'd discovered something about the clinic's practices that necessitated contacting the state medical board. Not once, twice.

But what? And how did it affect her? *Call me if the baby moves before three months.*

"I tried," Amoreena sighed glumly.

"You what?" Luis Rafael stood in the room.

She hadn't even heard the door open. "Nothing," she said. "Just talking to myself."

There wasn't the witty rejoinder or cheerful smile she would have expected in the past. Only a silent nod as the doctor moved about the room setting up the instrument tray.

Amoreena wondered where his assistant was. She didn't ask.

"The baby's moving a lot now," she said.

He nodded again, checking the Doppler. She thought he appeared ten years older. A day-old beard gave his face a Homer Simpson look, though there was nothing comedic about the dusky shadows under each eye or the wrinkled haphazard way he was dressed. If she didn't know better, she'd have guessed he just stepped off a plane after a red-eye flight. The alacrity in his bedside manner wasn't the only thing missing. His intense gaze that made Amoreena feel cared for was absent. It was as if a candle had been extinguished from behind his eyes.

She had no idea how wrong her impression was.

In ten minutes, the examination was complete. With due diligence, he checked her blood pressure, pulse, listened to her heart, lungs, and palpated her abdomen. His fingers firmly probing her skin caused no discomfort though junior didn't seem to relish the outside disturbance. A sharp lacerating pain shot down into Amoreena's pelvis. She winced.

"Hurts, huh," was all Dr. Rafael said.

"I think he's going to be a kicker in the NFL." Still no smile. She was beginning to hate his silent nods.

After a knock, a nurse entered and handed Dr. Rafael some laboratory slips. He scanned each cursorily.

"Everything okay?" Amoreena asked.

Another nod. He dropped the results on top of a chart. Amoreena noticed he hadn't touched the Doppler yet to check on the baby. The instrument still lay coiled on the tray beside an open tube of lubricating gel.

Amoreena watched him scribble a few lines in her medical chart and shut it. This man was definitely not the same Dr. Luis Rafael she'd come to trust. She'd have almost been more comfortable with Dr. Becker, regardless of any investigation. At least he talked.

"What do you think about the move?" she asked.

Amoreena saw it etched in his face as soon as his eyes met hers. *Everything wasn't okay.* Not the move and especially *not her baby.* A cold blanket engulfed her, and she gasped for breath. It felt like all the air had been sucked from the room.

"What is it?" she barely croaked, struggling to sit up. Suddenly nothing else mattered except the tiny life inside her. She pushed the tears away from her cheeks with both palms. "What?" she gasped again, refusing to accept what she'd sensed for some time.

Still he did not respond. He came to her.

Amoreena had no idea how long she sobbed with her head held against Dr. Rafael's chest. As his fingers slowly stroked her hair, the air gradually returned to the exam room. Her breathing came easier, and her tears ebbed. The baby moved, and no horrible images cascaded before her eyes.

She pulled her face away from his shirt and looked into his eyes. She opened her mouth to speak.

His index finger pressed over her lips stopped her. He bent close to one ear. "Don't say anything. Meet me in my office."

Her puzzled expression was met with a single shake of his head. Again he silently mouthed "my office."

She dressed quickly and waited for the nurse to escort her down the hall. She passed several other exam rooms: one was closed, and inside she heard muffled voices, but she paid no attention.

Dr. Rafael met her at his door and motioned her in, locking the office behind her. He moved to the window and gazed outside before stepping to his desk.

"Can I talk?" Amoreena demanded, her anguish controlled but no less poignant.

"Yes."

"What the hell is going on?"

"Sit down."

"No. Is my baby okay or isn't it?"

His failure to respond wasn't what floored her. It was the foreboding look in his eyes. *God, he's more scared than I am.*

"Amoreena," he began before having to stop.

She stood frozen in place, raising a silent shield to protect her from the worst. She hadn't experienced this sense of helplessness since Dr. Gillespie had initially broken the news about her mother's cancer.

Prepared for the blow, she waited, not fully realizing it's the punch you don't see that inflicts the most damage.

Dr. Rafael started again. This time he sounded more in control. "There's not much time," he said, and handed her a cardboard envelope one foot square.

"What's this?" she asked, sliding the packet in her purse.

"Your sonograms."

"But I already saw them."

"Just listen. The ones I showed you were normal films."

"I know."

"But they weren't of *your* baby."

"What—"

"Shut up and listen to me. Show these to your mother's doctor. He'll know what to do."

"What the hell do you mean? Not of my baby."

"The sonograms you viewed were from another clinic patient carrying a normal fetus. The same fake sonogram is shown to all the program surrogates."

"I don't believe you. You're lying."

Dr. Rafael used a key to open a drawer and dug inside. Amoreena saw droplets of perspiration glistening on his forehead. He withdrew a tiny prescription vial. He placed it in the palm of her hand.

"When you get to the hospital, I want you to take these. It's very important."

Amoreena opened the container. She counted six tiny blue pills. "What are these?"

"Medicine."

"For the baby?"

"Yes. But you must take them in a hospital."

"What if—"

Dr. Rafael virtually lunged across the desk, grabbing her by both shoulders. His eyes glared with the intensity of a trapped animal. "Do you want to die?"

Amoreena pushed back. "Are you crazy? No, I don't want to die."

"Then follow my instructions. Explicitly."

"What are those pills for? Goddammit, tell me."

Before he could respond, it suddenly dawned on her. She stared down at the pill container and wanted to scream. With a mouth as dry as parched sand, she said, "You want to harm the baby."

"Amoreena, please. You don't understand. If you allow this pregnancy—"

"You're asking me to destroy a part of me."

"It's not a part of you."

Amoreena saw his hand reach for her and she spun for the door. "Don't touch me," she cried.

Disengaging the lock, she threw open the door and dashed into the hall. As she ran for the elevators, she averted a collision with a tall Hispanic woman.

"Ms. Daniels," Polita said.

But Amoreena had heard enough.

If the light didn't turn in five seconds, she'd run the damn thing. Four. Three. Amoreena's foot inched off the brake.

Green. She squealed through the intersection, ignoring the stares from sidewalk pedestrians. A traffic citation was the furthest thing from her mind.

"It's not a part of you." Dr. Rafael's words had emotionally blindsided her. She'd panicked, no doubt, but there was also no doubt that at the time all she could think about was getting away from the clinic. She felt betrayed, angry, frightened, all of the above, suffocating under the weight of a thousand doubts and questions. Only after isolating herself in Silver had her respirations begun to normalize—barely—though her heart still might bounce out of her chest if she didn't get a grip on her speeding pulse.

Slow, slow, slow, she tried coaxing, but it wasn't working.

She began to feel faint. She spun into the nearest gas station and braked. Still gripping the wheel, she closed her eyes and forced herself to hold her breath. She counted to three, then exhaled. She repeated the same maneuver a second time.

Amoreena barely heard the tapping on the glass. She lowered the window to the smell of motor oil and gasoline.

"You okay?" the attendant asked.

Amoreena nodded. The dizziness was lessening. "Yeah, I think so." At least she felt able to drive again.

She pulled back into the traffic lane, making a conscious effort to hold to the speed limit. In fifteen minutes she'd be at Dr. Gillespie's office.

She'd always trusted Dr. Rafael, yet what had been so easy before she found excruciatingly difficult now. If he was so concerned for her health, why had he asked her to abort the pregnancy? Was her condition *that* serious? She let one hand wander to her purse, ensuring the sonograms were still there. She hoped the oncologist would provide the answers.

Dr. Gillespie's waiting room was empty when Amoreena approached the check-in window. She rang the bell.

An unfamiliar woman slid back the glass partition. "May I help you?" she asked.

"I need to talk with Dr. Gillespie."

"Are you a patient?"

"Yes, I mean no. My mother's a patient. Look, this is sort of an emergency." Amoreena felt her self-control slipping.

The receptionist gazed at Amoreena's midsection. "Dr. Gillespie no longer sees obstetric cases. If you'd like a referral—"

"I don't want a referral. I want to speak to Dr. Gillespie. Now."

"Please wait." Abruptly, the window slid shut.

A moment later, a nurse entered the waiting room. Amoreena breathed a sigh of relief. She recognized the woman. She'd assisted in drawing her mother's blood on more than one occasion.

"Hello, Amoreena," she said. "I was told you need to speak with the doctor."

"It's very important."

"I understand. Unfortunately, Dr. Gillespie will be in surgery the entire afternoon. Does this pertain to your mom?"

"No, I just need to talk to him."

"I can have the doctor contact you as soon as he's available."

This wasn't what Amorena needed to hear. Her sonograms felt like a lead weight dangling from her neck, growing heavier every second. Only sheer willpower prevented her from cursing out loud.

"You have my pager," she said.

The nurse smiled. "I'll relay the message."

"Please tell him it's urgent."

Amoreena's last final exam ended at four that afternoon. Before the test, Dr. Gillespie had called and agreed to meet her at the hospital after his last case.

The package arrived in that day's mail. Millie sifted through the assortment of bills, promotions, and holiday greeting cards, setting aside the flat bubble pack along with a pile of coupon booklets and advertisements. It wasn't addressed to her.

In her bedroom, Amoreena sat at her desk, staring at the check for ten grand. Dr. Rafael had slid the second installment on her surrogacy contract inside the ultrasound envelope. At least he'd remembered to pay her.

The baby moved in several places at once, forcing Amoreena to cradle her abdomen. She was getting used to the sharp pains but not the weight gain. She'd put on three pounds in the last day alone. Next to the computer monitor sat the little vial of blue pills. What kind of clinic would purposely prescribe medicine to harm a fetus? Several, times she'd attempted to discard the pills in the sink or toilet, but each time something held her back. She knew she'd never use them, yet she couldn't throw them away either. She'd tried calling Risken, but he'd been unavailable. She'd left a message with his secretary.

Her outlook seemed smothered by gloom. She missed the ebullience and insouciance that came with the completion of final exam week. Though she felt she'd done well, there was no sensation of accomplishment or pride. Over the last weeks, medical career goals had slowly slipped from the top of her priority list and, worse, she really didn't care. She wasn't even looking forward to the holidays. Tomorrow would be her first day for shopping. Just two days before Christmas!

With much effort, Amoreena rose and grabbed her sonograms, along with her purse. Byte followed her to the front door.

"There's a package for you," Millie called after her.

"It can wait."

Amoreena gently coaxed the pup back inside and shut the door behind her.

After depositing the clinic funds in the bank, she drove straight to the hospital. She found two nurses at the central station, but neither had seen the cancer specialist. She inquired about her mom.

"No change," one nurse said.

At least Geneva Daniels wasn't worse. Amoreena's attention shifted to the elevators and the two people moving her way.

"There he is," a nurse spoke behind her.

Amoreena's relief was tempered when she saw who the person was accompanying him. Rosalind Cates lumbered along beside the oncologist like a personal bodyguard, and Amoreena found herself wondering if the woman ever changed her suits. She had on the same drab gray colors she'd worn during their initial meeting. Only now she'd added a holiday green-and-red scarf to her sartorial repertoire. Merry fucking Christmas.

"Amoreena." Dr. Gillespie extended his hand in greeting. "I apologize for not getting back to you sooner, but that last case was more involved than I'd anticipated. You remember Ms. Cates."

Amoreena gave the utilization chairperson a curt nod. If Cates noticed Amoreena's pregnant condition, she gave no indication.

"I'll be in the conference room with the charts," she said to the oncologist and departed.

"I hate that woman," Amoreena said, watching her picking over the chart rack like a greedy vulture.

"I must admit she's efficient."

"Like a wrecking ball."

Dr. Gillespie led Amoreena a little way down the hall. "Have you visited your mother?"

"I'm going there now."

"We started another IV. Geneva's developed a small cardiac effusion, fluid in the sac surrounding the heart. Not serious, yet, but something we'll need to keep an eye on. She's scheduled for another echocardiogram tomorrow."

Amoreena shook her head disconsolately. So much for no change.

The oncologist patted her on the arm. "Keep your spirits up. Her intracranial pressure remains normal, and ophthalmology is still cautiously optimistic. Now what did you wish to discuss?"

Amoreena removed the sonogram envelope from her purse. "I wanted you to look at my ultrasounds."

"Everything okay?"

"I'd just feel better with a second opinion."

"I'd be happy to." The ward nurse interrupted him. She held the phone in one hand.

"Doctor, the ER needs you stat."

"Inform Ms. Cates and tell them I'm on my way." He tucked the sonograms under one arm. "I'll be in touch, Amoreena."

She watched him hurry toward the elevator. If the oncologist found anything abnormal with this fetus, only then would she broach the issue of the tiny blue pills.

Amoreena found her mother staring at the ceiling through blank eyes. The television was on, the volume muted. An intravenous line wound from a bag of clear liquid into Geneva's right wrist.

Amoreena pulled a chair beside the bed. "Dr. Gillespie says the eye doctors are hopeful about your vision," she said.

Geneva smiled, erasing years from her face. "How's the baby?"

"Fine."

"Still moving?"

"Every day."

"I want to feel."

Amoreena stood and placed her mother's palm against her abdomen. The movements appeared on cue, fast and jerky.

Geneva giggled.

"Mom, she's just a baby."

"I worry so about you, Amy. Did Dr. Sheffield talk to you?"

Amoreena nodded quietly, momentarily forgetting. "Yes," she said quickly.

"You're not angry?"

"Never. I love you."

"Give your mother a big hug."

Amoreena did and saw her mother was crying.

Later, when she arrived home, Byte was waiting at the front door and greeted Amoreena with gleeful yelps and a frolicky dance that consisted of running in sharp circles. She wished there was some way to sneak the happy dog into her mother's room. She was sure the pup's antics would have a positive effect.

A note on the fridge said Millie and Daryl had gone out with some friends to celebrate the end of hell week. Though an address was included, Amoreena wasn't in the mood.

The answering machine had recorded several messages but none from Dr. Gillespie. She thought he would have gotten back to her by now regarding her sonograms.

Reminded of her medical facility's impending move, she decided to call the Women's Clinic. She listened to a prerecorded message referring her to a 619 area code number. San Diego. She called, and a live operator answered. Amoreena hung up. At least they had someone manning the phones.

Her eyes passed over the brown packet sitting on the counter and nothing registered until she'd entered her bedroom. She stopped with a jolt in front of her mirror. She'd seen *that* handwriting style before, the funny way the two zeros in her address were scribbled.

A spark of electricity raced through her as she dashed back and examined the envelope more closely. Though no return address and a mistake in the spelling of her first name, one e instead of two, there was no doubt in her mind. The packet had been mailed by Ronald Godinez.

She found the computer disk inside.

Chapter Twenty-five

The note read:

This is the proof. I'm returning to Ensenada. Leave the clinic, Amorena.

I'll be in touch.

Ron G.
P.S. It's far worse than I thought.

Amoreena set the scrap of paper next to the disk. The postmark on the envelope was dated Monday, three days ago. Either the postal date was in error, which she doubted, or Ronald Godinez had been alive a full four days after he supposedly overdosed on drugs.

She shivered. Which meant the two people at Godinez's apartment on Saturday had lied to her, further lending credence to her supposition that Godinez's disappearance was somehow intricately twined to the Meechum Corporation. When the Senior Godinez had inquired about any recent gifts his son might have given her, she'd attributed the odd question to a distraught parent. If that assumption was false, then the couple were, in all likelihood, not even members of his family, and certainly not his parents. Who were they? Possibly the same two who'd followed her on the freeway in the mysterious gray van. Yet the couple had seemed so sincere in their grief. Could she be fooled so easily? Was she that gullible? Obviously, she was.

Anger pushed aside some of her obfuscation. She thought about the purported burglary of her own home the same day. *Nothing missing.* The ultimate goal of the break-in had likely been the retrieval of the disk. The same computer disk she now held in her possession.

Her anger gradually surrendered to fear. She felt Byte push against her leg. She petted him with one foot.

The puppy whined.

"Yeah, me too." Systematically, Amoreena went through the house, ensuring all the windows and doors were locked.

Feeling only slightly more secure, she returned to the kitchen table and reread the note. "This is the proof," the word "the" underlined for emphasis. She was confident the proof in some way alluded to her baby, but had no idea what the relationship was. She knew where the answer would lie.

Amoreena reached for the disk. It looked no different than any other disk she'd seen, until she slid it from its cardboard protector. Taped to the disk's back side was a life-size photograph of a human eye. The edges of the photo appeared roughly cut as if the image had been taken from a much larger photograph. Looking remarkably lifelike, Amoreena could count tiny flecks of gold in the green iris and follow the thread-thin blood vessels coursing across the pale white conjunctiva. For a scary moment, she imagined she recognized the eye.

With one fingernail, she carefully removed the tape and set the eye photo aside. Folded inside the cardboard protector she found a second note. Also in Godinez's script, it included just two words.

You'll Need

She turned it over. Blank. Maybe the intern had been in too much of a hurry to complete his instructions. Yet he'd taken the time to mail the diskette to her. Why risk the postal service, though, if the material the disk contained was so important? What if it'd been lost? Or stolen?

Because he didn't trust anyone. Nobody. Except an entity as large as the US government, and her. Amoreena lamented he hadn't had the time to hand-deliver the material. There were just too many questions, the largest now being—was Ronald Godinez still alive?

Amoreena reached for the phone and dialed his number from memory. A phone company recording confirmed what she'd already suspected. The number was disconnected. She replaced the receiver. Godinez's whereabouts would have to wait until tomorrow, when she'd go to the police.

Grabbing the disk, she returned to her bedroom. Byte padded at her heels. Sitting at her desk, she briefly hesitated before flipping the computer's POWER ON switch. In a moment, she'd discover just *what* was far worse than Godinez had thought.

Forcing her breathing to remain normal, she slid the disk into the port. The screen flashed.

WHO ARE YOU?

Amoreena silently mouthed the question appearing on the monitor. Her fingertips hovered above the keyboard. She typed in her name, then jabbed Enter.

ACCESS DENIED

"Shit." she mumbled. Byte pressed against her calf. "Let's try . . ." she entered LUIS RAFAEL.

ACCESS DENIED

"How 'bout . . . ?"

IRENE LEGGETT

Enter.

CONFIRM

"Oh boy."

Three options appeared—DIGITAL, AUDIO, OPTICAL. She moved the cursor to DIGITAL and pressed Enter.

NO CONFIRMATION

Two seconds later, the screen went blank. She repeated the sequence, using the administrator's name and the audio and optical choices, with similar results. Next she tried Dr. Becker's name and again came to a dead end after getting the NO CONFIRMATION message.

Amoreena stared at the blank monitor.

The baby kicked. "Quiet," she whispered. She removed the disk and reinserted it, repeating the entire process, only to be thwarted again by the software's built-in security program. Unless she could overcome this protective obstacle, retrieving the information on the disk would be impossible.

Her eyes drifted to the prescription vial. She shoved the bottle behind some paper so she wouldn't have to see the tiny blue pills.

She was still mulling other options when Byte suddenly began to bark. Amoreena heard someone fiddling with the front door lock. She raced toward the kitchen phone.

"Who is it?" she screamed.

She'd completed the nine of the 9-1-1 sequence before Millie stumbled in.

"You still up?" Her roommate wore a crooked grin.

Amoreena hung up. "Are you drunk?"

"A little."

"I need your help."

While Millie calmed the yelping pup in her lap, Amoreena succinctly explained the significance of the data on the disk.

Millie's expression turned ghostly. "You think there's something wrong with your baby?"

Amoreena didn't answer directly. "Can you hack in?" she asked earnestly.

Her roommate had sobered considerably. "I can sure as hell try. Show me what you've done so far."

Amoreena demonstrated her aborted attempts.

"Let's try my computer." Millie removed the disk. "I doubt it'll make a difference, but no two systems are identical."

Both girls watched the screen as Millie attempted to break into the system. After fifteen minutes she gave up.

"It's futile," she said.

"What about a password?" Amoreena asked.

"Passé. Besides the program didn't ask for one. You see these." She returned the screen to the DIGITAL, AUDIO, OPTICAL options. "The system's security is based on biometrics?"

"What the hell is biometrics?"

Millie advanced the cursor to DIGITAL. "The study of distinct differences in human physical traits. Here the program's asking for fingerprints. Audio would require voice prints, and optical, could be either retinal or iris scans." After three seconds, the screen went blank. "Unless you can identify yourself as—."

"Jesus."

"What?"

Amoreena rushed out of the room, Byte in tow, and returned with the odd photo. "Look at this."

"It's a picture of an eye, so?"

"No, an *iris*."

"I'll be damned." Millie snapped the photo from Amoreena's hand and examined it closer. "You're right. This came with the disk?"

Amoreena nodded. "Godinez tried to tell me with a note."

"Who's Godinez?"

"The guy who mailed me this disk." Amoreena quickly explained while Millie studied the photo from different angles. "You think it'll work?" she asked.

"It's worth a try." Millie set the photograph on a clean sheet of paper. "Now all we need is an iris scanner."

"Are they expensive?"

"Only about two grand."

Amoreena groaned.

"But I know where I might be able to access one a lot cheaper than that?"

Amoreena's expression lightened. "Where?"

"The computer lab."

"It's past ten."

"Open till midnight every night for final exams."

Amoreena's eyes drifted to her abdomen. She felt the baby move. "Can we go now?"

Millie popped out the disk. "What are roommates for?"

Amoreena drove. Every few seconds she'd check the rearview, realizing picking out a tail in the dark would be next to impossible. She'd already decided if she spotted a gray van, she'd drive straight to the police, even though she doubted they'd take her story seriously.

"You expecting company?" she heard Millie ask. Her roommate sat with a thermos of coffee clutched in her lap.

"Just looking."

"You're making me feel like *Mission Impossible*."

"I wish Risken had returned my call," Amoreena said, shooting a glance in the passenger-door mirror. "Maybe I should have tried him again."

"He's the medical investigator?"

Amoreena nodded. Pulling into the student lot, she saw more cars than she would have expected, until she recalled finals didn't officially end till tomorrow. "What if the lab's locked?"

"It won't be."

Amoreena ignored the baby's jerky kicks, even the painful ones, as she followed Millie to Henderson Hall. The night was cool and clear, and, in the distance, she heard the lilting voices of holiday carolers.

"This way." Millie directed her into a spacious room partitioned by three long continuous counters topped with individual computer workstations.

Most were occupied with students. Other than intermittent hushed voices and the occasional sounds of pages being flipped, the room was quiet.

"Fantastic," Millie whispered.

"What?"

"It's not in use. Come on, hurry."

Millie led them down an aisle toward a separate smaller cubicle. She flipped on the light. "Give me the disk."

The workstation, though similar in basic appearance to the others, consisted of a larger monitor and additional hardware that Amoreena didn't recognize.

"You know how to work this?" she asked, watching Millie seat herself before the keyboard.

"Just like mine, only with a faster chip and more gigabytes of storage. A lot more." She waited while the system booted up. "Every semester a government security specialist lectures us on advances in software security technology. See that?" She pointed out a small device about five inches long that looked like a tapered banana, only white. A flexible cord led from one end to the computer console. The other end consisted of a single black orblike lens approximately one inch in diameter.

"The iris scanner," Amoreena said.

"Actually it's a tiny camera that takes a high-resolution image of the iris," Millie explained as she carefully wiped the photo clean with a soft cloth. "By comparing the contrast between each pixel in the image, the scanner determines if the programmer really is who he says he is."

"Or she."

"Yeah, or she. Ready?"

Amoreena nodded.

Millie passed her roommate the disk. "You do the honors."

"Here goes." Amoreena slid the disk into the port. Instantly, the screen flashed for identification.

WHO ARE YOU?

"Who should we be?" Millie's fingers paused above the keyboard.

"Try Irene Leggett?"

"You think that's whose eye's in the photo?"

"I remember she had green eyes. God, I hope she wasn't wearing contacts."

"Me too." Millie typed in the name then hit Enter.

CONFIRM

She shifted the cursor to optical. "Okay, take the photo and position it directly in front of the lens. Make sure your fingertips are out of the way."

Using one hand for manipulating the scanner, Amoreena followed Millie's instructions. "Set."

Millie activated the lens with the mouse and then pressed Enter.

The response took only a fraction of a second.

HELLO, IRENE

"Bingo," Millie beamed at the monitor.

Amoreena's heart jumped. "Godinez, you're a genius."

Millie responded with a typed hello and pressed Enter. A menu appeared.

SEARCH MENU

GENE POOL—HOMO SAPIENS—GENERAL
GENE POOL—DISEASES/ORGANS
GENE—SUS SCROFA
GENE—PAPIO ANUBIS
DRONE CENSUS

Millie frowned. "What is all that?"

A pit had begun to form in Amoreena's stomach. The disease category looked the most intriguing. "Try gene pool, diseases and organs."

Millie entered the request. The data rolled down the screen.

ORGANISM—HOMO SAPIENS
Eukaryotae, mitochondrial
Metazoa, cordata, vertebrate,
Eutheria, Primata, Catarrhini,
Hominidae, Homo sapiens

Location/Qualifiers/MAP
Gene

    Alzheimer's
    Breast Cancer
    Colon Cancer
    Atherosclerosis
    Cystic Fibrosis
    Diabetes Mellitus
    Huntington's Chorea
    Neural Tube
    Parkinson's
    Depression, Endogenous
    Obesity
    Schizophrenia
    Tay-Sachs

The list went on and on.

"Continue?" Millie asked.

Amoreena studied the electronic file. "Hit diabetes." She waited while the screen filled.

```
ORGANISM - HOMO SAPIENS
ORGAN - Pancreas
DISEASE - Diabetes Mellitus
CHROMOSOME - 17
MAP "7p22"
GENE ICAp69
/translation="MVQPKETLQLESAAEVGFVRFFQGPEKPTTTVRLF
DRGDFYTAHGEDALLAAREVFKTQGVIKYMGPAGAKNLQSVVL
SKMNFESFVKDLLLVRQYRVEVYKNRAGNKASKEND
WYLAYKASPGNLSQFEDILFGNNDMSASIGVVGVKM
SAVDGQRQVGVGYVDSIQRKLGLCEFPDNDQFSNLEALLIQIGP
KECVLPGGETAGDMGKLRQIIQRGGILITERKKADFSTKDIYQDL
NRLLKGKKGEQMNSAVLPEMENQVAVSSLSAVIKF"ICAp69.
```

Millie shook her head. "Mean anything?"

"I suspect this refers to the gene that causes diabetes in humans. See, it even includes the specific genetic tag."

"Looks like alphabet soup to me."

Amoreena leaned closer to the screen. The pit was growing. "Can you return to the menu?"

"Done."

Amoreena reviewed the options. HOMO SAPIENS, GENERAL would probably be a listing of the forty-six human chromosomes, the Human Genome Project rehashed. She'd already been exposed to much of that data in her Human Genetics lectures. And she'd just sampled the DISEASES category. However, the last three options, she'd never heard of.

"Give me Gene-Sus scrofa," she said.

Millie entered the instructions. The data moved down the screen.

```
ORGANISM—Sus Scrofa
        Eukaryotae, Mitonchondrial
        Animalia, Cordata, Vertebrata,
        Mammalia, Artiodactyla,
        Suidae, Sus Scrofa
GESTATION—114 days
CHROMOSOME 6 locus ×1
MAP 10289–91
GENE—PAG—Accelerator Gene
CODON—Start = 1
PRODUCT—P protein—Accelerator gene
/db xref="PID:g727172"
/translation="YHRTNPTGTQDLLEIADYLLEQIRDNCTGNED
HTYSLRVIGNIGRTMEQLTPKLTSSVLKCIKSTQPPLLIQKAAIQAS
RKVELGDQVREVLLQTFLDNVSPGEKRLAAYLMLMRAPSQS
DINKVTQLLPGEKNEQVKNFVASHLANILHSEESYIQEL
/G E N E="PAG"
```

"Sus scrofa?" Millie asked incredulously.

Amoreena made no comment as she read. She guessed most of the data would require a PhD to fully understand. She made a mental note of the line delineating 114 days. Did that number correspond to the gestational time period of *Sus scrofa*, whatever the hell that was? Something

Godinez had told her clicked; however she was too engrossed to grasp it.

"I need more information," she said.

Millie's finger worked the keys back to the main menu, where she selected the next option.

This time the screen took longer to fill.

> ORGANISM Papio anubis
>   Eukaryotae, Mitochondrial, Animalia,
>   Cordata, Mammalia, Primata,
>   Cercopithecidae, Papio Anubis
> GENE BG—Wraparound Deoxyribonucleic Acid /
>   Nonspecified—see #137

"Papio anubis?" Amoreena stared at the screen. "You don't have a zoology text handy?"

"Not on me."

"What is #137?" she asked.

"Must correspond to another disk." Millie pressed Enter several times with no results.

Amoreena wondered if this was the reason Godinez had returned to Mexico.

"Let's try drones," she said.

"What the hell are drones?"

Amoreena slowly shook her head. "I don't know." A part of her wanted to look away and remove the disk. The other part won out.

"You want this printed?" Millie asked, bringing up the DRONE CENSUS.

"All of it," Amoreena said.

Millie directed the output to the printer as the data scrolled down the screen.

> MEECHUM CORP / GENECLONE PROJECT
> 1996–to date
> DRONES—Generation 1–3 CENSUS
> TOTAL COUNT
>   6/96–12/31/96

                    Generation 1—1,042
        1/97–12/31/97
                    Generation 1—678
                    Generation 2—14
        1/98–12/31/98
                    Generation 1—316
                    Generation 2—200
        1/99–current
                    Generation 1—17
                    Generation 2—98
                    Generation 3—127
                        8/16/99—Delete two Gen 3
                        Drones

"Stop," Amoreena said. She pointed to the date. "This is around the time Godinez said his fiancée was killed in an accident. And look. Around the same date, the Geneclone Project deleted two Generation 3 drones, whatever the hell they are."

"Coincidence?" Millie said.

"Yeah, right. What's the next page show?"

Millie advanced the screen.

        CENSUS BY CLINICS
                Guatemala / Las Canas
                Brazil / São Paolo
                Mexico / Mexico City
                Mexico / Ensenada
                USA / Santa Ana
                USA / San Diego

"Can you give me the data in the Women's Clinic only?" Amoreena asked.

Millie adjusted the cursor and hit Enter.

        MEECHUM CORP / DRONES
        Santa Ana Clinic
                1—Vivian Cortez—211326
                2—Olga Sales—211327
                3—Constance Siguero—211128

                    4—Angie Murgia—211329
                    5—Arecilia Ramos—211330

The list stopped at twenty-five. Amoreena recognized none of the names.

"Try Olga Sales," she said.

The data filled half the screen.

```
OLGA SALES—VACA 211327
Alien / Hispanic
HT—5'0" WT—121
HR—BR EYES—BR
BLD TYPE—O+
HLA—MATCH
DRONES—2 GEN2
        Term—140 days
        Delete Genes ICAp69/Chromosome 17
        Add Gene PAG — 1%
                BG — 10%
Disposition—Guadalajara, Mexico
—Universidad Hospital
—Diabetes Research/Misc Organ harvest
```

"Jesus Christ," Amoreena murmured, recognizing the word *"vaca."* She hurriedly scribbled down the deleted diabetes gene on chromosome 17, and the added genes, PAG and BG.

"Give me another name. Quick," she said.

"How 'bout Angie Murgia?"

"Fine." Amoreena felt her mouth go dry as she waited. A picture was beginning to form, and it made her cold inside. The baby hadn't moved in fifteen minutes.

Millie brought up the fourth name on the list.

```
4—ANGIE MURGIA—VACA 211329
Alien / Hispanic
HT—5'4" WT—148
HR—BR EYES—BR
BLD TYPE—O–
HLA—MATCH
```

```
DRONES—2 GEN2
      Term—140 days
      Delete Gene—None
      Add Gene PAG—1%
                    BG—10%
Disposition—Mexico City, Mexico
         —Cuidad Hospital
         —Organ—Heart, kidneys, brain, pancreas
```

Amoreena jotted down her notes. In this case, no deleted genes but again, the PAG and BG genes had been added, 1% and 10%, respectively. Also no mention of any first-generation drones, just two second-generation ones. How significant was this?

A woman poked her head inside the cubicle. "Ten minutes."

Millie swore quietly. "We gotta hurry. The lab's closing."

"Shit." Amoreena studied the monitor. There was too much information to assimilate in so short a time. She scrolled down the names on the screen. If these patients were past surrogates, why was there no reference to the babies? "I'm looking for two more names," she said.

Millie advanced the list.

Gretchen Bayliss occupied the thirty-seventh slot. As Amoreena expected, all the data had been deleted. The girl was classified as deceased. There was no mention of the two missing drones.

She found her own name at position forty-three. Reading each line, she had the vague sensation she was looking at the obituary of a stranger.

```
43—AMOREENA DANIELS—VACA 211368
USA / Caucasian
HT—5'8" WT—119
HR—RD/BR EYES—BL
BLD TYPE—O+
HLA—MATCH PENDING
DRONES—3 GEN4
      Term—110 days
      Delete Genes NONE
```

Add Gene PAG—5%
BG—10%
Disposition—Las Canas, Guatemala

Amoreena sat back with a start, the pen dropping from her fingers. The realization struck her square between the eyes. She suddenly understood. The drones *were* the babies. And she was carrying three!

Chapter Twenty-six

Amoreena glared at the phone. "Try him again," she ordered in her most threatening tone.

The paging operator hesitated. "Ma'am, it's past midnight."

"I don't give a damn, keep paging him till he answers." She slammed down the receiver.

Under the kitchen table, Byte cowered at Millie's feet.

Amoreena rubbed her temples. The tension had given her a monster migraine.

Millie set two extra strength Tylenol and a glass of water before her. "Try these."

The capsules felt like horse tablets in her throat. The water helped some. "It's unlike Dr. Gillespie not to answer his pages," Amoreena groaned.

Millie glanced at the digital clock on the microwave. "It *is* late."

"Damn, I need my ultrasound results."

Amoreena rested a palm on the stack of computer printouts. Before the lab closed, she and Millie had run off as much of the disk's data as possible. The lab proctor had even let them stay an extra fifteen minutes. Now, more than ever, she wanted the oncologist to call. Her sonograms could prove or disprove what she irresolutely suspected. She prayed she was wrong. *Three babies*. God, she wasn't that big.

First thing in the morning, she wanted to try to locate Godinez again. Or at the minimum, confirm that the man was still alive and breathing. She'd also contact Risken. The data she'd collected would be sure to interest the medical investigator.

Inside, she wanted to sit and cry, but her anger buttressed her emotions. There were no parents. There were never any parents. That much she was confident of, at least in her case. Everything also was just conjecture. Some of the data had seemed so bizarre, it had tested the limits of her disbelief. She planned on staying up most of the night to analyze the information.

The baby, now babies, moved jerkily under her sweatshirt. She refused to consider the word "drones."

The phone rang.

Amoreena jerked it up, expecting to hear Dr. Gillespie's voice. It was the paging operator. Amoreena hung up after less than half a minute.

"His pager's no longer in service," she said despondently. "The operator said it could be his batteries. I doubt he'd shut it off purposely."

On a whim, she dialed the oncology ward. The clerk who answered sounded like she'd been dozing. The night nurse sounded only slightly more awake. Geneva Daniels was sleeping, her condition unchanged, and Dr. Gillespie had last made rounds at seven that evening. The nurse also reported she'd tried paging the physician on another patient with similar unsuccessful results. Amoreena left a message to have him call her at home if he checked in for any reason.

"That's odd," she said, replacing the receiver. She watched Millie yawn.

"Go to bed," she said. "I'll wake you if I need to talk."

"Promise."

"'Night." Amoreena waited until her roommate had trudged down the hall before spreading the printouts across the table. For the next several hours, she pored over the data. Byte studied her with an intent puppy stare as she made her notes.

By 5 A.M. her hypothesis had begun to crystallize. She

shuddered, reviewing what she'd collated. Of the fifty-plus Women's Clinic cases she'd retrieved from the disk, all had been terminated prior to term; term being relative, as in each instance no pregnancy had gone beyond 140 days. And in every patient more recent than Gretchen Bayliss, the lengths of the gestational periods had been gradually decreasing.

Amoreena's was listed at 110 days. A mere three weeks away. Impossible.

No less significant, the destinations of three-quarters of the cases were large medical centers specializing in organ transplants, or private research laboratories, most foreign, and all described as conducting clinical trials in such diverse disease processes as cancer, diabetes, and Parkinson's. And gene therapy.

The remaining cases, seventeen drones in all, were received by Meechum's Ensenada facility, Clínica de la Baja.

What had been most unsettling, though, was isolating the gene deletions. One-half of the surrogates' data summaries had demonstrated isolated gene deletions in their respective babies or drones; for example, Olga Sales. Only after referring to last semester's notes on inborn errors of metabolism had she grasped the significance of this seemingly arbitrary finding. Genes coded for specific proteins that controlled how the human body functioned. In essence, they formed the blueprint by which every human organism developed.

If a specific gene was missing, or deleted, then the resulting organism would be defective. Amoreena flipped back through the printouts. For instance, Olga Sales's babies would be missing the gene that coded for insulin, thus all would be born with diabetes mellitus. Was it just coincidence that all Ms. Sales's offspring had been dispersed to a major diabetes research laboratory in Guadalajara, Mexico? If so, the *coincidences* were rampant. Drones with deleted genes for Parkinson's and Alzheimer's went to laboratories and medical centers specializing in neurologic disorders; deleted genes controlling obesity, arthritis, hypertension, and breast cancer to other specialized research facilities.

Amoreena cringed at the idea. The bastards were purposely manipulating the genetic code to clone disease-specific individuals to be used in medical research. The perfect *white mice*.

And if that wasn't iniquitous enough, it appeared many of the term drones, those without specific gene deletions, had been targeted for organ harvesting. Like hers.

Amoreena picked up Godinez's note. "It's far worse than I thought." How could she disagree? She suspected Meechum Corporation was not only a major player in the business of fetal tissue for experimentation but also a prominent producer of fetal and infant organs for transplantation purposes. And at a handsome profit, she mused.

She was still in the dark regarding the PAG and BG genes. She went back to her notes. *Sus scrofa* and *Papio anubis*.

"What the hell . . . ?" she muttered, reaching for her freshman biology syllabus. She thumbed to the index but failed to find either *Papio anubis* or *Sus scrofa*. She was about to slam it shut when her eyes settled on *Homo sapiens*, followed by a long list of pages. One in particular drew her attention, a taxonomic table of vertebrate organisms, categorized by their genus and species titles.

The table covered two complete pages and was laid out alphabetically. Amoreena drew in her breath when she reached the Ps and Ss. *Papio anubis* was the taxonomic name for an olive baboon and *Sus scrofa*, a domestic pig. Was Meechum cloning pigs and baboons, too? That was the only *acceptable* explanation. She was aware pigskin was used in the treatment of human burns, and baboon and chimpanzee organs were occasionally substituted for their human counterparts.

Amoreena couldn't ignore the other possibility, though. What if the small percentages of pig and baboon genes noted on the printouts indicated true gene additions? The thought was too monstrous to consider rationally.

Though she realized it was far too late for Risken to be in, she dialed his office anyway and left a second recorded message for him to call ASAP. She wished there was some way to contact Godinez, but she knew that was impossible.

Next, she grabbed the purloined disk and went to her bedroom. Byte was awake now and followed, but she noted the puppy kept at a distance. Searching through her desk, she found a blank flexible diskette. She slid the Meechum disk into the port and instructed the computer to begin transferring the information to the computer's hard disk. Then she transferred the same data back to the blank diskette. The second copy she'd place in her mother's safety-deposit box for safekeeping.

With the transfer complete, she placed both diskettes in her purse and returned to the kitchen. Dawn had arrived pink and cloudless, and from the window she could see birds dancing around the bird feeder. Too wired even to consider sleep, she drank a glass of juice and refreshed Byte's water and food bowls.

After letting the puppy out in the backyard, Amoreena showered and dressed. At seven she called the hospital to inquire about her mother's status. The AM shift nurse reported Geneva had spiked a temperature around 5 A.M. and intravenous antibiotics had been initiated by the on-call physician. More disconcerting was the news that Dr. Gillespie had not arrived for morning rounds.

Amoreena tried paging the oncologist herself, only to have the operator reiterate that his pager remained out of service.

Where the hell was he?

"Millie, you up?" she called out. She heard movement from her roommate's bedroom.

"I am now." Millie emerged wrapped in a flannel gown.

"Mom spiked a temp," Amoreena said. "I need to go to the hospital."

"You get any sleep?"

"No. And Gillespie seems to have taken an early Christmas vacation."

"How you feel?"

"The baby's kicking up a storm." Until she heard from the oncologist on her sonograms, Amoreena refused to entertain the thought of three babies.

Byte yelped from the backyard.

"Oh shit, I forgot." Amoreena opened the back door, and the pup bounded in.

She waited until Millie had finished pouring a cup of coffee before speaking. "Get dressed, and I'll give you a lift to your parents'."

The cup stopped midway to Millie's lips. "Why?"

"Because I don't think you should be staying here alone."

Millie eyes moved suspiciously to the stack of computer printouts. "What did you find?"

"I think Meechum Corp.'s producing genetically altered babies for medical research and organ transplantation."

"*Genetically* as in Dolly the cloned sheep. You gotta be kidding."

"And they might take it upon themselves to return here looking for their precious disk."

"At which time I'd be better served to be someplace else." Millie set the unfinished cup on the counter. "Give me fifteen minutes." She turned and rushed back down the hall.

Amoreena gathered her notes and folded them so that they'd fit neatly in her purse. She was worried about missing Risken's call, but she'd try reaching the investigator again from the hospital. Checking her bedroom once more, she hesitated when she spied the tiny vial of blue pills Dr. Rafael had dispensed to her. No matter what she'd learned so far, she still couldn't imagine actually killing her own offspring. Though she empathized with Gretchen Bayliss's situation, discovering a child was missing a certain gene did not make the fetus inhuman.

Is that all Gretchen Bayliss discovered?

Amoreena palmed the pills in one hand and started to flush them down the drain but changed her mind while the faucet ran. Instead, she dropped the pills and vial in her purse. She'd save the poison for Risken. The tablets might help in building a case against Becker and his corporation.

While Millie finished dressing, Amoreena stole a look out the front window. The street was quiet. No gray vans parked curbside.

"Ready." Millie carried a small suitcase and her portable computer notebook.

"You look like you're going on a trip."

Millie set the luggage next to the front door. "I decided to stay at my parents' for the holidays. You're welcome to come along."

"I'll be okay. I might sleep over at Mom's apartment."

Byte dashed between both girls, his small claws sliding along the wood floor.

Millie reached for the dog, but Byte reversed directions. "What are we doing to do about him?" she asked. "Dad's terribly allergic to animal dander, and we can't leave him here."

Amoreena agreed. "I'll take him with me. Mom's apartment has a small porch. He'll be safe there."

"You sure?"

"I'll watch him." She called the pup her way. Byte made it to her ankles, then bounded away, eliciting a weak grin from Amoreena. "He's not bad company," she said.

"He tries."

"Let's go."

Silver fired on the third attempt. Amoreena had just thrown the car in reverse when she heard faint ringing from the house.

"The phone!" both exclaimed simultaneously.

Millie unlocked the door, making way for Amoreena to get inside first.

She lifted the receiver an instant before the fifth ring triggered the answering device.

"Hello," she said, expecting and hoping for either Dr. Gillespie or Risken. It was neither.

"Are you all right?" Irene asked. "You sound out of breath." Amoreena winced at Millie. "I'm fine," she said.

"Dear," Irene began, "I don't want to alarm you prematurely, however a small abnormality was detected on one of your blood tests."

The news did not affect Amoreena nearly to the extent that it would have if she'd heard it a week ago. Or even twenty-four hours ago.

"What kind of abnormality?" she asked, playing along.

"It's not serious, but a follow-up test will be required. Can you come in to the clinic in say an hour?"

"I saw Dr. Rafael yesterday. He reported everything as fine," she lied.

"We only received the results today," Irene said.

Lying bitch. Unless a missing computer disk could be classified as an abnormal test result.

Amoreena forced her voice to remain calm, with just the right amount of tension to make her excuse plausible. "Irene, my mother's taken a turn for the worse."

"I'm so sorry."

"I can make it in, but it'll have to be closer to noon. Will that be okay?"

"We'll be expecting you then, dear. And don't worry. Everything will be fine."

Irene's last statement came across cluttered with background traffic noises, giving Amoreena the impression the clinic administrator was speaking over a cellular phone line.

She set the receiver in its cradle. "Irene wants to see me."

Millie looked aghast. "Surely you're not going."

"Do I have 'fool' painted across my forehead? Let's get the hell out of here."

Polita turned the corner and meandered slowly down the quiet residential street, checking for the correct address. As a young girl in Central America she'd dreamed of growing up in a neighborhood similar to this, where children could safely play soccer in the street or fly a kite from the front yard.

It wasn't too late, she told herself. At least her children, when she decided to have any, would be given the opportunities she never had early on.

She pulled to the curb in front of a small two-bedroom house and double-checked the street address. This was the one, though she looked with chagrin at the empty carport.

Before exiting the car, she studied the street, both in front and behind her, and saw nothing to raise her suspicion. Though still a member of the 'fraternity,' a word Dr. Becker frequently used, it would be imprudent to abandon all caution, especially in light of the sudden tightening of security at all the clinics. And now there was talk of postponing the opening of the new San Diego facility. She'd been given no reason why, just explicit instructions to return to Guatemala.

She'd been unable to contact Luis, and no one else at the Santa Ana facility was aware of any problem. So they stated.

Polita walked to the front door and knocked. The Anglo

would have to be told the truth. If the girl needed proof, Polita would show her the photographs, though this would be used as a last resort.

She waited a moment and knocked again, this time more forcefully. No one was home. Damn. She had time for one more pass by the girl's college before catching the 10 A.M. flight out of LAX.

Chapter Twenty-seven

The apartment expelled a depressing solemn smell that as soon as Amoreena unlocked the door and peered inside, she knew she'd never forget. Everywhere, the stale air carried subtle redolent reminders of her mother's presence—the soft scent of the perfume she'd been wearing when the paramedics had tramped across the rug, the fragrance of her mom's favorite potpourri, and the pungent odor of overripe fruit stocking a past holiday gift bowl adorning the kitchen table.

Byte leaped ahead and dashed under the dining room coffee table. Much of the room's furnishings still lay in moderate disarray since being hastily rearranged by the EMTs to make room for the stretcher.

Amoreena had to coax the dog out and lead him to the cramped screened back porch. The plants appeared badly in need of water, but she was too hurried to gather the pitcher and wet them. She set out a water bowl and a plate of Puppy Chow.

"Don't disturb your neighbors," she said gently, before sliding the door shut. Through the glass she saw the pup stare up inquisitively from his haunches as if this were some new game. He yelped twice before padding over to sniff at one of the potted rosebushes.

When she looked again from the front entrance, Byte had resumed watching her, this time his nose held so close to the sliding door, she could see his breath fogging the glass. She waved once and relocked the apartment after her.

Amoreena maintained the same high level of vigilance driving to the hospital that she'd kept while dropping Millie off at her parents' place, but detected nothing suspicious, no tailgating gray vans.

She parked as near the front entrance as possible and rushed inside, choosing the first available elevator to the oncology ward. With each step, she felt the baby give an almost identical kick as if the fetus were mimicking her every move. Though not uncomfortable, the sensations evoked no pleasure either. Since seeing the disk's data, too much inside had *changed*. More than ever, she wanted to hear Dr. Gillespie's interpretation of her ultrasound images. She needed to be re-assured, both about the pregnancy and her mother. She felt certain by now, she'd find the oncologist near her mom's bed-side, evaluating the situation and issuing appropriate orders.

She suppressed the sinking sensation in her gut as the elevator rose. What if Dr. Gillespie wasn't there? What if the oncologist still hadn't checked in? She thought about having given him her sonograms. She prayed there was no correlation. Regardless, once she'd determined her mom was in no immediate danger, she'd drive to the bank to access her mother's safety-deposit box, then proceed to the police. If Irene Leggett was so eager to draw her blood, she could come down to the City of Orange Police Department and collect it there.

Amoreena's expression hardened as soon as she stepped off the elevator. Rosalind Cates and two other physicians she was unfamiliar with were gathered at the nurses' station. A nurse and therapist passed her in the corridor, both with dismay etched on their faces.

That all-too-familiar sinking sensation rolled over Amoreena. She strode by the utilization chairperson toward her mother's room.

Ms. Cates stepped quickly, blocking her path. "Ms. Daniels, I need to have a word with you."

Amoreena moved around her bulky form. "After I see my mother." She proceeded down the hall.

"Your mother's been transferred to ICU," Cates called after her.

Ignoring the woman, Amoreena didn't stop until she'd entered what had been Geneva Daniels's room. She froze just inside the doorway. The bed lay empty. She watched briefly as a cleaning woman disinfected the handrails with a cloth rag.

"Why wasn't I paged?" Amoreena fumed, marching back to the nurses' station.

Cates ushered her to a private cubicle. She held a newspaper under an arm. "Dr. Brettner didn't have your pager number."

"Who's Dr. Brettner? Dr. Gillespie's Mom's doctor," Amoreena spit back. Out of the corner of one eye, she noticed the two physicians exchange uneasy glances.

"Ms. Daniels," Cates began again, "as of this morning, Dr. Brettner will assume all Dr. Gillespie's duties. I have some unfortunate news."

"That's not your decision," Amoreena cut her off. She started to move away, but a firm grip on her forearm stopped her. "Let go of me," she wrenched her arm away.

"You're making this difficult."

"I'll show you difficult." Amoreena reached for the clerk's phone. She punched 0. "Give me hospital administration," she demanded.

Cates dropped the newspaper on the desk in front of her, opened to page three.

"Administration can't help you, Ms. Daniels. As I attempted to tell you, Dr. Gillespie was killed yesterday evening. I'm sorry, as is the entire staff." She strode quietly away.

The headline read like a bad dream.

PROMINENT ONCOLOGIST VICTIM OF ATTEMPTED CARJACKING

Amoreena felt like all the wind had been sucked from her lungs. Even the sharp jab in her abdomen failed to break through her mask of confusion and anguish as she languished over the story.

The details were sketchy. While carrying some last-minute holiday gifts from a local department store back to his car, the cancer specialist had been accosted in the parking lot and fatally stabbed. There were several witnesses who described the assailants as two males in ski masks, medium height and build. After breaking into the physician's blue Lexus, both had departed the scene in a gray or white van. No license plate was given. Anyone with information was requested to call a Detective Jim Clark of the Santa Ana Police Department. A phone number followed.

Amoreena sat paralyzed, thankful to be left alone in the medical ward's conference room. She couldn't accept responsibility, she wouldn't accept responsibility, yet her refusal did nothing to clear away the black stain of guilt spreading over her psyche.

Had she unwittingly contributed to Dr. Gillespie's demise? What had been evident on her sonograms? She tried to recall who'd witnessed her giving the ultrasounds to the oncologist. A ward clerk, a nurse, an orderly—no one significant came to mind. Or was his death just a terribly horrific coincidence?

Every nerve in her body screamed otherwise.

She watched her fingers claw toward the phone cord as if her hand belonged to a stranger. She tugged, pulling the phone across the conference table until it lay within her reach.

She dialed the number listed in the paper. She asked for Detective Clark and was promptly placed on hold.

"Dr. Gillespie, please forgive me," she grieved, waiting.

Amoreena was still on hold when the conference room door flew open. A nurse waved frantically with one hand.

"Dr. Brettner needs you in ICU. Now."

"I'll be right there."

"It's your mother," the nurse said gravely. "You better hurry."

A man's gravelly voice came on the line. "Hello."

"I'll call you right back," Amoreena said, and hung up.

Please don't let Mom die, Amoreena pleaded silently, as the nurse escorted her to the hospital's intensive care unit. Once inside, a large-statured man identifying himself as Dr. Jarvis Brettner led her toward a cramped X-ray viewing chamber.

Over the doctor's shoulder, she watched as a respiratory therapist, several nurses, and an anesthesiologist hovered over a patient's bed. She recognized her mother's red veil scarf draped across a tray.

She started to break away.

Dr. Brettner touched her arm gently. "Ms. Daniels, your mother's in the process of being stabilized. I'll take you to her as soon as she's ready."

Amoreena allowed the doctor to steer her to the unit's radiology bay.

As he arranged a series of CT films on the viewing windows, he spoke candidly. "We're all very sorry about Dr. Gillespie, he was a fine colleague, but at the moment, we're in the midst of a serious crisis. One of the tumors in your mother's brain has eroded into a rather large blood vessel." He pointed. "All the white you see in the ventricles is blood."

Amoreena felt like her heart died. The entire film looked white! "I thought she just had a fever."

He explained further. "I've consulted with neurosurgeons and, because of the vessel's precarious location and your mother's underlying condition, there is no safe surgical procedure for this type of intracranial emergency."

"What *can* be done?"

"I promise you we'll do all that's necessary to make her comfortable."

Amoreena grabbed his sleeve, his meaning clear. "Mom's dying, isn't she."

"I assure you, she won't feel any pain. I'm terribly sorry to have to break the news this way." The oncologist stared uncomfortably across the ICU a moment. "Under any circumstances, this kind of outcome is devastating for all concerned, but especially today. Following periods of lucidity, which will gradually taper off, she'll eventually lapse into a comatose state."

"How is she now?"

Dr. Brettner shut off the light of the viewing window. "At this time she's coherent. I didn't tell her the specifics regarding Dr. Gillespie's absence, though she asked. I'll leave that up to you."

"I can go now?"

He nodded awkwardly, obviously distressed.

At the exit, Amoreena paused. "I appreciate all you've done."

The oncologist shrugged. "I wish it could've been more."

The nurse had arranged a rolling partition around her mother's bed, lending the corner more privacy. Amoreena squeezed between an opening and up to the bedside. Geneva Daniels lay motionless, buried under a mound of blankets. A single IV entered her chest just above the right clavicle, and the incandescent lighting gave her skin a ghostly, pallid appearance. Its texture looked as thin and fragile as tissue paper.

"Mom, I'm with you," she said softly.

Geneva's eyes remained closed.

A panicky flutter jolted Amoreena. "Is she . . . ?"

A nurse checked the radial pulse and shook her head, before stepping out. Amoreena did the same, taking several attempts to locate the barely perceptible beat under her fingertips. It was so weak.

The baby moved inside her, and this time she despised the sharp stabbing pains. Had everything she'd done been for nothing? She squinted her eyes shut, stifling the urge to scream out loud. Though tears warmed her cheeks, she buried the sobs within. She promised herself she'd remain strong. No matter what.

"It's Amy, Mom," she said, squeezing her mother's hand.

The contact elicited no response. However, she could hear a faint rhythmic gurgling coinciding with Geneva's irregular respirations.

Amoreena pulled a chair close. She didn't want to miss a detail. For a period of time, she didn't know how long, all else was forgotten. If she shifted just a little, she saw how the dim light would smooth the wrinkles and negate the blotches, giving her mother's face an ethereal quality. She lifted the scarf from the tray and placed it back over Geneva's bare scalp, just the way she would have preferred.

Amoreena saw no pain, only a woman resting comfortably after waging a war no human could have waged with more honor and dignity. It would be next to impossible to love and respect a person more. In vivid pictures, past images flashed before Amoreena's eyes—proudly bringing home that first straight A report card, her first bra, their first mother-daughter talk, her first date, her first driving lesson together, they went on and on. The high school graduation, her mom's waiting up after parties until she was safe at home, career discussions, college, and finally *the* diagnosis.

The gates swung open, and this time she was powerless to curb the sobs. Amoreena cried quietly, her face buried in her hands.

"Don't go yet," she choked. "There's so much I haven't told you. Oh Mom, I don't want to be alone."

"Amy." Geneva's voice rose above the sobs.

Amoreena gripped the slender fingers. "I'm here, Mom. Please don't go." The last words came in a whisper.

Her mother's eyelid fluttered open, only briefly, before closing. "Baby, we tried, didn't we."

"Our very best."

"How is the baby?"

"Moving more every day. Mom, I wanted to tell you—"

Geneva's grip stopped her. "Take care of her, Amy, just like you took care of me. I'm so very proud of you."

"I will."

"Promise me."

"I promise."

"You'll make a fine mother and physician, Amoreena. I'm gonna miss you so terribly, baby." Geneva shuddered suddenly. "Hold me. Hold your mother tight."

"I love you," Amoreena said, scooping both arms around the shaking frail body.

She heard her mother begin to hum.

"Remember?" Geneva whispered, interrupting a bar.

"I'll never forget."

"Sing it with me?"

"Don't leave, Mom."

Together, they sang Amoreena's namesake song, as they'd sung together since she was a tiny child.

> *Lately I've been thinking*
> *How much I miss my lady*
> *Amoreena's in a cornfield*
> *Riding in the daybreak.*
> *Rolling through the haze, oh,*
> *Like a puppy child.*

Amoreena continued to sing softly, long after the humming had ceased.

Dark had descended on the medical center when Amoreena left the hospital. The doctors had been gracious enough not to rush the finalities at the end. There'd been a few papers to sign, and after Rosalind Cates and the oncologist had offered their condolences, she'd been allowed as much time as she'd needed with her mother. She didn't remember how long she stayed, clasping the slender, cold hands, nor could she recall gathering up the few belongings in the small suitcase. She did recall feeling so utterly insignificant and alone, just a minuscule spot on the fabric of time. And how one less spot was going to create such a monstrous hole in her own life.

The funeral would be sometime next week.

Amoreena shut off the radio, disinclined to listen to someone else's holiday cheer. In her mind she kept hearing the obscure Elton John number. "Amoreena" was the first song she remembered learning, her mother singing it to her as a lullaby and then later when she'd learned to walk and talk.

> *Amoreena's in a cornfield*
> *Riding in the daybreak.*
> *Rolling through the haze, oh,*
> *Like a puppy child.*

The baby kicked.

"Stop it," she snapped.

She felt trapped in a daze, her emotions shrouded in a heavy fog of gloom and despair. She'd failed to return Millie's repeated pages and attempting to contact Risken or the Santa Ana detective had seemed out of the question in light of the day's events.

Her mother was dead. Dr. Gillespie was dead. Amoreena wiped at her eyes. In a way, the cancer had licked all three of them. How could God be so cruel?

Her mother's apartment was dark when she parked on the street. As soon as she unlocked the door, she heard Byte's barking, and somehow the puppy's eager greeting gave her sustenance. She dropped her mother's suitcase near the kitchen table. "I'm back," she said, her timbre reflecting more vigor than she felt inside.

Amoreena slid open the porch door and watched the rambunctious dog ricochet across the living room carpet like an errant billiard ball. She decided a leash was in order. On top of everything else, she didn't want to risk losing Millie's pet in a strange neighborhood.

"Wait here," she said.

Silver sat where she'd parked the Mustang, near a security lamp. Returning to the car, she slowed halfway down the sidewalk. The passenger door was partially open. Panic swept her. Hastily she jerked the door open all the way, fearing and knowing what she wouldn't find.

The computer printouts and the envelope holding the two disks were missing from the front seat.

"Damn it," Amoreena cursed, sliding her hands around the cushions and along the empty floorboard. How could she be so stupid? She'd made it so easy for them. She hadn't even locked the car doors.

The voice came from less than five feet away.

"Are you looking for these?" Irene asked.

Chapter Twenty-eight

"Step away from the car," Irene ordered.

Amoreena remained where she stood, partially shielded by the open passenger door. "I'm going to the police," she said.

"Not tonight, dear."

Irene took a purposeful step nearer. Besides the envelope and her purse holding the computer printouts, Amoreena saw her ultrasound jacket and another object concealed in the administrator's hand.

"We missed you in the clinic today," Irene said casually.

"I had an emergency."

"Yes, I'm aware. Your mother's death is regrettable, though by no means unforeseen." Irene moved closer.

Amoreena opened her mouth to scream for assistance but a strong hand from behind clasped over her lips, preventing her from producing anything more audible than a muted gasp. Simultaneously, she felt a sharp pain in her right thigh and looked down just as Irene withdrew the syringe.

The effects of the drug were immediate.

For a terrifying two seconds every muscle in her body contracted violently out of sync, making it impossible to catch her breath. At one point, Amoreena thought she would actually rend apart, and the escalating activity in her abdomen told her she wasn't the only one adversely affected by the injection. Just as rapidly, the convulsions passed, though not the terror. Her surroundings began to spin out of control, and she was falling, tumbling helplessly through space, though she could see perfectly well she was still standing, albeit supported by a pair of thick forearms around her chest.

"Close your eyes," she heard Irene order.

She did, and her equilibrium rapidly stabilized.

"Better? Don't nod."

The warning came too late. As soon as Amoreena moved her head, the intense vertigo returned, whipping between her eyes like a tiny cyclone.

She froze, afraid to even talk, petrified of the incapacitating spinning. She feared she'd miscarry if it returned, or suffer a heart attack.

Irene issued an order in Spanish.

Amoreena felt herself being escorted away from Silver. She was too frightened to resist. She peeked with one eye and saw a broad-chested man just off her left shoulder. He smelled of garlic.

"If you move, move very slowly," Irene instructed. "Nothing abrupt. Don't open your eyes because any stimulation of the eye muscles will precipitate the drug's effect. You can talk, but do so with little exertion and very slowly."

"What is . . . ?" She couldn't complete the sentence.

"It's called Naldonone," Irene said. "Very disruptive to the vestibular system. In higher doses, its quite lethal. It will not harm the drones, though if they become excessively agitated, I cannot guarantee *your* safety."

Amoreena heard a van door slide open and felt herself roughly positioned in a cushioned seat. Byte's frantic barking sounded like the puppy's yelps were bouncing off the walls of the Grand Canyon.

"Vincinio," Irene ordered, *"mata el perro."* Her tone had turned vehement.

Heavy footsteps drifted away.

A panic she hadn't known before struck Amoreena.

"What did you tell him?" she asked.

The inhuman coolness in Irene's voice frightened her even more.

"I said, kill the dog," the administrator answered calmly.

"No!" Amoreena gasped. She lunged for the door and found herself writhing on the floorboard, the van suddenly cartwheeling around her. An overpowering nausea threatened to empty her stomach.

"Don't be a fool," Irene said.

Amoreena no longer heard the puppy's barking as she tried to clear her burning throat of gastric acid. She retched, spitting saliva onto the van's carpet.

"Here, sip this," Irene instructed.

Amoreena felt a plastic straw between her lips and she sucked in a mouthful of water. The liquid was cool and carried a slightly minty taste. She found she could open her eyes but only one at a time, and only if she didn't move her head too quickly.

Irene assisted her back to her seat.

Amoreena listened. However, she could hear no noise coming from her mother's apartment. Using one eye, she saw that all the lights inside the unit had been extinguished. Momentarily, she recognized Silver's rough idling, then it too faded.

"Don't hurt the dog," Amoreena whispered hoarsely. "He's just a puppy." She began to shiver.

Irene placed a blanket over her. "Puppies are relatively inexpensive and can be replaced easily."

"You're a goddamn bitch."

Irene patted Amoreena's wrist and stepped outside, sliding the door shut after her.

In the dark, Amoreena attempted to peer out the window, but was thwarted each time by the vertigo. What little she did see indicated the street was deserted. Silver was no longer parked at the curb. She sucked in her breath to scream and again found her equilibrium turn acutely askew. If not for the seat belt, she would've tumbled sideways. It required all her will to prevent herself from vomiting.

A heavy fatigue descended over her, and she wondered if that was another of the drug's effects.

She never heard the van door open. She just knew that it did because garlic assaulted her nostrils. She felt a large hand grab her wrist at the radial pulse.

"How is she?" Irene asked.

The man said, *"Bien."* He climbed in beside Amoreena, while Irene slid in behind the steering wheel.

"Watch her carefully, Vincinio," the administrator said. "This *vaca*'s unlike the others."

"El gusto es mio, señora."

He moved closer, and when one of his hands brushed against Amoreena's breast, her attempt to twist away was met with more vertigo. The second time he touched her, she realized it was not accidental.

The van began to roll.

"We'll be in San Diego before ten," Irene said.

Vincinio grunted his approval.

Each sharp turn the vehicle made precipitated more sensations of disequilibrium and after a brief stop and go, Amoreena knew she could no longer resist.

"I'm going to get sick," she said.

The van slowed, and something light landed in her lap.

"Hold that over her mouth, Vincinio," Irene ordered.

Amoreena groped the two hairy wrists, helping to adjust the plastic bag, and promptly vomited. Immediately she felt better and savored the water offered her.

"Better?" Irene asked.

"What happened to Byte?" Amoreena asked.

Vincinio held one hand out in front of her face. His skin smelled of stale sweat.

"El perro bite me. See, *señorita."*

Using one eye Amoreena saw an ugly gash running diagonally across the dorsum of one swollen knuckle. Coagulated blood caked its rough edges.

"What you think about that?" he asked.

"I hope you die," Amoreena said hoarsely.

Vincinio laughed. "El perrito bite no mas."

Irene said, "Try to rest, dear."

"Where are you taking me?"

"On a little trip."

"Kidnapping wasn't in my contract."

"Page twelve, paragraph two," Irene reminded her. "Surrogate may be required to deliver child in a foreign country. At the corporation's expense, of course."

"I won't go."

"You're in no position to negotiate. Who else saw the disk?"

Amoreena didn't answer until another wave of nausea passed. "A medical investigator," she said with as much bravado as she could muster. "He has a copy."

"You're lying," Irene said. "Go to sleep. We'll discuss this later."

The van entered the interstate. The vertigo lessened considerably with the straight shot south. Powerless to hold her lids open, Amoreena settled back in the seat. Though the fetuses continued to move jerkily under her clothes, she experienced no real discomfort. A profound sadness descended over her that was as thick and real as the darkness in the van's interior. She wept quietly within herself, unsure of how much of the melancholy was due to the drug and how much was situational. Her own mother's death tore at her insides, creating an ugly festering wound no amount of sedation could conceal. The puppy's wanton murder only exacerbated her pain. Just the thought of Byte frolicking after the birds in the bird feeder brought on another round of tears. She never would've believed a dead puppy could have affected her so.

She fell into an uneasy sleep, her shoulder resting against the door panel and, when she awoke, she found herself alone in the backseat. The fine vibrations and low din of the vehicle's engine told her the van was still moving at a steady speed. The nonexistent fetal activity in her abdomen was a welcome relief.

She tested her equilibrium by opening one eye. She looked out a window and saw a swath of stars dotting the black sky. The brief abrupt obliteration of the Milky Way by a freeway overpass stimulated only a fraction of the vertigo. Maybe the drug's effects were wearing off.

Irene still sat behind the wheel. In the ebb and flow of the traffic beams, Amoreena saw wrinkles and crow's-feet spiking from the corners of the administrator's eyes. Vincinio sat in the passenger side, his large head wedged between the headrest and window. His snoring sounded like the purring from a sleeping tiger.

She drew in two deep breaths. It dawned on her that arrangements for her mother's funeral would need to be made. The thought of her mom's body lying in a local mortuary over Christmas brought on new waves of gloom and urgency. She'd wait until San Diego before attempting her escape.

Quietly, Amoreena practiced flexing her arms and legs. Though her muscles felt weak and sore, some of her coordination and strength had returned.

She began to formulate a plan.

"You're awake," Irene said, hearing the activity from the backseat.

Amoreena groaned. "So dizzy. How long will this last?"

"You were administered a small dose. Several more hours."

Amoreena refrained from asking more questions for fear of alerting her captors of the status of her improved mental state. She groaned again and sat back, aware of her seat-belt restraints. Her attempts to release the clasp were in vain. She was strapped in.

"I need to lie down," she moaned.

"We're almost there, twenty minutes."

"I'm getting sick again." She gagged.

Irene nudged Vincinio and said something in Spanish. Groggily at first, the big man twisted around and, using a small key, released the clasp.

Amoreena tumbled supine on the cushioned seat.

"The doors are locked," Irene warned. "Any attempted escape will be dealt with severely."

"I just want to sleep." Amoreena yawned, keenly aware of the increasing traffic noises outside. She guessed they'd entered the city limits. Somehow she had to get the van stopped. A trickle of perspiration coursing down her thigh gave her the excuse she required.

"I think I'm bleeding," she groaned.

"Are you sure?" Irene asked.

"I feel something wet on my leg."

"Damn," the administrator cursed softly.

Amoreena heard Irene talk briefly on a cellular phone, before saying "Dr. Becker will examine you at our San Diego clinic. Are you cramping?"

"A little," she answered, though her abdomen felt more empty than anything else. Still no movement. She began to worry the Naldonone might have accomplished what Dr. Rafael's tiny vial of pills had been designed to do.

She shifted gently when the van swerved down an exit ramp. She counted five turns before feeling two sharp bumps. The van descended a shallow decline, then rolled to a standstill. From the window, Amoreena could see a concrete column and cement ceiling. They were stopped in an underground parking garage. Her best and only chance would be to reach the street.

"How do you feel?" Irene asked.

"Sore." She heard both front doors open and close. Drawing her feet up along the cushion she waited. If she could somehow isolate Irene one on one, her chances of success would be greatly improved.

Luck was with her so far. The door facing her feet slid open. When Vincinio reached in to grasp her ankle, Amoreena gasped.

"I'm cramping real bad," she said. The vertigo returned but with little of its prior intensity. Amoreena screamed. "Hurry!"

Nearly dropping the cell phone, Irene regained her grip and dialed. "Get a doctor to the parking garage. Stat!" she added, followed by, "Where the hell is he?"

Amoreena cried out a second time, ignoring the spinning. She made herself pant.

Irene and Vincinio exchanged a few rapid lines in Spanish.

Amoreena gasped again clutching her midsection. She could actually feel movement inside her.

"I'm getting Becker," Irene said. "Watch her."

Amoreena heard her sprinting steps echo on the hard concrete. So she'd have to take her chances with Meechum's hired gorilla.

She saw the ugly scar punctuating his right cheek curl lasciviously as his eyes leered at a spot between her thighs. Drawing him into position would be the easy part.

"Please," she pleaded, holding out one palm.

Vincinio never hesitated. Spitting out a sunflower seed, he leaned inside the van. She waited until his face drew even with her shoe, before shooting her foot upward. She caught him flush below the Adam's apple. The blow felt like she'd stomped on an aluminum can full of sand. In rapid succession, she used her other foot to nail him on the forehead. He fell backward hard on the garage floor, landing with a heavy thud.

Sliding off the seat, Amoreena's feet hit the cement first. She tried to push herself upward with her hands but buckled forward when a wave of vertigo spun her out of control. She landed facedown on the cold concrete.

She felt thick fingers clawing into her calf and frantically pulled herself out of their reach.

"Help me!" she screamed, scrambling forward on hands and feet.

Vincinio stumbled after her, wiping bloody saliva and seed fragments from his chin with the back of his hand.

Amoreena made for the nearest concrete column and struggled to her feet. With cramps doubling her over, she half crawled, half walked to the next one. Behind her, Vincinio rapidly closed the distance.

"*Vaca!*" he cursed.

She could actually see headlight beams on the street above. Waving her arms, she screamed again.

His impact knocked her sideways, sending her sprawling on the cement floor. Vincinio's bulk crushed the air from her lungs. She couldn't resist his knees prying her legs open. His big, rough hands pressed into her flesh.

He's going to rape me.

Intense fear mortified her. Freeing one arm, she struck at his face, striking only air. She saw two faces, then three, four, all spinning uncontrollably counterclockwise—above her, to her left, right. A searing pain ripped at her insides, so acute she thought she'd been shot.

Running footsteps converged upon her.

She heard Dr. Becker's voice echo as if from some great distance.

"Get off her before you destroy half a million dollars."

The weight was gone. She could finally breathe. The next wave of vertigo, though, sent her tumbling into a deep black abyss.

Somewhere south of the border Amoreena awoke. She was sitting outside in a wheelchair on an asphalt drive. The cool night breeze felt like a thousand rose petals brushing against her skin. It smelled of ocean and fish.

For a terrifying moment, she was afraid to move her head, but gradually, with weak attempts at first, she determined she could look around her without precipitating any untoward effects. Under her clothing, the fetal activity continued, jerky and inconsistent.

On either side of her stood two guards. Both were armed.

Fuzzy and circled by yellow halos, a string of Malibu lights illuminated the entrance to a modern, four-story, gray-concrete building. She saw no windows. Beside the entrance on a grass terrace stood a sign constructed in large block letters.

CLÍNICA DE LA BAJA

She knew the words were significant, yet couldn't place them. Her brain felt like overcooked oatmeal. In her foggy sensorium, the names Ronald Godinez and Ensenada floated in and out of focus.

Figures moved in the shadows. She couldn't be sure they were real. She began to separate different noises—the waves crashing against the rocks, a more constant rumble, perhaps an engine, and a sound that chilled her to the bone—a prolonged shrill scream. This last sound left her feeling frightened and helpless.

Amoreena tried to stand, but a palm on one shoulder resisted her attempt.

"No, por favor," an orderly said.

Irene appeared before her. "Amoreena, you're going to receive another injection before the flight."

"Wha . . . flight?" Amoreena felt like her tongue had swollen to the size of a plum.

Irene spoke sharply and an orderly held a glass to Amoreena's lips.

"Drink, dear," the administrator said. "We can't have our prize surrogate becoming dehydrated."

The water tasted refreshing. She barely noticed the pinprick in her left deltoid. A calm settled over her, squashing down any fear and anxieties. She couldn't recall what Irene had just said. Something about flying. She felt like she was already flying. She couldn't even remember whether her mother was alive or dead.

The wheelchair spun a quarter turn and began to roll. The constant rumble echoed louder, drowning out the sounds of the ocean. She passed several smaller buildings and one security gate before stopping.

Silhouetted on the tarmac, Amoreena could make out the outline of a small passenger jet. A fuel truck was parked behind one wing.

More figures rushed by her. She recognized Dr. Becker and Dr. Luis Rafael. Though Becker made no effort to acknowledge her, Luis looked upon her with profound sadness in his eyes. She thought Dr. Rafael's face appeared bruised, especially under one eye.

Hushed conversations swirled past her ears. She understood little.

She watched with disconnected interest as two men exited a nearby one-story structure and approached, guiding a loaded stretcher toward a van parked just off the tarmac. One stopped beside her to light a cigarette. She recognized the ugly, raised linear mound of flesh scarring his cheek.

Vincinio eyed her disdainfully. Then she felt something in her hand. He forced her to grip the object, which she saw was the handle of a large knife. Then he removed it and pushed on, but not before a gust of wind had raised the sheet covering the corpse.

Amoreena stared at the dead man's face, the eyes gaped obscenely open, the bloody lips retracted from his teeth. She knew she'd seen this man before, but couldn't place the name.

Midway through the six-hour flight, her memory returned.

Chapter Twenty-nine

Millie pulled her coat tight around her waist and stepped back under the sheltering eaves of her parents' front porch. Though nowhere near freezing, the night breeze still carried a bite that chilled her, even with the additional layers of clothing.

Inside, the light remained on in the den. Her mother would continue to read until she'd returned safely home.

Millie checked her watch. Almost midnight. Daryl had sounded about three-quarters stoned when she'd called earlier. After listening to her explanation over the phone, he sobered considerably.

Twin beams from a Ford Bronco slowed and stopped in the middle of the street.

Millie pulled open the front door a crack. "I'm leaving."

"Don't be late."

"Mom, it's already late."

She dashed across the lawn and climbed into the front seat.

"What took you so long? I've been waiting over an hour," she complained, turning the vent so the heater fan hit her face.

"Why'd you page me so late?" Daryl asked.

"I couldn't sleep. Where were you?"

"A party."

"The night before Christmas Eve?"

"It was a Christmas party."

"Thanks for the invitation."

Daryl grinned sheepishly. "Where to first?"

"You okay to drive?" Millie asked, cracking a window to rid the truck's interior of marijuana scent.

"Nerves of steel."

"Okay, Superman, let's get to the medical center. Something's up with Amy's mom, and they won't tell me over the phone."

"You called?"

"Only about fifty times. Amy's not answering any of her pages either."

Daryl shifted into first and made a sharp U-turn. "You think she'd spend the night at the hospital?"

Worry lines creased Millie's forehead. "Only if something really serious happened to her mother."

Daryl shot his passenger a quick look. "You hear about that oncologist, what was his name?"

"Gillespie. It was on the news. He was Ms. Daniels's doctor."

"No shit."

Millie watched a police car zip past them, then glanced at the Bronco's speedometer.

"I'm not speeding," Daryl said defensively.

"Just checking." She tapped her foot impatiently when Daryl was forced to stop at a red light. "If she's not at the hospital, we'll check the house. If not there, she said something about sleeping over at her mother's apartment."

The light switched, and Daryl released the break. "What if she's not at any of those places?"

"She will be. She has Byte." Millie curled her fingers into a fist. "Man, when I find her, I'm going to kick her ass for worrying me so."

Daryl grinned. "You kick Amoreena's ass. Now that I gotta see."

The Gulfstream IV cruised smoothly at thirty-one thousand feet. An hour earlier the corporate jet had hit some turbulence, forcing the pilot to deviate several hundred miles west to avoid a high-pressure system building over central Mexico.

Outside her window, Amoreen could barely make out inter-mittent patches of night sky sandwiched between billowy mountains of obsidian clouds. Below her, nothing but a sea of blackness.

She settled back in her seat, aware she'd witnessed a death in Ensenada, but was still vague on the name. She was getting close, though. She willed herself to relax. It would come.

The cabin's interior was dark, with the exception of an overhead light two seats up where Dr. Becker continued to read. Directly in front of her, she could hear Vincinio's light snoring, and across the narrow aisle, Irene dozed with her head propped against a small pillow. She thought Dr. Rafael occupied one of the seats behind her but didn't know which one. She had no idea how many other passengers the airliner carried, if any.

The jet yawed to the right several degrees, dropped, and then smoothly leveled off. Amoreen experienced an instant of weightlessness which disappeared quickly, leaving a low-grade pressure sensation over her bladder. If she didn't relieve herself soon, she'd wet her pants.

Unbuckling her seat belt, she swiveled her knees into the aisle. Even with the constant adjustments of the jet, her own vestibular system reacted normally, and there was none of the incapacitating vertigo. She looked aft. The only illumination, other than an exit light, came from a blue light. She recog-nized the same type bassinet she'd seen in the clinic. She counted four, two on each side of the fuselage, mounted on specially designed shelves with restraints. Only one sat bathed in the eerie blue glow. Behind the bassinets, she saw a collection of strange-looking accoutrements that gave the en-tire tail section a medivac appearance—cylindrical canisters, tubing, monitoring equipment.

Immediately behind her she could make out six seats, three on either side of the aisle. Guards occupied two of them, both dozing in their green livery. The remaining four were vacant. Not seeing Dr. Rafael added to her disquiet. She could have sworn she'd seen him board the plane, even in her drugged-inebriated state.

She looked forward in the cabin. Still no sign of him.

The jet lurched in midair and settled back on an even plane, the drone of the two engines remaining constant. She could no longer wait. Rising on thighs that felt molded from rubber, she steadied herself by placing one hand on the overhead compartments. She shuffled forward toward a narrow door situated just behind the pilot's cockpit.

Becker looked up over his bifocals. "Where are you going?" he asked.

Amoreena motioned with her free hand. "Is that the bathroom?"

He nodded and went back to his reading.

The room, only a stall, barely yielded enough space to sit. She didn't know what she'd do if she had to vomit. She'd have to do it standing up. At least the seat was clean, and the basin smelled of disinfectant.

She finished quickly and started back down the aisle.

Relieving herself somehow focused her mind and when she reached the medical director's seat, she paused using both hands to maintain her balance. If she did develop the urge to puke, she'd found her first target.

"Why did you kill Dr. Gillespie?" she asked.

He glanced up with a blank stare. "I suggest you return to your seat, Ms. Daniels. Turbulence in a small jet can be quite unsettling when you're not strapped in."

She suddenly remembered the name that had eluded her. "If that question's too difficult, care to give Ronald Godinez a try?"

"Vincinio," she heard Becker say.

The security chief sputtered and coughed like a cold locomotive before piercing Amoreena with a steel gaze. If the man hadn't been breathing, she'd have thought he was dead. She saw absolutely nothing living behind his brown irises.

"What are you going to do, throw me off the plane?" she asked.

"Sit down, Amoreena." Irene had risen and was standing beside her seat. "You're blocking the aisle." The administrator had just begun a step forward when the plane dipped suddenly, sending both women clutching for a handhold.

With felinelike reflexes, Vincinio caught Amoreena under

an arm as her feet lost all sensation of gravity, but not before she glimpsed Irene's lips part in a silent O. For a fraction of a second, the administrator appeared to be suspended by tiny invisible strings, then she spilled sideways, caroming off the armrest and back into her seat.

Like a braking elevator, the flooring quickly returned under Amoreena's shoes, and her knees buckled only minimally, thereby avoiding a nasty fall, courtesy of Vincinio's steadying grasp.

She mumbled a weak "thanks" and returned to her place, fumbling to secure the seat belt.

The door to the cockpit swung open and a man wearing a military uniform poked his head out. Behind him, Amoreena could make out the glowing dials and gauges on the instrument panel.

"*¿Esta bien?*" he asked.

"Try to warn us next time, Esteban," Becker said.

"I sincerely apologize," the pilot atoned, switching to flawless English. "I promise to make the remainder of the trip more accommodating." His eyes hung on Amoreena a moment, then he pulled himself back inside and shut the door.

Amoreena watched Irene struggle to her feet and make a second attempt to move down the aisle. The administrator's skin had taken on a peaked green color, and she walked with one hand touching her abdomen. Inside, Amoreena relished Irene's discomfort. The turbulence obviously wasn't agreeing with her, though she hoped Irene made it to the bathroom before she became sick. The last thing she needed was a firsthand account of Irene's last meal.

As the pilot promised, the flight smoothed considerably, and Amoreena adjusted her seat so she could lean back and stare out the window. She focused her attention on the green light mounted on the starboard wing tip. In microseconds, its flash would vanish and then reappear as the jet's airfoil sliced through the dense blanket of clouds. Soon, the vanishing portion lessened, until the light no longer disappeared at all. She gazed down and saw isolated patches of lights where the overcast had begun to break.

She raised her wrist to check the time and silently cursed.

The bastards had taken her watch. She glanced across the aisle, and found Irene perusing a screen of numbers on a laptop.

Amoreena mustered up the courage to ask for the time, then vetoed the entire idea. She turned back to the window. What the hell did it matter? One, two, or three o'clock. She still wouldn't be missed at home for several more hours.

Millie would sound the alarm first. In the morning her roommate would call the hospital, find out Amoreena's mother had expired, then try to call the apartment because she knew Amoreena wouldn't return to the house. Then her roommate would drive over to Geneva's place when no one answered.

One seat up, Amoreena could hear Vincinio's rasping snore. She wondered how he'd disposed of Byte's corpse. Or if he'd even disposed of it. Millie would have to notify the landlord.

The hypothetical scenario stopped rolling there. Regardless of what Millie and the landlord discovered inside the apartment, a dead strangled pup or an empty unit, Amoreena was sure of one thing. Irene would have made it appear as if Meechum's recalcitrant surrogate had departed voluntarily.

Amoreena sensed a small deviation in the jet's course. Was the sky lightening to the east or was that only her imagination? Amoreena picked out four clouds and assigned the souls of the recently deceased to each—Byte, Ronald Godinez, Dr. Gillespie, granting her mother the largest and most intricately shaped.

"Fly away, Mom," Amoreena whispered. "You're free."

She felt hollow and empty inside, like a mannequin on which her skin had been stretched and glued, living tissue on the outside, dead beneath the plastic.

She dozed and when she awoke the cabin was as still as a windless night. Even the babies lay quiet within their fluid-filled chamber.

Thirty minutes later, the aircraft began its descent.

*   *   *

"*Dios mio*, you're bringing the Anglo here, to Las Canas?" Polita stood dumbfounded and exhausted from having gone almost twenty-four hours without sleep.

Antonio Calientes reached across the expansive teakwood desk for his ornately tooled humidor, one of several in his possession, each designed to hold a different type of premium cigar. He lifted the top and removed a *Donlino*.

"She came voluntarily," he remarked as he stroked the cigar with his slender, almost elegant fingers.

His delicate actions reminded Polita of a sex act, and she wondered if this was his intent. She was too tired to be riled, so she simply watched him with a bemused expression. She'd choose dealing with the elder Calientes brother any day over his younger sibling, Vincinio. Antonio was just a snake, quick to anger and quick to be appeased. In contrast, Vincinio was a true *monstruo*, a monster.

Antonio rose, searching for his matches. "The doctor has allowed me two of these a day."

"So you start before breakfast," Polita said.

"This is my breakfast."

Polita smirked, watching him rifle through his drawers. A small, agile man, he was built the exact opposite of Vincinio. So much so, she wondered, as did everyone else at Las Canas, whether the two men were in actuality really brothers, though she would never make her doubts known. While insulting a general in the Guatemalan military might make you disappear, angering Vincinio would guarantee you a slow, horrible death.

The rich aroma of burning tobacco permeated the room.

"Sit," Antonio said, motioning and dispensing the match in an ashtray in one fluid move.

Polita took three steps across the plush carpet to the nearest chair and did as she was told. All requests from the undisputed chief of Las Canas were treated as commands. She needed little reminding that she was no longer in the United States.

She felt his appraising stare and rose to meet his gaze. She was thankful the air-conditioning in the plantation house was functioning, or she would've been perspiring. General

Calientes had not sent for her so soon after her return to discuss the recent drop in price of sugarcane.

"How was your trip to the land of milk and honey?" he asked.

Polita was always amazed at the general's precise command of the English language, even down to the subtle nuances of sarcasm. You did not truly own a language until you could express yourself sarcastically in that language. Antonio had demonstrated his ownership many times over.

"All the proper accreditation papers for the new San Diego facility have been filed," she answered truthfully, though she knew this was not what he intended to discuss.

Antonio gave her a thoughtful nod before shifting his attention to the burning ember on his cigar. "A computer disk was stolen from one of our clinics in Mexico," he said calmly. "The individual responsible was apprehended. However the disk was no longer in his possession."

"How can you be so sure?"

"Vincinio questioned the young man."

God, Polita thought, squirming under her clothing. She'd overheard Tom Volkman discussing an incident with Irene regarding an irate client, or perhaps it'd been the boyfriend of an irate client. She'd not been made privy to the details. Regardless, she was positive Antonio's use of the word apprehended was a euphemism for murder. She'd never heard of anyone *participating* in one of Vincinio's interrogation sessions and surviving to tell about it.

"Where is the disk then?" she asked, more out of a sense of obligation than any desire to know. She already knew. Why else would the American be brought here?

Antonio lifted a fax. "Señorita Amoreena Daniels had the disk. Two, actually. One was a copy." The general had switched to his native language.

Polita did the same. "International kidnapping cannot be taken lightly. The consequences for our country will be severe."

Antonio raised one eyebrow. "As I already said, she's come voluntarily."

Polita stood suddenly, her anger bubbling to the surface. "Jesus Christ, Antonio, do you expect anyone to believe that? Her own mother was dying. For all we know, she's dead now.

And the Anglo was a responsible student. Would she just up and leave?"

Antonio smiled wickedly. "You have your mother's fight. If I were not fifty-two, I might marry you."

"No, Antonio, you would never marry me. Have me for a mistress, maybe, but never marry."

The smile eroded from the general's face. "I had your mother."

"Yes," Polita said, letting herself back down into the chair so he wouldn't see her wobbling knees. She'd known that for years, thanks to her cousin Luis, but this was the first time Antonio had been so blatantly direct. Just hearing the words made her feel dirty inside. But if not for her *madre's* sacrifice, and a sacrifice it surely must've been, Polita's education would have been nonexistent. Perhaps she, too, would've ended up a *vaca*. Or a Meechum housekeeper like her oldest aunt.

"You will guide Las Canas through the legal maze, Polita." Antonio was talking again. "Irene and Dr. Becker assured me the Anglo's departure will not be unexpected."

"The *Americanos* are not imbeciles."

Antonio grunted while he took a moment to savor the *Donlino*. "Kidnapping will not be the primary issue, though if it is, it will not be as you presuppose."

Polita listened in silence, deeply troubled by the general's circumlocution.

Antonio abruptly ground out the cigar. "Were you aware that five of the ten richest people in the entire world live in the United States?"

"America is the wealthiest nation on earth," Polita responded.

"And that the world's richest human is also an American, worth almost one hundred billion dollars. He could literally buy our country."

"He would never make such a foolish investment," Polita said ruefully.

"*Mi querida*, you don't speak the truth."

"No," Polita said, hurting inside that she'd even utter such a lie. She loved her home unconditionally, with its bountiful natural resources and rich history, and relished the day she'd see Guatemala rise above the political turmoil to emerge a world leader in Latin America. If only . . .

Antonio went on, oblivious to her musings, "And by opening up the lucrative markets to the north, Las Canas can do more for our own people than any government assistance program."

Just don't ask the vacas *how they feel.* Polita kept the thought hidden.

"For that very reason," Antonio continued, "nothing and no one will be allowed to jeopardize our operation."

She'd heard this all before. Polita let her eyes roam over the hand-carved teakwood desk and the general's expensive antiques, representing the work of artisans from numerous countries, museum-quality antiquities that any executor would drool over. Yes, the operation, as Antonio had so succinctly phrased it, demonstrated without a doubt that Las Canas had most definitely done well for the Calientes brothers and Meechum Corporation's private investors.

"But she is an American," Polita said before she realized she'd spoken.

"What of it? Does that place the Anglo above you or me?"

Polita recognized an unwinnable argument when she heard one. "As Las Canas's legal counsel, I will undertake whatever legal maneuvering is necessary to protect our interests," she said, backtracking. "When does she arrive?"

"Today." The general showed her to the door. "Above all, we must avoid any international incident."

"I understand your concern."

Polita waited until she was alone before allowing herself a tiny smile. An international incident. The Anglo may have just provided the very blade with which to slit the great plantation's throat.

Chapter Thirty

Amoreena laid her head back and inhaled in slow succession. The jet had just completed a brief layover in Guatemala City, Guatemala. There in the Central American nation's capital, she'd watched Dr. Rafael and Dr. Becker disembark with several of the bassinets. They'd loaded their cargo into a medivan and driven away across the tarmac. They didn't return for takeoff.

In their places, two young Latin American women had been escorted onto the jet by the attendant. Neither had smiled or talked. They'd taken their seats in the rear of the cabin.

Amoreena adjusted her legs to relieve an ache in her back. She felt dizzy.

"Here, drink this." Irene was holding a plastic glass half-filled with a clear liquid. "It's only water. You can't let yourself become dehydrated."

Amoreena sipped once. It tasted like water. She drank the rest in long swallows, admitting to herself she was genuinely thirsty. She returned the glass.

"More?"

Amoreena shook her head and found the window. The overcast had burned away, leaving the sky virtually cloudless, a brittle blue sheet draped from horizon to horizon. Below, the vanishing city and airport had transformed the landscape into a tessellated patchwork of farms and small villages. Rivers and roadways scrawled haphazardly across crops and ranch-land as if drawn by a child's hand. Far in the distance, Amoreena could see the land buckling skyward, forming an escarpment of peaks and ridges. The mountain range looked purple under the golden sun.

"What's going to happen to me?" she heard herself asking, her eyes glued to the changing geography ten thousand feet below.

"After you deliver, you'll be returned to California," Irene said.

Amoreena twisted in her seat. "After I deliver—I'm not even four months pregnant."

Irene's expression remained inscrutable. "Then I suggest you accept our hospitality. Must I remind you're still bound by the terms of the contract."

"But my finals, graduation." Amoreena sounded phony, and she knew it. She'd never make a good actress. She could feel Irene studying her profile.

"The disk, Amoreena. What did you see?"

"I couldn't get in," she lied. There was no way she was going to drag Millie into this.

"You're lying. The disk was encrypted to record how many times the data is accessed. Two times, Amorcena. Since leaving our Ensenada facility, the disk was hacked into twice. Ronald Godinez and who else?"

"Ask Godinez."

"He's dead, and you know it."

"Then you should've inquired before murdering him."

Irene came as close to a smirk as her pursed lips would allow. "Vincinio did. He possesses quite a persuasive personality. Godinez said he mailed the disk to you."

"I don't believe you," she said, though inside she did. She dredged up from her memory the hideous scream she'd heard at the airport in Ensenada. God knows what Vincinio had done to the poor man before he'd killed him.

Irene waved to the attendant for a drink. "Anything?" She shot a look across the aisle.

Amoreena declined, her mind struggling to redecipher what she'd gleaned from the disk. *One hundred and ten days.* She made a quick mental calculation. If what she interpreted from the data was accurate, that meant she would deliver in ten days. She stifled a shiver. It was never Irene's intention to keep her in Guatemala for three months. In less than two weeks the terms of her contract would be fulfilled. Then what? Godinez had seen the data, and he was dead. She realized she could never reveal what she knew, though questions hounded her at every turn. What kind of pregnancy came to term in three months? And the pig and baboon genes, were they genetic markers of some type? Yet, just asking the questions would prove she'd seen the disk. She couldn't risk it.

She decided to try a different tack. "What will happen to the baby?" she asked, making sure she used the singular form.

"They'll remain here," Irene answered, oblivious of using the plural pronoun.

"To be with the parents?"

"Of course."

Though Amoreena didn't believe the administrator for a second, just hearing the word "parents" made her feel slightly more secure. Any sense of relief evaporated with Irene's next question.

"Why did you show Dr. Gillespie your sonograms?"

Amoreena stiffened with anguish, precipitating a tiny, sharp kick in her abdomen. She loosened her seat belt. "I wanted a second opinion," she said tersely.

"Who gave you permission?"

"I borrowed them on my own," she answered, feeling herself sinking deeper into a state of despair. If she hadn't given Dr. Gillespie her ultrasounds, he'd be alive now. She hated herself for her mistake. But how could she have known?

"You didn't trust our medical staff?" Irene asked. Amoreena turned back for the window. She couldn't bear any more of this Inquisition-style conversation.

"I need to rest," she said weakly.

"We'll talk more on the ground," she heard Irene say.

When Amoreena opened her eyes again, she found the

landscape had undergone a mystical transformation. From the air, it appeared the earth had been carpeted in thick shag. Green stretched in all directions as far as the eye could see. Lush valleys basked in the sun, and wisps of low-lying white clouds shrouded the tips of several of the highest tree-covered ridges. She saw no villages, roads, nothing man-made—only miles and miles of rain forest. The vista was breathtaking. She'd never seen anything like it. Momentarily, she became frightened. If the plane crashed, she knew they'd never be found.

She glanced about the cabin and saw everyone else mesmerized by the view, even Irene and Vincinio. The plane banked to the east, and she felt herself slide against the seat's armrest. The descent accelerated, and she consciously touched her midsection, but the jet's maneuver elicited no untoward response from inside other than a strange fluttering sensation. It was not uncomfortable.

She looked down again and saw huge rectangular plots of cleared land cutting wide yellow swaths through the dense greenery as if a giant lawn mower had made three errant passes, then vanished. Two were parallel, and the third formed the bottom of the topographic U. Forest ran right up to the field's edges.

A guard in back mentioned "*Cana.*"

When their altitude dropped below the highest ridge, Amoreena saw people working the fields. The crop looked like corn.

The jet made another sharp bank and all whispering ceased.

A short distance from the U's bottom, though from the ground it could easily have been a mile, and surrounded on all sides by jungle, a compact cluster of buildings appeared. Under the sun's rays, their skin glistened alabaster white, and they formed a kind of semicircular pattern like short, thick spikes on a wheel. Their architectural lines appeared ultramodern, sharp, impersonal, and functional, and Amoreena recognized the largest one, the one with a large radar disk on top, from the pamphlet she'd received during her orientation. Forming the centerpiece of this tropical Shangri-La, she picked out a stately house, magnificent and rambling with wraparound verandahs and Doric pillars, and shadowed by huge trees. The scene was reminiscent of a pre–Civil War plantation house from the Old South.

Circling the complex, she saw other structures, some appearing more timeworn, even dilapidated, but one in particular commanded her attention. Situated directly behind the radar-disked edifice sat a huge circular concrete building. It looked like one of those cement holding tanks constructed at oil refineries, except this one exhibited a series of odd skylights deforming its flat roof. The sun reflected brightly off the glass domes, and as the plane passed directly over the structure, Amoreena thought she detected an ocean blue tint beyond the glass—the same blue color she'd seen emanating from the bassinets.

One more turn and the runway, an asphalt strip almost half a mile long, came into view. The landing gear locked in place with a gentle jolt, and moments later the Gulfstream touched down smoothly, racing past a military helicopter, jeep, and a pair of aluminum towers, before coasting to a stop in front of a small hangar.

The attendant unbuckled her seat belt and rose.

"Bienvenidos a Las Canas," she wished.

Then bowing her gaze toward Amoreena, she said, "Welcome to Las Canas, *señorita.*"

Chapter Thirty-one

Initially she'd thought the speck against the azure sky was just a bird, maybe even a quetzel, Guatemala's most famous fowl, but rapidly the dark spot had grown into a small plane. With heightened fascination, Gabriella had watched the small jet make a semicircle and float down over the jungle canopy, finally coming to rest on a concrete apron where the runway widened and abruptly terminated in front of a maintenance hangar and a row of fuel pumps.

She hung back and found a shady spot against the wall of the commissary, letting the other girls, *vacas*, proceed ahead down the asphalt road back to the *dormitorios*.

Gabriella watched Antonio and his retinue welcome the passengers as they disembarked the aircraft. She spotted Polita and Humberto observing the same scene from the front seat of a jeep parked next to the hangar. She saw more security personnel milling about, pretending to be on duty yet drawing closer and closer to the parked plane and casting furtive looks at the short flight of stairs descending from the jet's fuselage. She noticed the other *vacas* had slowed and were watching the new arrivals, too.

Gabriella's curiosity was piqued. She'd seen the plantation's private jet land numerous times, and never in the ten months she'd been at Las Canas had she witnessed such a welcoming committee. She brushed a few strands of hair off her forehead and crossed the road to a shallow dirt field for a better view. She could feel her breakfast of *huevos rancheros, tocino, jugo,* and *leche fuerte*, a vitamin-mineral-fortified drink all *vacas* were required to imbibe, churning in her stomach.

She recognized the *gringa prima*, one of the plantation's elite from the United States. She'd heard the women called Irene by Antonio and *La Jefa* by some of the guards. Behind her, plodding down the steps like a two-legged rhino, lumbered El Diablo himself, Vincinio. If she lived to see the day the Las Canas security chief lay lifeless, facedown on the earth in a pool of his own blood, all her pain would have been worth it.

Gabriella shielded her eyes to observe better the two women descending the stairs. Surely this pair wasn't the impetus behind the morning's impromptu reception. Though dressed better perhaps than she'd been upon her arrival, and looking more refreshed, which was understandable since flying in on a jet was far less taxing than enduring a thousand miles of rough road and inclement weather on a broken-down unair-conditioned bus, nonetheless the women gave the impression of being nothing more than typical *vacas*. She watched a stout guard lead them across the tarmac toward the jeep. Humberto's job would be to deliver them to the medical ward for their physical examinations. Within a week the newcomers would be seeded.

The jeep lurched forward and had just begun a sharp turn when it abruptly stopped. Even across the hundred yards of distance, Gabriella saw Humberto jab Polita in the shoulder and point to the jet. The steady buzz of conversation from the other *vacas* stopped. Every pair of eyes, including those of the guards and everyone else on the tarmac, was directed toward the figure standing in the doorway just behind the cockpit.

Gabriella noticed first the unruly mane of thick hair, almost red in the sun, pulled harshly over one shoulder. The girl was tall and carried herself erect, using just one hand on the thin metal railing as she descended the stairs. With a sudden urge to get nearer, Gabriella tore off her sandals and ran halfway across the dirt infield. The Anglo was dressed in blue-cotton maternity pants and a fashionable blouse similar to ones Gabriella had seen modeled in women's magazines. Unlike any other *vaca* at Las Canas, though, this woman conveyed an air of confidence when she moved, from the way she took in the entire scene of ogling stares with a single sweep of her head to the manner in which she passed by Vincinio, almost brushing his arm, yet never acknowledging his presence. She walked directly up to the *gringa primera* and stopped.

The teenager stood, her arms at her sides, and watched this woman, Irene, and Vincinio climb into a second SUV and follow Humberto toward the medical building. Without a doubt, this individual had to be the Anglo Polita had referred to several months ago. *That means she is a* vaca. *Just like the rest of us. But she really isn't like the rest of us*, Gabriella realized. *This* vaca *is from America*.

Gabriella felt a tiny thread of jealousy tug at her heart. She also understood any plans for an escape had suddenly changed.

From the backseat of the SUV, Amoreena could see the beady eyes of the driver, a Hispanic man who looked older than most of her university professors, eyeing her from the rearview. She averted his lubricious stare. Ever since disembarking the jet, she'd felt like the newest fish in a tropical aquarium exhibit.

Amoreena just wanted to sleep, which is what Irene promised, once the physical exam was completed. Any adrenaline rush had dissipated, so Amoreena was confident that once she reclined she'd have no difficulty collecting some much-needed rest. The vehicle's jostling had even failed to ignite the babies. Small wonder. Twenty-four hours of constant disturbances was bound to affect them, too.

"Over there is La Casa de Plantación." Irene was talking again, pointing with one hand and acting more like a docent on a field trip than an abductor. "We simply call it The House. Imagine, it was built during the last century. Beautiful, isn't it."

Amoreena couldn't disagree. Constructed in a shallow rise

overlooking the airfield and central commons, the mansion could have been plucked off the set of *Gone With the Wind*. Six magnificent pillars with thick shafts rising from huge concrete pedestals connected the first and second floors. A wide, airy verandah ran across the entire front of the structure and was met on each side by end gables featuring mullioned windows and pavilions of stuccoed brick. The second-floor entablature included a massive balcony with cast-iron railing.

"There's seventeen rooms," she heard Irene say.

Green. Green. Green. Huge trees with swaybacked limbs sheltered the plantation house in deep shade. Colorful gardens blossomed on all sides, rife with shrubs and poppy flowers and smaller trees, many of which carried orange and yellow fruit.

Even the air smelled richly tropical, sweetly pungent, as if it, too, were alive. The aroma gave Amoreena a head rush. She wondered if she might be experiencing some delayed effects of the drug. She tried to lower her window but found the electronic tab nonfunctional.

Irene spoke to the driver. Amoreena heard a single soft snap.

"Try it now," Irene said.

Amoreena pressed the tab until the window dropped half-open. The warm, humid breeze cleared her head, enabling her to focus on the myriad of hummingbirds and butterflies she saw dancing across the prismatic petals. The colors were vivid and included every shade imaginable. She picked out one insect species with large chartreuse wings that was twice the size of any of the birds. She also noticed a constant, low-pitched buzzing sound that seemed to come from all directions, and it took a moment to realize she was listening to the drone of millions of insects—wings, legs, feet, moving, vibrating, rubbing together in discordant harmony.

She felt an itchy sensation and slapped her neck. In her palm she found the squashed remains of a small black fly.

Irene handed her a tissue but not before glancing at the insect.

Vincinio looked, too, and mumbled. *"Mosca."*

"They're not poisonous," Irene said, "but it might be best if all the windows remained up until we reach the center."

Amoreena returned the window to the closed position, any miniscule sense of serenity vanquished.

The *center*, as Irene had referred to it, was the impressive collection of multistory concrete structures Amoreena had seen from the jet just before landing. The buildings, four in all, stood at the far southern boundary of the compound, away from the plantation's other structures, which included the resident mansion and a hodgepodge of hangars, guard towers, shops, dormitories, an open pavilion, a helipad, and other buildings, some of which appeared as if they'd withstood eons of the indigenous tropical showers—barely. Their rotting clapboard walls and rusted sheet-metal roofing stood out in sharp contrast to the polished fortresslike facade of the research facility which the SUV approached.

The main building was the largest, four stories and at least fifty yards in length, rising out of the ground like a modern-day Mayan temple, replete with four Toltec motifs and carved stone *stelae*. The architectural lines were sharp and angulated, yet blended smoothly with the dark, heavily jungled landscape that gazed down upon the center and seemed only to be held at bay by a twelve-foot-high metal perimeter fence. Amoreena wasn't sure if the enclosure was designed to keep animals out or people in. The fence continued around the compound as far as she could see.

Two of the other three buildings were noteworthy only for their prevalence of windows. Each was two stories, and they were connected by a partially sheltered corridor, open on the sides and with a wood roof infested with tangled masses of vines.

The fourth structure was the odd-appearing one that had caught her attention from the plane, circular in shape with the blue skylights. It was located behind the main building and attached at the first level by a concrete-enclosed walkway. There were no windows that she could see.

The driver parked in front of the largest building, and Irene escorted Amoreena up a series of shallow steps to the lobby entrance. Inside, the cool air-conditioned environment was a welcome respite from the humid air outside. The view was

even more welcome. Walls of Yaxchilan stone lintels, lime-
stone murals, and rare *Jaina* figurines made her feel like she'd
stepped back in time five centuries. The floor consisted of rec-
tangles of white marble with inlaid strips of black onyx polished so bright it made Amoreena blink. Potted plants and
trees reached fifteen feet to the ceiling. She'd never been in a
room so elaborately decorated. The quality surpassed anything she'd ever seen in a museum.

There were no chairs, just a guard station situated in front
of a set of closed double doors. Besides the pair of guards
dressed in their military uniform replete with sidearms and
AK-47's, the only other person present was an elderly cleaning woman watering a shiny plant laden with large purple
flowers.

"Antonio Calientes, Vincinio's older brother, collects rare
artifacts," Irene explained. "His primary interests lie in antiquities of past Mesoamerican civilizations."

"He must have gobs of money."

"Meechum Corporation provides him with the necessary
funding."

"In return for what?"

Irene smiled smugly. "Antonio's a general in the
Guatemalan military."

"Oh," Amoreena said, as if the statement explained everything.

At Irene's direction, she waited while the administrator and
Vincinio approached the guard desk. Amoreena could understand nothing of their conversation, so she diverted her attention to the partial view of five security monitors mounted on a
wide console. The glare off the glass screens prevented her
from making out any images.

She heard a short buzz, and one of the double doors
opened. Out strolled a short robust man in a white lab coat. He
strode directly up to Vincinio and, after producing a pair of
surgical scissors, he cut away the makeshift dressing from the
security chief's left hand. Amoreena could see the digits were
swollen and red from the dog bite. Silently, she prayed Byte
hadn't suffered too much. She also prayed for the security

chief's hand to rot away, though she figured a place that could manipulate the human genetic code could surely rustle up a therapeutic supply of antibiotics.

The man led Vincinio down a narrow corridor. She watched them until they disappeared around a corner.

"Amoreena." Irene was holding a file under one arm. "They're ready for us upstairs."

Passing the security station, Amoreena spied a cellular phone on one of the guard's belts. What she would give to make one phone call. It wasn't going to happen now.

The pre-Columbian splendor of the lobby vanished beyond the double doors, and Amoreena suddenly found herself immersed in the heart of an ultramodern medical and research facility. Procedure rooms and exam rooms, many occupied, lined both sides of halls that fed into a central triage area; the layout was similar to the medical wards she'd seen in the United States, only much cleaner. Every surface, the countless instrument trays, even the floor, appeared to shine independently with its own aseptic sheen. Colors were soft—whites, beiges, and pale greens. Even the air smelled as if it had been scrubbed pure with some sort of disinfectant.

The second-floor plan was identical to the first. Medical personnel all wore white lab coats, or green or white scrubs, and conducted their duties in robotlike efficiency. She heard no talking other than what might have passed as brief instructions or information passing. Certainly nothing friendly. They reminded her of zombies. It was scary. Most appeared Hispanic, though she saw a few Caucasians and Asians, and still fewer blacks. The number of employees was less than what she would have expected working in a facility this large.

Above the nurses' station a large flat monitor was mounted. In digital format with green lettering, Amoreena counted twenty-eight names, most of Spanish origin. Hers wasn't one of them. Beside each name, she recognized notations similar to what she'd witnessed on the Godinez's computer disk— drone numbers and encryptions she presumed alluded to gene deletions or additions. She picked out the BG and PAG symbols. Again, she refused to let herself wonder why they were there.

Irene passed her off to a nurse. "This is Myra," she said, introducing the girl. "She speaks no English, so don't attempt to communicate."

Amoreena tried to smile. The woman was not much older than she, at the most late twenties, and was plump, with a round flat face. She received the chart from Irene, turned and walked to the nearest room.

"Just follow her," Irene instructed. "I'll be outside if you need anything."

Amoreena took that as a warning not to try anything foolish.

Her examination room was like the others, spotless and well equipped with an exam table, sink, bathroom, sonographic machine, and minilaboratory. The nurse placed Amoreena in a gown and proceeded to take her blood pressure and pulse, and collect tiny vials of blood and a urine sample. She wrote several times in the chart.

Amoreena could feel the babies moving, but their activity was not uncomfortable. It was the cool air that made her shiver. The vent was aimed directly down on the exam table.

Ignoring Irene's instructions, she asked, "Do you have a blanket?" Amoreena gestured by folding both arms across her chest and shaking them.

The nurse's expression broke into a grin.

"So you guys do know how to smile," Amoreena said, watching as the girl opened a cabinet and withdrew two sheets.

"Thank you," Amoreena said. She draped both sheets across her shoulders.

EEIOUUUU. The shrill, high-pitched cry splintered the air, nearly driving Amoreena through the ceiling. A second louder, truncated caterwaul briefly followed. Both echoed as if originating from just down the hall. A deathly silence ensued.

Listening, but hearing nothing else she could consider threatening, Amoreena took several seconds to regain her composure.

"What was that?" she asked, sure she looked as pale as the sheets. She stared at the door, prepared to flee if some animal busted down the hinges. She wouldn't have been too surprised if a jaguar or panther had leaped inside the room. The screams had sounded that inhuman.

Unperturbed in the least, the nurse began to spin down the two vials of blood in a small centrifuge.

Amoreena started to repeat the question when she saw the door handle begin to turn.

The door opened and two men in lab coats entered. Both were dark-complected, bearded, and carried clipboards. While the nurse continued preparing the samples, the men approached the exam table.

"No mueve, vaca," one said tersely.

"What the hell does that mean?" Amoreena asked, angered at the intrusion. She was still disturbed by the screams, identical but stronger versions of the ones she'd heard at the Women's Clinic in Santa Ana.

"Don't move," the same man ordered.

Stay cool, they're only looking, Amoreena told herself. Her breaths came in shallow quick succession and a light perspiration had broken out on her skin.

"Lie down," the second man said. His accent was thick and difficult to understand.

Even before her head touched the pillow, she felt her gown roughly pulled up to her chest. Purposely, the men palpated her abdomen and each listened for fetal heart tones. She despised their brusque probing and the crude manner in which she was forced to lie exposed.

The men conversed rapidly, not a word in English, and exited without so much as an *adios* or *gracias*. Their entire exam lasted less than thirty seconds.

Amoreena covered herself and sat up too quickly, precipitating a round of dizziness. She lowered her head until her equilibrium returned to normal, noting that all activity in her abdomen had ceased.

The nurse responded with another blood pressure check.

"I need a telephone," Amoreena said.

The nurse dropped the cuff on a tray and scribbled a line in the chart.

"You understand me," Amoreena said. "I know you do. I need help. Please."

The girl filled a cup with water and handed it to her.

"No!" Amoreena said, shoving the cup away. "Telephone."

She mimicked using a phone with her left hand. *"Teléfono,"* she repeated.

The nurse simply looked at her with an opaque stare.

Her frustration mounting, Amoreena slid off the table. She towered over the much shorter woman. She reached for one sleeve of the girl's uniform.

The nurse's expression erupted in fear. She darted for the door.

"Don't leave!" Amoreena lunged after her.

The door swung partially open just as the frightened woman grabbed for the handle. She scooted into the hall like a scared rabbit, leaving Amoreena feeling angry and vulnerable on the cold tile. Any inclination to give chase evaporated, though, when the haggard figure of Dr. Rafael filled the doorway.

"Buenos dias, Amoreena," he said.

He stepped into the room and closed the door.

Chapter Thirty-two

Amoreena couldn't decide whether to race across the floor and embrace him or cock her right fist back and swing at him. She did neither.

Dr. Luis Rafael walked to a stool and sat down.

"The nurse looked afraid," he said casually. "What did you say to her?"

His accusing stare helped Amoreena define her emotions. "I only threatened to kidnap her to a foreign country in the middle of the night," she answered venomously. "Of course, I'd wait until after her mother died first," she added. "But then, you'd know nothing of that."

"Please, Amoreena, sit. You shouldn't be standing so much. You've been under a tremendous strain."

She hated his condescending attitude. It wasn't like him. "Strain? Look who's preaching. At least my head is in one piece."

Luis seemed to wince at the barb. Or more likely, Amoreena thought, he was reacting to the profuse bruising under his left eye and over his left cheek, spreading like a spilled bottle of ink.

"What happened to your face?" she asked, unable to mask the genuine concern in her tone.

"This." Luis touched the swelling, this time without so much as a flinch. "Just an accident."

"You're not the clumsy type. Was his name Vincinio?"

Dr. Rafael's expression sombered. "Amoreena, you're no longer in the United States."

"Is that supposed to be news?"

"Please, listen."

"No, you listen! The bastard murdered my roommate's pet. Byte wasn't even four months old! Then he tries to rape me. And you stand there and try to tell me it's okay because 'Toto we're not in Kansas anymore.' Give me a fucking break."

Luis stood and approached to within one foot. He continued as if she hadn't spoken. "You must be very careful what you say."

"Or what? I'm dead. Is that the big Las Canas secret that nobody's supposed to know? People open their mouths, and they die?"

"Get dressed."

"When do I go home?"

"Soon."

"After the babies are born?"

She didn't like his hesitation. "Yes," he said.

Amoreena studied how his eyes seemed to find her and hold her. "I don't trust anything about you," she said.

"I'm to escort you to your room." His face had become a mask again, undecipherable and impersonal.

This only provoked Amoreena. "They killed Ronald Godinez," she said, as she slipped off her gown and dropped it to the floor. Her anger buried any feelings of shame.

Luis made no effort to look away. "You're badly mistaken," he said.

"I saw his swollen, bloody face at the Ensenada airport. I wasn't *that* drugged."

"You're under a tremendous strain. Probably the pregnancy."

"Are you goddamn nuts?" Amoreena fumed. "I've been kidnapped, for godsakes."

"You're fulfilling the contract."

Amoreena couldn't believe what she was hearing. She

leaned back against the exam table, shielding herself with just her pants. "You're acting like a fucking robot," she said.

For the first time since entering the room, Luis's tone conveyed genuine emotion. "I work for Meechum Medical Corporation, Amoreena."

"You know about the murders, the drones, the . . ." Her voice rose. "Weird noises in the hall. What the hell was that I heard earlier?"

"It was nothing," he said, but she saw his skin had paled.

"Bullshit. I bet you even knew I was going to be kidnapped, didn't you? Didn't you?" she screamed.

"Calm down."

"Fuck you, Luis. Fuck Vincinio, and fuck Las Canas!"

Luis lunged and grabbed her by her bare shoulders, digging his fingers into her flesh. "Quiet, please. Do you hear me? Quiet," he hissed.

"What are you covering up?" Amoreena reached for him, and he shoved her hand away.

"Goddammit, don't push me," she said. She thought he looked more frightened than angry. "You've become a zombie. Just like all the others. What's happening here? You can tell me. I'm not going anywhere."

She hadn't realized they were no longer alone until she heard Irene's voice.

"We'll handle it from here, Dr. Rafael," the administrator said. She stood in the open doorway, flanked by two guards. They swaggered in behind her, looking all too eager to perform their duties.

Luis reached for Amoreena's face. "I tried to warn you," he said.

She blocked his hand. "You're pathetic." Her eyes darted to Irene. "Get the hell out of my room."

Irene's expression remained impassive. "Dr. Rafael, your services are required in the nursery."

Without a second glance in Amoreena's direction, Luis retrieved the nurses' chart and exited the room.

In his place, another man appeared.

"I'd like you to meet General Antonio Calientes, dear," Irene said as she closed the door.

Amoreena heard the lock engage with a soft click. She acknowledged the man with the tiniest tilt of her chin. He was thin and wiry and dressed sharply in a military uniform with creases so sharp they looked like they could slice paper. Bright shiny medals and colorful insignias adorned his vest. She noticed both guards giving him a wide berth, their lascivious grins no longer evident.

General Calientes didn't proffer his hand. Instead, he spoke to Irene in fluent English as if Amoreena didn't exist. "Vincinio was quite accurate in his assessment of the Anglo. She is a pleasure to observe."

"I apologize for her insolence, General," Irene said.

"Accepted." Antonio took a crisp half step closer.

Amoreena desperately wanted to dress but was afraid to move. There was something cold and reptilian behind the general's beady eyes. She felt like she was trapped in the lair of a hungry snake, and if she even blinked, she would be consumed. With both arms she positioned the pants to conceal as much of herself as possible, which wasn't nearly as much as she would've preferred.

The general's gaze was almost hypnotic. "I visited your country once, Ms. Daniels," he said. "Washington, DC, a splendid metropolis. You should feel proud."

"I am," Amoreena said, aware of the guards' salacious stares once again.

Antonio gave a perfunctory smile. "Of course. All Americans are proud. They require the best. Especially for their offspring. That is what makes Las Canas such an important service provider. We provide what is not available anywhere else in the entire world, for any amount of money. And you've become an intricate spoke in our wheel, if I may paraphrase an old English idiom."

Amoreena was too cognizant of the guards, who had spread out on each side of her, to be impressed with the general's mastery of her birth language.

"May I get dressed?" she asked, her eyes darting from the General, to Irene, and between the guards.

"Please do, Ms. Daniels," Antonio bent down and retrieved the gown. He proffered it with one hand.

When she reached for it the guards struck like hyenas. Grappling with each of her arms, she felt the pants wrestled from her grasp and her naked body hoisted up onto the exam table.

She screamed, not unlike the hideous cry she'd heard from the hall, until a cloth blanketed her face. She detected a distinctly animal odor to the fabric that made her gag. She tried to fling her head sideways but was prevented by two strong hands clasping her ears in a viselike grip.

"No, Irene!" she cried out. "I'm not going to run!"

"Of course not, dear," Irene said soothingly. She issued her orders in Spanish.

Amoreena winced at the sharpness of the guard's fingernails as they dug into her skin. She felt a hand pry her right hip to one side.

"Luis!" she screamed. "Dr. Rafael!"

For a few intense moments, it felt like burning embers exploding in her pelvis as the tiny lives in her womb exploded in ferocious activity. The sheer magnitude of the pain emptied the air from her lungs. Perspiration spewed from every pore.

She never felt the sharp jab of the needle into her right buttock. This time, though, she welcomed the drug's rapid onset of action. Her struggles, and the pain, quickly melted, left behind in a science-fiction world of which Amoreena wanted no part.

She began to float.

"How do you feel?" Irene asked. The cloth no longer covered her eyes, and Amoreena could see Irene's face.

"Better." She couldn't be sure she'd actually spoken the word, but that was how she felt. Better. The smoldering in her pelvis was only a dull ache now.

"Ramona Perez wishes you well," the administrator said, while mopping the sweat from Amoreena's forehead with a damp towel. "She says our clinic in Santa Ana has been inundated with calls regarding your whereabouts."

Amoreena attempted to focus through a thickening mist of blurred images. "I want to go home," she moaned.

"Sure you do, dear."

The ensuing darkness came swiftly, descending upon Amoreena like a cloud of swarming locusts.

* * *

Antonio waited until the servant had replenished everyone's wine before asking, "How much does the American know?"

Savoring the dining hall's plethora of lingering exotic aromas, Irene drank thirstily, noting the red Chardonnay was a Napa Valley series. She wondered if the general's choice had been made for her and Dr. Becker's benefit.

"Not much," she said. "And what she does suspect is only conjecture on her part. Ms. Daniels is not a researcher or doctor."

"Yes, only a second-year premedical student."

The general's sarcastic use of her own words sent a shiver across the nape of her neck. She looked to see if Dr. Becker was going to back her up, but saw the Meechum medical director too busy tackling his second serving of brown rice and *pollo frito* to contribute anything. After completing transactions at two of Guatemala City's most prestigious hospitals, he'd flown in on a small commuter plane in time for the sumptuous banquet of chicken, stewed *tepezcuintle, plátanos fritos,* and *ceviche*.

Only Vincinio had completely cleared his plate of three servings, though Dr. Becker was proving a worthy culinary opponent.

"Of far greater concern," Irene continued, "is how she obtained the sonograms. It would be unfortunate if our years of work were publicly revealed too prematurely. The bioethicists would have a field day."

"I am not familiar with the term 'bioethicist,' " Antonio said.

Vincinio grunted.

Irene waited for him to speak, but the big man reached for more wine. Perhaps he'd simply belched.

"Bioethicists," Irene explained, "are scholars who form opinions on what is morally and ethically right and wrong, especially in the arena of medicine and research. I highly suspect the drones would receive an extremely negative review."

"To hell with the bioethicists." Becker had finished and motioned to the servant to remove his plate. "They're basically a bunch of narrow-minded bureaucrats, mostly theologians and philosophers, who try to squelch all advancements in science."

"Will they prove an insurmountable problem?" Antonio asked.

Again Vincinio grunted.

"Give it time," Becker said. "In the future, the drones will be widely accepted, the 'standard of care' so to speak. Until then, we continue to expand our markets north."

"Is the American market so large to risk early exposure?" Antonio queried.

"If we are to legitimize our product, we must move now to establish these markets." Becker initiated a toast. "With the US dollars we'll receive from the sale of the drones, you and your brother can purchase enough antiquities to fill three plantation houses. I promise you that."

This time both Caliente brothers grunted. Irene guessed the short, deep snort was an hereditary trait, though not many other physical characteristics between the two siblings were similar.

As she listened to the general and Becker discuss demographics, gene pools, and *vaca*-implantation frequencies, Irene took a moment to study Vincinio's almost simian features. When she'd first met the Las Canas security chief eight years ago, her initial impression was she'd just shaken hands with a lowland gorilla. His grip had been like a vise. She watched as his forearm muscles bulged grotesquely in coordinated contractions while he grasped and raised his wineglass, emptying the red liquid down his twenty-inch gullet. This was one man she'd never want to cross even if she was *La Jefa*.

Vincinio wore a six-inch diagonal scar, easily visible in the flickering candlelight, that ran midway down his forehead, across the bridge of his nose, and terminated on his left cheek. When he smiled the cheek portion mounded into angry red welts. Antonio had told her his brother had received the scar as a young teen and subsequently killed the knife-wielding attacker with his bare hands, but not before emasculating the man first.

Primitive and efficient, the Calientes brothers could be trusted only to the extent they were recompensed. The opulent furnishings of the banquet hall—the high cathedral ceilings, the elaborate carvings and moldings, the handsome pier mirror with its espagnolette ornaments, the ornately decorated and inscribed antique vases and sculptures, all bespoke of the partnership's profitability. No one entered or departed Las Canas without the Calientes brothers' consent.

Amoreena Daniels would be no exception.

"Could the Anglo have received these sono images from her male accomplice?" The question came from the general and was directed at her.

Irene caught Vincinio's malicious gaze and looked away. "Ronald Godinez, no," she said. "Only someone within the medical facility would have access to the patients' medical files."

Antonio examined his cigar in deep rumination. "It is your impression, then, we have a traitor employed by the organization."

Irene tensed under the scrutiny. She noticed Becker and Vincinio had grown extremely quiet, too. "That appears to be a distinct possibility, General," she answered.

"Then I will look into it," Antonio said casually.

To avoid disturbing her digestion, Irene decided it would be best not to dwell on how the Calientes brothers looked into things.

Chapter Thirty-three

The heavy night air, laden with moisture from an earlier cloudburst, hung oppressively over the sugarcane plantation, touching objects, inanimate and animate alike, with its wet tentacles.

Amoreena woke once, lying prostrate and thirsty on a damp, narrow mattress. Her clothing clung to her skin in a clammy and inhospitable way. From the absolute darkness, muffled claps of thunder vibrated a windowpane, and when she turned toward the noise, she detected a stagnant and sour smell as if a sack of rotting lemons had been stashed under her bed.

Groggy and feeling like her head was encased in cement, she attempted to sit up but stopped when bombarded with intense waves of vertigo. As she reclined on her back, a rumbling sensation coursed through her pelvis, precipitating abdominal muscle spasms and forcing her to roll to one side. The relief was immediate.

The high-pitched wail of a dying animal was the last sound she heard before falling back to sleep.

When she awoke a second time, she knew she was no longer alone.

A hand blanketed her mouth.

"If you scream, we're both dead," he whispered coarsely.

Amoreena nodded once, and the fingers departed. She parted her lips to speak but a dry, thickened tongue prevented her uttering anything coherent.

Two firm arms eased her to a sitting position. Surprisingly, no waves of dizziness returned. A glass was placed in one perspiring hand.

"Drink," he said.

"Luis?" she said, her voice raspy and full of gravel.

"Yes, now drink. The fluid will dilute the drug's effects."

The cool water seemed to shrink her tongue, and after three long swallows her throat no longer felt packed with sand.

"Can you stand?" he asked, gently guiding her to her feet.

"Yes, I think so."

"Dizzy?"

"I can walk."

Using a penlight, Luis helped her into a pair of thick-soled leather sandals.

"Fit okay?"

"They'll do," Amoreena said. She could see that her quarters were a squalid cramped room with cinder-block walls. There was no table or chairs, only a cot, which served as a bed. Above the cot a cracked mirror hung canted off center.

A red glow touched her face, and Luis quickly forced her back down on the mattress. He put a finger to his lips and pointed across the room.

The window reflected a deep red, almost a fuchsia, then the light vanished, but not before highlighting the series of vertical iron bars just outside the pane.

"We'll have ten minutes. Hurry," he said.

"What was that light?" she asked, following him across the room to the shelf.

"The guard tower."

Amoreena watched him scoop a single pile of clothing into a rucksack. She recognized her jeans and the shirt she'd worn at her mother's bedside.

"Can I change?" she asked, realizing for the first time the clothing she had on, a pair of loose-fitting cotton pants cinched above her abdomen and a pullover smock, was not her own.

"No time," he said, glancing cursorily once around the room. "How do you feel?"

She caught him staring at her protruding midsection. "If you mean the babies, they're still asleep, I guess."

"You never took the pills."

"No," she said, unable to read his eyes in the dark. "Where are you taking me?"

She must have said it with more suspicion in her tone than she meant because he grasped her hand roughly and pulled until their faces were only inches apart.

"Do you want to go home?" he asked.

"Yes." She could actually smell the intensity on his breath. And something else. Maybe fear.

"Then follow me."

Amoreena felt the adrenaline surge in her nerves, triggering a fleeting flurry of activity in her abdomen. She heard the door creak, but not open, and sidled next to him, holding on to his hand as if it were a lifeline.

She sensed him listening.

Then he closed the door.

"What?" she whispered.

"Sssh."

The padded footsteps approached rapidly in the hall, stopping just outside the door.

Luis waited for a knock, two soft raps barely discernible to Amoreena, before releasing the latch.

Shifts of pale yellow light entered the room, silhouetting the waifish figure standing in the corridor. Outfitted in boots and camouflage khaki pants and shirt, he resembled a miniature soldier. In one hand, he gripped a wooden club.

Humberto grinned up at Amoreena with a smile disproportionately large for his narrow face, before slipping back out of the doorway.

Luis guided her into the hall. Amoreena had to step around the sprawled guard slumped against the wall. She saw a large ugly welt deforming one cheek.

"Is he dead?" she asked.

The boy's eyes flashed. "Alfonso like donkey. Too stupid to die." He returned the club to Luis. "Dr. Rafael make home run." Then he swung with one arm, imitating a smooth arc in front of his thin chest.

"You hit him?" Amoreena said, watching Luis stripping the guard of his pistol, rifle, radio, and a set of keys from one pocket.

"Humberto exaggerates," he said. "It was only a triple." He slipped a key in the door and locked it before pocketing the key chain. *"Listo,"* he said to the boy.

"Listo."

Amoreena felt the boy take one hand and begin to lead her down the hall. Over her shoulder, she saw Luis checking the rifle's magazine. Then, tucking the club and pistol under his belt, he quickly caught up, handing the boy the portable radio.

The corridor terminated in a narrow stairwell illuminated by a flickering lightbulb suspended from the ceiling on a short cord. Moths, some nearly as large as a man's palm, gyrated in tight circles, casting giant shadows along the walls.

Luis led, slowing at the first-floor landing. "What about the other guard?" he whispered back to the boy.

Humberto shrugged. "He getting laid." He cast Amoreena a look registering disgust. "Juan take what *vaca* he want."

"I'm sorry," she said, her newfound respect for her bilingual diminutive companion mushrooming by the minute.

Entering the lobby, Amoreena recalled neither the threadbare brown carpet nor the enclosed alcove that served as the dormitory's watch post. She guessed she'd been carried upstairs because she saw no wheelchair ramp or elevator. Overhead, the majority of the bulbs in the chandelier were burned out or missing, and the copper wall sconces were stained with the green patina of decades-old oxidation film.

Smothered voices erupted from behind the alcove's security door, followed by what sounded like a sharp slap. She heard repetitive creaking, either wood or springs, another slap, and then a girl's pitiful mewling.

The girl's obvious rape made Amoreena sick, even more so because she was powerless to intervene. She understood Humberto's earlier disgust even more.

Seemingly satisfied the guard's attention was directed elsewhere, Luis ushered the threesome across the lobby and out into the night. Quickly, in single file, Amoreena occupying the middle position, they scurried around the back side of the dormitory.

She had no idea of what time it was, just that it was late. A moon hung low in the sky, like a giant yellow saucer. Under the soles of her sandals she felt leaves and tiny branches, and as she walked, moist uncut blades of grass swept across her ankles.

They reached the corner and waited, while the infrared beam of another security beacon swept across the ground, before dashing ten yards to cover behind an identical building. No lights were visible, and Amoreena presumed the structure was another dormitory.

"Okay?" Luis had stopped and turned to check her pulse.

"I'm fine," Amoreena said, though the short sprint had left her huffing for air. She was thankful the activity in her midsection was limited to intermittent kicks, nothing uncomfortable, only bothersome.

Beside her, Luis and Humberto talked in hushed tones. She detected alarm in both their voices, though comprehending nothing they said.

She caught Humberto's furtive glance her way.

"¿La Americana hor caminado por las selvo, de noche antes?" he asked, his attention directed back to Dr. Rafael.

Replying in Spanish, Luis shook his head.

"What did he say?" Amoreena asked, displeased with what she saw in Luis's face.

Luis placed a calming hand on the boy's shoulder, then said, "He asks if you've ever been in the jungle at night before."

"Hell, I've never been in a jungle during the day before."

"That's what I told him."

"Why would he ask that?"

Luis made an adjustment to the strap of the AK-47 where the leather crossed his collarbone. The gesture looked more like a stall to Amoreena.

"In order to reach your vehicle," he said, "you'll be required to hike through some undeveloped plantation land."

A disturbing image began to crystallize in Amoreena's mind. From her vantage point, she could see the ground sloping evenly downward approximately fifty feet, ending at the perimeter fence. Beyond that, a living wall of vegetation blocked a full one-third of the sky.

"How undeveloped and how far?" she asked, sure any answer would be anything but reassuring.

"Rain forest and less than a mile."

"At night? Tonight!" Any residual sedation from Irene's drug flew from Amoreena's system.

"Believe me, it's your only option. Unless you're capable of piloting a chopper."

Amoreena could feel the weight of both their eyes on hers, as if measuring her.

Luis gripped her palm. "Humberto's experienced in the jungle, he'll make a good guide. If there was a safer way, we'd take it. There isn't."

"And if I stay?"

"Señorita, you not leave Las Canas alive." The boy said it, and in his words, Amoreena saw the bare-knuckled truth, something she'd suspected since gazing into Ronald Godinez's lifeless face, maybe before.

"God, I'm not even up-to-date on my tetanus," she said.

"Try not to cut yourself," Luis said, taking Amoreena's sarcasm literally.

"The moon," she heard Humberto mumble.

Deep shadows bathed in silvery lunar luminescence suddenly became giant organisms waiting in ambush, forcing Amoreena to look away from the opaque bulkhead of gently swaying trees and tangled mass of vines and epiphytes.

"*Reze por nubes,*" Luis said. "Pray for clouds." He handed Amoreena the rucksack. "Humberto will take you to an area concealed from the guard towers. Keep to the shadows and don't wander off. Tonight the moon favors the eyes of the guards."

"What about you?" she asked.

Luis shot the boy a look. "There's someone else I must try to help."

"We'll wait."

"No," he hissed, clutching Amoreena by both shoulders. "This will be your only chance. There will be no seconds."

"But—"

Luis silenced her with two fingers across her lips. "If I'm not back in twenty minutes, go with Humberto." Then he said, "And tell the world what you know, Amoreena."

"What do *I know*?"

"*Prisa*," he ordered the boy.

Amoreena felt Humberto's tug at her arm. "Luis," she said. Her feet felt encased in lead.

Luis raised one hand in farewell and smiled, the lunar rays augmenting the brilliant white of his teeth. But it was a deeply sad smile. Then he whirled and disappeared around the brick edifice's corner.

"*Por favor, señorita*, we go." Humberto began to pull at her again like an impatient child.

Side by side, they crept along the back side of the dormitory, stopping once when a swath of red touched the perimeter fence. The ground was soft and spongy in places and smelled pungently earthy. A myriad of odd noises flew at them from every quadrant—cackles, screeches, buzzing, crawling sounds.

In the moon's glow, she saw fragile winged creatures dancing in sharp crisscrossing paths just above the forest canopy.

"*Murciélagos*," Humberto whispered. "Bats?"

The pair continued without stopping. Humberto deliberately kept the pace moderate, only a brisk walk, using the moonlight to avoid the slender tropical vines snaking across the ground and stealing up the brick.

Before crossing between buildings, they would always wait for the tower beacons to swing away. The brief respites gave Amoreena a chance to regain her breath. So far the exertion hadn't adversely affected the fetal activity. It was persistent but tolerable.

When she caught Humberto's questioning looks, which were many, she'd whisper, "I'm okay."

What bothered her most were the flying insects. She was constantly swiping flies and bugs away from her face and ears. On more than one occasion she had to spit them from her mouth.

"How much farther?" she asked.

Humberto shook his head. He hadn't understood.

Amoreena tried again. "How far?" She gestured with one arm.

He grinned and nodded.

"Not far." He pointed.

A long football field away, Amoreena recognized the multistory silhouette of the main research center. Behind the center, she picked out the ghostly blue iridescence on the roof of the building she'd seen from the jet. In the darkness of night, though, she could also see this same blue light emanating from a series of windows midway up its curved walls. Under the near full moon and with the rain forest canopy serving as a vibrant breathing backdrop, she had no difficulty imagining she was observing an alien spacecraft from a foreign solar system.

"What is that?" she asked, leaning next to the boy.

"Keep *bebés*. I climb inside."

"The nursery," Amoreena said, aware of a new tingling in her gut. She fixed her gaze on one of the windows. Each was at least fifteen feet from the ground. "Humberto, did you see the babies?"

The boy didn't answer.

"What is it?" she asked, witnessing the same profound sadness in his eyes that she'd seen in Luis's. As well as fear.

"I promise, Dr. Rafael," he said, shaking his head with exaggerated force. Then grasping her wrist, he quickly pulled her out from the building's shadow and down a gentle declivity toward the perimeter fence. They moved as one, picking their way carefully. The grass was so saturated with condensation, their feet made little more noise than if walking on a wet carpet.

Amoreena worried about snakes. Her sandals offered little protection, and she wasn't sure which type she feared more, the tiny venomous ones invisible until they struck or the huge serpentine monsters with bodies the girth of tree trunks.

They saw no snakes, only a few small mammals that scurried away with such lightning quickness, Amoreena questioned whether her eyes were playing tricks in the dark.

Reaching the fence, they stopped. The metal links were six

inches wide, far too narrow for a human to slide through, even one as thin as Humberto. Twelve feet above her head, Amoreena could barely make out the razor wire entwined in tropical vines and lianas. She pushed against the metal, detecting little give.

Beyond the barricade, the jungle rose skyward, blocking the stars and moon, like a cresting green tidal wave. All around her she could smell the sweet pungent odor of damp earth and sugarcane, leading her to believe—falsely—that the cane fields were nearby.

Humberto nudged her with one elbow and pointed through the fence. *"Chigiro,"* he whispered.

For a fleeting instant, Amoreena detected a dark form the size of a small dog standing in the tall grass, before it turned and vanished. She heard a splash.

"Is it dangerous?"

"No problema," the boy said. "Leopard food."

"Wonderful."

They followed the fence until they stood directly behind the nursery. Looking uphill, Amoreena could see the blue light escaping the roof's skylights and a single tall tree embracing the building with thick, dark tentacles.

Humberto squatted low and began to tear away some vegetation growing at the base of the fence. Amoreena waited. Miraculously, she watched him tug a portion of the metal links free, creating a gap about two feet square. She could see where the metal had been previously cut.

"'Reena, you." He indicated her to go first.

She didn't correct his mispronunciation. Instead, she crawled through the opening on her hands and knees, careful to avoid the sharp metallic spines.

He passed her the rucksack and a small canvas bag he had cinched at his waist and slipped through behind her.

"No move." In a flash, he vanished behind a clump of ferns.

A few brief seconds of terror gripped Amoreena until she realized she still retained possession of both packs. The boy wouldn't have deserted her without his supplies. Regardless, standing and shivering in the cool damp air surrounded by swarms of buzzing and crawling insects, toothed and clawed creatures designed specifically to kill and maim, miles of rain forest, and no way out, renewed the waves of panic. She had no identification, no money, no credit cards, nothing, not even her visitor's passport. Irene had confiscated them all. And no weapon.

"Damn," she wanted to scream. It came out as a coarse groan.

" 'Reena." She heard his voice before she saw him.

Humberto bounded over a fallen log. In one arm he clutched a rifle, not unlike the model the guards carried, however this one appeared in a far greater state of disrepair— cracked wood stock, rusted magazine, and it was an older bolt-action model. She wondered if it would even fire.

She was still looking at the gun when another figure, a young girl, stepped into the clearing. She stopped beside the boy, her chin even with the boy's scalp.

Wearing dark pants, cinched around her slender waist with an elastic band, a black top, and with her hair tucked beneath a similarly black cap, she gave Amoreena an appraising stare. An insect touched her cheek and with a swift arc of her hand the teenager crushed the bug and tossed it to the jungle carpet. She didn't say anything.

"Do you speak English?" Amoreena asked, vaguely, aware she'd seen her face before.

"Yes, I talk English," she said disdainfully. "You talk *español*?"

"No."

The girl commented to the boy in Spanish, and both giggled. Then Humberto's grin dissolved. He said, "Gabriella *vaca*, too."

The teenager cut an elbow into the boy's side, sending him faltering a half step. "I not *vaca. No mas*."

"Your name is Gabriella," Amoreena said.

"*Sí*, Anglo."

"I'm Amoreena."

The girl walked closer, barely making a noise. In the moonshine, Amoreena could see she would be very pretty if she ever smiled.

"Dr. Rafael tell me about you," she said.

"Where is Dr. Rafael?" Amoreena asked.

Humberto tugged at Gabriella's sleeve. *"Vamonos."*

"Cállate."

Amoreena heard the boy mumble under his breath. It sounded like he'd said "bitch."

Gabriella lifted both packs from the ground. "Dr. Rafael try to save Polita. She dead meat." Though the words had come out sounding tough, Amoreena detected genuine concern in the teenager's voice. Just as rapidly, all concern evaporated. "You carry Las Canas babies, Anglo?" the girl said.

Humberto leaped in front of Amoreena. "Gabriella, she not know."

"Know what?" Amoreena asked, feeling that same odd tingling sensation return to her belly.

Gabriella slowly reached out and touched Amoreena's midsection. "I carry Las Canas *bebé* once." She jerked her fingers away as if shocked by an electric charge. *"No mas."* She began to walk away.

Amoreena moved to follow, but Humberto blocked her path. "We go, *señorita. Rapido,*" he pleaded.

She clutched at the boy. "Tell me what? What about the Las Canas babies? Please, Humberto, I must know."

"No. *Me prometi a* Dr. Rafael."

Amoreena pulled the boy closer by his arms. He resisted and slipped away. For a second, she thought he might turn and run.

"Humberto," she said. "Please. Tell me."

Gabriella brushed the boy aside as if he were yesterday's newspaper.

"Anglo," she said. "Maybe you want see Las Canas *bebés.*"

Chapter Thirty-four

Any second thoughts about returning to the plantation grounds withered as soon as Amoreena set eyes on the strange blue lights.

While Amoreena changed into her clothes, Gabriella removed a wire cutter from one of the packs and enlarged the hole in the fence, snipping the links as high as she could reach. She repeated a parallel cut, then kicked the loose segment of mesh onto the ground.

Humberto started to protest but was quieted with one lancing look from the girl.

"Espera aqui," she said. She turned to Amoreena. "I tell him wait here."

Humberto shrugged, his pride knocked down a notch or two, yet in his doleful expression Amorcena could see what a giant crush he had on his teenage heroine.

Gabriella confiscated the rifle, checked to make sure a shell was chambered, and stepped across the revamped opening first. Amoreena followed, barely having to duck.

Starting up the slope, Garbriella moved silently and sleekly and looked as if she could slip out of her sandals and sprint like a deer if the need arose. Midway up the rise, she stopped and crouched low, waiting for Amoreena to catch up.

Both looked back and saw Humberto squatting in the opening, smoking a cigarette. Amoreena could barely make out the burning ember floating to his lips.

"What if the guards patrol the fence?" she asked, supporting her abdomen with one palm.

Gabriella confidently poked at the wristwatch on her wrist. "All sleeping. No problem."

Amoreena checked the time: 3:40. At home it would be an hour earlier, and she would have been missing over a day. Surely a massive manhunt was in progress.

"¿Lista?" Gabriella asked, instantly halting and correcting herself. "I mean, ready? My English not perfect."

"Beats the hell out of my Spanish," Amoreena said, and, for the first time, she saw the girl grin.

"We go," Gabriella said.

"What if Dr. Rafael returns?"

Her smile melted. "He busy."

Amoreena followed the teen up the remainder of the slope until both stood pressed against the concrete wall of the nursery. They waited while a searchlight cut a swath of red between the main research center and one of the dormitories, illuminating an asphalt roadway and some farm machinery, including a tractor.

Once it passed, Gabriella followed the curve of the wall and stopped again at the gnarled trunk of a huge tree. High over their heads, its twisted branches rose well above the nursery's roof.

Amoreena wondered how they were going to get inside the building. Climbing the tree was definitely not an option, at least in her condition, though she guessed the girl could probably shimmy up the trunk like an acrobat.

Amoreena waited, listening to the chirruping crickets and singing cicadas, and slowly became aware of another noise. Crying. Though faint and muffled by concrete and wood, there was no mistaking the inhuman shrieking, lasting less than one or two seconds. It was the same wail she'd heard in the clinic in Santa Ana and just outside her exam room in the main research center.

Gabriella touched her arm. "You still want see Las Canas *bebés*?" she whispered.

Flutters of trepidation exploded inside Amoreena's chest. She felt her own babies moving jerkily within her. "Yes," she said, though some undecipherable quality about the wails made her want to return to the isolation of the jungle.

The girl nodded and climbed around the wide trunk, indicating to Amoreena to be careful traversing its thick, serpentine root system. Their pace quickened.

They circled the entire back side of the nursery, where the grass and dirt gave way to a flat concrete apron. This, in turn, led to a raised loading platform.

Gabriella slunk up and crouched below the upper lip of the dock. One vehicle was parked on the drive. Amoreena had seen an identical unit taking on one of the bassinets at the airport in Guatemala City. This one appeared empty.

A single floodlight illuminated the loading platform and drive area. The concrete driveway descended and split, one fork servicing a subterranean entrance to the research center while the other appeared to provide access to the other structures in the complex. Momentarily, a red beacon bathed the side of one building, then swung away.

After ensuring that no guards were present, Gabriella took Amoreena's hand and both girls mounted a short series of steps. They stopped before a double metal door emblazoned with bold black lettering.

Amoreena didn't have to understand Spanish to gather the gist of the warning. She sensed her nerve dwindling. "Have you done this before?" she whispered.

A metal key flashed in the girl's hand. *"Sí."*

Amoreena heard the lock disengage and felt Gabriella tug at her wrist. Together they ducked inside, letting the door swing shut quietly. The ululations, which from outside had sounded so muted, now echoed loudly. She had to force herself to shut the cries out and concentrate on her immediate surroundings.

Once Amoreena's eyes grew accustomed to the deep gloom, it was apparent they'd entered a medical storage room. The only illumination came from fifteen feet away, where some of the blue light from the nursery seeped in under a second set of doors. The air was cool and carried an aseptic odor,

very much like a medical ward. On each side of a narrow concrete aisle, Amoreena recognized IVAC respirators, pressur-
ized gas canisters, intravenous feeding tubes, rows of
insulated containers of various sizes and configurations, and,
occupying one entire section of wall, stacks of the infant
bassinets and shelves holding packages of powdered infant
formula.

Gabriella led Amoreena midway up the aisle and indicated
for her to wait while she continued to the second set of doors.

She watched the teenager crack the door, peek, and shut it
again. Then, setting the rifle aside, she removed a small coin
from one pocket and flicked it through the crease at the floor.
Between the cries, Amoreena heard the fleeting tinkle of
metal on the nursery tile.

Almost immediately, someone approached, walking with
soft purposeful steps.

Amoreena held her breath.

The door opened halfway, revealing an elderly Hispanic
woman in a drab peasant dress. She and Gabriella spoke
briefly in hushed voices.

Amoreena felt the woman's baleful stare. Gabriella turned,
and said, "She ask if you read note?"

"What note?"

Gabriella translated. "She place on *carro*."

"Silver," Amoreena whispered. In a sonic burst, the words
returned—*Lo siento por tus bebés, vaca*. I feel sorry for your
babies, cow. "Why did she write it?"

The woman required no assistance, answering with a malicious grin. "You see."

Amoreena's heart jumped, suddenly recalling when she'd
seen the craggy-lined face. This woman had been one of the
custodial crew at the Women's Clinic. If the note had been
some form of warning, why had Luis so casually brushed it
off?

The woman's lips tensed into a tight string. She pushed
aside an infant feeding tray and moved aside.

"You hurry," Gabriella said to Amoreena.

"You're not coming."

"I wait."

Amoreena moved forward but held back at the doorway as if an invisible net spanned the entrance. The force against her was that tangible. The keening in the nursery rose much louder and when she glanced down at the feeding tray, she noticed the nipples on the bottles were not conventionally shaped. They were much wider and more elongated than a natural nipple.

"If no want see, we go," Gabriella said.

"I must see." Amoreena ignored the old woman's glower and stepped inside under the blue lights.

The room was large. The bassinets, all covered with gray blankets, were arranged in three rows. There appeared to be at least a hundred, maybe more. Most of the bassinets were linked to monitors and intravenous setups, and many had their own oxygen canisters, though not all. The one closest to her had no blanket and looked vacant.

Above the clamoring of the hungry mouths, which seemed to erupt in odd intervals, she could hear a constant low-pitched hum from a series of fans suspended between the skylights. These kept the air, which-smelled faintly of eucalyptus, in a continuous state of circulation. One-half of the opposite wall was comprised of two wide viewing windows. Beyond the glass she could see another room with more monitors, their green digital faces glowing eerily under the blue luminescence. The room looked empty.

Even though the nursery temperature seemed warmer, upper seventies or low eighties, it felt less humid than outdoors. Regardless, she couldn't suppress the goose bumps prickling across her skin. If she didn't know a tropical rain forest grew just hundreds of feet away, she'd have sworn she'd entered an ultramodern neonatal care unit somewhere in the United States. The fact that what she was witnessing lay in the middle of a jungle in a third world country only added to the incongruity.

She resisted casting Gabriella a backward glance and pressed toward the nearest aisle, the one directly before her. She passed a medicine cart and a table mounted with two microscopes and a centrifuge. Out of the corner of one eye, she caught a movement and froze. The disturbance had come from a bassinet midway down the row to her right. She watched and waited. Nothing happened. Then to her left another motion. This time she saw a portion of a blanket bounce up and then drop down. She stepped closer and more movement erupted right in front of her. Across much of the field of bassinets nearest to her, brief bursts of activity bounced the blankets unpredictably, varying from one bassinet to another. There was no rhyme or pattern, except that as she moved closer, the activity always seemed confined to the bassinet nearest her. It was as if *they* sensed *her* presence.

She felt similar activity in her own abdomen and suppressed the urge to turn and run. Something was dreadfully wrong under the blue lights, and she was suddenly afraid to confront what lay concealed at the opposite ends of the intravenous tubes.

Did Ronald Godinez enter a similar nursery in Ensenada, Mexico? How many more such blue rooms were spread across Central and South America? Did they all echo loudly and smell of eucalyptus?

Amoreena wiped a trickle of perspiration from her temple. From behind her she heard Gabriella whisper, "Hurry."

Amoreena looked for the older woman and found her beside a heavy metal door. She held a small paring knife and no longer appeared overtly hostile. She avoided Amoreena's gaze and pretended to busy herself with a tray of mangos and oranges.

The first three bassinets were empty.

The fourth one was covered with a warming blanket. Amoreena's pulse matched her anxiety. From under the blanket, which was jerking as if mechanically alive, she heard an intermittent sibilant sound. Breathing. She detected a hoarse cough from a neighboring bassinet one row over, and this time when the blanket bounced, she glimpsed five stubby fingers balled into a miniature fist. The flesh looked roughened and wrinkled and inordinately hairy for a newborn. Her breath caught in her throat and she made herself look away. Make it be the lighting, she prayed.

From the nearest bassinet, she removed a clipboard from a metallic hook. Amoreena scanned the index card seeking any information that would tell her Las Canas was doing nothing more than manufacturing babies. *Normal* babies.

She read rapidly, noting similarities to the data encrypted on Irene's computer disk.

```
VACA—97 / DELIA SANCHEZ
Blood Type — O+, HLA — MATCH
DRONE — 2 GEN3
        Gestation — 119 Days
        Aninsulinic
        PAG — 5%
        BG — 10%
Disposition — Diabetes Research Institute
              University Center
              Sao Paulo, Brazil
              Organs — All
```

Amoreena returned the data card to the bassinet, shuddering at the realization. An *aninsulinic* drone. Becker and Irene had actually succeeded in cloning a newborn totally devoid of insulin. On purpose. The significance of the rest of the data remained buried in undecipherable numbers and percentages.

Ignoring the warning lights flashing in her brain, she reached for one corner of the blanket and peeled it back.

The infant exploded in a riotous flurry of flailing arms and legs. It squealed like a pig and attempted to roll over, but a thin strap bound its chest in a supine position.

Amoreena dropped the blanket as if it were on fire. By pressing her palm over her mouth, she barely stifled her own scream. It *was* squealing like a pig. Yet the creature looked like nothing from the pages of a *Sesame Street* script.

The tiny body appeared swollen and disproportioned, with a thick trunk far too large for the squat muscular limbs. The skin, wrinkled and excessive, was a mosaic pattern of bald areas and patches of bristlelike hairs. The skull was malformed with far too much bone, and in its wide set eyes she saw a malevolence far beyond the infant's tender age. She was sure this last observation was only her imagination, yet when the baby opened its mouth to squeal, she reared back in revulsion.

It *already* had *teeth*. And its fingernails were well developed, too, thick and brown, indicating the raised scratches on the baby's face and abdomen might well have been self-inflicted.

The infant looked less than human. Or *only part human*. An aninsulinic drone monster.

Gross disbelief filled Amoreena's face. She replaced the blanket and moved to the next crib. Another hybrid stared up at her, and when it splayed its fingers and reached up, Amoreena jumped, bringing a sneer to the infant's lips.

She leaped down the row. More of the same. Yet all different—some with more hair, some less, some with simian facial characteristics, others more porcine. And as she stared in horror at each child, a realization began to dawn on her like a sunrise over a nuclear holocaust. Meechum Corporation had moved far beyond manipulating the human genetic code. There was a reason each Las Canas infant looked so *subhuman*. The data sheet on every crib confirmed her worst suspicions.

Every child had incorporated into its own genes and DNA a small percentage of pig and baboon DNA.

Amoreena virtually ran to the next row, praying for a normal infant. There were none. All were male, squealing, and she felt for sure some would have grabbed her if their torsos had not been restrained.

Her heart raced. Becker and Irene weren't selling babies. They were manufacturing little monsters. Gargoyles. By manipulating genes, they could clone drones with specific defects, the ideal research guinea pigs. The ideal infant organ donors. Hearts, lungs, kidneys. You need a liver, call 1-800-LAS CANAS.

A metallic clanking rose above the cacophony of squeals. Amoreena froze, thinking she'd triggered some type of alarm. The noise was coming from behind the door where the old woman stood. It couldn't be an alarm because the clanking came in irregular bursts. It sounded almost like *chains*.

Amoreena dodged a bassinet, refusing to look down, and approached the single door. It appeared heavy and impregnable. At eye level, she saw a small viewing window and more of the blue light beyond the glass.

A panicked look swept the old woman's face. She attempted to bar the way.

Amoreena moved the tray aside along with the woman. "I must see." As she shielded her eyes with both hands, she heard footsteps rushing behind her, clapping smartly on the tile.

Amoreena squinted into the wire-laced glass. Only her own reflection stared back. She reached for the handle and yanked.

"No, 'Reena!" Gabriella shouted.

The door swung open smoothly and a blast of fetid air blew out, bringing with it the smell of feces and rotting fruit.

Screams, she couldn't tell how many, exploded around her, and two dark forms flew directly at her, causing her to stumble backward.

The metallic restraints pulled taut and the pair of subadult drones fell to the concrete floor, clawing and scrabbling to reach the exit.

Amoreena gasped in horror. The creatures, there must have been ten or fifteen restrained in the high-technology dungeon, were virtual clones of the infants, only much more imposing. Each looked at least a hundred pounds and capable of inflicting serious damage if given the opportunity. With small heads, disproportionately stout trunks, and short muscular limbs, the drones squatted in twos and threes, fixing their pale yellow eyes on Amoreena.

She stared back, and beyond their hideous countenances and genes run amuck, she saw something more human than primal and an intense sorrow and grief overwhelmed her. She hated Irene and Becker for what their science had created, no matter how profitable the technology was or how many human lives were prolonged.

She dug the heels of both palms into her eyes and wanted to weep.

A hand touched her shoulder. She barely flinched.

"You shouldn't be here," Luis said.

Amoreena fell into his arms. "Get me away from this place, please."

Chapter Thirty-five

Amoreena struggled to wrestle the macabre images from her mind. As she trailed Luis from the nursery, she would have welcomed the return of the drug's incapacitating vertigo, the lethargy, the loss of consciousness, anything to rid herself of any memory of having experienced firsthand what genetic engineering could do when carried to grisly extremes. The Las Canas children of the future—gargoylic guinea pigs.

A fetal kick rocked her midsection, chiseling a cold spot all the way to her spine. She tried to catch her breath. Even as she fled the nursery though, Amoreena realized no matter how far or fast she ran, she would never be leaving the Las Canas drones behind her. Because the horror was actually *inside her*. Growing nails and hooves and bristles. Had Gretchen Bayliss experienced the same sensations? Of terror, revulsion, and pity? Yes pity; after all, the drones were part human. Or the frightened Mexican girl in the park? *My baby isn't human.* Now Amoreena understood. And she wanted to scream.

They aren't human. Not totally.

The air on the loading dock hung heavy and dank. Amoreena reached for Luis's elbow, and he brushed her hand aside.

"Not now, Amoreena," he said.

She desperately needed to talk. His brusqueness quieted her.

Gabriella rose from the shadows of a trash bin where she'd been ordered to wait. Moonlight traced thin wet lines from the corners of her eyes down across her cheeks.

Silently, the three moved down the steps. On the second floor of the main research center, Amoreena saw two lights. She couldn't recall whether the rooms had been illuminated earlier.

Cement gave way to asphalt, then grass. She no longer feared stepping on the back of a coiled snake. She only wanted to distance herself from the hideous artificial products of conception. She prayed the hapless creatures didn't think, didn't feel. She refrained from praying they would all die. She already knew they would.

Humberto squatted in the tall jasmine grass next to the fence. He leaped to his feet when they approached. Amoreena held the boy's gaze long enough to realize he saw in her face what she'd witnessed behind the nursery's cement walls. She noted an odd combination of pity and disgust reflected in his eyes, then he looked away as if she carried some contagious disease.

Luis and Humberto exchanged quick words in Spanish while Gabriella gathered the rucksacks. Amoreena saw an additional leather-bound carryall, which Luis retrieved from the ground. He moved beside her, so close that his eyes appeared only as dark holes in his heavily shadowed face. They used no flashlights.

She felt the need to touch him, but resisted. An insect buzzed near her ear, and Luis knocked it away.

He handed over the carryall. "This will explain much of what you observed inside. These are Polita's records. Don't lose them."

"I saw Irene's disk, the one they killed Ronald Godinez for," Amoreena said, accepting the records.

"I know."

"I hate the bitch."

"Hate can be constructive at times. You'll need every ounce of it to escape Las Canas." His jaw muscles tensed into golf balls. "Amoreena, if you're apprehended, they'll kill you."

Her calmness startled her. "Now why doesn't that surprise me?"

Traces of a smile played at the corners of Luis's mouth. He reached out and touched her hair. "I knew you were different the first time I set eyes on you."

"How so?"

"Intelligent, arrogant . . . beautiful."

Amoreena clasped his hand. "Will that be enough?"

"You'll make it enough."

In spite of what she'd seen, with all her heart Amoreena wished to hurl the carryall deep into the rain forest and embrace this man risking his own life to save her. Yet she stood frozen in place like an artist's sculpture. And she knew why.

"They planted those *babies* in me."

"Yes."

"Were you also aware of this minor fact when you first set eyes on me, touched me, put your hands on me?"

He acted as if he were mute.

"Answer me, dammit."

"It makes no difference now."

"The hell it doesn't. You're sick," she hissed. "This whole fucking place is sick." She held up the leather carryall. "What's in this? More of your goddamn contracts."

"Records of the financial transactions. Hospitals, research laboratories, some even in your own country, purchased the drones for experimentation and organ transplants. My cousin risked her life gathering the evidence."

"And what am I supposed to do? Deliver it to the *New York Times*?"

Luis stood sheepishly like a small boy caught with his hand in a cookie jar. "For what it's worth, not all of the Meechum surrogates carried drones. Some were legitimate pregnancies."

"Like that's supposed to make it right. You're as guilty as Becker and Irene," she said.

"The drones save lives, Amoreena. Human lives."

"But you're not carrying one of these *things*," she spit back.

"*Doctor*," Gabriella said, stepping between them just as a truncated scream drifted across the commons.

Amoreena heard Luis curse. He herded the group away

from the fence to the very edge of the jungle. The earth smelled damp and alive.

"*Prisa*," he said, handing Gabriella a small-caliber revolver. She stoically stashed the weapon in one of the packs.

Amoreena wondered why he'd given the pistol to the girl and not kept it himself.

The reason quickly became apparent.

"Good-bye, Amoreena," Luis said.

She stood dumbfounded. "You're not going?"

"I'll stay and do what I can for my cousin."

"Polita."

"Without her conscience, the atrocities of Las Canas would remain buried with the sugarcane."

Another scream punctuated the night. This one, similar to the previous, was definitely of human origin, unlike the squeals and grunts from the nursery.

"'Reena." Humberto had heaved the rifle over one shoulder and was already slipping deeper into the shadows.

Amoreena locked eyes with Dr. Rafael. "I must hear it from you. Did you know?" She had to hear the truth.

His expression remained inscrutable. "Go," he snapped.

"Not until you tell me."

"There's no time to explain."

"That's no answer."

"It is tonight."

Amoreena reached for him only to have her hand sharply parried.

"Leave, Amoreena," he said, "before they butcher you and your babies."

"You bastard. You planted those monsters in me. *And you knew it!*"

Luis's face had become a mask. He nodded curtly to Gabriella, then ducked back through the gap in the fence.

"Didn't you?" Amoreena cried. She started after him, the tears brimming over her lower lids. "Didn't you?"

She watched Luis until she could no longer see him. It was Gabriella who turned her and led the way back into the trees.

Amoreena cast one last horrified look at the nursery and its

eerie blue lights. Then the thriving arms of the jungle
wrapped around her.

Though the temperature was only in the low seventies, the humidity trapped beneath the forest canopy made it seem they
were hiking through a giant sauna. Sweating profusely,
Amoreena was forced to take frequent rest breaks. The babies' activity, in her mind she still referred to *them* as babies,
held steady, with occasional bouts of kicking. Fortunately, she
experienced no significant discomfort. The serrated edges of
leaves, insects, vines, and tree limbs provided enough of that.
Her senses had never been so inundated. It felt like she was
walking on overdrive. The flying insects were the most an-
noying, clamoring around her head like a living invisible
cloud.

Thirty minutes into their trek, Humberto used his machete
to clear an area at the base of a huge *ceiba* tree. He offered
Amoreena a seat on a thick root knot, after first inspecting the
spot with his flashlight.

She accepted. Using both palms, she leaned back against the
trunk to relieve the pressure on her midsection. The bark possessed a firm spongy texture not unlike a desiccated dish pad.

"You good?" Gabriella asked.

Amoreena slapped at a crawling insect on her ankle. "I feel
like an old woman."

"No, you *muy bonita*," the teenager said.

Amoreena saw Humberto's exaggerated nod in agreement
and smiled wanly. "You should see me on my good days." She
noted their puzzled expressions. "Never mind," she said. "It
was a bad joke."

Humberto studied a cleft of sky barely visible in the
canopy roof. *"Lluvia,"* he said.

"What is *lluvia*?" Amoreena asked.

"Rain," Gabriella interpreted. "Later."

Amoreena swatted away another mosquito. She touched a
tender red welt left by the insect's proboscis and winced.

"'Reena." Using his machete, Humberto sliced off a leaf

from a succulent and spread some of the viscous liquid on her forearm where the insect had bitten her. "Help keep *fiebre* away," he said.

Humberto and Gabriella demonstrated how to spread the natural repellent over any exposed skin. The clear sap spread easily and smelled similar to aloe vera. Amoreena was careful to keep it away from her eyes and mouth. The relief from the flying pests was immediate. She was tempted to apply the unguent to her abdomen, but just thinking about what lurked in her womb rekindled nauseous waves of futility, forcing her to relive the nightmarish images of the nursery. Behind every moss-covered hummock or vine-infested tree trunk, she saw a Las Canas drone, sneering contemptuously in the dark with its ochre eyes and peeled-back lips.

She offered no protests when it was time to move again. Instead of gene splicing in secret laboratories and aberrant products of conception, she concentrated on the physical sensations outside her reproductive tract, which were mostly aches and pains in her ankles, thighs, and lower back.

Taking the point, Humberto purposely kept the pace tolerable yet appropriate to the dire nature of their situation. The path seemed to be a natural animal route, zigzagging through the trees and underbrush in smooth arcs and curves. Amoreena tried not to think about the hungry jaguars or pumas, stealthily stalking their prey nearby, or the boas and pythons coiled invisibly on low-hanging boughs and vines. If any attack came, she doubted she'd see it coming.

Everywhere, she smelled the active fermentation of rotting wood and decomposing vegetable matter. The earth was perpetually moist and allowed the trio to move in virtual silence. That was in stark contrast to the cacophony of sounds inundating them from all sides—chirping frogs and insects, birds in flight, and the occasional dying wail of an unseen victim of the jungle's process of natural selection at its harshest.

Amoreena felt about as safe as being stranded in a New York City subway at 4 A.M. during a summertime hot spell. And about as alone.

In the tendrils of moon rays, the dense growth surrounded

them in layers of silvery shadows. In the predawn hours, the vivid colors of the tropical orchids and passion vines were lost in hues of grays and blacks.

"How much farther?" Amoreena asked just as she deflected a stray branch away from her head. She'd given up picking the debris from her hair, and her feet were killing her.

"Close," Humberto said, slashing a hanging vine with his machete.

"Need rest?" Gabriella asked from immediately behind her.

"No," Amoreena said. She adjusted her pack so the straps didn't dig so deeply into her shoulders. She noticed neither of her companions asked about the *babies*.

The plan, revealed to her midway along their circuitous route, called for reaching an abandoned cane picker's bus before dawn. Choosing to hike directly through the jungle at night would be totally unexpected. The rain forest provided Las Canas with an impenetrable barrier. Or so the guards fervently believed.

Amoreena listened with keen interest to Gabriella's version of her first attempt at leaving the compound. Shortly after being apprehended, the girl had taken up sides with Polita.

"I rather die fast in jaws of big cat," the girl vowed, "rather than be caught again and suffer death by Vincinio."

During the periods of silence, which were many, Amoreena devised her own list of priorities. Number one, excluding surviving the immediate and real dangers of the jungle, was getting to a phone. She desperately wanted to contact the US Embassy. Gabriella thought the consulate might be in Guatemala City. Then she'd call Millie, though she guessed by now her disappearance would have at least caught the attention of the local authorities. Except it was Christmas Day.

She groaned. Her case would not even be seriously considered until after the holiday. And it fell on a Sunday to boot. That meant at least another day before the first team was called in. If she'd tried, she couldn't have devised a worse set of circumstances—pregnant, hiking through the jungle with no identification, and dependent on two children to pull her through. In the parlance of Rosalind Cates, the odds of a favorable outcome were daunting enough to make her consider waving the white flag. But she'd never quit anything before. And she wouldn't quit now. If her mother had waged an unwinnable battle with such class, so could she.

They traversed their fourth stream just prior to 5 A.M. In less than half an hour daylight would arrive in full. The eastern sky already glowed with the pink stain of the approaching dawn.

Amoreena slid off her sandals and followed Humberto and Gabriella down the gentle bank into the soft muck. The water was only inches deep and brimming with water lilies. Tiny frogs leaped like pinballs from pad to pad. They made the crossing unfettered and, once on the opposite bank, checked their feet and ankles for leeches before resuming their trek. There were none.

As if a wand had been waved, the jungle had magically exploded in greens and purples and yellows. Momentarily, Amoreena was awed by the myriad colors and forms and moving shapes—screeching yellow-and-green birds, long, flourishing vines rife with flowers and fruit, and isolated blankets of mist hovering above the swollen wet earth. She saw howler monkeys performing tricks in the treetop canopy and parrots cracking nuts with their powerful beaks. For twenty minutes, no one spoke.

The road materialized out of nowhere behind a towering wall of ferns. Humberto waved his machete high over his head in a victory salute before assisting Amorena up the steep embankment.

"*Ya estamos aqui,*" the boy said sheathing the machete.

"We here," Gabriella said. Though she appeared to try to hold back her emotions, a huge smile formed on her lips nevertheless, and she gave both Amoreena and Humberto a high five.

The packed dirt was a welcome change from the wet, spongy floor of the jungle. Their pace quickened considerably, and before the sun had cleared the horizon Humberto was pulling the branches used for cover away from the decrepit orange bus. The hood rose with a rusty squeak and while the boy snapped a missing distributor wire in place, Amoreena and Gabriella climbed aboard and stashed their gear under the two front seats.

"*Feliz Navidad,*" Humberto said, jumping in and throwing both girls a flower.

"Merry Christmas," Amoreena wished back. She placed her flower in Gabriella's hair.

Humberto slid into the driver's seat and guided the key into the ignition slot.

Amoreena crossed both fingers.

The engine sputtered once and came to life.

Chapter Thirty-six

Antonio toyed distractedly with the glowing ember of his cigar until, with one final flick, the burning tobacco broke free and fell into the ashtray.

"Is it serious?" he asked.

Dr. Becker's brow furrowed as he examined the documents. He continued to read.

Irene sat at the opposite end of the couch from the medical doctor, choosing to watch the general seated behind her desk instead. She sipped at her coffee, wondering why the plantation overseer appeared to be so wound up. After all, it was just a fax.

Becker finished and looked up. "How many pages reached the embassy?"

"Only the first two," the general answered. He stood and walked stiffly to the window. "The remaining were intercepted before they could be transmitted."

"And pages one and two?" Becker's tone drifted toward the caustic, which, in Irene's mind, wasn't prudent.

Antonio seemed to take little offense. He forced a smile and returned to his chair. "You forget. It's Christmas Day. I've already placed a call to our contact at the American consulate, and he's assured me no eyes but his saw the fax. Rest assured, pages one and two have been destroyed."

Becker's expression softened. "Then no damage has been done. But a leak of this magnitude could have been very serious, General. This document summarizes the cloning and gene-splicing techniques involved in creating the research subjects. If this information ever became public, the international ethics community could shut us down. Our markets would contract seventy-five percent, and we could say *adios* to transacting any business in the United States for at least five years."

"That would not be acceptable," Antonio said.

"I agree," Irene interjected. "That is why Polita must be dealt with very severely." She waited for Antonio's response, suspecting more bad news. She and Becker weren't escorted to a sequestered meeting in the general's private suite because one of his staff was caught faxing classified information.

She studied how Antonio gently rested the cigar in the cradle of the ashtray. Almost like a woman. So different from his beastly brother. Which raised another worrisome point. Where was Vincinio? If this was a security issue, which it most definitely was, then why wasn't the security chief present?

The general rose again. "Polita is awaiting her interrogation session," he said. "Unfortunately, I have more unfavorable news. The American is missing."

"What do you mean by *missing*?" Becker asked.

The revelation caught Irene totally unprepared as well. She'd been awakened an hour earlier by the helicopter's powerful motors but didn't think it of much significance. Nothing more than a routine patrolling mission, perhaps. Listening to the general's words, the disturbance carried far greater portent.

"A guard was found outside her room unconscious." Antonio explained. "Dr. Luis is treating him at this moment."

"I don't care about the goddamn guard," Becker blurted out. "That woman is carrying over half a million dollars of corporate merchandise. The first-generation fours."

Clearly intrigued, the general asked, "What is so special about these drones?"

Becker looked almost apoplectic. "Generation fours mature much faster, thereby decreasing carrying time while simultaneously increasing carrying capacity. With the G-four drones, our product output will increase thirty percent each cycle. They'll also grow faster into subadults. This will eventually cement our monopoly in the adult transplant and research markets. Now where the hell is she?"

"We're still gathering information, Doctor." Antonio said. "However, you can feel confident the situation is under control. Must I remind you, we've never lost a *vaca* before."

As far as Irene knew, what the general said was true, though for the US operation there'd been several close calls. Gretchen Bayliss, the most memorable. But then . . .

"Ms. Daniels is not your typical *vaca*, General," she found herself saying.

Antonio grunted. "The Anglo will never leave Guatemala alive. This I promise you."

Overhead, the Sikorsky's mighty rumble tracked across the ceiling.

The Sikorsky Black Hawk's massive rotors cut a fifty-four-foot swath of swirling turbulence through the heavy, moisture-laden air. For all their torquing power though, the spinning foils couldn't begin to match the tempest building inside Vincinio.

For two hours, the air search had taken them over every square acre of the compound grounds, including a twenty-kilometer radius out from the perimeter fence. He'd even instructed the pilot to follow the main and only plantation road as far as the Itzimté Ruins, at least fifty *kilómetros*, about thirty miles, and still nothing. Only jungle, jungle, and more jungle, with the exception of the plantation fields, which were relatively easy to scour since the *cana* was in its mid-growth cycle, barely four feet tall.

Vincinio lowered the binoculars to the level of his bushy mustache and scanned the far horizon where the blue met the deep green in a smoothly rolling line. They were far too low to see the placid surface of Lake Petén, where he'd once swum as a child. Thirty meters under the chopper's sweltering cockpit, the canopy roof coiled and recoiled from the gale-force downdrafts of the Sikorsky's rotors.

Vincinio shifted his gaze downward through the starboard window and felt a pit of desperation begin to grow in his stomach. He started to wonder if this was the same plot of earth they'd flown over thirty minutes earlier. A huge green ocean. If the Anglo had chosen the jungle as an option of escape, he realized any chances of spotting her from the air were virtually nonexistent. At night, with a thermoscanner, his chances might be somewhat improved, but it wasn't night, and he didn't have any sophisticated search surveillance equipment. Only a pair of 8×50 binoculars and his eyes.

"Me lleva la chingada," he cursed, ramming his elbow against the cockpit side panel. The force of the blow caused the pilot to make a minor adjustment in the cyclic.

"Commandante," the aviator said, motioning to the fuel gauge.

Vincinio saw the needle dipping dangerously to the left and grunted his approval. The unthinkable had occurred. He'd lost his quarry.

What masqueraded as a road was really nothing more than a red ribbon of turgid soup slashing its way through a monotonous sea of green. With the end of the rainy season, the dirt had become mud, puddles had swollen into narrow lakes, and shallow furrows had widened to form deep valleys.

Humberto navigated the muddy *carretera* in quiet reserve, keeping both hands glued to the steering wheel. Directly behind the driver's seat, Gabriella dozed, her head lolling against the window in rhythm with the vehicle's constant flux of accelerations and decelerations.

Amoreena occupied the seat across the aisle from the girl, but found the riding too rough to fall asleep. Not that she wasn't tired. She felt dead on her feet. At least the terrible fear of capture had lessened to a degree. They hadn't heard the *wump-wump-wump* of the security chopper for some time. Her pulse had returned to normal, and the activity in her midsection was a discomfort she was learning to tolerate. As long as she didn't think too hard about what the movements in her

womb represented. More than once she regretted not taking
Luis's tiny blue pills when she'd had the chance.

A myriad of strange scents drifted in from the open windows. Most were sweet and emanated from the thick garlands
of blue-and-white orchids weighing down the hanging vines
like bunches of giant grapes. Some of the vines coursed skyward over two hundred feet to the forest canopy, and the hummingbirds seemed as plentiful as bees.

They crossed several wooden bridges. All appeared to have
been constructed during some past civilization. The wood was
jet-black and splintered at the joints, yet with Humberto's
careful maneuvering, the bus made it to the other side each
time. Under the planks, water rushed over glistening mud-
flats choked with crawling plants and reedy grasses.

Rounding a bend, the bus abruptly slowed. Amoreena
sucked in her breath. To the side of the road, resting on a
fallen limb, perched one of the most vibrantly colored birds
she'd ever seen. The boy honked, and the bird rose in flight,
displaying its shimmering green-and-red plumage and long
snaking tail.

"Una quetzal," Humberto beamed. He braked to watch the
majestic fowl, its feathers radiant in the sun.

"It bring us luck, 'Reena." Gabriella had opened her eyes in
time to see the quetzal, too, before the large bird vanished in
the cobalt blue sky.

On the outskirts of Ixcocal, the bus broke down.

So much for the quetzal's magical spell, Amoreena thought
ruefully, sharing a bottle of soda with Gabriella in the shade
while Humberto negotiated with the village mechanic.

Adobe structures lined both sides of the unpaved thorough-
fare, and Amoreena decided more dogs and cats resided in the
town than people. Everywhere she looked she saw a mangy
stray.

The humidity hung in the air like a heavy wet blanket, and
she could feel the beginning of a headache developing behind
her eyes. They'd been traveling for six hours.

"Is it always this hot here?" she asked, pressing the bottle to
the bridge of her nose.

"Mostly yes," Gabriella said. "Not in America?"

"Sometimes."

"We have rain later," the girl said, trying to sound cheerful

Wonderful, Amoreena thought. Just what this country needs—*more rain*. She watched a car, a rusted relic that once had been somebody's VW Beetle, pull into the front lot of the garage. It settled in nicely with the motley collection of other relics.

"What about police?" she asked, trying another angle. The locals had already informed them the phone lines were down courtesy of a storm three days prior. It'd be another week before service was restored to the village.

"*La policía* no good," Gabriella answered, making a foul face. "All corrupt."

"Maybe we can buy them," Amoreena said, mostly in jest. Damn, what she'd give for a Tylenol.

The girl smiled awkwardly and rose. "I go check on bus. I be back."

Amoreena followed Gabriella's svelte walk across some flat stones to the garage. In the United States, the teenager would have been some high school football team's homecoming queen. She'd wondered about the tattooed number on the girl's neck but didn't ask. She also recalled where she'd seen her face. In Irene's surrogate catalogue. She kept the knowledge to herself.

"I need to walk," Amoreena said out loud. Cramps were developing in her calves, and she wanted to stretch her legs. She picked out the most modern building in her immediate view, a dirty brown double-story brick-and-adobe abode with a weather-beaten red-tile roof. A columned verandah ran its entire front, and a melancholic neon sign declared the structure the Hotel Topacio.

Amoreena secured her sandals and crossed the street to the small inn. A placard, *cuarto Libre*, hung askew in the window. A wrinkled woman wearing a faded shawl and *huipile* rocked in a wood chair next to the entrance. Beside her, assembled in a wicker basket, was a Nativity scene of handmade papier-mâché figurines.

"Hello," Amoreena said.

She responded by slowly swiveling her head and in the woman's searching gaze Amoreena saw the asynchronous stare of the sightless. At the foot of the chair sat a brass pot holding a few small coins.

"I have no money," Amoreena said, knowing the woman couldn't understand her.

"'Reena." Gabriella bounded up and tugged at her arm. "The bus ready."

"She's blind," Amoreena said, poignantly reminded of what the cancer had done to her own mother.

Gabriella pulled a single *centavo* from her pocket. "Not much."

The coin made a forlorn tinkling sound.

"Merry Christmas," Amoreena said, feeling anything but joyous.

While Gabriella took her turn behind the wheel and Humberto dozed, Amoreena made one attempt to examine Polita's leather carryall. However, the combination of trying to read, the bus's bouncing and sliding, and her pregnant condition made studying the documents next to impossible. Much of the written material was in Spanish, and trying to decipher the English portions only increased her headache or brought on new waves of nausea. At the first opportunity, she'd suggest mailing the entire carryall to the Santa Ana Police Department in the US or maybe the California Medical Board. Anything to get the repugnant material off her hands. Just holding it made her feel filthy inside.

She still refused even to consider any formal decision regarding her own unborn. She realized this would have to change once she reached the States. Her priority now was just getting home. She could only handle one nightmare at a time. Line 'em up.

Amoreena downed the last of the soda. Her throat felt parched. Even with the windows down, the air in the bus was stifling. "How far to the next town?" she asked hoarsely.

"Next Machaquila," Gabriella said, using the rearview to make eye contact. "No good. Much *vacas* go through Machaquilá to Las Canas. No safe. We not stop."

"I must get to a phone."

"Poptún better."

"How long?"

"Two hours. If rain, three."

"Will they have a phone?"

"Many *teléfonos* in Poptún, 'Reena. I promise."

Two hours, Amoreena thought. She prayed the long distance operators spoke English.

Chapter Thirty-seven

The screams began soon after the guards' midday *siesta*.

Initially, Polita had refused to cooperate. However, with Vincinio's talents for persuasion, Irene was confident the Las Canas counsel would be singing like a songbird in short order.

Information. That's precisely what they lacked and required most at the moment. Unfortunately, the wounded guard, the sole known witness, still lay unconscious in the infirmary. Perhaps his head wound was more severe than Dr. Rafael had at first intimated. And a second ground search had failed to turn up anything substantial. The very composition of the escape party was still in question, though a census of the *vaca* population had revealed one absentee—a Gabriella Torrez, with a history of one escape attempt. And she'd been seen learning English from Polita.

Another prolonged scream floated on the wet breeze, wafting in through Irene's third-floor-office window in the research center. Reaching octaves she thought no human voice could hit, the piercing cry sent cold shivers across the administrator's neck. The anguish was so different from the grunts and squeals the drones made, so *entirely* human.

After two more cries, she'd heard enough. She rose and shut the window. Weren't there drugs that could be used to extract information from recalcitrant subjects? It would be so much less barbaric.

The closed pane and ceiling fan only muted the screams. Polita's voice had become hoarse, and the poor miserable wretch was crying out for mercy or her mother now. Irene couldn't decide which.

The entire situation made the administrator sick and nauseous. Yet it was a vulgar necessity. If Amoreena Daniels's escape was successful, Meechum Corporation would suffer immeasurably, not to mention the thousands of lives that might be lost. Lives like Jerome's. Her son would be twenty-seven if he'd been able to obtain the liver transplant he'd required. But because his name had been randomly placed lower on the recipient list than another patient's, his much-needed surgery had been delayed. The wait killed him. *No, the system did*, Irene mused bitterly. If Las Canas had been in existence then, Jerome would be walking around today.

Tough luck, Polita.

Ignoring her perspiring palms, Irene checked her computer and roved ahead six days on her electronic day planner. The grand opening of Meechum's San Diego facility might have to be delayed, yet the postponement couldn't be helped if things remained twisted here.

She dialed a private number and waited for Ramona Perez to answer. After a brief insincere holiday greeting, she issued a new set of orders. Ms. Perez wouldn't understand some of them, but the assistant would follow them nonetheless, undercutting the chance that anyone would accept the validity of Ms. Daniels's claims, if the American did happen to beat the extreme odds stacked against her.

Irene made a second call and finished just as a young guard appeared.

"The general is ready to see you," he said in timid Spanish.

"The Anglo has been found then." Irene noted the screams had ceased.

"*El Jefe* requests your presence."

Becker was already seated in the private suite when the guard escorted Irene in. She saw Vincinio standing beside his brother in front of an expansive wall map. His massive form took up almost twice the space as the general's, and Irene observed with disgust the dark splotches staining the security chief's clothes. The animal hadn't even bothered to change uniforms. She knew by their bloody abundance that Polita was dead.

Antonio waited until all were seated before beginning. "As suspected, Polita Salinas was deeply involved in the Anglo's disappearance. Regrettably, the American was included only at the last minute, *after* arriving in Las Canas." His beady eyes bored into Irene.

She shifted uncomfortably under their gaze. "There was no other choice but to bring her here. She already knew or suspected too much."

"Blame will be credited in due course," the general said with a perfunctory grunt. "Vincinio informs me with certainty the Anglo is not acting alone. Along with the other *vaca* Torrez, a boy named Humberto accompanies them. Dr. Rafael might be involved as well. The most disturbing news pertains to the extensive collection of documents they carry concerning the Las Canas organization."

"You're positive they've left the plantation?" Becker interrupted, new panic etching at the edges of his voice.

"With the aid of Señorita Salinas's confession, we've discovered a breach in the security fence, Doctor. The escape took place during the night. And we believe they might have transportation. That is, if they survived the jungle."

"Is that possible?" Irene asked.

"Humans have lived in the rain forests for thousands of years," Vincinio answered. "The Anglo's party has little experience; however, I must assume the worst and believe they are somewhere south of Las Canas heading toward the capital." His cold eyes blazed. "The plan is to intercept them well before Guatemala City. The net is being tightened even as we speak."

"How so?" Becker asked, obviously infuriated.

Careful, Irene thought.

Antonio delicately touched his mustache. "The local agencies have been informed, as have all our contacts at the bus and train depots. Also the two airports in Flores and Guatemala City have been issued descriptions. They cannot leave the country except through your embassy. And we have that covered."

Becker stood thrusting his finger threateningly at the general. "You better be right on this one."

Vincinio rose and stepped in front of his smaller brother. His sneer was enough to wipe the pale off the dead. "Merry Christmas, Doctor. Now go back to your laboratory."

Irene caught up with Becker outside his research station. "Stay off the general's toes, Ross. Have you already forgotten Polita? There is no Bill of Rights here."

Becker frowned. "Have you also forgotten that kidnapping an American citizen is a federal crime?"

Irene saw she had him, though. Becker's scowl had disappeared at the mere mention of Polita's name. Neither she nor he had ever been so near the cold-blooded torture of another human being before. Neither would ever forget.

"I made some calls," Irene said. "Ramona Perez has been instructed on how to handle the press while Tom Volkman formalizes the charges against Ms. Daniels. These will be presented to the DA on Monday."

"The FBI will become involved."

"If not already. But Antonio assures me our man at the consulate can handle the fireworks."

A cramped concrete bunker located under the Casa de Dolor housed the security cells. There were five such rooms, each measuring eight by eight feet.

Luis Rafael's cell occupied the middle position next to the central stairwell leading up into the interrogation chamber. The stale underground air smelled of wet mold and rat feces. Today a new odor permeated the oubliette's dankness—blood.

Sitting on the floor with his back against the wall, Luis watched the single yellow bulb in the corridor flicker. It did that each time the door to the stairwell disengaged. He heard the guard's boots echo on the concrete steps. Was it his turn upstairs now?

He held no grudge against his cousin. He'd listened to her cries of agony and knew it was only a matter of time before she gave up his name. At least she'd given him the opportunity to inject the guard in the infirmary with enough sedative to make him sleep for twelve hours or more. By the time he awoke to tell what he knew, Amoreena would be miles from the plantation.

Luis cursed himself for not having listened to Polita a year ago. But his lustrous desire for a slot in an American residency program had blinded him, and Dr. Becker's promises had been too tempting. Now Polita was dead, killed in the most vile way imaginable, by the hands of a madman.

Until Amoreena Daniels, they had only been drones. Not anymore. Somehow she had changed his priorities. Or maybe he just changed on his own. *God, don't let it be too late*, he thought.

He felt the heavy vibrations from the Sikorsky's rotors through the cement walls. Vincinio was heading south. It would be dark soon, hindering the search effort considerably. How much distance had Gabriella and Humberto covered? San Juan. Sabaneta. Ixcoxal. Machaquilá. If they would reach Poptún by nightfall, Guatemala City would be within their grasp.

The guard stopped outside his door. He was alone, a large keg of a man who walked with a rigid knee. Luis was on his feet when the key released the lock.

The guard motioned him out, with the hand gripping the revolver. "*El Jefe* wants to talk," he said.

"Where is my cousin?" Luis asked, praying for a single chance.

"Maybe you can help her, Doctor." The overconfident guard pointed the gun up and grinned. "She asks for you," he said, unaware he'd just answered the prisoner's silent entreaty.

Luis kicked, catching the larger man's wrist, and the pistol spiraled across the uneven concrete, caroming off the opposite wall.

Far faster and more agile, Luis reached the weapon first. When he spun and fired, the bullet and the hard bone above the guard's left eye collided in midair.

*   *   *

The three helicopters cut diagonally across the Peten Highway like roving birds of prey.

Humberto's curse snapped Amoreena awake, before the chopper's monstrous drones drowned out all other noises except the engine backfires as the bus tried to accelerate.

A fourth chopper appeared to zero in on them, before zooming low overhead. Every loose nut and bolt in the bus's rusted chassis began to vibrate until Amoreena feared the vehicle would split apart. She sat petrified, unable to move or speak.

Humberto swerved sharply from behind a diesel, but held back, unable to pass. A flatbed heaped with cattle hides whisked by in the opposite direction, the two driver's side mirrors missing by inches.

"*¡No te preocupes!*" Gabriella screamed, pointing at the four gray silhouettes growing smaller against the clouds stacked along the horizon. She swung to Amoreena. "Only militia, 'Reena, no worry," she said.

As the bus decelerated, Humberto said sheepishly, "Sorry."

Gabriella slapped him on the shoulder. "You *loco*, boy." The two shared a tense grin.

Amoreena forced a smile and rested her head against the metal window frame. The sight of the helicopters had electrified her with genuine terror, leaving her more enervated than before her nap. The pain in her neck persisted, and she felt a little dizzy. She shifted her position to make the movement in her abdomen more tolerable. If she'd needed an excuse to miscarry, this false alarm would have been a suitable opportunity. She'd felt totally helpless. When the time came to react to a real threat, she hoped her responses would be as quick and instinctive as the boy's.

She reached over and patted Humberto's arm. "Nice driving," she said.

The boy's face swelled with pride.

Amoreena leaned back in her seat and stared out her window. Sometime while she dozed, the jungle had given way to a vast stretch of banana fields. The road was wider, too, though still heavily rutted with long stretches of standing water.

"Where are we?" she asked. There was also more traffic.

"Poptún, not far," Gabriella said.

The *carretera* began a gradual ascent. The air smelled of rain, jocotes, mangos and banana groves, which rapidly thinned out as the elevation increased. Soon lush forests of pine surrounded the road, and where the trees had been cleared, avocados and mangos thrived. Along the far horizon, magenta-colored hills rose to meet vertical bundles of blue-gray clouds. The sun was barely visible, only a scimitar slice of orange.

The evening temperature had dropped considerably, offering a welcome respite to the hot, humid jungle. Amoreena looked down over the rolling land and saw the lights of a village nestled in a verdant valley of ferns and orchards.

Panic tugged at her insides. The collection of wood-and-adobe dwellings was already behind them. "Is that Poptún?" she asked.

Gabriella was busy reading directions to Humberto from a torn scrap of paper. "*Sí,*" she said, without looking up.

The road curved and became much narrower. There was no such thing as a shoulder, and angry branches whipped and clawed at the bus's windows and roof. Amoreena desperately wanted to protest but held her tongue when Humberto pulled to stop under a high brick archway. A festooned sign declared the property the FINCA IXOBEL.

The boy and girl whooped and exchanged a high five.

Gabriella leaped to her feet. "'Reen, Polita say we okay here."

"Is there a phone?"

"We find."

Beyond the gate, Amoreena saw a cluster of camping sites. All appeared unoccupied, though she could hear music and voices wafting in the cool breeze.

Humberto released the brake and drove by a row of wood-framed cabins and a small lake. Not far from the water's edge a rope ladder descended from a huge tree house partially con-

cealed in branches and leaves. Past the campsites, more land
had been cleared, allowing crops of bananas and coffee to
flourish. A spacious two-story house constructed of brick and
masonry marked the working farm's headquarters.

Humberto parked on the gravel drive. Men in ranch clothes,
tending to stables of cattle, horses, and sheep, seemed to pay
the newcomers no mind.

A wave of fresh homesickness assaulted Amoreena. The
place reminded her of the old American West. She wiped the
grime from under her eyes and waited while Gabriella exited
the bus to meet an older man with a brown face of leather
who stood on the porch. He wore a red bandana, long-
sleeved cotton shirt, and Levi's. His boots looked alligator or
ostrich.

When Gabriella turned and waved, Humberto leaped from
behind the wheel. "We go, 'Reena." He landed with a gravelly
splash and sprinted for the farmhouse.

The man, introduced as Señor Salinas, led them inside. The
entrance foyer opened into a spacious living room with wood-
paneled floors and intricately patterned woven rugs. The furnishings were spartan and clean, and all seemed to revolve
around a huge stone fireplace hearth, large enough to stretch
out on. Seasonal decorations gave the room a festive atmos-
phere. A large Christmas tree filled one corner.

Señora Salinas was a tall, sylphic individual with sad, delicate features. Gabriella introduced her as Polita's mother. If
the daughter followed after the mom, Amoreena guessed
Polita was a strikingly beautiful woman. This impression was
confirmed by the series of family portraits hanging in the hall.

Señora Salinas escorted them into the kitchen, where the
fresh-baked scent of bread emanated from a brick-domed oven.

A series of rapid exchanges in Spanish ensued between
Polita's parents and Gabriella and throughout the entire conversation, Amoreena could see the woman was profoundly
distraught.

"Why is Polita's mother so sad?" Amoreena asked the boy
in a hushed whisper.

"She afraid for Polita. No call on Christmas," Humberto
said.

"What does Polita do?"

"She work at Las Canas," was all the boy said, with a shrug.

Amoreena heard Dr. Rafael's name on several occasions and the mere mention of the name seemed to precipitate angry reactions from Señora Salinas. When the older woman began to weep, Gabriella ushered Amoreena from the kitchen.

"Polita's mother blame Dr. Rafael for her daughter's troubles," the teenager explained. "She also blame us."

"Me."

"You American, 'Reena. Sorry."

The phone hung in the hall mounted under an imposing crucifix. Parched palm fronds from previous Lents stretched behind the Savior's crown of thorns.

"What do Polita's parents know about Las Canas?" Amoreena asked.

"Little, maybe, I don't know." Gabriella began to dial.

"I want to reach the American Embassy," Amoreena said.

"I get number—" the teen broke off and spoke in Spanish to someone on the line. Then she handed the receiver to Amoreena. "Operator put call."

On the second ring, a male voice answered. "Embassy, Post One. Merry Christmas."

"Hello," Amoreena said, stifling a wide grin. He sounded so official. And so close.

"How may I assist you, ma'am?" he asked.

"My name is Amoreena Daniels. I'm an American citizen." From that point the words flew from her mouth.

"Ma'am, ma'am, please. Not so fast," he interrupted.

She barely heard her own phrases and run-on sentences.

"Ms. Daniels, stop."

"Don't tell me to stop!"

"Ms. Daniels. I'm only a Marine sentry. Now I'm going to place you on hold—"

"No!"

"And transfer you to the duty officer."

"Dammit, don't—" A thick interminable silence followed.

Amoreena waited. She could feel her own pulse in her fingers gripping the phone.

"Ms. Daniels." It was a different voice. A man.

"Yes," Amoreena virtually screamed.

"Ms. Daniels, I'm Arvis Taggert."

"Are you the ambassador? I want to talk—"

"The ambassador is not available. It's Christmas."

"Then make him available, please. I'm an American citizen. I've been kidnapped."

"Amoreena." Something too familiar in the way he said her name made her stop.

"Amoreena are you still there?"

"Yes," she said, aware of a new chill in the hall.

"Ms. Daniels, we're aware of your circumstances and believe me everything is being done diplomatically to ensure your safety. Mr. Horwitz, chief of the American Citizen Service Section, has been informed of your status via transmittals from the United States. Unfortunately, you're on foreign soil governed by foreign laws. We cannot just call out the Marines."

"Why not?" she cried out.

"Where are you, Amoreena?" Taggert asked.

"A farm outside Poptún," she said. Her voice felt like dry carpet.

"That's approximately twelve hours from Guatemala City. Do you have transportation?"

"A bus."

"That's good. Now I want you to drive to Rio Dulce. That should take you about an hour. Report to a Lieutenant Rios. Is that clear?"

"Yes."

"He will escort you to Guatemala City. Are you alone?"

"No, I'm with two friends."

"And you're pregnant, correct?"

"How did—"

"The fax indicated you were pregnant, Ms. Daniels."

"Yes, I'm pregnant," she said. "I escaped from Las Canas."

Amoreena could almost picture Taggert assessing the situation. The conversation was going nothing like she'd envisioned.

"Write down the embassy address," the officer instructed. "Avenida La Reforma 7-01. We'll be expecting you sometime tomorrow. Amoreena, keep a low profile and try to avoid any interaction with the local militia. Guatemala and our administration are currently not on the best diplomatic terms."

Fear gripped Amoreena like a tightening glove. "I'm scared, Mr. Taggert," she said. "They want to kill me." Her voice cracked.

"Lieutenant Rios will take care of you, Ms. Daniels," he said. "But it's imperative you reach the embassy grounds." He sounded a million miles away.

"I'll be there," she said, her eyes falling on the crucifix. Just hanging up required every ounce of will she could dredge up.

She gritted her teeth. "I need to make one more call," she said. With Gabriella's assistance, she got through on the fourth ring.

"Amy," Millie's squeal broke past the static. "Shit, I've been worried sick. Where the hell are you?"

"Poptún, Guatemala."

"Goddamn, is this for real?"

"Millie, I just spoke with the embassy. They said they're aware of my situation."

"I bet they are. Girl, you're famous. TV, radio, even the FBI's involved. Two detectives came by—on Christmas Day! And that medical investigator, Risken, called as soon as the news broke."

"What news?"

Millie's pause dragged forever. "Roomie, Meechum Corporation has implicated you in the death of Ronald Godinez."

Chapter Thirty-eight

The slatey clouds lay thick and folded like a black sheet. The incessant drizzle had started soon after departing Poptún. On the outskirts of Mendez the rain shower began in earnest.

Only one windshield wiper worked, thankfully the one on the driver's side, yet Amoreena still wondered how Humberto was able to keep the bus on the road. The drops were so large and so many, the wiper blade barely kept up with the torrent of water sluicing down the glass. Other vehicles, some with missing headlights, honked if the bus slid too near their side of the road.

Huddled in her seat with Polita's leather carryall tucked against one side, Amoreena caught Humberto's stare in the rearview. It was dark out, and the lightning reflected the moisture off his small face. She waved weakly.

"You good, 'Reena?" he asked.

"Yes," she said, though in fact she was feeling pretty lousy. The headache behind both eyes hadn't lessened, and, if anything, the pain in her neck and back had grown. Her face felt flushed, and she was experiencing more chills. Her conversation with Millie hadn't helped. On the plus side, the restive activity in her midsection had taken a break from the constant punching and kicking.

Slouched on the seat directly across the aisle, Gabriella

dozed. The teenager's window was cracked, and strands of wet hair clung to the glass, forming Medusa-like patterns.

Amoreena watched Mendez come and go. All in five minutes. The village was identical to the three or four previous hamlets—one story brick-and-adobe residences, a service station, a motel, and one or two street markets. She saw no indication of any police presence.

Next on the list, according to the roadside signs, Semox, then Sahila. They'd already been driving over an hour, and Amoreena was beginning to wonder what map Taggert had consulted. Of course, she realized the inclement weather conditions would affect any travel-time estimates. Rio Dulce couldn't be too far ahead.

With each mile that passed, the shock of her roommate's revelation lessened, only to be replaced by more rage. She couldn't believe the PR scam Irene and Becker were trying to pull. Her blood boiled. Had she really touched a knife at the Ensenada airport, or had that memory only been a dream? She couldn't recall, she'd been so drugged at the time. Regardless, she was confident any homicide detective would be able to see through the ruse. She wasn't a murderer. No one would take the charges seriously. Unless they thought she'd cracked up.

The bastards, Amoreena thought, painfully aware of how situation might be made to look. She could almost read the bold print. Surrogate mother goes psychotic and commits murder. She could easily see the stunned faces of the medical school admissions committee. Her MCAT scores could be through the roof, and they'd still recommend she see a psychiatrist. In prison. *Adios* medical career.

Under the carryall, she felt the babies jostle for position. The discomfort was enough to make her grimace. God, if she could just rewind her life six months, God, if she'd just been born rich, God, if her mother hadn't been diagnosed with cancer. God, God, God . . .

"Goddammit," she cried, crashing the heel of her fist against the window. The tears streaked her cheeks with rivulets of dust and grime.

"'Reena, it okay," Gabriella said, sliding in next to her and draping an arm over her shoulder. "I cry, too. Many times."

"Why me, dammit?"

"You save Las Canas. You American," Gabriella said. "Good things in America. Strong things. You strong."

"*Sí*, 'Reena, you *Americana*," Humberto voiced, waving a tightly packed fist over his head.

"No," Amoreena said, holding back the sobs. "I'm not strong. I'm not smart. I'm just so . . . fucking desperate."

Gabriella pushed closer. "I tell you secret. I see *mi bebé*. When come out, no crying, only sound like pig. And head real ugly and mouth moved like fish on riverbank."

Amoreena could feel the girl's guilt and anguish and in a small way, this seemed to lessen hers. She listened.

"I no hold him, 'Reena. I no want to. I look at *mi bebé* and say, I no want you, *bebé*. You not part of me. I no make you, *bebé*. Then nurse take away." Gabriella's gaze turned distant. "Later I cry. Every night, I cry for *mi bebé*. But I never see again, 'Reena. Never."

No one spoke. Amoreena felt the teenager's hand slide into hers.

"'Reena." Gabriella said suddenly, her tinny voice barely audible above the clatter of the rain and squeaking wiper blade. "Why *mi bebé* no look like me?"

Amoreena clasped the girl's fingers. "They're not real babies, Gabriella. Not like you, me, or Humberto. They're . . ." How did you begin to explain the genetic manipulation of the human genome to a teenager?

"Evil?" Gabriella finished.

"No, not evil. But the people who run Las Canas are evil."

"I no hate *mi bebé*."

"I believe you. And one day you'll fall in love and have another baby."

"And this one will look like me?"

"Your baby will be beautiful."

"Like me," Humberto said with a sly grin.

"Ooooh." Gabriella giggled. *"Cállate."* She jumped up and slapped the boy on the back of the head.

Amoreena laughed, too, and it felt okay. How long had it been since she'd laughed? Or smiled?

She embraced Gabriella. "Thank you."

"Why you say thank you?"

"Because you made me feel good."

The girl stood and pumped her fist against the roof. The collision resounded with a sharp whop. "We win, 'Reena."

Another whap from Humberto's fist. "Win!" he yelled.

Seeing their innocent exuberance, Amoreena couldn't resist balling up her own fist. "Yeah, we're gonna beat those bastards."

Against the oncoming beams of light, the rain fell at sharp angles, pummeling the lakes and rivers in the road. Along either shoulder, Amoreena could just make out the darker silhouettes of trees bent beneath the wind. In a way, the storm, or *tormenta*, was a godsend. It'd take a maniac to fly a chopper in these conditions.

Rio Dulce appeared in the bus's beams as if the village had suddenly dropped from the clouds with the rain. One moment, banana fronds whipsawed by the gusts, the next a narrow road lined with structures. There were no lights in any of the houses nor any illumination in the markets and gas station they passed. Decorations of the Nativity sat in ghostly darkness. Amoreena saw the flickering glow of candles through several windows.

"No electricity," she murmured.

"La tormenta," Gabriella said.

"Where is the *federales*?" Amoreena asked, straining in the darkness to read the writing on the street signs and seeing nothing but her own warped reflection in the glass.

"Polita say no go to *policía,* 'Reena," Gabriella warned.

"We need to find Lieutenant Rios," Amoreena said, aware of a new onset of chills. She clutched her arms tightly around her chest.

"Polita say—"

"Just get me to the fucking police station," Amoreena snapped. She wiped at the perspiration beaded on her forehead.

Gabriella shrugged. "Sure, 'Reena." The teenager and Humberto exchanged worried glances.

They drove two blocks until they found a street vendor camped on the corner under his parka. Baskets of avocados, mangos, and crates of vegetables and cartons of dried fruit

and candy formed a barricade around his impish figure
Amoreena saw he was only a child.

"¿*Como esta, amigo?*" Gabriella greeted with a friendl
smile.

"*Hola.*" The boy stood. Up close, Amoreena saw he wa
older, early teens. Thin wisps of hair covered his upper lip
and crude tattoos decorated his forearms. He stepped out from
under his shelter, oblivious to the rain plastering his hair fas
against his neck. He grinned lewdly at Gabriella, ignorin
Humberto's jealous eyes.

She produced a bill from one of the packs and handed it t
him through the bus's open door. From his surprised reaction
Amoreena guessed the amount of money was large.

They spoke rapidly. The conversation ended with Gabriell
giving the boy a light peck on his acne-prone cheek. He
saluted and returned to his fruit stand.

"One block, take right," Gabriella instructed Humberto. He
shifted into gear. "*La Policía* on left, two-floor building." She
faced Amoreena, waving one finger negatively in the air. "He
say no Lieutenant Rios *aqui*. Give two names of magistrates
none Rios."

"Maybe he was wrong?"

Gabriella shook her head adamantly. "With what I pay, he
not wrong."

Amoreena pursed her lips. Did these goddamn headache
make her misunderstand Taggert? She was sure he'd said asl
for Lieutenant Rios.

"Show me the building," she said.

Humberto eased right around the next corner, careful to
avoid losing a wheel in the thick mud.

Amoreena looked left. "I see it," she said.

The federal magistrate's station was the only building or
the block with a steady light inside. Mounted on a table, a
Coleman lantern filled the window with a yellow glow. Two
vehicles were parked outside, both late models. One was obvi
ously law enforcement, the other an unmarked SUV.

Humberto pulled up until their view improved.

Gabriella spoke softly and the bus's headlights went dark.

Three men sat around a desk. Two were dressed in uni

forms while the third was draped in a dark green poncho. His
back was broad and moved as he talked. The other two appeared to be laughing, as if all three were sharing some old familiar joke.

Abruptly all the levity vanished. The uniformed man behind the desk picked up the phone. He listened a second, before transferring the receiver to the ponchoed man.

Shifting on his feet so that he half faced the window, the
man in the poncho scratched at the ugly burn scar on his neck
and ear as he spoke.

Amoreena's eyes filled her face. "Get us out of here," she
whispered.

"What?" Gabriella said.

"Move!"

Taggert.

Vincinio punched the power off button, then passed the cellular phone back to one of his men seated in the Sikorsky's bay.

"Get this thing lower," he ordered, scanning the chopper's
search beam below and seeing only silver streaks and blackness.

"Any lower and you'll get a *real* good look at the ground,"
the veteran pilot said, instantly mincing his words.

The wind screamed, and the aircraft yawed sharply to the
left, sending the men scrambling for a handhold. Supplica-
tions to the Virgin Guadalupe filled the hold as the Sikorsky's
rotors struggled to find support.

Vincinio clutched both hand rests, his knuckled fists white
under the strain. The windows were nothing but sheets of water, and the constant gyrations were even beginning to affect
his cast-iron stomach. Crashing into the Peten jungle was not
an option he wanted to experience.

He glanced sideways at the pilot, admiring his skills in
maintaining some semblance of control over this hulking
metallic bird. He would let the man's earlier insolence pass.
The cabin was leaking like a sieve, and just getting the chopper back on the ground again in one piece under these unsavory conditions would be worthy of a bonus.

Vincinio checked the flight panel. According to the radar screen, they were the only object in the air. That didn't surprise him. Angry thunderheads threatened to crush them from all sides, and the unpredictable wind gusts made it feel as if they were captive in a giant Ping-Pong ball floating on a roiling sea.

The men in the hold sat stoically, too tense even to pray.

The pilot pursed his lips. "It will be impossible to land in Rio Dulce in this storm."

Vincinio accepted the man's expert judgment. If the Anglo did show up, which so far she and her coconspirators hadn't, Rios had been instructed to resort to any means necessary to apprehend them, short of killing the American. That job would be his once the products had been delivered. Vincinio planned to make the most of it. First he had to find her.

Below, he picked out beams of headlights on the Peten *carretera,* but cascading walls of rain made identifying a specific make and model next to impossible.

"Where can you land?" Vincinio asked.

The pilot punched in a code on his navigator. "The storm's breaking apart over La Ruidosa," he said.

Vincinio nodded. Perfect.

Chapter Thirty-nine

La Ruidosa, the "noisy place," sat at the junction of the Peten Highway from the north and the Atlantic Highway from the west. Anyone traveling by road from the rain forests of the Peten to Guatemala City had to pass through La Ruidosa.

Vincinio wondered if his prey were aware of this little bit of trivia regarding the Guatemala freeway system. It didn't matter, he decided. If they attempted to reach Guatemala City, he had them. All he had to do was sit. He couldn't wait to see the Anglo's expression when he pulled her from the bus. That would only be the beginning of her painful ordeal.

As the pilot had predicted, the last storm of the rainy season had broken and moved west. Overhead, the sky twinkled with the constellations of Orion and Capricorn. The night air smelled of fresh earth, blooming jasmine, and fried *pollo* from a street merchant's smoking *cabaña*.

Vincinio rose from the hub of one of the Sikorsky's wheels and stretched. From his vantage point, no one could pass through La Ruidosa junction without undergoing a visual inspection. The square had been cleared of all parked vehicles and the evening Nativity mass postponed three hours until midnight.

The local magistrate had been quite cooperative. You didn't argue with a man and his Sikorsky.

Vincinio watched his men wave through a truckload of feeder cattle on their way to slaughter. A tourist bus backed away from a *pensione* and was delayed twenty minutes while the passengers' visas were examined. All cleared.

Anytime now, Vincinio surmised. If the swollen road from Rio Dulce hadn't swallowed the fugitives up first. He hadn't heard of any accidents. He considered sending a car to look.

He rechecked his most recent surveillance calls. Semox—no sighting, Sahila—*nada*, Rio Dulce—bingo. A street vendor had reported being paid two hundred quetzals by a pretty girl in a rusted yellow bus for information on a man named Lieutenant Rios. The vendor didn't recall seeing the *Américana*, just a boy driving. He didn't see the bus leave Rio Dulce, so he couldn't elaborate on what direction they'd taken. The point was moot. If the traitor's goal was the embassy in Guatemala City, then they'd be driving south toward La Ruidosa. Rios would cover any retreat north.

One of his men shouted.

Vincinio saw the single beam approaching even before the bus entered the square. He smiled, thinking about the Christmas present he was about to deliver to his brother. He ground out his cigar and, resting a huge palm on the butt of his revolver, sauntered toward the blockade.

From his perspective, the driver appeared to be a female. That didn't bother him. What counted was this had to be the bus. Mud caked its sides from wheel rim to roof. Closer up, he saw that both headlights were functional, it was just that one was buried in road slush.

Flashlights danced over the rusted relic as if the vehicle were on a Broadway stage. One of his men had the door open and was gesturing wildly with the barrel of his rifle.

One, two, three passengers disembarked, all women. Then a fourth, carrying a baby. Vincinio frowned and broke into a jog. Now a fifth, another woman also draped in white.

"Me chingado," he cursed.

One of his men turned, embarrassment coloring his young face. "They claim the bus was given to them. A donation for their church."

Vincinio felt like the top of his head was going to explode.

He glowered at the nuns, temporarily resisting an impulse to place a bullet in each of their bowed skulls.

"I apologize for this inconvenience, Sisters," he said. "We won't keep you long."

The twenty-eight-foot *Gaviota* rode low and stable in the water, taking the two-foot swells at a forty-five-degree angle across her beam. The conditions were a vast improvement from the five-foot crests pounding Lago de Izabal when the schooner departed El Relleno ninety minutes earlier.

Amoreena rested on a cot in the dingy cabin. The window was open, but still the air reeked of fish offal, diesel fuel, and stale tobacco. She didn't complain.

Gabriella tended to the packs and supplies, drying some of their clothing and sorting through the false visas and papers Luis had given her.

"Polita arranged all that?" Amoreena asked.

The girl nodded without looking up. In the cabin's light, her face glowed like an angel on the Sea of Galilee. "She very intelligent. Like you, 'Reena."

Amoreena raised one palm. "You mean this boat. It was pure luck." If *this* could be called luck.

"No, you and Polita much alike. Beautiful, intelligent, and hate Las Canas."

"No argument on the third point."

Gabriella shrugged and returned to her work. Above the cabin roof, Amoreena could hear Humberto conversing with the boatman. From the boy's tone, he was obviously enthralled with the seafaring way of life.

Amoreena faced the window and sucked in the salty breeze off Lake Izabal. The lights from the shore were no larger than stars, though far more varied in color. The luxurious resort hotels—Izabal Tropical, Catamaran, De Rio—all twinkled like faraway Christmas trees. Her mother would have sat for hours just admiring the view.

Amoreena tried to pick out the single beacon from the Castillo de San Felipe fifteen kilometers away. One of the nuns had said the tiny fort had been built by the Spanish to protect the lake from British pirates. She gave up searching for its singular pulsating guide among the myriad of other lights.

It had been luck. Pure and simple. Since she'd told Taggert they were driving a bus, there'd really been no other option than to ditch the vehicle. Vincinio would be expecting to find them in a yellow bus. She realized that as soon as she'd recognized Rios as one of the security guards at the Women's Clinic, the tall one who'd threatened the frightened Mexican girl in the park. Thank God she'd seen him first. She wondered who else at the embassy was on the Las Canas payroll.

Coming upon the nuns and their broken-down van outside El Relleno worked out perfectly. In exchange for a lift down to the River Dulce, the nuns were given the bus as a donation to their Church of the Virgin Mary. Not wishing to risk passing through La Ruidosa, Humberto had found the fisherman docked under a suspension bridge and, with Gabriella's assistance and a hundred quetzals, been able to persuade him to transport them across the inland sea to Marisco.

Before sailing, Amoreena suggested wrapping the leather carryall securely and mailing its contents out of the country. The boat looked like a dinghy pounding against the wharf in the rough surf. She didn't want to see Polita's efforts wasted at the bottom of Lago de Izabal. Humberto and Gabriella had vetoed her idea, citing the inefficiency and fraudulences of the Guatemalan postal systems. The records were kept in their possession.

The rolling seas affected Amoreena very little—she was already nauseous to begin with—and she felt sure the constant waves of wracking chills indicated she was febrile. She pressed the back of her hand against her cheek, and beneath the sweat and dirt, her skin smoldered.

She was thankful when they finally docked.

Marisco was a sleepy port village at the foot of gentle hills covered in tropical forests and rubber plantations. The beaches were lighted magically in observance of the Nativity.

The rifle was too heavy to lug, so Humberto gave it to the fisherman as a gift. They tramped up a dirt road to the bus stop, which was nothing more than a stone bench and a wood placard posting the arrival and departure times. The night was cool and dark, except for the moon, which hung over the western hills bathed in a yellow halo. Not another soul was in sight.

While Gabriella deciphered the bus schedules, Amoreena sat with her palms in the moist stone beside her. She was light-headed and wanted to cough but couldn't. The babies hadn't moved since stepping off the boat, and she wondered if they were dead. She saw a coiled shape under a clump of ferns roll to its feet. An immature gargoyle hissed and smiled at her. She gasped and watched the feral cat slink out of sight.

"God, I'm hallucinating," she murmured.

"'Reena, drink." Humberto passed her a small bottle of water.

Amoreena finished the thirst quencher in five swallows. "Sorry," she said, handing the empty bottle back.

"*No problema*, you more important than me."

The words felt like needles in her heart. "No, Humberto," she said, pulling him against her in a tight embrace. "No, baby, we're all equal. Do you understand? We're all the same." He smelled like a young, healthy boy should, wet and sweaty and dirty, like he'd been playing football all afternoon in the rain. She didn't want to let go.

Humberto patted her on the back twice, then slipped out of her arms. "You okay, 'Reena?" he said.

"Yes, I'm okay," she said.

Gabriella plunked down on the bench. Consternation masked her face. "No bus till six in morning."

"Tomorrow!" Amoreena said.

The girl nodded. "Wait or . . ." she raised one thumb.

"We can't stay here."

Gabriella stood defiantly. "I get ride."

"Where?"

"On road." She undid the top button on her blouse and folded the collar open, exposing her shallow cleavage in the moonlight.

Humberto couldn't contain his grin. "*Cállate*," the teen scolded the boy.

Amoreena watched her traipse out to the road, swinging her

lithe hips in exaggerated fashion. The girl had grown up far too fast.

The first vehicle that stopped was going in the wrong direction. Ten minutes later an open-bed diesel hit its air brakes and slowed to a standstill. Amoreena saw Humberto rise with his hand concealed in one of the packs. He walked out and stood behind Gabriella while the negotiation proceeded.

After the requisite bills exchanged hands, the trucker, an elderly *ladino* with arthritic wrists and hands, assisted Amoreena onto the truck bed, loaded half-full with sacks of grain and baskets of avocados, tamarinds, membrillos, and mangos.

He shoved a light in her face after she slumped against the wood planking.

"She need a doctor?" he asked Gabriella in broken English.

Amoreena heard him and said, "No."

"You *Americana?*" he asked.

"Yes," Amoreena said.

He shrugged and returned to the cab.

Gabriella and Humberto tossed the rucksacks and carryall up next to the grain and scrambled in.

"We in luck," the girl said. "He take us as far as El Progesso."

"How far is Guatemala City?" Amoreena asked.

"Only three hundred kilometers," Humberto boasted.

Amoreena groaned. A hundred and eighty miles. As the truck pulled off the shoulder and accelerated, she looked back at the silver-streaked waters of Lago de Izabal. Only she saw the moving search beacon cruising westward along the path of the departing storm.

The heavily traveled Atlantic Highway stretched from Guatemala City east all the way to the Caribbean coast town of Puerto Barrios.

Cruising one thousand feet above this sparsely populated landscape of isolated villages and *fincas,* Vincinio ordered the pilot down midway to the capital. He spent fifteen minutes on the ground at Rio Hondo. He made two calls, then proceeded on to Guatemala City.

Arvis Taggert removed the silk handkerchief from his shirt pocket and cleared his nose. With the bougainvilleas in early bloom, his allergies were running rampant.

The embassy official crossed the marble patio and approached the Marine on duty.

"Merry Christmas," the corpsman wished.

Taggert checked his watch. "Yes, for two more hours, I suppose. All quiet?" he asked. He smelled more rain in the air.

"Yessir."

"I'll be taking all American Citizen Service calls tonight," Taggert said. "Notify me immediately of any communication with Ms. Daniels."

"What about Ambassador Goins?"

"Your explicit orders are to notify me."

"Yes, sir."

Chapter Forty

Around midnight, the fever broke. Sweat poured from Amoreena's pores as if her skin had been squeezed like a wet sponge, dampening her clothing and the bed of burlap she rested on. The cool night air only brought on more rigors and chills.

She had no idea where they were. They'd passed towns with names like Quirigua, Los Amates, Doña Maria, and Zarzal. Broad valleys and imposing hills flanked both sides of the highway, appearing more like paintings under the moon than actual landscape. She could smell bananas and coffee, along with manure and cattle. Overhead, the sea of stars was occasionally broken by black islands of clouds.

Gabriella and Humberto slept. Neither had spoken since leaving Marisco. In the deep shadows, she could see their arms and legs twitch. She hoped their dreams were pleasant. The gentle vibration from the pavement was soothing.

With her temperature normal again, Amoreena experienced a new sense of vigor. And hope. She crept to one of the rucksacks and dug until she found Gabriella's flashlight. Using her knees, she focused the narrow beam down upon the carryall. She shuffled the papers, culling those documents in English.

Polita had been meticulous in her record keeping. Amoreena found herself mesmerized by the entire diabolical process. The original drone embryo was conceived over a decade earlier. Polita was unsure of the origin; she hypothesized a political prisoner or a local farmer. There'd been rumors that Becker had paid a small fee for the retarded teenage son of a local prostitute. The boy's body vanished within months of the transaction and was never recovered.

The isolation and cloning procedure was straightforward. Once a male diploid somatic cell was collected, its nucleus was removed and implanted in the unfertilized egg of a normal female whose nucleus had also been removed. Any female would suffice since the female DNA was never involved in the procedure. The key was to resynchronize the cell cycle. This was achieved by first starving the cell of nutrients, then fusing the male nucleus into the recipient female egg. A small electrical current was then applied to mimic the microburst of energy that occurred during the fertilization process. Shortly after the charge, the hybrid egg would begin to divide normally, forming an embryo. The process was repeated many times. Becker maintained a collection of male cloned embryos in all his research labs.

More recently, *transgenics* had been incorporated into the process. This involved the transfer of genetically engineered segments of DNA from other species into the genetic material of the cloned human embryos.

Amoreena shuddered when she finally fully comprehended what she'd seen on Irene's computer disk. The pig accelerator genes (PAG) were used to shorten the period of gestation (nine months down to four). However, the process required wrapping or camouflaging the pig genes in a carrier much closer genetically to humans, thus the baboon gene (BG), before the pig DNA plug could be successfully indoctrinated into the human genome. The result—mature babies with inhuman characteristics in less than 120 days.

It was almost too fantastically horrible to believe. Meechum Corporation had actually succeeded in combining DNA from different species to produce a viable organism. *Drones*.

Polita had documented many of the transactions in a concise, orderly fashion. From the onset, it became obvious the drones served two purposes—as research subjects and organ purveyors. The donor program was by far the most profitable, hearts auctioning for upward of half a million dollars. Parents would sacrifice anything to save their dying child. The research drones sold for less but moved in vastly greater numbers, depending on the gene manipulated. Diabetes, cancer, and lipid research were in the greatest demand. Using information updated daily on the Human Genome Project website, Becker and his scientists would alter the basic clone to produce drones made to order for laboratories specializing in such diverse fields as obesity, mental illness, and even Alzheimer's. The possibilities were limitless once they knew the location of the gene locus.

Amoreena experienced little relief in realizing the drones she carried were totally independent of herself, DNA wise. Her mental and physical attributes had been irrelevant from the onset. Her only purpose was to serve as the incubator, indicating what Irene had previously insinuated about her contract's value had been pure bullshit.

Amoreena scanned more of the pages. Some were typed, others written in longhand. According to the notes, the Las Canas victims were lured in with promises of food and money. Once they became fertilized (or seeded) they were not allowed to leave. Amoreena read through a list of names Polita had been compiling. Some had check marks by them with arrows leading to other names. Amoreena wondered if these other names were relatives or contacts. She couldn't be sure. Most of the names had lines drawn through them. Polita indicated in several places that many of the women who entered Las Canas did so under aliases. Others were runaways or were homeless. If someone did come looking for a particular girl, the Las Canas security (Vincinio) would promptly forward them to the corrupt local authorities, who would steer any investigation away from the compound. The women of Las Canas were truly prisoners.

The women were never allowed to view the drones during the delivery (rare exceptions occurred, the source of the Las Canas monster rumors) and were always informed their babies had died or were severely ill, requiring specialized care elsewhere. It was Vincinio's job to deal with any *difficult* surrogates. Many of those women simply vanished.

One of Polita's more recent entries dealt with the subject of subadult drones. The impetus for allowing some of the drones to mature was Becker's belief that the adult and children transplantation market would be more lucrative than the neonatal. Far more children and adults required transplant organs than newborns. He steadfastly fostered the premise that he could someday legitimatize the drone trade. And when the drones were finally accepted he wanted to be well established in the most lucrative market—the United States. The subadult drones also provided a continuous supply of diploid somatic cells for future cloning.

Meechum Corporation's initial foray north of the border consisted of bona fide surrogacy transactions—contracts and payouts upon delivery of normal healthy infants. Only gradually were the drones phased in. Women were chosen strictly on financial need. Meechum clinics had always treated mostly Hispanic patients, and this practice continued upon opening the Women's Clinic in California. However, any race was acceptable as long as the women were healthy and free of any gynecological ailment.

By offering contracts, the corporation maintained a legitimate face. However, since the drone surrogate pregnancies were terminated early, these contracts were considered *breached* since there was never delivery of a *healthy viable infant*. This practice saved the corporation significant amounts of money.

Polita's insight gave Amoreena reason to pause. Irene and Becker had never planned on honoring her contract to its fullest because they knew she was never going to deliver a full-term, healthy baby. The realization made her despise the entire concept even more and further solidified her resolve to expose what Polita had tried in vain to expose.

Amoreena scanned Polita's list of laboratories and research centers purchasing the drones. Most were in foreign locales, though she did see more than several in the US, two affiliated with prestigious university medical centers. Once this data became public, the political repercussions would stretch internationally and force new legislation regulating biomedical research.

"You no look good, 'Reena." Gabriella was seated watching her. The girl motioned to the carryall. "Real bad, yes?"

Amoreena wiped at one eye. "Yes." She didn't want to talk about it. She felt movement under her clothes and wanted to hurl obscenities at Becker and Irene. She reshuffled the documents and strapped the cover back in place. She wouldn't look at it again.

The truck slowed and made a wide turn into an all-night *tienda*. While the attendant refueled, she and Gabriella went inside to use the rest room. Humberto relieved himself on the pavement.

"Telephone?" Amoreena asked the clerk upon exiting the bathroom. She wanted to try the embassy again. She'd stay clear of Taggert this time.

The clerk pointed to a pay phone outside, without taking his eyes from the small television screen mounted over the register.

Amoreena waited for Gabriella by the phone. The chirruping crickets were deafening. A second truck pulled in and stopped. She began to wonder what was taking the girl so long and looked back inside the market. She found both Gabriella and Humberto glued to the television. Both their faces appeared unnaturally pale.

Neither looked at her when they stepped outside. The trucker honked.

"We go, 'Reena," Gabriella said.

"I want to use the phone."

"Please, 'Reena." The teenager was crying. She hugged Amoreena and coaxed her back to the truck.

Humberto was hyperventilating like he was suffering from asthma.

"What's wrong?" Amoreena asked.

The boys face filled with fear. "They dead, 'Reena. All five."

"Who's dead?"

Gabriella's eyes were as large as saucepans. "The Sisters." Her voice cracked. "*La policía* say we do it."

* * *

Luis Rafael touched the dial, ridding the frequency of some static. With pure incredulity, he listened to the news bulletin. Five nuns of the Church of the Virgin Mary were accosted on their way to a Christmas service. All were shot more than once. Only an infant survived, left uninjured. Brief descriptions of the perpetrators were included. All three were considered to be armed and dangerous.

Cursing, he downshifted Polita's Jeep Comanche and plowed across a lake of mud. The charges were so preposterous he wanted to laugh, yet he knew the broadcast spelled serious trouble for Amoreena. By daylight, the entire country would be on the lookout for a fair-haired fugitive and her two young accomplices.

Luis was forced to slow when he felt the wheels begin to hydroplane. The road would improve past Rio Dulce. He'd make up time then. And with God's help, much more.

At 11:45 P.M. Pacific Time, Ramona Perez took her final break. The coffee, no cream, only sugar, was stale and cold. She drank it nonetheless.

The last of the surrogacy medical records were packed, taped, and ready for shipment out of the country. The job was complete. The UPS man was dollying the final boxes into his truck as she sat.

The phone rang. She answered, half-expecting a call from another Santa Ana Police detective or that intrusive medical investigator Risken. Prying eyes never seemed to sleep.

It was Irene. Ramona listened, assimilating what she heard, though the news defied belief.

"Maybe our girl is going *loca*," she thought, hanging up.

Ramona flipped through her Rolodex and found the numbers to the *LA Times* and *San Diego Tribune*. The Amoreena Daniels story was going prime time.

Crying together helped, but only minimally. So much unbridled rage consumed Amoreena's emotions, even the remorse seemed secondary. She prayed that God would give her one chance to enact retribution on the Las Canas security chief, for Byte, and for the nuns. And the scores of other lives he'd savagely dealt with. She doubted God answered such misguided entreaties but if He did, Vincinio was a dead man. She swore it.

The diesel began a slow deceleration. Gabriella scrambled up a stack of grain sacks and peered out over the cab's roof.

More anguish marred her face when she slid back to the truck's bed. "All stop. Maybe one mile," she said.

Amoreena and Humberto crawled to the rear of the trailer where the side panels were not as high and peered around the wood planks.

The line of brake lights extended away from them like a long beaded snake. At the head of the column, flashes of red and blue sliced the darkness, indicating either police or fire. Beyond the roadblock, the coruscating lights of a small village spread haphazardly down a hillside.

"Rio Hondo," Humberto murmured.

With the hiss of its air brakes, the truck lurched to a complete stop. The night was suddenly still, and Amoreena noticed that the drizzle had returned. The cab door opened and closed with a sharp crack. Humberto grabbed Amoreena's hand and ushered them back to their places against the grain.

"Shshsh," Gabriella whispered. "Pretend sleep."

Amoreena slumped with her head on Humberto's shoulder. She willed herself to appear relaxed though a new wave of cramps swelled inside her abdomen. Through her closed eyelids, she could sense the flashlight's beam playing across the sacks of grain and fruit. It moved up to her face and seemed to hang there momentarily, then leave.

When it was dark again, she opened one eye. The old trucker was no longer at the rear of the diesel. But they could hear his departing footsteps on the pavement. First a walk, then a slow, steady jog. A hundred yards up the column they heard him yell.

"*La Americana. Aqui!*"

Gabriella sprang to her feet. "We go!"

Amoreena tucked the carryall against her chest.

* * *

With each step, another layer of mud glued to a previous layer, increasing the weight of the sandals so that Amoreena felt she was sporting the latest style in lead boots. The intense burning in her calves and thighs raced up her back, shoulders, and neck. Only minutes after diving into the wall of banana fronds, she was forced to stop and rest. Drenched in perspiration, she literally couldn't suck in enough air. Along with the cramping, she was experiencing another round of rigors and chills. She cursed the fever devouring her bones.

Even the numbing realization that if they were caught, she was dead couldn't make her lift her legs another step.

More sirens.

"Hurry, 'Reena," Gabriella cried.

"I can't." *I'm dying.*

Insects, clouds of no-seeums, mosquitos, flies, buzzing things, and crawling things bit at her skin as if she was coated in honey. She wanted to die. The banana plantation would become her mausoleum.

Keep going, keep going, keep going.

Another step. Two steps. Three steps . . .

Another mile. Two . . .

Amoreena had no idea how long she'd lain in the dark, sprawled and unconscious on the pile of decaying leaves and humus. She inhaled the pungent wet odor of decomposing vegetable matter and opened her eyes.

She was alone.

When she drifted off again, she was dining with her mom and Millie in their backyard in Orange. They watched Byte chase the mourning doves around the feeder. Her premed school advisor was there, too, and Daryl and Dr. Pike. Someone tapped her shoulder. She turned and welcomed Ronald Godinez. Cradled in the crook of each arm, he held a baby drone. One of the drones squealed and offered her a cool Corona.

The vision was fleeting, smashed to bits by another wave of intense pain. She groaned, arching her back. Her breaths came in short pants. The cramps passed slowly, never quite going away completely, leaving her abdomen hard and achy.

She propped herself to a sitting position, waiting for the lightheadedness to evaporate. She tried not to make a sound. A guard could be standing not three feet away, and she wouldn't know it, so thick and dense were the banana trees. In every direction, she could reach out and grasp heavy drooping fronds.

Gabriella and Humberto were gone. She couldn't blame them. In the distance she heard sirens and thought she detected a dog barking. There might have been more than one dog.

Amoreena stood, using the fronds to guide herself to her feet. She was surprised her legs felt as steady as they did.

About to take a step, the air froze in her lungs. Footfalls. They advanced rapidly. There was no place to run.

The wall of vegetation quivered and shook, and two banana tree stalks split apart.

Gabriella squeezed between them. " 'Reena," she said, embracing her.

"Where's Humberto?"

"We find road. Follow."

"How long was I asleep?"

"No long."

"I hear dogs."

Gabriella cocked her head, listening. "*La Policía* have *perros*. We hurry." She pulled Amoreena's hand.

Amoreena searched the ground. "The carryall."

"With Humberto."

They crossed five cultivated rows, clearing the fronds out of the way with their hands and shoulders, and slid into a shallow irrigation channel. They sloshed through the mud and silt until they arrived at a two-foot concrete culvert. Humberto waited on top and helped both girls up onto the macadam road. Ten yards across the crushed shell, the plantation fields resumed.

"Which way?" Amoreena asked, realizing they had no choice but to proceed to their left. On the right, the road dead-ended at the banana field.

They walked a quarter mile until they saw two structures silhouetted against the sky. The cramping and fever and chills forced her to stop twice, yet they covered the distance quickly. The ground was solid as paved concrete under their feet.

Even before Amoreena saw the small biplane parked next to a hangar, she had suspected they weren't hiking along an ordinary road. Ordinary roads didn't stop in the middle of a fruit plantation with no turnoffs.

The private runway widened into an asphalt tarmac. A drive led to the one-story residence.

Without so much as a snarl, the Belgian Malanois launched its steely body from the porch like a sleek black rocket.

"Run!" Amoreena screamed.

Instantly, all three were bathed in the wide yellow beams of a floodlight.

"Shep!" A man's voice commanded. His accent was cajun, thick, and the dog's name came out sounding like *sheep*.

The watchdog clawed to a stop not four feet from Amoreena. Saliva dripped from his open mouth.

Humberto's hand slid inside one of the packs.

"Don't do it, sonny," the man said.

"No, Humberto," Amoreena said. She could see nothing in the light's blinding glare. She reached for Gabriella and the boy and shoved them back a step.

The dog growled once, and they stopped.

"If you move," the man said, "Shep might mistake you for monkeys or thieves. He despises thieves. Monkeys just plain taste good."

"We're not moving," Amoreena said, resisting the urge to peel strands of wet hair from her forehead.

"See, Shep, these aren't monkeys." A figure materialized outside the light's radius. The floodlight exaggerated his features, giving him the appearance of a circus clown. "Thieves, perhaps."

"We're not thieves," Amoreena said. The cramps were pummeling her inside and if she didn't lie down soon, she was going to pass out. "I'm an American and—" Before she could complete the sentence, the tarmac began to spin.

"Goddammit, Josh," a woman's voice rang out. "Can't you see the girl's ill. Get her inside, you old fool."

The face, blotched with brown age spots, was *latina* but Josh Lableau's wife spoke fluent English. "How far along are you, dearie?" she asked, wringing out a rag over a metal wash pan.

"Almost four months," Amoreena said. She lay on a couch in a small room that smelled of leather and lemon oil. Another cramp reached down from her abdomen into her pelvis. She thought she could actually feel the ligaments stretch. She grimaced when the babies jerked. "Where are Gabriella and Humberto?" she asked pursing her lips.

"They're fine." The woman placed the cool rag across Amoreena's forehead. "Josh," she called. "Better get *El Halcón* fired up. This girl's got the fever in a bad way."

Gritting her teeth, Amoreena stifled a groan midway through a second round of spasms. She tried to pant the way the pregnancy manual had instructed. The fever and cramps were too much, though. She felt like her lungs were filling with water. The paroxysm of chills sent slivers of ice through her bones.

"You're burning up," the woman said, running a finger over Amoreena's arm. "Where did you get all these bites?"

"The jungle."

Other figures gathered around the couch. She could hear Gabriella and Humberto talking rapidly in Spanish, interrupted every so often by the woman and the man called Josh. She heard her own name and Las Canas more than once.

She felt a touch on her belly and looked down. A drone with wrinkled features and squat arms sat perched at the end of the couch licking its lips. It squealed and scurried toward her face.

Amoreena screamed and flailed her arms.

"'Reena." Gabriella was at her head. "It okay." She and Humberto helped restrain her.

The drone vanished, and Amoreena stopped struggling. She tried to moisten her mouth. "I'm sorry. I thought I saw . . ." She was unable to finish, her lips were so parched.

She watched Josh and his wife exchange worried looks. In

the soft lamplight, Amoreena could see Josh was much older than what her initial impression of him had been, and with his wide neck and flat nose, his countenance was not one to put a person at ease. Both forearms were thick as pieces of firewood and laced with tattoos and veins.

The gruffness left his voice sounding gravelly. "You must see a doctor," he said.

"No," Amoreena started to protest.

"Missis," he said, *Meeses*, more firmly. "If I don't get you to a hospital, you might lose your baby."

"I don't care. Please, they want to kill me. And Gabriella and Humberto, they need your help."

"Ms. Daniels." The familiar way he said her name reminded her of Taggert, and all the strength ebbed out of her.

She stared fixedly across the room at the six paintings depicting vintage WWI fighter planes—Sopwith Camels, Nieuport Scouts, Fokker Scounges—all frozen in the midst of aerial combat. Oddly, she would remember them as the most beautiful paintings she'd ever seen.

Josh Lableau squatted beside the couch. "You're gravely ill," he said. "You could die without the proper attention. Malaria still kills, even in the twenty-first century."

"Malaria." Amoreena found herself chuckling inappropriately. "Are you a painter?" she asked, unaware of her own denial.

"No. I'm a pilot."

The *soldado*, a member of the military police stationed outside Cabanas, heard the distant low-pitched drone of an engine and reached for his binoculars. He'd been told to report any unusual activity. The homicide suspects were still unaccounted for.

Against the black clouds, he strained his eyes but saw nothing. Farther west, toward the capital, lightning ripped the sky with blue electricity.

Was a light plane heading into a storm unusual enough to wake his superior? He checked his watch, then reached for his radio. At half past three in the morning it sure as hell was.

Chapter Forty-one

The modified Beech Staggerwing dipped suddenly, stirring up a fluttering sensation in Amoreena's stomach and precipitating a burst of activity lower down. She sucked in her breath until the discomfort passed. At least the acetaminophen capsules Josh Lableau's wife had given her were controlling the fever with modest success. The rigors had weakened, and Amoreena could feel her sensorium clearing. She feared her lucidity would not last long.

She still found it hard to accept the Lableaus' lay diagnosis. American girls from Orange County, California, didn't get *malaria*. Colds, maybe, and menstrual cramps, and bad hair days. But not malaria.

Amoreena sat in the copilot's chair—it had offered the most leg room in the cramped biplane's cockpit—while Gabriella and Humberto occupied two makeshift seats in the small cargo hold, along with the four thirty-pound sacks of *Jorge Fernandos* coffee beans Lableau had planned on delivering to a merchant in Santa Rosa. The delivery time had been postponed indefinitely.

Outside the windows, now streaked with drizzle, the sky hung low and dark, blotting out the ground below. The ride was relatively smooth, but from the consternation squeezing Lableau's face, she guessed they were in for some rougher times ahead. According to the air traffic controller at Aurora International, the storm's westward course had stalled over the capital.

"How will you see to land?" Amoreena asked, aware of the ominously thickening cloud cover.

Lableau snorted. "See? We're going in on instruments, young lady. No time for a flight plan." He scanned the air-speed indicator. One hundred and eighty knots. "Been flying this route for fifteen years. Do it with my eyes closed."

Lightning arced between two towering thunderheads. The echo of thunder sounded like sticks of detonating dynamite. From the hold, Gabriella and Humberto screamed.

"Jesus Christ." Amoreena gasped. "That was close."

"Hold on to your seats," Lableau said.

The air traffic controller at Aurora International Airport watched the tiny blip on the radar screen descend through ten thousand, seventy-five hundred, and level off at five thousand feet.

Multiple times he'd attempted to convince the pilot to turn around. Without success. The man must be a lunatic, he de-cided. The entire airport was enveloped in clouds, and rain sluiced diagonally to the ground in showers of silver. Cross gusts were hitting forty knots.

"Flight 2066, you may begin your descent to runway 0-1-0," the controller instructed. "Please respond."

He repeated the instructions three times in English and Spanish. When there was still no response, he reached for the phone and dialed the four-digit emergency code.

The cramps were coming every fifteen minutes and lasting thirty seconds. Initially, the pain had been confined to her lower back and abdomen. Now it radiated into her legs. The fever and chills only magnified the discomfort. Amoreena felt the overwhelming urge to *bear down*.

"Get me on the ground," she gasped.

Lableau cast her a worrisome look. "Won't be long," he said.

The 1933 Beech pitched and spun as if suspended from a long spring. The ceiling broke at two hundred feet, and the lights on the ground appeared suddenly, rising upward toward them in leaps and bounds. Another fifty feet, and Amoreena saw the whipsawing tops of trees and power lines under the plane's landing gear.

Lableau tried once more to radio their position but the lightning-damaged VHF transmitter just spit back static. He checked his airspeed. A hundred knots. A powerful cross gust threatened to flip the plane on its back side, necessitating reflex-timed adjustments to the flaps.

The maneuver sucked the wind from Amoreena's lungs. She heard Gabriella cry out and felt the teenager reach around the seat and clasp her arm. Humberto sat hunched over his knees in stoic silence.

Amoreena arched her back with the onset of more cramps.

"Lableau, I don't see the runway!" she cried out.

"It's down there somewhere, believe me," he said. "Just hang on to what you got. I can't land this plane and be a midwife at the same time."

A crash of thunder split the sky, and the cockpit seemed to sink beneath them. The 450 HP engine whined as the propeller grabbed more air. The staggered wings bent under the sheering stress.

Amoreena groaned through clenched teeth as tiny hands clawed at her insides. She could feel her thighs damp with moisture.

"Hold on," Lableau said.

"It goddamn hurts!"

"Breathe, 'Reena," Gabriella coached.

Amoreena forced her air out in brief whistling gasps.

The Staggerwing bucked and rocked.

"*Aqui!*" Humberto yelled triumphantly, pointing toward the ground.

The trees vanished, replaced by a thin double line of blue runway lights. A final sharp dip, and the wheels hit solid ground, but only momentarily.

"Stay down, *mi amor*," Lableau said. His fingers gripping

the yoke looked carved from alabaster, so prominent were the
tendons.

With a sharp *thunk*, the landing gear hit again, jarring the
cabin's interior. This time, the *El Halcón* remained earth-
bound, coasting past a hangar and two jumbo jets before
rolling to a rough stop. Lableau reduced power and returned
the flaps to their neutral position.

Humberto and Gabriella let out repressed cheers of relief,
while Amoreena gazed out the window in disbelieving
shock.

"We made it, Mom," she whispered.

Outside, the raindrops looked like nickels and dimes
bouncing off the concrete. She heard Lableau unsnap his
seat belt.

"Welcome to Guatemala City," he said.

Amoreena smiled wanly. "I think my water broke."

The guard watched the emergency scene unfolding on the tarmac from the dry comfort of the nearly deserted terminal. His
seemingly indifferent observation lasted only long enough to
confirm the small biplane's occupants. The boy was off first,
followed by the girl. The third passenger was being assisted
by an older man, presumably the pilot. The storm was not
making their efforts run smoothly.

The guard smoothed his medic's uniform and turned away.
His instructions had been explicit.

Everyone was talking at once in staccato bursts of incomprehensible syllables. An attendant slipped a pillow under
Amoreena's head. Rain pelted her face, the drops sizzling
against her burning skin.

Amoreena began to drift until another wave of cramps exploded within. She tried to sit up.

"No, 'Reena," Gabriella said. "*Médico* say lie down." She
tucked a blanket around the stretcher.

Amoreena slid her hand over her belly. The skin felt as hard as an overinflated basketball. The grotesque images of Las Canas floated everywhere in the clouds above. A huge gargoyle leaped away from the small plane's fuselage. It was only Lableau.

He followed the stretcher to the medivan. "They'll be taking you to the hospital. The doctors are good. My wife delivered our only child there."

Amoreena heard only the word hospital. "No," she protested. "The embassy. Please tell them."

The grizzled pilot sadly patted her hand as he would a sick daughter. Then an airport official escorted him away.

"Lableau!" she screamed.

The two attendants hoisted the stretcher inside the van. The compartment seemed too small. One attendant climbed in, and the rear door slammed shut. On a shallow shelf, Amoreena saw five Las Canas bassinets. She slammed her fist against a window and struggled to sit up. The attendant shoved her back down.

She heard the engine fire. "Take me to the fuckin' embassy," she cried. Across oceans of rain and thunder, she heard the feable voices of Gabriella and Humberto calling her name.

The medic reached for one of Amoreena's arms. An IV needle and tubing hung suspended from the van's roof.

"Get the hell away from me," she said, shoving the man's hand aside.

"Por favor, señorita." He was thwarted a second time.

A siren wailed somewhere behind her head. They began to move.

"Luis, Luis, I need you," she called out.

The Beech Staggerwing looked like a child's discarded toy as they pulled away. From the medivan's rear window, Amoreena glimpsed Humberto and Gabriella being herded into a police cruiser. And next to his vintage aircraft, Lableau appeared as tiny as an ant against the expansive gray tarmac.

A second ambulance arrived moments later.

Vincinio set the headset aside and watched triumphantly as the medivan swung around the east corner of the long military hangar and sped toward them. For the past two hours he'd monitored all of the incoming radio signals, including those of the air traffic controller, and now in one smooth operation, he'd recovered the prize and her precious living cargo right from under the noses of the *policia*.

Refusing to share one of his men's umbrellas, he stood in the rain next to the rented sedan. The Sikorsky Black Hawk was refueled and ready for takeoff. The worst of the storm's fury had passed, and the controller had already cleared them for liftoff.

What choice did the *cabrón* have, the Las Canas security chief gloated.

"Embassorio," Amoreena tried again, making the word *sound* Spanish.

The man ignored her, choosing to stare intently at the passing small planes and military jets outside. She saw Polita's leather carryall resting on his lap, and she realized she'd lost.

The Sikorsky had just come into view when a second siren wailed behind them.

The medivan accelerated. Amoreena caught the flashing light of the police cruiser carrying Gabriella and Humberto as the *policia* sped to catch up.

She heard the attendant curse and watched in horror as he removed a pistol from under his white coat and aimed. The shot exploded like a bomb, blowing out the back window.

The police cruiser swerved suddenly and skidded sideways. The man leaned across the stretcher and aimed again.

Oblivious to the trickle of warmth coming from one ear, Amoreena grabbed the attendant's wrist and jerked backward with all her strength. The barrel swung toward her face, and she ducked as a second shot blasted out the glass behind her. The ambulance's tires squealed as the van spun, sending the attendant falling against the compartment wall, pulling racks of intravenous tubing with him.

The out-of-control police cruiser careened toward them. Amoreena managed to cover her head just before impact. She felt the van begin to roll and struggled for a handhold on the

stretcher. The empty bassinets tumbled over her as the medivan slid on its side across the concrete.

The jolt of the crash killed the sirens and engine and forced
the rear door open. The odor of gasoline instantly mixed with
the smell of cordite as the van came to an abrupt stop.

Amoreena pushed an arm out of her face and tried to sit up.
The cramps returned, forcing her to stop momentarily, as she
gasped from the pain. Then, prying herself out from under the
stretcher, she managed to squeeze around the unconscious
guard. A large purple bruise had formed behind his right ear.

The gasoline smell grew stronger, and panic overwhelmed
her threshold for pain. Kicking the bassinets aside, she scrambled for the exit.

The ringing in her ears lessened, and she heard a scream
just before the acrid stench of burning flesh filled her nostrils.

A figure climbed in beside her.

" 'Reena," Gabriella cried.

With the girl's assistance, Amoreena scooted out from under the stretcher and felt her feet touch the tarmac. Flames
leaped at the corner of her vision, and she turned to find the
front half of the medivan engulfed in fire. Black smoke bil-
lowed from the windows, and the flames hissed and sparked in
the steady drizzle. The driver's screams stopped.

Amoreena watched as the guard in the ambulance compartment came to and began to cough and spit. Polita's carryall
had split open and papers and documents littered the medivan's interior.

Gabriella pulled at her arm. "No time," she said, as the entire vehicle exploded in flames.

The police cruiser had done a 360 and faced a long hangar.
Amoreena had to step around the young *policia* lying beside
the driver's open door. He moaned in agony, clutching his
right upper chest.

Humberto helped her into the backseat while Gabriella un-
holstered the *policia*'s pistol and climbed in behind the wheel.
Amoreena heard an engine whine and saw a black sedan leave
the dark silhouette of the Sikorsky and speed toward them.
The cramping sent vise-grip waves of pain across her midsection, but she refused to lie down.

"Can you drive this thing?" Amoreena asked.

"I learn." Gabriella turned the ignition key.

Humberto leaped in the passenger side and slammed the door.

A side window exploded in shards of glass just as Gabriella hit the accelerator.

"Wait!" Amoreena yelled.

Gabriella braked long enough for Humberto to assist the police officer in. He slumped against Amoreena, his face ashen and his uniform smelling of blood and perspiration.

A second shot missed as Gabriella fishtailed back around a row of small storage depots and hangars, the black sedan in close pursuit. She aimed for an emergency exit and accelerated past the deserted security post, splintering the wooden barricade.

"Can you find the American Embassy?" Amoreena asked, panting through another wave of contractions. Her face felt on fire, and she noticed one ear was bleeding.

"Where?" Gabriella said.

"Avenida La Reforma something. *Ask the federale?*"

"¿Como puedo llegar al Embajada Americana?" She had to repeat the question two times before the injured man understood what she wanted.

Listening to his instructions, Gabriella steered past two more security checkpoints and bounced across an esplanade to the city streets.

Another bullet shattered the driver's side mirror, and Humberto lowered his window and returned fire with the *policia's* pistol, getting off three quick shots in succession.

Amoreena looked behind them. The driver-side front wheel of the sedan was deflated and spewing off chunks of black tread. She could hear sirens converging from all directions.

Gabriella braked around a corner, sliding out of control briefly and bouncing off the curb, before accelerating through three intersections and around the Plazuela España. Traffic was light and at Avenida La Reforma she hooked a sharp left at forty miles per hour.

Five blocks away, Amoreena saw the three-story, white-concrete building with the large red-tile seal of an eagle holding an olive branch. From the top of a tall pole, the United States flag hung limply in the rain. She'd never seen a more beautiful sight.

"There!" Amoreena shrieked.

Hearing the shots, the night-duty Marine had already sounded general quarters.

Six across, the uniformed men waited, accompanied by the night security detail, each armed with an automatic assault rifle. A fifty-caliber machine gun provided additional firepower, should its use become necessary.

The early-dawn sky was a sultry pink where the clouds had broken, and the rain had tapered to a fine sprinkle.

"Think it's her?" the post Marine asked.

A sergeant flipped the safety off his weapon. "We don't want a war, but if she's American, she's one of us."

From the safety of the marble patio, Taggert watched the police cruiser screech to stop in front of the protective concrete planters. The deputy chief of mission, defense attaché, and the ambassador had all been notified in order to cover his ass.

Reluctantly, he started down the stone steps. Sirens wailed everywhere. He had hoped it wouldn't get this nasty.

Even before Gabriella had shifted to park, Amoreena swung open the door and tumbled out into the street. Thirty feet away stood the ten-foot-high security gate. Pushing herself to her knees, she crawled up the curb and hobbled between two of the large rectangular planters bursting red with blooming bougainvilleas.

"I'm Amoreena Daniels!" she screamed.

The cramps were excruciating and caused her to fall forward. Using a concrete bunker for support, she reached the pedestrian walk on sheer willpower.

More tires skidded behind her, but she didn't turn. Her vision was fuzzy at the edges, and her lungs were devoid of air.

She choked and spit out a glob of blood. In one of the planters she saw her mother transformed into a huge drone, and she cried out in dismay.

Lunging, she felt her fingers close around the cool wrought iron.

"Open up," she gasped.

A young Marine moved forward, but Taggert motioned him back with a curt wave. "I'll handle this, son."

"Open the goddamn gate," Amoreena said.

Taggert suddenly looked indecisive. "We need some identification," he said.

"Open up the fucking gate! I'm Amoreena Daniels." She was wheezing and felt a heavy pressure drop between her legs.

"She's pregnant, sir," one of the Marines said.

"I can see that"—Taggert frowned—"but this *is* the United States embassy. We must have some form of identification."

"Are you Taggert?" she asked.

"Yes, I am."

"You bastard, open the goddamn gate!" Amoreena thrust her arm through a gap between the bars at the slight man.

Taggert moved back a step. The situation was getting far too awkward. Fifty grand suddenly didn't seem quite so much.

"Señor Embassy Official." Vincinio's voice broke the standoff.

Amorena whirled, pushing against the immobile metal for support.

Vincinio made a conciliatory gesture of goodwill with both hands and stepped between two planters. "Gentlemen, at this precise moment Ms. Daniels stands on Guatemalan soil. This criminal is a fugitive from justice in our country for the murders of five Roman Catholic Sisters and is also wanted by my superiors for stealing corporate property. Let's not turn this event into an international crisis. *Por favor.*"

Amoreena balled up both fists and flew off the embassy gate. "You worthless piece of shit!" she screamed, rushing the Las Canas security chief. "I'll see you dead."

Vincinio easily sidestepped the assault and watched her fall pitifully to the sidewalk.

The ocean swelled in her ears, and Amoreena rolled to her

back. All she could feel were the labor pains. "Oh, my God," she groaned.

"'Reena." Gabriella and Humberto knelt beside her.

A scuffle broke out, and Gabriella cried out, "Dr. Rafael!"

Luis bounded past the *soldados* and charged the gate, shoving a wallet at one of the Marines. "This woman is an American citizen kidnapped by a foreign corporation. Here's her identification. Now, unless you want these babies born on foreign soil, I suggest you open the gate."

Vincinio reached for his pistol, but with the *policía* behind him and the Marines not ten feet away, rationality overcame rashness, and he unwillingly backed away.

Amoreena cried out. *"They're coming!"*

"I need some towels and warm water," Dr. Rafael ordered. "And blankets. Hurry."

Amoreena grasped Luis's hand. Tears traced grimy, crooked paths down her cheeks. "Promise me, Luis. Don't let me see them. Please," she cried. "Don't make me see my babies."

"Amoreena, close your eyes and push when I say."

Chapter Forty-two

Other than wisps of gray in his beard, the man looked too young to be an infectious disease specialist. He lifted the temperature chart from the foot of the bed.

The patient stirred and opened her eyes. He noted that the yellow in her sclera was fading and the conjunctivas were no longer injected.

"I see you're back with us, Ms. Daniels," he said.

"Yes," she said.

"Your temp's down. Finally." He perused some laboratory values, "You gave us quite a scare. Those Group B arboviruses are tough bugs to lick. Superimpose a pneumococcal pneumonia, and you're cooking up a recipe for disaster."

"It wasn't malaria then."

"No. Yellow fever. Similar symptoms, different mosquitos."

She noticed he hadn't mentioned the pregnancy. Surely, he knew.

Amorecna took in the abundant vases, fruit baskets, and bouquets spread across the room. Somehow the tropical orchids smelled the strongest.

"What day is it?" she asked.

"Wednesday, January eleven." With one hand he waved at the bountiful array of gifts. "You're a popular young woman."

"I don't feel so popular."

He grinned and slapped the chart shut. "You will. I promise. We'll shoot for an early discharge next week."

"Thanks, Doctor." She watched him leave.

Over two weeks. Amoreena tried to collate the last sixteen days into some semblance of order, but there were too many gaps and blanks in the puzzle. She had no recollection of the actual births, and only bits and pieces of the embassy debacle remained, though she did recall screaming obscenities at an embassy official. On the way to the embassy hospital, she suffered multiple seizures owing to her high temperature, so she'd been told, and the doctors hadn't expected her to live. All concerned agreed that luck played a major role in her miraculous recovery, and once she was stable enough to travel, Uncle Sam arranged the medivac flight back to the States. That was six days ago.

What became of the newborn *drones*? She had no idea. She could use the word now in relation to herself since they were no longer a part of her. They were never a part of her. She'd never touched their tiny fingers. Never heard their cries.

Many times over the past week she'd even begun to wonder if the events of the last four months had actually taken place. She knew they had. Risken and two detectives had been by numerous times. Their conversations were still murky. In time she knew this would clear.

Amoreena gently palpated the arca below her navel. The skin and underlying muscle felt soft and flaccid. As soon as her strength returned, she'd begin a sit-up regimen.

The door opened following a soft knock. Millie tiptoed in like she was walking on broken glass.

"You're not crying again, are you?" she asked.

Amoreena shook her head. "No." In her dreams, she saw three perfect little faces with perfect little noses and perfect little mouths, grotesquely mounted on the bodies of pigs and baboons. She would awake and sob. The dreams were becoming less frequent, too.

"Byte sends his greetings," Millie said, clearing a fruit basket off a chair and plunking herself down.

Amoreena tried to smile. It didn't feel natural yet. Receiving the news that their pet had survived the ordeal, though, had been a major psychological turning point in her recuperation. A puppy outsurvive her? Never.

"He still crapping in Ms. Landers's front yard?" she asked.

"Right next to the old bag's rose garden."

Amoreena wanted to laugh. It didn't quite materialize. "I miss him," she said. She thought her roommate looked strained, like she hadn't been getting enough sleep.

"He'll be there when you get home," Millie said, producing a copy of the *LA Times* from her backpack. "Brought you some reading material for later. You won't believe how big this thing is getting. CNN's left three messages at the house, and some lady from *60 Minutes* called. And yesterday, I fielded two requests for interviews from a couple of agencies representing two major-league movie producers. I mean we're talking Cameron and Spielberg big."

Amoreena shrugged. She wasn't up to negotiating screen rights at the moment.

"Hey, girl," Millie went on, "those film execs live out of wallets bigger than our house."

"Any word on Gabriella and Humberto?" Amoreena asked. Since regaining consciousness, she'd inquired about their whereabouts daily. Those two occupied her thoughts more than anyone else. Except her mom. And Luis.

Millie shook her head. "Nothing. Last I read, some journalist reported they'd been deported back to Mexico."

"They saved my life."

"I know."

Millie opened her purse and removed some papers and an envelope. "Here's the stuff you requested from the mortuary." She dropped the papers on the newspaper. "Geneva had a nice service."

"Her only child wasn't there."

"She'll understand. Talk to her when you get out." She rose and placed the sealed envelope on the bed. "These arrived the first week in January."

Amoreena read the return address, and her stomach churned. She tossed the MCAT scores aside.

"You're not going to open them?" Millie asked.

"They're not important."

"They're important. They're just not important today." Millie waited while a nurse hung a fresh IV bag. "Everyone at school's asking about you. Even Gladys Peterson. I told them you'd be back to finish the spring semester."

"Classes already started."

"You're smart. You'll catch up."

"If I was so smart . . ." Amoreena couldn't finish. The tears welled in her eyes, and the uncontrollable sobbing began again. She could feel Millie's arms, and still she couldn't stop.

"Hey, Amy, it's okay. You're back."

"They weren't human, Millie. I saw them wedged in this stinky room. They were chained like prisoners and looked at me with these big, sad eyes," Amoreena cried. "They had feelings. They weren't human, but they still had feelings."

"Of course they did."

It wasn't the words but Millie's tone. *Of course they did.* Amoreena tensed. Parents used the same tone with their children all the time. *Mommy, I saw Santa Claus in the chimney. Of course, you did, dear.*

Millie didn't believe her story.

"The drones exist," Amoreena said, pulling away. "I carried three of them inside of me for godsakes."

"I know."

"You don't know."

"Amoreena, I talked with your doctors. Your illness causes hallucinations."

"Goddammit, Millie, I saw them."

"Amy, I love you, but these stories about pigs and monkeys and humans—"

"Baboons."

"Okay, baboons and humans. Saying this sort of stuff—"

"*Stuff!*"

"Let me finish, please. If you persist in telling these stories, you might hurt your chances for medical school."

"You think I'm crazy."

"No, Amy, you were very ill. You almost died."

"You saw the disk."

"The night you were kidnapped someone broke into the house and erased your computer's hard drive."

"All the records?"

"Yes," Millie said, dropping her eyes. The gesture looked awkward, rehearsed. When she began to play nervously with the straps of her purse, Amoreena suspected. She felt dead on the inside.

"They got to you, didn't they," she said.

Millie's face turned crimson. "I resent that insinuation."

"How much did they pay? Fifty thousand, a hundred."

"I'll come back tomorrow when you're rational." She strode for the exit, pausing briefly at the door. "For what it's worth, they destroyed my computer, too."

That afternoon, the nightmare returned, only this one included trees. Lots and lots of trees. Amoreena didn't mind the forests. In this particular dream, she could even climb the trees, and as skillfully as her animal friends. High in the forest canopy, she felt safe from intruders, safe from those on the ground who would wish her harm. She still saw the cloned porcine and simian minotaurs, but having the trees helped.

When she opened her eyes, Amoreena smelled chicken noodle soup. The cup sat next to an anemic plate of fruit on the hospital tray.

She saw the medical investigator seated in a chair next to the door.

"Can I come in?" Risken asked.

"You're already in." Amoreena felt nauseous and shoved the tray away.

Risken pulled the chair next to her bed. "The doctors upgraded your condition to stable."

"Does that include my mind?"

"Pardon?"

"Nothing."

Risken rearranged his briefcase beside the leg of his chair. "You don't want to know how many reporters I counted in the lobby."

"Don't tell me."

"Fifty-one."

Amoreena shut her eyes. She couldn't find the trees.

"Just wanted to fill you in on the various investigations," Risken said, helping himself to a pitcher of water. "Did you know Meechum Corporation was selling its products to laboratories and hospitals in over thirty countries?"

Amorcena's lids snapped open. "You mean the drones."

"No, I'm referring to their pharmaceuticals. Agents and reagents and automated gene-splicing equipment for medical research."

"What about the drones?"

Risken paused to take a long sip. "The Guatemalan government is stonewalling any neutral party inspections of this so-called jungle research station. They label your assertions as totally insane."

"Las Canas exists."

"Yes, as a sugar plantation. So they say."

"Get out."

"Hey, I'm on your side. I do have some good news. All international charges against you have been dropped, and you've been exonerated of any wrongdoing in the death of Ronald Godinez."

"I feel wonderful."

"Those were serious charges."

"And Dr. Gillespie?"

"Case is still open."

"What about my babies?"

Risken removed an apple from the nearest fruit basket and took a generous bite. "Officially, there never were any babies."

"What?" Amoreena tried to sit up.

"No, relax. I'll explain it the way I heard it from the State Department in Washington. You were barely sixteen weeks pregnant, and anything born that premature would not be considered viable."

"We're not talking about *normal* babies."

"Two, what was delivered was delivered on foreign soil and immediately transported under the jurisdiction of the local medical authorities."

"In other words, they vanished."

Risken shrugged. "We don't have access to them."

"This is bullshit."

"We have nothing tangible. No documentation, no eyewitnesses, no physical evidence that these *drones* actually exist."

"Find Gabriella and Humberto. They'll tell you."

"The Mexican officials are not demonstrating an eagerness to give them up."

"What about the Marines?"

"They remained within the embassy perimeter. You delivered outside their immediate line of sight. We're still trying to arrange an interview with Dr. Rafael, but so far he's been a tough individual to pin down. He's as slippery as Irene Leggett and Dr. Ross Becker. I presume they remain somewhere in Central America."

"So it's business as usual."

"Ah," Risken said, raising the apple. "It's not *all* bad news. Meechum's new San Diego facility has been denied accreditation. The technicality was minor, but it will hold up under board scrutiny. Dr. Luis Rafael was an unlicensed physician in the state of California."

"He was my doctor." Amoreena felt a tug at her heart when she said this.

"True, but practicing medicine without a license is against the law."

"They'll appeal."

"Of course. But for the present, they're out of California. We're rounding up former employees and patients to try to strengthen our case."

"Contact Ramona Perez."

"She's on our list." He finished the apple and reached for his briefcase. "You're big news, Ms. Daniels."

"So I've been told. But you'll find the real news in the Las Canas nursery. The drones aren't fiction. They're as alive as you and I." She watched him to the door. "My memory's going to return, Mr. Risken. Everything—patients' names, genetic codes, laboratories, all of it. I read that disk. *I was there.*"

The medical investigator stopped and pulled a folder from his briefcase. He removed a blank piece of stationery and dropped it in the empty chair, along with his fountain pen. "Write it down, Amoreena. All of it. This thing is far from over."

She couldn't tell whether he believed her or not, but it really didn't matter. Las Canas did happen, and she would remember.

She found the envelope weeks later, buried under a stack of old well-wishers' cards. There was no return address or postmark date. The note was brief.

> *Because an act might be considered ethically wrong, does not make it morally wrong, if the act saves lives.*
> *The drones save lives. Three young lives, in your case.*
> *Think about it, Amoreena.*
> *You're going to make a fine physician.*
>
> *Irene*

Amoreena reread the missive once, then sealed both the letter and envelope in a clear plastic Ziploc bag. She would turn the evidence over to the FBI, though she doubted it would assist in their investigation. Irene was far too clever to make a careless mistake at this stage in the game.

That night Amoreena slept more soundly than she had in months. She dreamed of three tiny roughly hewn gravestones half-buried in an impoverished cemetery far from home. She saw her mother spreading orchid petals on the freshly turned earth. And when she awoke, she began to write.